MAX AND THE REGENT SUPREME

D.P. BOWKETT

Dippy Bee

First published in 2024 by Dippy Bee Publishing

Cover illustration by Alex at IndieBubble
Interior Formatting by Kelley at Sleepy Fox Studio

A very special *thank you* to my beta readers who encouraged me to get this far.

eBook ISBN: 978-1-7395583-3-8
Print ISBN: 978-1-7395583-2-1

BISAC codes YAF019040, YAF056010, YAF001000

Dear Friend,

I've lived on your planet for more than two thousand years, but people keep asking me how and why I came here and what my life was like on my home planet, Zephyrion.

Sorry, I'm forgetting my manners. My name is Max, and I was born and named Maxo on the planet of Zephyrion around 45 years before coming to your planet. By the way, only my mother ever called me Maxo, and that was when I did something wrong.

My early career saw me become Maxorani before changing careers and becoming Maxoraxin. I'm sorry, but I'm jumping ahead again. On my planet, our name has two parts: the first is your known name, chosen by your parents, and the second part is your job. In my case, I became an engineer or a rani. After my brother got injured investigating corruption, I enrolled as an enforcer, a raxin, to try and catch the Deceptors involved. Oh yes, Deceptors are what we call criminal Shadowers, and Shadowers are what the most significant race of people on Zephyrion were called until the rebranding to Zephyrions after the Grand Formation when the planet unified under one government to try to save us from a collapsing planet. Eventually, I was promoted to a hal, like one of your police officers in charge of an entire local or specialist force. If you made it to a position of power and control, you were made a member of our Elite Council, the ultimate governing body of our planet, and your job name would start with an e, which was how the phrase "look at them acting like a jumped-up e-name" came from.

Our scientists, under Elite control, built solar domes to block solar radiation. Then, they found a way to extract our energy souls from our physical bodies. This meant whilst our dense atmosphere left us looking the same, holding our energy soul together, we were no longer organic or needed organic food.

But everything was far from perfect under the Elite Council.

When you create positions of ultimate power, like our Elite Council, you invite people who will do anything to seize that power. They even used creatures called Daxson in their pursuit of that power. I'm doing it again. A Daxson is a Shadower who, due to genetic mutations, was born needing intense amounts of power to survive. They were virtually uncontrollable and were often used as executioners as they were ruthless, incredibly wild energy souls.

After coming to your planet, I've had to learn new languages, different ways to behave, and even different measurements. When I first came to Rome, they had an uncia, which is 0.97 of an inch or 2.46 centimetres. It's about the same size as one macon, a measure we had on Zephyrion.

But there have been some crazier units of measurement during my time here. In 1958, the Massachusetts Institute of Technology (MIT) students used the height of a first-year student, Oliver R. Smoot, to measure the length of the Harvard Bridge at 364.4 Smoots long. In the 19th century, loggers in the American Midwest used the bloit, a distance of about 16 feet. This was the length of a log that they said two men could move.

Even time has the 'Warhol' measure, referring to Andy Warhol's quote, 'In the future, everyone will be famous for 15 minutes.' However, I'll let you get on and experience the craziness of my life on Zephyrion and in Ancient Rome, which was more than a Warhol ago.

1

FRACTURED FAMILY

'You need to talk to him. He's your brother,' Lin snapped as she packed her bag in the living room of their twenty-third-floor apartment.

'Yes, okay, but you know how stubborn he is,' Max replied. 'He's such a proud Shadower and a damn good enforcer until the accident.'

'I know all that, but his refusal to transition is crazy. He'd have his leg back, be able to move about easily, and no longer be mortal.'

'What you mean is he'd be able to move out.'

'Well, if he did transition, we could move into one of those luxury new apartments. But we're stuck in this dump because it has a kitchen so he can have food. Even the furniture is old fashioned and made of plastic and foam.'

'I wouldn't call this place a dump. It's only a few years old and has a great view across the park,' Max protested.

'Once upon a time, it might have had a great view across the park. Now it's got a view across brown barren soil. Those new apartments have an indoor atrium with fountains, and some even have real plants inside,' Lin replied. 'If he transitions, we could move, and I suppose he can move with us until he finds his own place. Just tell him.'

'You tell him, you're one of the experts on Operation Exodus. Dazzle him with the science.'

'That's half the problem. I'm the Deputy Project Leader, and my partner's brother still needs to transition and prepare for interstellar migration.'

'Morning, Linaxani, morning, Max,' Zym said as he walked into the living room, assisted by his support cage.

'Morning, Zymraxin,' Lin replied curtly. 'I need to go, Max. Please just do it.'

Their conversation was interrupted by an electronic voice, 'Good morning, Zephyrions.'

'Cogi, off,' Max snapped at the round two-inch deep black disc hovering above a shelf and projecting an image of the Zephyrion flag onto a blank wall from a large round lens at the front of it.

'I'm sorry, Maxoraxin. This is an important global message from our Supreme Leader, Timezel. Due to the current climate conditions, please stay home, do not travel, and protect your friends and family.'

The image changed from the flag to a scene of buildings shaking violently as the ground cracked and opened, letting lava break through the surface.

'Oh great,' Lin sighed. 'Cogi, can anyone travel today?'

'Certainly, Linaxani. You and Maxoraxin are authorised to travel as normal. This directive only applies to Zymraxin within your household. Have a glorious day.'

'How did he ever become our Global Supreme Leader?' Zym grumbled. 'I remember when he was just one of us, plain old Timraxin. What did that slimy toad do to get an e-name, never mind rise to the top? I bet it involved corruption.'

'Zymraxin, you are fined fifty credits for breaking the social courtesy code and a further forty credits for making a false allegation against our beloved Supreme Leader,' Cogi stated.

'Well, there goes your daily social credit income. Well done, brother,' Max glowered.

'Why's it my fault? I told you not to get one of those Cogi things.'

'You know full well you can't exist anymore without them. Our banking, mobility, homes, and jobs rely on Cogi,' Lin said. 'Max, I've got to go. Just sort it.'

'And the fact it means the Elites have total control over our lives is just an added bonus?' Zym shouted as Lin slammed the front door on her way out.

'Zymraxin, you are fined five credits for spreading malicious gossip,' Cogi stated.

'Do you want some food before Simo arrives and we go to work?' Max sighed.

'I can sort myself out if you need to rush off. I don't want to burden anyone,' Zym replied.

'It's okay. Besides, we need to talk. How does one of my frittata specials sound?'

'It sounds like you're trying to soften me up for something Lin wants you to tell me. However, please don't let my cynicism stop you from cooking. You know I love what you do with eggs.'

A little later, Zym is sitting at the table in the small kitchen, eating the food Max has prepared. Cogi hovers from the living room and rests on the worktop.

'For a tough guy, you sure know your way around a kitchen,' Zym said as he finished his food. 'Don't you miss eating real food instead of those energy things?'

'Of course, I do, but look at yourself. Only having one leg would have been tough in the old days, but the atmosphere is now so dense you need that support cage to do even the most basic of movements.'

'If you're talking about transitioning to an energy soul, forget it. They claimed it would save the planet if we all transitioned. All those scientists showed us charts and models proving that if we shed our physical forms, which meant no more need for food and associated waste products, we could reverse the damage done to the planet. But they forgot to model all those billions of discarded bodies decomposing at once, and all those farm animals released to fend for themselves or, in most cases, die.'

'Yes, Zym, I know they lie.... erm, I mean the modelling proved inaccurate,' Max said, watching Cogi glow but then return to rest mode.

Zym followed Max's eyes and snarled, 'Cogi, leave us.'

'I'm sorry, Zymraxin, but I am not allowed to leave you unattended in case you need anything. I'm here to ensure you have a glorious day.'

'Zym, come on, you know Zephyrion is dying. The animals and plants are disappearing so rapidly. Lin tells me the mass production of Exodus machines is in full swing to evacuate the planet within a year or so, and you can't be evacuated unless you're an energy soul.'

'They've been saying the planet is dying since they started the transition process thirty-odd years ago. Yet somehow, we're still here.'

'Are you honestly saying things haven't gotten any worse in all that time?'

'Oh no, of course, they have. First, we had the global rebranding calling us Zephyrions instead of Shadowers, following the Grand Formation of the Elite Council and the creation of our Supreme Leader and his deputy to bring the planet under one government. Then we had the mysterious infection that would wipe us out but never did; they just used it to introduce new restrictions. Before long, social credits replaced proper money, which they can now give, take or restrict at will. Not forgetting these new travel restrictions where they control our every movement, unless you have plenty of credits, in which case you simply buy travel permits and do what you want.'

'Zymraxin, I must caution you that your speech may be considered inflammatory.' Cogi glowed.

Zym glowered at Cogi as if he was about to say something but then ignored it. 'Max, our parents are buried here. We grew up here. How can we join Operation Exodus to abandon the planet and leave like it means nothing?'

'Of course, it means something, but we can't change history. Our parents always said don't let your past torture your future. The one certainty is that Shadowers have stripped this planet of everything, and we will die if we don't leave. We've tried to engineer solutions, which just made it worse. The atmosphere has changed so dramatically because of our behaviour that the planet is crumbling, and everything is dying around us. Even our moon is being drawn closer by Zephyrion's increased gravity. Yes, I wish our parents could have lived long enough to see transitioning as they might still be alive as energy souls now, but it wasn't to be.'

'I wish you'd seen them in action, but you were too young. When I first became an enforcer, they were already legends. They brought down some big Deceptor crime syndicates back when space travel involved real spacecraft, unlike this zapping to different planets by machines you have now. You young'uns have it easy,' Zym sighed thoughtfully.

'Easy? Have you seen how much crime has soared?'

Criminal Shadowers have been called Deceptors for as long as anyone can remember, but neither Max nor Zym could deny that transitioning had increased illegal activity.

'That's because I'm not still enforcing and keeping you slackers in order,' Zym laughed.

'You may be my big brother, but I can still give you a slap, you know,' Max chuckled.

'Hang on, and I'll just turn my support cage off to give you half a chance.'

'That's why you should transition. You'd get your leg back and be able to move faster.'

'How can you be so sure? Look at you and Lin; you've both transitioned, but you look the same, apart from your bodies, which now have a glowing aura around them. Who's to say I don't transition and still look like an old man with one leg?'

'Because it doesn't work like that. Any damage to our physical bodies doesn't impact our energy souls. How many times have you tried to scratch your missing leg?' Max challenged.

'Hmm, I see what you mean, but I'm still not sure.'

'Promise me you'll consider transitioning. I don't want to lose you, too.'

'Fine. You can tell Lin you've convinced me to at least think about it.'

'Thanks, Zym. Do you want me to prepare anything for your lunch?'

'No, it's okay. I thought I'd treat myself to a Zingles burger.'

'I'm sorry, Zymraxin, you have exceeded your unhealthy food limit for this week, but I can recommend some healthy plant-based alternatives. Would you like to hear more?' Cogi interrupted.

'*No, I don't*! Max, does it mean leaving them behind if I transition and join the migration programme?' Zym asked, nodding in Cogi's direction.

'Only energy and energy souls can be migrated with an Exodus machine. Anything that's not energy, like animals, machinery, etc., must be migrated by craft.'

'I'm warming to this transitioning idea. Cogi vision on.'

Cogi pointed towards a blank wall and started to project a television image.

'Welcome to Zingles. Whether you're looking for an energy burger to boost your soul or a mega Zingles burger for our organic customers, we have what you need,' the advert promised.

'Anyone would think we're being spied on,' Zym groaned.

The seismic activity had long since made travel via the old underground network impossible, and only the foolhardy would consider using the few remaining public transport vehicles running on tracks. This led to personal tube transport, small one-person cylinders shaped like a can but with a domed roof, which you could summon with your communication device. Each tube would open at the front and allow the passenger inside. It would detect your height and weight and adjust the seat accordingly before a safety harness is lowered over the passenger. The door would close, and the front screen allowed the passenger to see their surroundings or watch a film or television show.

After her argument with Max, Lin didn't feel in the mood for overhyped reality dramas and fast-food adverts, so she selected the window option and settled back.

As the tube hovered above the electromagnetic field embedded in the road, Lin watched the scenery change from the tired, smaller apartment blocks in the area where she lived with Max to the huge superscrapers of the main city centre. The city underwent a significant restructuring when transitioning began. They had called it a new future for a new Zephyrion at the time. Nature had other ideas on days like today. The tube juddered as seismic activity rumbled around her, and the streets were filled with mist as water and gases mixed with the usual street haze.

As the tube slowed, Lin could see the looming cylindrical glass and metal building of the One World Research Centre. In the middle was the largest superscraper in the city, at 285 floors, with four more superscrapers of 200 floors surrounding it to the sides and the rear. At the front was a 10-floor domed glass and white marble building. The buildings were connected by sharing the first five floors before separately continuing upward. The entrance to the complex was through the marble-domed building with One World Research Centre emblazoned in shimmering gold lettering on a black background above the main doors. The whole complex was set to the back of a large pedestrianised square surrounded by shops and stalls.

After the ten-minute journey from home, Lin exited the transport tube and walked across the square towards the centre's main entrance. The flower beds surrounding the entrance were now barren, a poignant eulogy for a bygone ecosystem, contrasting with the brightness of the glass and marble entrance.

The advertising screens scattered around the square flashed like a supernatural disco amongst all the decaying flower beds. 'Sign up now for the Migration Lottery,' the signs encouraged passersby. 'Get to the front of the migration queue and be among the first to enjoy a fresh new world.'

The screen flickered to a new advert, 'Start your day with our super deal, a Zingles energy burger and energy shake for only eight credits. We have what you need.'

'Welcome, Linaxani. Are you going directly to your office?' the Cogi voice asked as the main doors opened.

'Yes, and ask my sister Julirani to join me.'

'Certainly, Linaxani. Please use chute three. Have a glorious day.'

Lin walked across the marble floor to the chute area, where a metal-based glass cylinder was waiting with welcome Linaxani illuminating the back wall. She walked into the chute, and the glass door closed behind her with a gentle hiss before the chute started to move sideways along a corridor until it was underneath a long, thin shaft of blackness above. Despite the statistics that reminded her of a higher likelihood of death from armed robbery than from a malfunctioning chute, Lin always had a rush of relief every time she emerged from the chute onto her floor.

Ten minutes later, after unpacking her bag and getting set up for the day, Lin looked out of her 80th-floor office window along the corridor of sentinel superscrapers that she had only recently travelled between, towards the setting red moon at the far end of the road. Below her, the travel restrictions meant the glow of energy souls and transport vehicles were few and far between. However, they still illuminated the permanent street-level haze like some ethereal beast emerging from the underworld. For some reason, the haze always looked denser up here than at street level. A knock at the door broke her concentration.

'Door open,' Lin shouted, turning to face it.

'Morning, Lin. One Energycreds double shot energy shake for you,' Juli said.

'Thanks, Juli, I need this.'

'I thought so. I wasn't far behind you when you arrived and snapped at the door Cogi,' Juli laughed. 'Trouble in domestic paradise?'

'Just the usual. Max's flaming brother, but I don't want to talk about him. How's the Supreme Leader's Exodus machine going?'

'It's on track for the Grand Gathering, but I still don't understand why it needs to be so powerful when the entire government are only going to Astral 5.'

'Because even though they've been establishing a city on Astral 5 since the first spacecraft were sent there forty years ago, Deceptors control parts of it.'

'That still doesn't explain it. The power built into the SL's machine exceeds anything we've ever built. It would get him to Astral 5 in less than ten percent of the time of our current most powerful Exodus machine.'

'Eight percent of the time, if my calculations are correct, but it's about something other than getting him or the Elite Council there faster.'

'Come on, sis. I didn't get you that shake just so you could hold back on me now.'

Lin looked around and said, 'Cogi, security code arc, dash, zero, nine, twelve, shad.'

'What does that mean, and why hasn't Cogi replied?'

'It shuts Cogi down in this room. It doesn't hear or record anything.'

'I'm going to remember that code,' Juli laughed. 'It'll make bedroom time much more fun.'

'Sorry, Juli, that code only works with my voice, and even then, only in government and security buildings.'

'Spoilsport. Anyway, what's so hush-hush?'

'They want us to send a Daxson across first so the local enforcers can use it to wipe out the Deceptors.'

'A Daxson? But they're lethal. They'd kill everything on Astral 5.'

'That's the idea. Then once they run out of people to kill, they'd run out of energy and die themselves.'

'But there's Shadowers already living and working there with their families,' Juli protested.

'I know. It's unfortunate, but it's for the greater good. Let's go down to the chamber and see the progress,' Lin replied as she tapped a screen on her desk.

'Hello, Linaxani and Julirani. I'm here to serve your every need. Have a glorious day.' Cogi said.

Lin used her communicator to call for a double chute, which arrived in a few seconds. After boarding, the chute closed and shot down, dropping below the street level before heading along a corridor. It took several minutes before it slowed and then rose into a large glass-walled room with two huge, elaborately decorated blast doors in front of them and a corridor to the right. Behind them, they could see the towering One World Research Centre in the distance.

Lin and Juli left the chute and started walking down the corridor past various offices and lecture halls before entering the Grand Exodus room through a pair of less grand blast doors. In the centre of the room stood what looked like a cross between a giant telescope and a super-heavy artillery gun barrel pointing towards the ceiling. It was over thirty metres tall, with a circular illuminated Exodus Deck about three metres in diameter at the lower end of the barrel. Glass walls surrounded the deck with a glass door to the side. To the side of the deck entrance were some metal steps which led to a control platform about ten metres up the side of the barrel, with a bank of monitors and controls at the top.

'Good morning, esteemed Deputy Project Leader. Is there anything I can do for you or Julirani?' someone in a white coat asked.

'Good morning. I'm looking for Granxili,' Lin replied.

A few minutes later, Lin and Juli stood on the control platform talking to Granxili.

'Morning, Gran. I've been telling Lin we're on track for the Grand Gathering in a few weeks.'

Gran was jigging excitedly, 'Yes, esteemed Deputy Project Leader. We are about to do our first test exit.'

'You may call me ma'am. It seems our arrival couldn't be better timed,' Lin replied.

'Thank you, ma'am. Yes, we have identified an uninhabited planet and are about to send that energy meal and shake on the illuminated Exodus Deck down there to it. Our tracking machine here will show its condition when it arrives.'

Gran leant forward and pressed a button on a microphone, 'All personnel stand clear of the Exodus Deck and press your clearance button when in a safe viewing area.'

A scurry of personnel gathered in several areas designated by green chevrons on the floor as Gran watched the red lights on his screen turn green for each Shadower.

'Okay, ma'am, we are ready to start the exit process.'

'But there are still three red lights,' Juli pointed out.

'Those are for us. In the event of an explosion, this area is classified as at risk. May I recommend you join the senior team in the VIP gallery, please?' Gran indicated a raised area at the back of the room.

'Nonsense, I want to watch the action up close,' Lin replied dismissively. 'Besides, I want to see if they get there or if they're totally destroyed.'

Gran looked at Juli pleadingly, but she just nodded at him to continue. He went to press a button to seal the Grand Exodus room doors when there was a clatter behind them, and one of the doors flew open, followed by two Shadowers pushing a cleaning trolley.

Gran turned around and shouted, 'Who're you, and how did you get in here?'

'Oh, I'm sorry, have we interrupted something? We've just had this room added to our cleaning rota. I'm Claudurath, and this is my sister, Sabrath, Sir.'

'Well, shut that door, move into that green area, and stay there.'

Gran waited for the cleaners to shut the doors and turned to Lin. 'I'm sorry, ma'am. I've sealed the doors now. Shall I continue?'

Lin nodded her approval before giving the cleaners a look that could kill.

'Exit in five, four, three, two, one, exiting,' Gran pressed a button on a screen, and the machine sprang to life.

The ceiling split in two, leaving the upper end of the barrel aiming at the stars. With a low grumbling noise, the barrel slowly moved to the left and pointed higher into the sky before a siren sounded. The machine started to hum, and an electronic voice said, 'Target planet secured.'

'Permission to go, ma'am?'

Lin nodded, and Gran pressed buttons on separate screens simultaneously with his left and right hands. The electrical hum increased, and the Exodus Deck filled with a bright light as an electronic voice counted down from ten, followed by a flash of white light shooting out of the upper end of the barrel towards the stars.

'Well?' Lin asked impatiently.

'Sorry, ma'am, even though it's a small amount of energy, it still takes a few seconds. Wait, look at the screen, it says it's arrived, and it's perfect.'

'Excellent, Gran. I had every confidence in you,' Juli said excitedly.

'So we'll be able to reassure our Supreme Leader in a few weeks that we have safely sent Shadowers to distant planets and in numbers rather than one at a time?' Lin asked.

Gran looked nervously, 'We can start multiple energy exits immediately, but when you say Shadowers to distant planets, how distant are we talking? Sending a Shadower via an Exodus machine over long distances could take weeks for them to arrive and for us to confirm their safe arrival.'

'How about KLT3.4e9.3?'

'Let me check.'

'That seems like a rather strange planet to pluck out of the blue, Lin,' Juli challenged.

'Oh, I've been given a list of habitable planets, and that was the one I was looking at when you brought me my shake,' Lin laughed.

'I've found it, ma'am. Could we try somewhere closer? That could take us three weeks to confirm the safe arrival of a Shadower.'

'Let me think for a minute. Oh, can you open the Exodus Deck door? I want to check it's clear, please.'

Lin watched Gran press a button to open the deck door. Then she turned around. 'You, yes, you, the cleaning people, go into the Exodus Deck and make sure it's clean and that none of the energy meal was left behind.'

Claudurath and Sabrath pushed their cleaning trolley forward and left it at the deck entrance before going inside and looking around for any signs of the meal, but the area was spotless. On the control deck, Lin leant forward and pressed the door button she'd seen Gran press, locking the cleaners inside.

'Hey, you locked us in,' Sabrath shouted.

'Sorry, I'm not sure what happened, just give me a second,' Gran apologised.

Lin stood between Gran and the control screens, 'If we send them now, we'll know before the Grand Gathering that the machine works with multiple Shadowers over long distances.'

'B-b-but we've yet to test it on Shadowers. Never mind multiple Shadowers or over long distances, ma'am.'

'That's okay. They'll be adventurers, blazing a trail for our esteemed Supreme Leader. Surely anyone would be willing to take a risk to earn such an honour.'

'Well-l-l, I guess so, ma'am.'

'Let us out,' the cleaners shouted in unison.

'Lin, it still needs to be tested. What if they die during the exit?' Juli pleaded, her face twisted in a dance of emotions.

'It's okay; we can soon get some new cleaners,' Lin joked, moving away from the controls. 'Gran, get on with it.'

Gran nodded slowly and repeated the exit procedure. With a low grumbling noise, the barrel slowly moved to the right and aimed at a lower point in the sky before a siren sounded. The machine started to hum, and an electronic voice said, 'Target planet secured.'

'What are you doing? Let us out. Please,' the cleaners begged.

'Permission to go, ma'am?'

Lin nodded, and Gran pressed the separate buttons for the second time. The electrical hum increased, and once again, the Exodus Deck filled with a bright light, and the electronic voice counted down from ten. There was the start of a scream from the deck before a longer flash of white light shot out of the upper end of the barrel towards the stars, followed by silence.

'Well?' Lin asked.

'Their exit appears to be successful, ma'am, but it'll be some time before we know if they're dead or arrived safely.'

'Excellent news, Gran. Come on, Juli, we've got a team meeting with the Project Leader in the 185th-floor conference room.'

A few minutes later, they stood by the chute area, waiting for some to arrive.

'I can't believe you did that.' Juli glowered at her sister.

'Why not? My job, correction, the job of all of us, is to get this machine up and ready for the Grand Gathering. We can't afford to tell the Supreme Leader we need a few more weeks of testing.'

'What's happened to you, Lin? The sister I know would never have been cruel like that.'

Lin dropped her voice to a whisper, 'Juli, the planet is in serious trouble, and time is running out. You're right. I would never have done that in the past, but I've been told we now have to take risks for the greater good. Besides, the Exodus technology has been around for some time, so we know travel that way is safe; it's just the distance that could be risky.'

'I hope you're right and those two cleaners survive.'

A single-person chute arrived, and Lin stood inside and turned to face Juli. Lin said, 'Stop worrying, Juli. We've just saved days of testing.' Then, the glass door sealed the chute closed.

'Or we've killed two colleagues for no reason,' Juli scowled as she watched the glass chute shoot downwards and away before stepping into another one that had just arrived.

2
ENEMY OF THE PLANET

'Simo, great to see you,' Max said, opening the door as he welcomed his friend and colleague into his dwelling.

'You too, Max. How's Lin and the grumpy old beggar?' Simo said, hugging his friend.

'The grumpy old beggar is doing well, thank you, Simoraxin,' Zym shouted from the next room.

Simo and Max walked into the living room, where Zym was watching a game show, and sat down.

'Cogi, vision off,' Zym said.

'I'd say you're looking well, Zym, but my mother taught me never to lie,' Simo laughed.

'What is it with you junior enforcers? Did they forget to teach you young'uns respect for your elders during training?' Zym smiled.

'Excuse me, but I'm not so junior nowadays. High Counsellor Jericesen has just appointed me as Simohal.'

'Simo, that's fabulous news. I guess you'll be getting a team of your own?' Max beamed.

'Stop right there. First of all, how the heck did Jericraxin get an e-name and become a High Counsellor? He was my partner, and I was his superior.'

'Just think it could have been you having absolute control over all the raxins and other enforcers if it wasn't for the...' Simo trailed off.

'It's okay, you can say if it wasn't for the accident,' Zym replied. 'So come on, how does a jumped-up bit of a kid get promoted to a hal and be responsible for a whole team of intergalactic enforcers?'

'Quality always rises to the top, Zym,' Simo laughed. 'Plus, they are setting up a new security squad to protect the Migration Lottery as they think Dronin will stage a protest.'

'Quality? More like desperation,' Zym joked. 'Dronin? As in Droninhal?'

'He left the enforcers a long time ago. He's now on the Elite Council's most wanted list for offences against the planet. Don't you watch the news?' Simo asked with a puzzled look.

'Why would I watch anything pumped out by the propaganda machine?'

'Be careful, Zym,' Max said, nodding towards a glowing Cogi.

'I just mean I'd trust Dronin with my life. In fact, I did; he was the one who pulled me out of the craft after the accident.'

'When did you last see him?' Simo demanded.

'Hey, I'm not some Deceptor, you know. I've not seen him since just after his promotion to a hal after my accident.'

'Sorry, Zym, but I had to ask.'

'Zymraxin, I must caution you that protecting an enemy of the planet is an offence carrying the maximum sentence of death by Daxson,' Cogi said coldly.

'Stand down, Cogi. Simo was only asking Zym out of curiosity and not as part of an enforcer investigation.'

'Understood, Maxoraxin,' Cogi replied.

'So what has Droninhal done to make him an enemy of the planet?' Zym asked.

'He's just Dronin now. He's been stripped of all titles and privileges. He claimed he was trying to expose what he called corruption between enforcers, the Elite Council and Zephyrion's House of Finance. But it was a plot to overthrow the government and seize power himself under military rule. Now he's under the radar of all our systems and running what we believe to be an underground network of rebels, but we are closing in,' Simo explained.

'Simohal, I must caution you not to discuss an ongoing investigation with a civilian,' Cogi said.

'Hey, I'm still a raxin, thank you,' Zym snarled.

'Zymraxin, you are permitted to retain your raxin title as a mark of respect following your retirement due to injury in action. You are not an enforcer,' Cogi informed him.

Simo tapped a device hanging from his waist, then said, 'Cogi, you are incorrect. Section 13c of the enforcer's guide of conduct, covering officers of the state injured in action and updated for the laws of transition, clearly states, "By the functionality bestowed by transitioning, any officers of the state injured in action remain an enforcer and may be reinstated from retirement should transitioning return said officer to full health."'

'I apologise for any misunderstanding, Simohal. Of course, you are currently correct.'

'I could do with one of them,' Max laughed.

'Hal issue only, junior,' Simo smiled. 'But I do have a favour to ask.'

'Which is?'

'I need a second in command I can trust, and I can't think of anyone better than you.'

'But we're intergalactic enforcers. We've had light and heavy atmosphere training and specialist Deceptor tracking coaching. It's what we know. How does that match security work?'

'Because my team has two roles. One is to prevent Deceptors and especially Dronin from interrupting the Lottery.'

'And the other?'

'To track Dronin down and bring him in. That's where you come in. I've inherited someone who will manage the Lottery security. Jericesen said he'd done some of the biggest security events, and I need you to help me track and capture Dronin.'

'Don't do it, Max. Dronin saved my life, and you are one of the best trackers I've ever known.'

'Zym, I'm sorry. I'm sure once upon a time, Dronin may have been a good guy, but if the Elite Council has declared him an enemy of the planet, he must have changed. It happens,' Max sighed.

'But, Max, you hate the—' Zym started.

'I hate the bureaucracy, but I support the Council,' Max interrupted.

'So, will you join me?' Simo asked.

'Yes, Simo, I'd love to join your new team.'

Simo lifted his device and tapped a few buttons, then said, 'Maxoraxin, do you wish to join Simohal's enforcer squad and accept and agree to comply with all orders issued by him?'

'I do so wish.'

'Do you also accept the responsibility of being his second-in-command and further agree that in the event of Simohal's inability to fulfil his duties, you shall stand in his stead?'

'I so shall do.'

'Welcome to the team, Max.'

'It looks like I'll have to go through this transitioning thing after all, if only to make sure somebody is doing the day job while you two are off playing security guards,' Zym laughed.

'Seriously, Zym? Would you become an enforcer again if you were to transition?' Simo asked.

'It's the only thing I know, so yeah, I would.'

Simo picked up his device, tapped a few buttons, and said, 'Let's make it official. Zymraxin, I formally offer you the role of enforcer when you transition and subject to you recovering the use of your missing leg. Do you accept this offer?'

Zym looked at Max, smiling proudly, 'I do accept.'

'It seems that subject to your transition, Zephyrion has us brothers back on the enforcer team,' Max replied.

'I'm not sure this world can survive much longer having that thrust upon it!' Simo laughed. 'Although saying that, Jericesen will probably have a hissy fit hearing you're back under his leadership.'

'Aww, can you hold off telling him? After all, I need to book myself in for transitioning first,' Zym laughed.

The following day, a figure shuffled down the streets of the Deserted Zone, a part of the city long forgotten because of the high radiation levels caused by the solar dome's absence. The solar dome was an electronic shield installed many years ago to protect the city's inhabitants from the worst of the direct solar radiation.

Once upon a time, the Deserted Zone had also been protected by the solar dome, but the shifting tectonic plates had released poisonous gases, long since dissipated, which resulted in the zone being abandoned and the dome projectors reallocated to other parts of the city.

The towering skyscrapers that once reached for the stars like giants now sagged of old age, crumbling as if the ravages of time had weakened their giant spines, leaving them almost mirroring the gait of the figure walking between them.

The offices that once bustled with the noise and vigour of trade were now reduced to feeble whispers, whilst abandoned and decaying vehicles lay strewn across the cracked mosaic-like street reminiscent of children's toys from a bygone era.

The lone figure shuffled along this eerie tableau, his movement slow and deliberate. His steps kicked up dust that swirled around him like memories reluctant to fade as he glanced around to ensure he wasn't being followed.

He stopped by a small stone building, one of the few remnants of the ornate buildings that used to adorn the zone before it became a world of glass and metal. He pressed a small button beside the door and stood back.

'I'm sorry, but this zone is now declassified and empty. You are recommended to return to the city. Please identify yourself and your reason for being here, and then depart. Have a glorious day.'

Zym scratched his head. How could Cogi be out here when the zone is declassified? He shrugged and said, 'Zymraxin, I'm here to ensure the area is safe.'

He could hear movement behind the door, and it opened slowly, revealing a large guard holding a weapon.

'Come in and stand inside that box,' the guard said, indicating a metal box behind him.

Zym entered the box, and the guard held out a large wire basket and whispered, 'Remove your watch and all other electrical devices and place them in here.'

Zym did as instructed, and the guard closed the basket lid and handed it to a colleague who placed it in a slowly vibrating cupboard.

'That's better. We can talk freely now. I'm Cal. That machine will relay information through your devices as if they have been updating and resetting, and it will use your home details to make it look like you are there. How long will it take you to get home?'

'Hi, Cal. I'm Zymraxin. About an hour if I can get a ride to the edge of the zone.'

'Blar set the extraction time to two hours,' Cal told his colleague. Turning back to Zym, he said, 'When you get home, stay there for at least another hour. This will allow the devices to fully reset and upload to your home Cogi, and it'll look like you never left home. Now follow me.'

As they walked down a corridor, Zym asked, 'How come you've got a Cogi on your front entrance? Surely that allows the Elite to track you?'

'It's not real, just a mock-up to distract any curious passersby. I hope you don't mind me saying, but you don't look well enough to be a raxin.'

'I had to retire due to an accident, but I'm still an enforcer at heart,' Zym replied.

'What is it with you ex-enforcers? Keri is exactly the same,' Cal laughed.

They stopped, and Cal knocked on a door. A voice shouted, and Cal opened the door to reveal a small room surrounded by full bookcases. In the middle of the room was a large leather-topped but well-worn wooden desk, and behind it sat a thin man wearing an old green jumper. He had clearly transitioned as Zym could see the faint aura surrounding him, but that aside, everything felt and looked like some bizarre old-fashioned detective programme.

'Zym, come in. Thank you, Cal. You can leave us and shut the door behind you.' Dronin stood and walked around the desk.

'Hello, Dronin, you're looking well,' Zym said as he struggled to shake hands.

'I wish I could say the same, Zym. Why haven't you transitioned?'

'After the accident, I lost any reason to carry on.'

'I still remember pulling you out of the craft's wreckage. You were such a fighter, even after losing your leg. I hated seeing you retreat into your shell, and I never found out why they stopped us from seeing you.'

'I'm sorry, Dronin. That was my fault. I started losing myself and got them to ban all visitors. I was convinced everyone was against me or out to get me. I didn't even trust Max. I pushed everyone away.'

'What turned you around?'

'Max did. He refused to give up on me and kept investigating what caused the crash. It took him a long time, but he never stopped the hunt.'

'Did he find anything?'

'Yeah. It turned out that the financial fraud I'd been investigating was tracked to a Deceptor Gang Lord with government links. They tampered with my craft, and when the crash failed to kill me, they started giving me drugs in the hospital, which made me paranoid. If Max hadn't been determined and refused to give up on me, I'd have never survived.'

'Did they catch everyone involved?'

'Yes. Max literally saved my life. I'd never admit it to him, but as an enforcer, I'd say he's as good if not better than our parents were.'

'I don't remember any of that. I must have left before then.'

'Why did you leave? I was convinced you would end up as Droninesen.'

'No chance. They'd never risk anyone as determined as me in that role. I hear Jeric is esen now. But I don't understand how he could become the High Counsellor of all enforcers when he rarely caught any Deceptors and was just a yes man. As for me, I didn't so much leave as I was persuaded to go.'

'Why?'

'Not long after your crash, I uncovered a plot to remove the Supreme Leader and replace him with a hereditary Regent Supreme. A position for life that gets passed down through that Shadower's children.'

'So no more elections? Not that they were that fair since only the Elite Council members voted on the SL. But at least the Elite Council elections are a bit more open.'

'Surely you don't believe that, do you?' Dronin challenged.

'What do you mean?'

'The voting has been rigged ever since it went digital. That was what your parents were investigating when they died in that crash. They got me involved as a junior raxin, and when they were killed, I swore to keep up their investigation.'

'They weren't killed. It was an accident. Max always claimed there was more to it, but their spacecraft crashed. It was a simple tragic accident.'

'Zym, join the dots. Your parents were investigating vote rigging and were killed in a crash. You've just told me you were almost killed in a crash when you were investigating fraud and corruption.'

'But if that's the case, how come you're still alive?'

'Because I woke up late, so my partner took our son to school in our landcraft instead of me.'

Zym sat there contemplating what Dronin had told him, 'Oh, Dronin. I'm so sorry.'

'It was a long time ago, but I won't give up until I understand who is involved in Project Cronis and bring them all down.'

Zym sat mulling over the crashes and absentmindedly replied, 'I'm not surprised.'

'Anyway, please excuse my manners. Can I get you a drink?'

'I wouldn't say no to a drink if you have something.'

Dronin tapped a button and said, 'Two bottles of Brackles Best and some snacks, please, for our guest.'

'You remembered? Where did you find some? Alcohol was banned after the Grand Formation.'

'Of course, I remembered. We had some great nights when we were younger, and luckily for us, the old brewery is in the Deserted Zone, and when they evacuated, they left a lot of stock behind. Anyway, why did you come here and more importantly, how did you find us?'

'The finding you bit was easy. Do you remember Keriraxin?'

'I shouldn't say this, but of course I do. Keri is part of our team operating in the city. Although she's not a raxin anymore.'

'Yes, I know. She's working at the local Zingles bar. I saw her early this morning and said I needed to see you.'

'Looks like I need to improve our security if people are handing out my address like calling cards,' Dronin laughed as Cal entered the room with the drinks and snacks.

After waiting for Cal to leave, Zym said, 'I told Keri I needed to see you urgently, and she knows we've been friends for as long as I care to remember.'

'Oh, absolutely. I'm constantly getting greeting cards from you and invitations to dinner parties. It's incessant. I barely get any time to myself,' Dronin chuckled.

'I'm sorry. I know I could blame my injuries and everything, but the truth is I've become a recluse. Since I moved in with Max and Lin, I've basically given up. Well, actually, I moved in with them because I had given up. I even refused to transition because I just wanted this misery to end. I didn't see a future when we're losing every one of our freedoms. The Elite control every part of our existence.'

'Blimey, I thought I was a misery gut! Get this down your neck and tell me what's changed to bring you here,' Dronin said, opening one of the bottles of Brackles and handing it to Zym with a smile.

'Cheers, Dronin. To the good old days,' Zym said, taking a large swig of the cool, refreshing green ale.

'No, my friend. To the bright future days.'

'That's why I'm here. I'm sure you're aware the Elite has declared you an enemy of the planet, but did you know they've assigned two top enforcers to track you down.'

'Yes, I heard I'd been bestowed that title. But how do you know about them assigning trackers to find me? I'm not bothered; they've tried it before, and it didn't turn out well for them. Why are you so worried?'

'Because the enforcers assigned are Simohal and Maxoraxin, and they believe you'll do something at the Migration Lottery next week.'

'Would that be so bad if I did? Besides, I've heard the top man involved in Cronis will be there, so I need to be there.'

Zym lowered his drink, 'Cronis?'

'Yes, I said earlier. The plan is to overthrow the Supreme Leader and install a Regent Supreme. Cronis is their codename for it.'

'Sorry, Dronin, but Cronis was the fraud I was investigating, and Max brought them all down.'

'Then this is an even bigger problem because the last communication we intercepted on Cronis was yesterday afternoon.'

'What did it say?'

'Test exit initiated. The final stage of Cronis is in motion.'

'Do you have any more information?'

'I've got some people on the inside helping me. I can't say much, but I'm sure it's linked to Operation Exodus.'

'In what way?'

'Your parents knew there was vote rigging to the Elite council. This ensured that only the wanted Shadowers made it to become the Elite. I'm joining the dots here, but I'm guessing the fraud you were investigating was some way for them to fund this all, and now we have Exodus.'

'But Max shut Cronis down.'

'Max just delayed Cronis by cutting off one of their funding routes, but the plan has stayed the same.'

'But what's the point of appointing someone as Regent Supreme when we'll soon be pushed out to other planets scattered across the skies? From what I've heard from Lin and Max, two planets will be devoid of civilisation, so having a

Regent will make no sense if we have to rebuild from scratch,' Zym said, swigging more of his beer.

'Because the Elite are so uptight, they don't want to lose control, especially on the one planet already having a Shadower civilisation.'

'Astral 5?'

'Exactly. From our information, the plan is to install this person as Regent Supreme on Astral 5 and only populate it with selected Shadowers.'

'So it will be an exclusive planet of the Elite without any of us normal Shadowers?'

'Not quite. The Elite will need workers who will be vetted and specially selected for their skill sets. No Deceptors or rebels will be allowed. Only those who swear allegiance to the new Regent Supreme will be allowed to go there.'

'But Exodus is sending Shadowers to two other planets as well as Astral 5,' Zym said.

'They will be feeder planets for Astral 5. The brightest and those with needed skills will be allowed to migrate to Astral 5, and those planets will also be backups for Astral 5 in case it develops any climate problems. All three planets swearing allegiance to the Triple Crown of the Regent Supreme. But I've said too much. You need to promise to keep this to yourself.'

'Of course, Dronin. If I can help in any way, let me know.'

'That's good to know, Zym, but in that state, I'm afraid you won't be able to do much.'

'I'm going to transition, and Simo has agreed to take me back as an enforcer.'

'That's great news, Zym. Get in touch when you have transitioned. In the meantime, I'll get Cal to take you home. I'm assuming he's taken care of your electronic devices?'

'Yes, he said I must stay home for a while to let them reset.'

'That's right. Do you have anything else on you that might confirm you've been away from your dwelling?'

'Keri sorted me out with a lift to the edge of the Deserted Zone, so there's no payment trail except this receipt from the driver to give back to her.'

Dronin took the receipt and threw it in the bin along with the empty bottle of Brackles. 'I'll make sure Keri is repaid, and I'll save this Brackles for when we are standing side by side after bringing down Cronis, my friend.'

3
THE LOTTERY

'You, yes you. What are you doing? Is this your idea of dancing, or did you attend the Chaos School of Art?' the choreographer spat in frustration at one of the dancers.

'Do we really need to be here?' Max sighed.

'I've got to make sure the team know what to expect,' Simo said. 'Besides, you're getting a free show. People are paying hundreds of credits to see this tomorrow.'

'This isn't a game; it's life and death, blood and tears, and you're behaving like you're strolling through a park,' the choreographer's voice sliced through the air.

'See, it could be worse. You could be a dancer instead of having the pleasure of easygoing me as your boss,' Simo laughed as he checked the position of a security camera.

'That's true, but if you dare to ask me to pirot or whatever it's called, I'm out of here.'

'It's pirouette, you heathen, and don't worry; I think you'd be better as one of the statues than as a dancer. Well, the cameras all look fine,' Simo said, inspecting the last security camera.

'I know I'm new to security enforcement, but those cameras look bulky.'

'That's because they include energy depletors like your weapon. My guys in the viewing gallery can point these at anyone using the built-in sight guides and shoot to within an accuracy of one macon.'

'One macon? Wow, that's about the thickness of my thumb. Are you sure? This place will be heaving tomorrow, and one false slip means heads will roll.'

'I'll prove it. See that energy shake at the back of the stage?' Simo said, picking up his device.

'No way, not with all those dancers jumping around.'

Max watched as one of the security cameras overhead rotated towards the stage. Simo tapped a button, and the energy shake imploded almost silently as if it had never existed.

'Wow, do you need a direct hit on a Shadower to wipe them out?'

'There is no way I'd have these set at terminal power. It only depleted that shake's energy because it was so small. Any shot to the body or head of a Shadower should render them unconscious, and a limb shot would paralyse the limb.'

'That's it. I'm an artiste, but I'm expected to work with amateurs. You boy,' the choreographer's shrill tone rang out.

'I'm Chadre—'

'Do I look like I care what your name is? Just get off the stage now. Frank..., Frank! Send out a backup dancer, preferably one not made of stone, and someone get me a drink.'

A few seconds later, someone came scurrying over with a drink.

'What is this rubbish?' the choreographer said, knocking the drink out of the person's hand. 'Just get me a plain energy drink, not this junk.'

'I'm not being paid enough for this,' the person said as they hurried away, heading toward Max and Simo.

'Stop right there. Can I see your pass, please?' Max said, stepping in front of her.

'Yes, Sir,' she said, holding it out.

'Keritrek, hmm, I recognise your face. Have we met before?' Max said, studying her.

'I don't think so, Sir.'

'What are you doing here?'

'I work for Zingles, Sir. They are the main sponsors for the Migration Lottery and are doing all the catering.'

Simo turned around, 'I'd know that voice anywhere. Keriraxin, what are you doing here?'

'Simo, wow, it's been a long time. I'm Keritrek now, and I work for Zingles. I left the enforcers ages ago. What are you doing here?'

'I've been promoted to a hal and put in charge of lottery security. Max, here is my deputy. Why did you leave?'

'My partner turned out to be a Deceptor, and under the new enforcer rules, you have to resign, even if you never knew and your partner has subsequently been killed. Death by Daxson in his case,' Keri sighed.

'I'm so sorry to hear that. The Elite Council have toughened up so many rules.'

'But for the greater good, though,' Max added.

'Max, you must be the only enforcer I've ever met who's ruthless at his job but still looks for the good in everyone!' Simo laughed.

'Nice to see you again, Simo, and nice to meet you too, Max. But I need to go and get the choreographer's drink before she kills someone,' Keri said, hurrying away.

'Good to see you too, Keri. Come on, Max, I'll introduce you to Lucraxin. He's my head of the security team.'

A few minutes later, Max and Luc exchanged pleasantries in the viewing gallery as Simo studied the array of screens.

'Do you have everywhere covered?' Simo asked.

'Yes, Sir. We can see and pick out any individual in the 75,000 audience with no blind spots.'

'And the performers?'

'End-to-end coverage of the stage, Sir.'

'And backstage?' Max asked.

'Why would we have cameras there? The audience is out front.'

'Luc, have you been in charge of many security jobs?'

'No, this is my first Max. Why do you ask?'

'No reason. I guess you just saw the opportunity to get some senior experience and applied?'

'I didn't apply. Jericesen pulled me off transport and gave me the job. I felt honoured, especially as it meant working with Simohal.'

Simo turned his attention from the screens, 'Did you say transport?'

'Yes, Sir. I'm a fast learner, though.'

'We need more cameras. Max, follow Luc to all the areas not covered by cameras, work out how many we need, and get them in place by tomorrow morning at the latest. Delaying the show isn't an option.'

'Okay, Simo.'

'But Sir, we don't have any more cameras. That was all we were sent.'

'Do we have any overlapping cameras that we can move?'

'No, Sir. The plans were detailed, and we had exactly the right number to match.'

'Who prepared those plans? Show me.'

Luc hit some buttons, and a schematic of the auditorium and camera positions appeared on the screen. He zoomed into the lower right corner, 'You did, Sir. Look, there's your code mark.'

'That does look like yours, Simo.'

'I've never seen those plans in my life.'

'Who supplied the cameras?' Max asked.

Luc pulled up the delivery certificate, 'It's the Council Procurement Office.'

'Max, take Luc and work out what we need. I'll contact the CPO and see how many they can get us and by when.'

An hour later, Max and Luc re-entered the viewing gallery.

'Covering all backstage areas, excluding changing rooms but including the Elite lounge and all entrances and exits, will take thirty more cameras as a minimum, Simo.'

'It's irrelevant anyway. The CPO said they could only get us more in five or six days,' Simo replied.

'We'll have to station as many enforcers as we can. That's our only option,' Max suggested.

'Excuse me, Max and Simo, sirs, I can get some cameras. Not like the others with built-in depletors and sights, but at least we'll be able to see what's going on back there. But it's not quite—'

'Shh, Luc. Cogis have ears. Take Max and get them. I need some explanations from Jericesen.'

An hour later, Simo stood in Jericesen's office, 'What the heck is going on, Jeric? You said Lucraxin was experienced in security.'

'That's what I was told, Simo. Our Supreme Leader, Timezel, personally recommended him. Apparently, Luc had impressed him at an event.'

'He was in transport. In what way does that make him a security expert?'

'I was told to put him in charge because of his experience,' Jeric protested.

'His experience in directing traffic, yeah, great choice. Hang on; I know someone who cooks a mean burger. Let's make them the next esen in charge of the enforcers, shall we?'

'Calm down, Simo. I wouldn't have made you a hal if I wasn't sure you could deal with problems. Things go wrong, and I'm sure you and Max can sort it.'

'Problems? Problems are when someone gets the time wrong for a pick-up or when a Deceptor changes their plan. This is a monumental screw-up, and that's ignoring the fact that my code mark has been forged on the camera plans.'

'What do you need to sort this out?'

'We need thir... fifty depletor cameras tonight and an additional sixty enforcers for the show.'

'Call the CPO to get the cameras, and I can get you ten more enforcers.'

'I've tried the CPO, and they've said no chance in the timescale and ten enforcers? Fine, just leave the Supreme Leader and Deputy Supreme Leader to Deceptors. I'm not responsible for their security.'

'Simo, you're lucky enforcer offices are one of the few Cogi-free locations because talk like that could be considered treason.'

'Thirty-five armed enforcers, or else, and I need cameras.'

'I've no control over the CPO, but okay, twenty officers.'

The magnificent Migration Lottery Arena glowed like a beacon of light amongst the city's gloom. Its outer walls were giant screens relaying the inside of the building, almost as if the walls weren't there, and you could see the crowds inside swaying to the sounds of a band playing enthusiastically on the stage. Multi-coloured lasers flickered towards the stars as if in battle with the light droids, dancing across the sky in a preprogrammed display of precision, showing the faces of the Supreme Leader and his deputy before switching to a giant Migration Lottery logo.

'Go home. The arena is now full. Nobody else will be granted access. Credit fines will be issued to everyone failing to disperse,' came a booming voice across the sound system outside the arena.

'I've got a terrible feeling about this, Simo,' Max said, studying the screens in the viewing gallery.

'Me too. I've got three other viewing galleries, with two enforcers in each. Luc and Jeric are stationed with three other enforcers at the Elite Council entrance. Including the twenty enforcers from Jeric, I've got about ninety stationed around the arena, including backstage. But it still doesn't feel enough.'

'I can't believe Jeric refused to give you more. We've got one continuous Zingles bar running around the perimeter of the arena, so you've got more chance of buying a burger than seeing an enforcer! It's a good job Luc came up trumps with the extra cameras.'

'He'll make a good enforcer one day. I just wish we had someone with more experience in that role.'

'What access have you been given to Cogi?'

'I'm told it's full access within the building, excluding the Elite Council and their guests.'

'Cogi, how much of the audience is wearing their own Cogi-enabled devices?'

'Hello, Maxoraxin. Currently, eighty-four-point-seven percent of the audience matches your criteria. However, one hundred percent have a Cogi-enabled glow band on their wrist.'

'Did you really think I could resist the opportunity to use the fad for glow bands to track everyone,' Simo laughed.

'You cunning little devil. Let's test it then.'

'Good idea. Cogi play the audio and video from glow band 17,236.'

The screen flickered and showed a waving image of the crowd as a voice said, 'I'll have two Zingles energy bucket meals, both with energy shakes, please, and —'

'Cogi, change the image to the glow band nearest the front and centre of the stage,' Max said.

The image changed to the band playing, but it looked like the camera operator was dancing along to them, 'They're so good, aren't they?'

A muffled voice could be heard replying, 'Yeah, but I wish they'd start the show.'

'Cogi, show the glow band furthest from the stage,' Max said.

'There are currently two glow bands in the same place. Which would you like to see, 9,346 or 9,347?'

'Show one on each screen,' Simo replied.

The screens flickered, showing shaky images of a wall from each glow band, 'Oh, Mic, please do that again. It was—'

'Cogi off. Blimey, we don't need to monitor some things,' Max laughed.

'You prude. You were young once, you know,' Simo chuckled.

Luc's voice came over a speaker, preventing further frivolity, 'Our esteemed guests are just arriving.'

Simo pressed a button and replied, 'Thanks, Luc. All enforcers be prepared. This is a level one operation, action status two.'

Several minutes passed, with Luc providing a running commentary of the guests as they were escorted to the Elite Lounge and given refreshments.

'Simo, Bobmaton has just come into the room. I've never met anyone famous before, and now I've met the Supreme Leader, Deputy Supreme Leader and Bobmaton,' Luc whispered excitedly.

Simo looked at Max and gently shook his head, 'He's like an excited youngster in a goodies shop.'

'Twenty credits says he'll have Bobmaton's autograph by the night's end.'

'That's such a certainty I'd need long odds to take that bet,' Simo laughed.

The band finished playing, and the lights in the arena went out. Only the glimmer from the surrounding Zingles bar provided any illumination, looking like a red and blue halo around the central blackness of Shadowers.

A ghostly voice boomed across the arena, 'Fellow Zephyrions worldwide and here in the Migration Lottery Arena, it's time for the greatest show of all time. But first, please show your respect for our Supreme Leader and the esteemed Elite Council as we hear All Praise Zephyrion.'

The global anthem played out as the Supreme Leader, Timezel, the Deputy Supreme Leader, Nicoeyel and the Elite Council ceremoniously walked onto the stage one by one, bowed to the audience and took up preplanned positions on the stage.

The anthem finished, and Timezel stepped forward, 'Zephyrions, we stand here on the brink of the end of our civilisation on this planet. We have worked hard to save our world but now face an insurmountable threat. Across the globe, we can see the devastating impact of climate change, so tonight, we start our journey to create a new future.

'Without the global effort to find new opportunities for us, we will reach a point where this planet can no longer survive as the atmosphere continues to become evermore inhospitable. Therefore, we have to start again to protect us all. First, I must beg you to stay home between sunset and sunrise. We have tried intermittent travel bans, but they are not enough. I thank you all for complying with these rules, but we must do more.

'From sunset tomorrow, there is a nighttime curfew. You may only leave your dwellings for specific purposes. Shopping for necessities is allowed, but you must do this no more than necessary and absolutely not more than every third day. Being outside in the hours of darkness for medical purposes, including transitioning and caring for vulnerable Zephyrions, is allowed. Travelling to or from work before sunrise or after sunset, where your job is classified as planet critical, is also permitted. Cogi has been updated with all jobs meeting this classification, so if you need more clarification on your job, ask your Cogi.

'You may no longer arrange social meetings with anybody who does not share your dwelling during the hours of darkness, either in your dwelling or elsewhere. If you disobey these rules, the enforcers have the authority to deploy their energy depletors at whatever level they deem appropriate, including terminal depletion.

'Except for energy or organic food shops, only retailers with remote ordering and delivery can trade during the hours of darkness. All ceremonies that take place after sunset are also now banned, without exception.

'No Supreme Leader has ever had to enact these measures, nor would ever want to, but we are in extreme circumstances. We will provide social credits to everybody affected by these rules until they migrate to a new planet. The future will be challenging, and I regret that some of us may not make it to the new dawn, but science is our friend. We are expanding our Exodus machine programme to make faster and more efficient machines. Those lucky tonight will be amongst the first migrated, but please be patient. You will all receive your personal migration dates.

'The time you give us by obeying these rules will provide us with the time to organise the safe migration of us all. I stand here today with a promise. My Elite Council and I are your servants. Your survival and future are our priority, and as such, we will be amongst the last to leave Zephyrion once you are all safe.

'I am honoured to be your Supreme Leader, and I know every one of you will rise to this final challenge because this is the last thing we must overcome on this planet we call home. So, I ask you all to stand together in this final task. The Great Exodus means we have a bright future ahead of us on different planets, but we will always be Zephyrions. May you all be blessed.'

Bobmaton burst onto the stage, bowed to Timezel, then turned and threw his hands in the air, 'Thank you, Supreme Leader and esteemed Elite Council. Zephyrions show your appreciation for—'

The screens around the arena flickered, and then a hooded figure appeared in front of an image of the Grand Exodus room, 'Yes, thank you, Supreme Leader and the Elite Council, for throwing the planet's biggest party before you kill us all. That is what tonight is, my fellow citizens. We have all been lied to. We know our planet is on the brink, but far from helping us all escape to new worlds, their real plan is mass extermination.'

Simo was screaming into his communicator, 'What the hell is this? Someone get that feed cut now.'

'Simo, I've just spoken to the broadcast executives next door. They have no control over anything,' Max said.

'Can they at least cut the feed to the rest of the planet?'

'They've got engineers working on it now. I've also told Luc to take some enforcers and see if they can find where that Deceptor is.'

'With Lin, by the looks of it,' Simo shouted, pointing at the monitors.

'You see, my fellow citizens, we've received evidence of a new extermination machine they've built. When they conned us into transitioning, they ignored the data about our bodies decaying. This time, they are killing us and sending our remains into space. What you are about to see is beyond shocking.'

The hooded figure disappeared to show the Grand Exodus room with Lin, Juli and Gran on the upper control deck.

'You, the cleaning people, go into the Exodus Deck,' Lin said.

The cleaners were shown heading into the glass-walled room, and then the image zoomed in on Lin pressing something on the console.

'Hey, you locked us in,' Sabrath shouted.

'Sorry,' Gran apologised.

The image moved to a wide shot of the room as Lin said, 'We'll know before the Grand Gathering that the machine works with multiple Shadowers.'

'B-b-but we've not tested it on Shadowers at all yet. Never mind multiple Shadowers, ma'am,' Gran said.

'For our esteemed Supreme Leader, surely anyone would be willing to earn such an honour,' Lin replied.

'Well-l-l, I guess so, ma'am.' Gran was heard saying.

'It's okay; we can soon get some new cleaners,' Lin joked. 'We'll be able to reassure our Supreme Leader that they're totally destroyed.'

'What are you doing? Let us out. Please,' the cleaners begged.

The Exodus Deck filled with light, and you could hear a scream before the glow subsided. The image zoomed in to show the deck now empty.

'Well?' Lin asked.

'It'll be some time before we know if they're dead.'

'Excellent news,' Lin replied.

The image froze on Lin's face as the arena was filled with an almost deafening gasp.

'What the heck was that?' Simo asked.

Max shouted down his communicator, 'Lin, have you been watching the Lottery? ... What do you mean it's not what... Well, did it or... What does sort of mean... uh huh... okay... well, the planet isn't going to think that... No, under no circumstances, leave our dwelling. I'll get some enforcers to you and to Juli and send me the address details of that man with... Well, make some calls and find out where he lives. All three of you are in danger.'

4

THE TRAIL

Several minutes after the interrupted transmission, the screens around the arena still flashed the same message, 'There is a technical fault. Normal transmission will begin shortly.'

An announcer's voice boomed around the arena, 'Zephyrions, I am sure you are all as shocked as we are by the lies told in that cheaply hacked-together imagery. While we prepare to resume tonight's history-making Migration Lottery, the esteemed Elite Council has agreed with Zingles that all refreshments will be free for the rest of this evening, so please place your orders at your nearest counter. In the meantime, our enforcers are in the process of capturing the Deceptor.'

From the viewing gallery, Simo and Max frantically communicated with enforcers to gauge the disruption caused by the Deceptor's message. A few fights had broken out, but these were quickly quelled, and the announcement of free food and drinks had further placated the crowd. But there were still plenty of reports of comments like, 'I knew this was too good to be true,' and, 'I said this climate change thing was a trick. They just want to get rid of us all.'

'Cogi, under no circumstances are you to issue warnings or fines relating to the social code or rumourmongering to anybody inside this arena,' Simo said sharply.

'Under who's authority? Simohal.'

'Under my authority as bestowed under the...' Simo tapped the device on his belt and then continued, 'Section 323 of the Elite Council's regulations on civil disturbance and disobedience in the event of a major crisis which may risk the lives of any Elite.'

'Very well, Simohal. This order will be invoked until the end of the current event, but it will require final approval by Jericesen. If such approval is not given within one day, all fines and warnings will be issued retrospectively.'

A junior broadcast runner appeared around the door into the viewing gallery, 'We've got full control back.'

Simo turned towards the voice, 'Well, that's something. Have you tracked where the signal came from?'

'There was a hard wire from the Zingles bar and then a series of relays, but it's so heavily encrypted using systems the Council banned years ago.'

'How many of those lies managed to get out beyond the arena?' Max scowled.

'Everything up to the point when those cleaners were begging to be let out. We managed to cut transmission before that scientist killed them.'

Max lunged at the door, grabbing the runner roughly. 'DON'T YOU EVER SAY THAT AGAIN. That scientist is my partner, and she has said that the shoddy little video was lies, editing bits and putting them out of sequence. Those Shadowers were volunteers to be the first sent via the latest Exodus machine to a distant planet. THEY ARE NOT DEAD.'

'Y-y-yes, mate, okay. I'm sorry.'

'Calm down, Max. That temper of yours will get you into trouble one day,' Simo said, prising the runner from Max's grip. 'The poor beggar only repeated what he had seen on the screen.'

Max turned away in frustration, 'Maybe so, but because of that Deceptor, my family's lives are now at risk. We need to get them protection.'

'Yes, we do. Get on the communicator to Jeric to get it sorted,' Simo replied. Turning to the runner, he asked, 'What is happening with the show?'

'The Lottery must go on. The Supreme Leader and his Deputy will make a joint statement, and then it's back to Bobmaton. In the meantime, we're showing a rerun of The Two Bobs to remind viewers that Bob is a really nice and funny guy before we restart the show.'

'Luc, it's Max. Where the heck is Jericesen? He's not answering his communicator.'

'He's currently with the Supreme Leader and the Elite Council. I'm not sure what they are discussing, but he mentioned he was coming up to see you and Simo afterwards.'

'Try to interrupt him. This is urgent.'

Luc turned towards the Elite Lounge, intending to knock on the door, when his path was blocked.

'You, enforcer, I demand protection? You do know who I am?' Bobmaton snarled.

'Yes, Bobmaton, of course I do. It is a great honour to meet you. I will see what I can do,' Luc replied, trying to sidestep him.

'Of course, it is an honour for you, but never mind "see what you can do!" I demand you place me immediately under your protection and arrange to get the commanding enforcer here with a protection team immediately.'

'I am sorry, Bobmaton, but the High Counsellor is busy with the Supreme Leader, his deputy and the Elite Council behind those doors. If you could return to your allocated dressing room, I will arrange for someone to see you as soon as possible.'

'Behind those doors, you say? Well, I am friends with Nicoeyel, so let's see about this,' Bobmaton said, marching towards the doors, where two armed security guards blocked his way.

'Get out of my way. I'm here to see our esteemed Deputy Supreme Leader,' Bobmaton ordered the guards.

'Nobody is allowed to pass, Sir. Order of the Supreme Leader himself.'

Luc watched the exchange between Bobmaton and the guards with amusement. The more the celebrity waved his hands like some crazed mythological beast, the more resolute the guards became. The predictable 'Don't you know who I am?' was met with a nod and a shrug, and an attempt to barge past resulted in Bobmaton being pushed down onto his backside. In one last desperate effort, the celebrity leant forward and whispered something to one of the guards.

'Are you sure, Sir?' the guard replied.

'Yes, and remember only to the Deputy Supreme Leader.'

A few minutes later, the guard reappeared with the DSL Nicoeyel and Jericesen, both looking angry.

'Who do you think you are, Bobmaton? That word is never to be mentioned in public,' Nicoeyel glowered.

'Sorry, Nicoeyel, but this enforcer refused to provide me with protection,' Bobmaton said, pointing towards Luc.

Luc went to respond, but Jeric indicated that he should remain quiet.

'Bob, you are here to present the greatest show anyone will ever see. But please remember, if you want to be included in our project, you must do as you're told and follow our rules. Am I making myself clear?' Nico said, calmly placing his arm over Bob's shoulders.

'Yes, but—'

'No buts, Bob. We can always send you to one of the other planets.'

'Understood, Nico. But can I at least have some protection in case there is more to come from that Deceptor?'

Nico smiled, 'Absolutely. Jeric?'

'Yes, Deputy Supreme Leader?'

'Can you personally escort Bobmaton to his dressing room and post an enforcer outside his door.'

'Not a problem, Deputy Supreme Leader.'

Bobmaton looked smug as he strode away with Jeric and Luc behind him.

'Oh, Jeric,' Nico shouted. Jeric turned, and Nico added in a lower voice, 'Once he's in his room, lock the door. Under no circumstances is he to be let out until we restart the show.'

'Yes, Nico.'

'Sir, Simo and Max have asked if you can contact them as soon as possible,' Luc said to Jeric.

'I was just about to head up to see them when Mister Ego there turned up. Let's get him secure, and then we can join them. I assume they're still in viewing gallery one.'

After settling Bobmaton back in his room, appointing an enforcer, and quietly locking the door, Jeric and Luc made their way through the crowds. The atmosphere in the arena was hot and humid as the building's atmosphere controls struggled to cope. It had been installed when the building was first built and before the significant deterioration in the climate over the last twenty years.

The air was rank with the smell of junk food. Even though most of the audience had now transitioned and were choosing energy meals and drinks, Zingles had found a way to make them smell and taste almost like real fried food. Unfortunately, the effect was considerably less convincing when that smell was mixed with the fragrance from the food prepared for the organic Shadowers who had yet to transition.

Jeric and Luc finally reached the viewing gallery, smelling far from pleasant.

'Blimey Jeric, have you and Luc been moonlighting as Zingles servers?' Simo quipped.

'Never mind that what the heck has been going on? Why didn't we know about this attack, and why wasn't it shut down sooner?' Jeric snarled, slamming his hand down on a desk.

'I did warn you that we needed more enforcers, and I'm sorry, but my prophecy implant isn't scheduled for a few weeks. So how were we supposed to know what would happen before it did?' Simo replied sarcastically.

'Don't turn this on me, Simohal. I appointed you because I thought you could be trusted, and I even approved Max joining your team so you could infiltrate Dronin's gang and bring him down before the event.'

'In fairness, Sir. I am making progress with Dronin, but to expect us to infiltrate and stop him in barely a week is impossible. By the way, can—'

'FAIRNESS? I'll tell you what's unfair, Max. I appoint two of my best enforcers to manage the biggest show in history, and you turn it into a screw-up.'

'You also said you gave me a right-hand enforcer who had "done some of the biggest security events." No disrespect, Luc, but Luc is nowhere near that experienced,' Simo interrupted.

'No problem, Sir. I agree with you,' Luc replied.

'So what's your grand plan then, Simo?' Jeric shot back.

'Max and I will go after Dronin as soon as the show is running smoothly. Luc and another enforcer will manage this viewing gallery and report to me if anything happens, and you can return to the Elite Council, Sir.'

'Not a chance. You're not leaving here until this event is over. Max, you said you've been making progress on Dronin. What do you know?'

'Dronin is living in the Deserted Zone. We're not certain where, but we've narrowed it down to within a few blocks, Sir.'

'Cogi, when was the last movement into or out of the Deserted Zone recorded today?'

'Hello, esteemed Jericesen. The last movement recorded was three young Shadowers riding their scootercraft into the area two hours ago.'

'Give me strength,' Jeric sighed. 'Cogi excluding young Shadowers playing, when was the last recorded movement?'

'Certainly, Jericesen and I apologise for the confusion. The last movement was by a large package landcraft approximately five hours ago, leaving the Deserted Zone into area Sixteen Street Three East.'

'That leads directly to where we think Dronin is,' Max replied.

'Cogi, has it been seen since?'

'Yes, Jericesen. From the moment it entered the city, it came straight to the arena, where two Shadowers disembarked and entered the Zingles bar. Would you like to see the footage?'

'Yes!'

The screens flickered and showed the package landcraft pulling up, and two Shadowers got out. They both went to the back of the craft, pulled out a heavy box, and went inside the arena. The camera changed to an internal one, showing the two Shadowers carrying the package to a side door into the Zingles bar. One of them knocked on the door, and a Shadower opened it, spoke to the other two and let them in with the box before the screens went blank.

'Cogi, where is the rest of the footage?' Jeric demanded.

'I am afraid that is all we have on them, Jericesen. The Zingles bar is a series of enclosed catering boxes, meaning the overhead cameras cannot see inside them.'

'What about the Cogi-enabled glow bands and security passes?'

'I'm sorry, Jericesen, but as they wore hoods over their heads, I did not have a facial image to reconcile to any glow band images.'

'And security pass images?'

'The security passes are not Cogi enabled, Jericesen,' Cogi replied.

'Do we know where the landcraft is now?'

'Yes, Jericesen. It is currently heading back towards area Sixteen on the same street. If it continues at its current pace, it will enter the Deserted Zone in under ten minutes.'

Jeric received a message on his communicator and, after reading it, looked up. 'Max, I want you and Luc ready to leave in ten minutes. Simo, call Trimhal and tell him I have authorised you to commandeer a team of fifteen of his enforcers to accompany Max under Max's leadership. I'll message Trim on my way to the Supreme Leader to approve it. The show is restarting in fifteen minutes. Don't mess this up for a second time.'

'Jeric, I need to speak to you about Lin, her sister Juli and the —'

'No need to worry, Max. As soon as that Deceptor started showing that video, the Deputy Supreme Leader immediately ordered a squad of enforcers to pick them up and place them in a Council safe house with armed protection.'

'Oh, that's kind of him to react so quickly. Can you let me know where they are?'

'Just get Dronin and his accomplices. I'll ensure Lin knows you've been told they're safe, and you can go to them when you get back. But I need to go. Before I forget, Simo, I approved your order not to issue penalty notices. Good thinking. The last thing we need are riots over fines.'

'Thank you, Sir.'

Max watched Jeric leave the viewing gallery and ensured the door was closed.

'Cogi, show the sequence where the Shadowers knocked on the side door to the Zingles.'

'What are you looking for?' Luc asked.

'Cogi freeze and zoom in to the Shadower opening the door,' Max replied.

The image froze and zoomed in. Max looked at Simo, who nodded in reply.

'Who is that?' Luc asked.

'Cogi, is Keritrek still in the arena?'

'Yes, Maxoraxin. Keritrek has appeared serving food at the Zingles bar on numerous glow bands and other cameras.'

'Cogi, place Keritrek under visual arrest. All movements are to be tracked and recorded, and any attempt to leave the arena carries an immediate alert.'

'Of course, Simohal. Would you like a restraint order added to any attempt to leave?'

'No, Cogi, just a priority one alert to me.'

Max and Luc headed towards the Deserted Zone, followed by several other enforcer landcraft. The stay-at-home order, which was due to start the following evening, meant the roads and streets were crowded, with Shadowers making last-minute dashes to do things before the curfew began.

'Sir, Simohal will be okay, won't he? Jericesen seemed very angry,' Luc asked.

'No need to call me Sir, Max is fine. As for Simo, he is tougher than he looks and certainly a lot tougher than Jeric.'

'Thanks, Max. I feel guilty for letting Simo down over the security. If I'd done everything right, you wouldn't have wasted yesterday correcting my mistakes and might have captured Dronin.'

'Luc, don't sweat it. Even I made mistakes when I was as new to the force as you. Yes, I know it's impossible to believe I could ever make mistakes.'

'Actually, Max, I was going to say you still do,' Luc replied with a smile.

'If it weren't for the fact you're in the control seat, I'd give you a slap,' Max laughed.

'That's okay, Max. I'd move slowly to give you a chance.'

'Excuse me, enforcers, I do hope I'm not interfering with your bonding session, but I just thought you'd like to know we are restarting the Lottery,' Simo's voice said through the landcraft's speakers.

'Sorry, Simo, I was just teaching this whippersnapper a thing or two about manners. Although I think he's a lost cause!' Max chuckled. 'Do we need to tune in to listen as I assume our Supreme Leader will be speaking?'

'No, it's fine. You're on enforcer business regarding protecting him and the Elite, so you have a legitimate excuse.'

'Any news on Lin, Juli and the others?'

'The enforcers have collected her and the others. The DSL insisted they stay in his dwelling on the city's edge. Let me know when you get into the Deserted Zone,' Simo replied.

'They're in the DSL's dwelling?'

'Yes, Max. Apparently, the DSL has been working closely with them on the new Exodus machines and felt one of his dwellings was the safest place for them. Didn't Lin tell you they were working together?'

'We never discuss work, Simo. Well, not the confidential stuff. It avoids arguments.'

'Hey, Luc, is it just me, or does it sound like Max has to behave at home?'

'I wouldn't know, Sir. I've not got a partner,' Luc said.

'Got to go, Simo, we're entering the Deserted Zone,' Max added.

Luc disengaged auto mode and slowed the landcraft. Despite the city's desolation caused by climate change, the Deserted Zone exaggerated that desolation to an extreme. Plants and trees were not just dead or dying memories of what once was; they had disappeared altogether. Buildings were beyond any hope of repair and were in danger of collapsing at any moment, creating a post-apocalyptic forecast of the fate awaiting the rest of the planet.

Luc manoeuvred the landcraft around the abandoned cars, then braked suddenly as young Shadowers shot across the road in front of them on their scootercrafts.

Max's emotions were on full alert as he opened his door and exited the landcraft. Instincts kicked in as he pulled out his depletor in case of danger.

'Oi, you lot get back into the city. It's not safe out here.'

'Why don't you go catch some Deceptors? You can't tell us what to do.'

Max aimed his depletor at one of the scootercraft and fired. The scootercraft's battery died, and its lights went out.

'Hey, you've killed my scootercraft.'

Max took a few steps towards them and smiled, 'Yes, and unless you go back to the city, I'll do the same to the rest of them, too.'

The young Shadowers shouted obscenities as they headed away, and Max got back into the enforcer landcraft.

'Where did you learn to shoot with such accuracy?' Luc asked.

'My parents. They always said accuracy in everything made the difference. They had me practising as soon as I could handle a weapon.'

'They sound like wonderful Shadowers, Sir. Which way should I go?'

'They were the best. It's that way.'

Luc headed the landcraft in the direction Max indicated. As they left, one of the young Shadowers opened his communicator, 'The enforcers are headed in your direction, Dronin. They'll be there soon.'

'Thank you for the update,' Dronin replied.

'Stop here, Luc,' Max said.

Before them stood crumbling skyscrapers, decaying and bent in various directions as if ready to shuffle off. In the centre stood a proud stone building, defiant amongst the decay. The enforcers gathered around the lead vehicle, waiting for instructions from Max.

'I want eight of you to enter round the back and the rest with me,' Max ordered.

A minute or so later, the enforcers barged the front and rear of the building. Inside, they found nothing untoward. The place was deserted.

'They knew we were coming,' Max said as he kicked the desk in an office in frustration.

'Could you have been given the wrong location? You did tell Jericesen that you had only narrowed it down to within a few blocks,' Luc asked as he admired the rows of books filling the bookshelves surrounding the room.

'Never reveal everything you know to your boss, Luc. Otherwise, they'll never appreciate your effort when you deliver. This is the right place. I planted the tracker on his support cage, and this is definitely the address he came to.'

'You've lost me, Max. Whose support cage?'

'Never mind, it's not important at the moment. What is important is how did they know we were coming?'

'Why don't we arrest the person you planted the tracker on? I'm sure we could persuade them to talk. Perhaps they found the tracker and alerted Dronin.'

'No, I removed the tracker before I left home this morning,' replied Max as he slumped into the chair.

'Before you left home? You mean—'

'Not now, Luc,' Max said, reaching into the bin and pulling out the empty bottle of Brackles and a rentalcraft receipt.

'What is that bottle for?'

'That, my young enforcer, is how we used to try to forget a bad day at work. And this bit of paper confirms this is the right building.'

Luc took the bottle off Max and sniffed it, 'Ugh, that smells disgusting. What is it?'

'The best ale ever. Far better than those fancy blue and red ones they came out with.'

'You mean alcohol? That was banned—'

'Just be very careful with your next words, young Luc. Or I may not be responsible for my actions,' Max laughed as he took the bottle back and savoured the smell.

'I was only going to say it was banned years ago. Almost in the dark ages,' Luc said with a grin.

'Sir, we've got a lead on the package landcraft. Cogi picked it up, entering the city to access an energy station,' an enforcer said, running into the room.

'Brilliant. I assume it was denied energy?' Max said, jumping up.

'No, Sir. The vehicle is not marked as blocked, and the energy cost was charged to a member of the Elite Council.'

'Which member?' Luc asked.

'We don't have access to that information, Sir.'

'Us oldies from the dark ages could have told you that, Luc. Good effort, though,' Max said. Turning to the other enforcer, he added, 'Get that package landcraft blocked immediately. Lock all its doors and cut its engine.'

'We've tried, Sir. But it is not on Cogi's register, so we can't block it.'

'How can that be true? Everything is on Cogi,' Luc stated.

'Very old landcraft didn't have Cogi capability, so that's not entirely true. But we've seen the images; this is a relatively new vehicle. So either Cogi has been hacked and the landcraft taken off the database or—'

'Or it's an Elite vehicle,' Luc interrupted.

5

HALF SQUARE THE CIRCLE

Juli looked up at the skyscraper towering above the surrounding buildings, 'Where the heck are we?'

'The Deputy Supreme Leader insisted we bring you to his edge of the city retreat,' the enforcer replied. 'The dwelling has been emptied whilst we were collecting you. The DSL said you're to make yourself at home.'

'You mean he owns this entire building?' Gran asked excitedly.

'No, Sir. The complex is one of many used by the Elite Council. This is the DSL's preferred one to get away from it all. His dwelling is on the top two floors.'

The enforcer escorted them into the building, followed by several other armed enforcers. After the hot, murky, foul outside air, which almost burnt the throat to breathe, the air in the building foyer was cool and refreshing. The foyer décor was incredibly elaborate to a point well beyond ostentation. Everywhere you looked were precious metals and jewels instead of simple buttons on wood or base metals.

The windows were opaque from the outside, but inside, you couldn't even tell there was glass as you looked out at the barren land once teeming with exotic trees and plants. What would have been an ornate pond was now a dried-out ditch, and fallen trees littered the gardens.

Juli sighed, 'How can they live in such isolated luxury when they look out at what our planet has become.'

'It's not their fault. How could they have known how quickly the climate would deteriorate when they built this,' Lin replied.

'It just feels morally wrong when so many Shadowers struggle to survive.'

'Oh, Juli. You're such an idealist. Remember, the Elite Council is arranging for every Zephyrion to be sent to new planets so they can have a new start.'

'And sometimes, big sister, you show such naïvety. If they are so wonderful, how come the Elite Council all get to go to Astral 5, you know, the planet now fully established with the comforts of hospitals, dwellings, roads, etc., whilst others are being sent to empty planets to start again!'

An enforcer walked over to Gran, who had been examining the indoor plants and escorted him back to Lin and Juli.

'We've finished uploading your details into the building's systems. You now have full access to the facilities and the DSL's dwelling.'

'What facilities?' Juli asked.

'There is a full exercise room and pool in the basement, a fine dining restaurant on the thirty-fifth floor, and the DSL's dwelling entrance is on the 90th floor. By the way, there is no Cogi here; everything is controlled by an Elite-only device called Argo.'

'Erm, can I cook my own food? Things are a little tight,' Gran asked nervously.

'It's okay, Sir. All the facilities here are free for residents and their guests,' the enforcer replied before summoning chutes to take them to the 90th floor.

'Why are they going to so much trouble? This is only temporary, isn't it?' Juli asked.

'No, ma'am. According to the DSL, this is your shared accommodation until your Exodus day,' the enforcer replied.

'But that could be a year or more,' Juli protested.

'It'll be fine, Sis,' Lin replied before stepping into a chute.

After a quick trip in the chutes, they stood by the entrance to the DSL's apartment, which looked unassuming compared to the ostentation of the rest of the hallway. Highly polished stone and gleaming crystals dazzled in all directions whilst a plain wooden door stood before them.

'Argo, open,' the enforcer said behind them.

The door hummed as steel bolts slid back into the surrounding frame and wall, and the door opened.

Gran gasped as they walked into the apartment, 'Have you ever seen so much greenery? I thought the reception was impressive, but this is like the old pictures of Zephyrion. Everything is so lush and green.'

'Never mind the plants. Did you notice the size of those metal bars in the door frame that slide through the door? Nobody is getting in through that,' Lin replied.

'Or getting out,' Juli added cynically.

'The bedrooms are upstairs, and if you need anything, just ask Argo. There will be enforcers outside the door, by the chutes and down in the lobby, so you won't be disturbed. I'll leave you to settle in and arrange for your bags to be brought up,' the enforcer said as he walked out of the main entrance, closing it behind him.

Gran headed towards the stairs. 'I'm off to check the bedrooms out.'

Juli laughed, 'I don't think Gran gets out much. Although I have to admit this place is incredible.'

'This place is even more impressive than the DSL's city centre dwelling,' Lin sighed.

'Is there something you're not telling me, Sis?' Juli challenged.

'What? No, of course not. The Project Leader and I were invited to meet the DSL a few weeks ago. That's how I knew we needed to accelerate Operation Exodus. We are talking months at the most rather than years to evacuate the planet.'

'Months? But there are around 3.5 billion Shadowers on Zephyrion. We would need to send eight million a day to clear the planet in a year, which means 450 days nonstop without a break.'

'It's not as daunting as you think. We aim to have almost a thousand Exodus machines ready within the next few weeks. Don't forget we have around half that amount already.'

'Yeah, for luxury travel to Astral 5 and other nearby planets, but we are talking about more powerful machines.'

'Based on my calculations, we should have around seven new machines in each of the one hundred and thirty major population groups across the planet. If we use the travel ones for those going to Astral 5 and the newer, more powerful machines for the more distant planets, then we are looking at around four hundred and sixty Shadowers per day, per machine.'

'Deputy Project Leader, Juli, have you seen the bedrooms? They're bigger than my dwelling,' Gran said excitedly, rejoining them.

'You can call me Lin when we're not working, Gran.'

'Thank you, ma'am...err Lin.'

A while later, Lin was unpacking in the master bedroom when she spotted a door keypad at the back of a wardrobe.

'Argo, open this door.'

'I'm sorry, Linaxani. Which door are you referring to?'

'The one at the back of this wardrobe in front of me.'

'I'm sorry, Linaxani, there are no doors at the back of any wardrobes.'

'But I'm looking at it.'

'I'm afraid I'm unable to comment on what you are looking at, Linaxani.'

___

'Shadowers, please give our incredible lottery winners a round of applause,' Bobmaton cheered.

The excitement of the Migration Lottery show had eased the tension from earlier in the evening, and the audience cheered and applauded enthusiastically. Glitter fell over the 200 winners gathered on the arena stage, and lasers flashed across the stage and into the audience as Bobmaton waved his arms to encourage further audience applause.

'Simo, the SL is going to make a further statement. Make sure enforcers are on standby to get him and the rest of the Elite Council away as soon as he comes off stage,' Jeric said into his communicator.

'Yes, Sir. Are you going with them?'

'I've been asked to go with the DSL to his dwelling to make sure Max's family have settled in.'

'Understood. Max reported that Dronin had evacuated their base before they got there.'

'I'm losing confidence in Max. Perhaps you were a little hasty in appointing him.'

'No, Sir. Max is a top-class enforcer like his brother and parents before him. He said Dronin is using an Elite landcraft.'

'His parents were weak, and his brother was a liability. Even as a junior enforcer, I had to carry Zym. It sounds like Max is no better. Are there any Elite landcraft reported as stolen?'

'No, Sir. But it was energised and paid for by an El—'

'Then it can't be an Elite vehicle, can it? I've heard enough excuses, Simohal. If you don't sort Maxoraxin out, then I will.'

'Yes, Sir. I'll speak to him in the morning.'

Back on the stage, Bobmaton signalled for the audience to quieten down, 'Shadowers, please welcome back to the stage our esteemed Supreme Leader and the Elite Council of Zephyrion.'

Bobmaton moved to the back of the stage, where the Deputy Supreme Leader pulled him to one side. 'Well done, Bob, you've hosted a stunning show.'

'Thanks, Nico. We recovered well from that early interruption. Have they caught the Deceptor responsible?'

'Not yet, but they are closing in. Talking of that incident, I need to give you some great news.'

The Supreme Leader raised his hands, and the audience cheered and applauded. A few dissenting voices were quickly silenced by a mixture of enforcers and shocks from their Cogi glow bands.

'Zephyrions, I think we can all agree tonight has been a fantastic show. Our gratitude goes to Bobmaton for hosting such a great event, and congratulations to our worthy winners on stage and all of you who have a lucky ticket around the planet. If you contact your local lottery office, they'll swap your ticket for migration pins for you and your immediate family,' the SL said, glancing back to see Bobmaton and Nicoeyel having an animated discussion.

The audience cheered again, and the screens flickered, showing excited Shadowers in their dwellings around the planet.

'Thank you so much Zephyrions. As your Supreme Leader, I am humbled to be your servant, and as simple Timezel, I'm excited at the prospect of us starting our new adventures across space in just a few weeks.'

The audience erupted into a frenzy of excitement in the arena and on the scrolling images of dwellings across Zephyrion.

'In a few weeks, we will hold a Grand Gathering in each of the one hundred and thirty population regions. There will be an Elite Council member hosting each event to celebrate the first winners in every region who will be sent to Astral 5, but —'

The noise from the audience reached a fever pitch as Timezel stood with his arms out, pleading for quiet.

'Please, bear with me, but I have even more news. There is one more winner in tonight's Migration Lottery who will get this crystal migration pin, which means this lucky winner will be the first Shadower sent via our newest Exodus machine.

'I'm sorry the new machine was revealed to you under such heinous circumstances earlier this evening, but these new machines can send a Zephyrion to Astral 5 in seconds instead of minutes. This will mean we can get to our new home planets quicker and safer.

'I hope you agree that the final winner fully deserves this honour after performing magnificently all evening and throughout his career. So please give a full-on Zephyrion cheer to our final winner and the Zephyrion who will start our official Operation Exodus, your host for this evening, Bobmaton.'

Timezel turned to see Bobmaton being unceremoniously pushed forward by Nicoeyel. Timezel grabbed Bob's hand, shaking it and pulling him forward simultaneously.

'Bob, don't be shy; you truly deserve this honour. Plus I have one more surprise for you. When you arrive on Astral 5, you will no longer be Bobmaton. I'm excited to tell you that arriving on Astral 5 will be Bobevrin. You will be the newest member of the Elite Council.'

The Supreme Leader's shock promotion of Bobmaton was a masterstroke of quick-thinking as the angry-looking presenter suddenly beamed.

'I'm actually lost for words, Supreme Leader.'

'About flipping time,' a heckler shouted, followed by a cheer from the audience.

Bob laughed and said, 'Sorry about that, everyone, that *was* my agent. I say *was* because he's now fired.'

Max threw the empty Brackles bottle across the room. 'So, we know what he's driving but can't block it. We know an Elite Council member funds it, but we can't find out who. Can anyone tell me what the hell we can do?'

Luc and the other enforcer jumped back at Max's fury.

'Sir, we are still tracking the vehicle on Cogi cameras,' the enforcer said almost apologetically.

The enforcer pulled out his communicator and opened up a city map. He pointed to the edge of the city nearest to where they were in the Deserted Zone, the energy station where the vehicle was charged and then to a moving dot.

'Why are we standing here? All enforcers into pursuit mode now,' Max snarled.

A few seconds later, the enforcers were heading after Dronin with Luc at the head.

Max grabbed his communicator, 'Simo, are you there.'

'Yes, Max. You'll never believe what's gone down here.'

'Not now, Simo. It's Dronin. He's heading back to the arena.'

Max explained what they had discovered, and Simo relayed the news to Jericesen.

'Jeric, it's Simo here. Dronin's landcraft is heading back towards the Migration Arena.'

'He shouldn't be coming back here. What's your intel, Simo?'

'We aren't sure yet, but his vehicle is heading quickly towards us.'

Jeric shut down his communicator and whispered to the Deputy Supreme Leader about Dronin's approach. Within seconds, the Supreme Leader, the DSL and the Elite Council were hurried to their waiting landcraft. As they headed outside, the skies also decided that the party was over as a storm broke. Zephyrions had become used to extreme weather, but this one exceeded the norm. Lightning crackled across the sky, creating lines of light beyond all laser shows, whilst the rumble of thunder sounded like gods of war fighting for their existence.

Buildings shook in fear as the ground beneath them rumbled and trembled like a wild beast.

'Zephyrions, the weather has deteriorated rapidly. You are welcome to continue enjoying the facilities of the Migration Arena until it passes,' the tannoy announced.

'Max! Jeric has confirmed the Elite Council are now travelling away from the arena, but the weather has turned nasty. Where are you?' Simo asked.

'We're in a landcraft and back in the city, heading towards you. We can see the storm ahead of us. It sounds loud.'

'Can you see where Dronin is?

'We are closing in on him, Simo. His landcraft automatically slowed as he hit the shopping zone, which is not a problem because we can override the speed limiter on our autodrive control. I think we can intercept him before he gets to the arena.'

The storm gathered momentum as lightning stabbed the ground around the arena. Glass from nearby buildings showered down as skyscrapers twisted in the storm. Shadowers in their skyscraper dwellings screamed as some of their windows shattered, and they cowered in the furthest recesses of their homes as they watched their furniture being sucked through broken windows. Inside the Migration Arena, bands took turns entertaining the audience and trying to muffle the noise of the storm.

'Jeric, are you and the DSL clear of this storm? What's happening with the rest of the Elite Council?'

'Yes, Simo, we've cleared it and are heading towards the DSL's dwelling. The Supreme Leader has taken some of the Elite Council to the Palace Compound. A few are coming to the same complex as us, and the rest are catching skycraft away from the city. I'll ensure the Elite Council is protected. You just intercept Dronin.'

'Yes, Sir. Are we authorised to use terminal apprehension?'

'Absolutely not. Dronin is a link to whoever is controlling the rebellion. We need him alive.'

'Understood, Sir.'

Simo finished the call to Jeric and relayed the orders to Max, who was being flung from side to side in the enforcer landcraft.

Luc swerved the vehicle around some furniture that had landed in the middle of the road. 'Max, these conditions are getting worse.'

The storm seemed to have become a living malevolent beast. As the rain lashed the towering skyscrapers, the winds turned into mini tornadoes, colliding with each other like pinballs in an amusement arcade until they merged and grew in ferocity. Debris flew through the air as the contents of the buildings were sucked out through the broken windows and combined with the street-level detritus.

Luc struggled to stabilise the landcraft after the autodrive failed due to the weather conditions, 'Can you see where Dronin is?'

Max looked at the enforcer tracker screen and squinted through the rain ahead. 'Slow down, Luc. I think he's stopped just ahead of us. All enforcers, the Deceptor's landcraft has stopped. The road appears to be blocked with debris. Set all depletors to stun. Under no circumstances is anyone to be killed.'

Luc stopped the landcraft a safe distance from Dronin's landcraft. The enforcers piled out of their vehicles and gathered around Max.

'Stay sharp, and follow my lead,' Max shouted over the storm's roar. His voice struggled against the raging torrent, but they nodded in acknowledgement.

As the enforcers encircled the landcraft, they could see the front of the vehicle had collided with a large sign that had blown off a nearby office block and sliced straight down the middle of the landcraft cabin, breeching the bulkhead separating the cabin from the cargo area. Max peered inside, but there was no sign of Dronin, and he cursed under his breath.

Max signalled for three enforcers to head to the back of the vehicle and instructed the others to prepare for action. Max slowly aimed his depletor at the split in the bulkhead, battling against the storm, which seemed intent on ripping the weapon from his grip. He fired and watched as the energy burst shot through the gap and bounced around inside the vehicle's cargo hold.

Once the energy burst had subsided inside the vehicle, he ordered the enforcers to open the rear doors, but there was no sign of Dronin, only some computer equipment, cameras, cables and other technical equipment.

Max pulled out his communicator, 'Simo, we've found the package landcraft, but there's no sign of Dronin.'

'I think I know how to find him. Keritrek has just left the arena. I've got some enforcers following her, and I'm about to join them. Check the vehicle over, then head this way. The storms slowing.'

'Okay, Simo. I wish it were—'

Max crashed to the floor as a box struck him across the back of his head.

'MAX, what's going on? Where are you?'

Luc rushed over to Max, who was lying unconscious. He checked him over and noticed his communicator was still open, showing Simo's face. 'Sir, it's Luc. Some flying debris has knocked out Max. He's alive, but we can't wake him.'

'Leave a couple of enforcers with him, check the landcraft for anything which could help, then head this way. I think Dronin is meeting Keritrek, who is heading in your direction.'

'Yes, Sir. We'll be on foot as the roads are impassable.'

Luc assigned two enforcers to take care of Max and ordered three more to check the back of the vehicle whilst he examined the vehicle cabin. After a few minutes of searching and collecting a few items, Luc ordered the enforcers to follow him, with instructions to the two enforcers to take Max to a medical unit.

Luc tapped his communication device, 'Cogi, where is Dronin?'

'I cannot be certain, Lucraxin. He does not appear to have a registered Cogi device or implant. However, an unidentified Shadower is approximately five minutes ahead of you.'

'Show me.'

'This is the last recording of that individual, Lucraxin. It was taken three minutes ago. I'm afraid the storm destroyed many of my traffic surveillance cameras, so I have to rely on landcraft and other domestic Cogi devices.'

One of the enforcers pointed ahead of them, 'Sir, look, there's the same Migration Lottery advert screen with that crack down it. We must be closing in.'

Not long later, Max opened his eyes, 'Where am I, and what happened?'

'You were hit by some debris, Sir,' the enforcer replied.

'Where's Luc and the others?'

'They're closing in on Dronin, Sir. We are waiting for the medicraft for you.'

'Stuff that, I'm fine. Come on, we need to get going.'

'But, Sir.'

'Don't but me, enforcer, cancel that medicraft and let's go.'

The storm was easing as Luc pushed ahead with his team of enforcers. Detritus blew through the air and danced like marionettes as the winds made one last attempt to bring down the city.

'Luc, it's Max. Where are you?'

'I'm closing in on Dronin. He's had to push through the wreckage, so it's an easy trail. How are you doing? What did the medicraft say?'

'I cancelled it. I've had worse injuries fighting with Lin. Have you spoken to Simo?'

'Yeah, he's following Keritrek. He thinks they're meeting up.'

It felt like stepping through a door between a dying storm and tranquillity as the storm disappeared almost as quickly as it had arrived, which Dronin appreciated. The road was an obstacle course of debris, but at least he only had to fight a path through the rubble now rather than also battle the weather. He heard a crash behind him and turned to see a pile of debris collapsing. Clearly, the storm had built some unstable towers of its own. Alarms were going wild around him, and through broken windows, he could hear Cogis advising Zephyrions to stay indoors and away from windows. If he could only get to Keritrek at the arena, she could hide him safely until he could meet his Elite Council contact.

Following the path cleared by Luc's team ahead of them, Max and the two enforcers rapidly closed the gap to Luc and the other enforcers.

'Luc, we are closing in on you. Have you found Dronin yet?' Max said into his communicator.

'We have a distant visual on him, but we are still too far away to engage,' Luc replied.

'Simo, it's Max. Where are you?'

'Max, I thought you'd be at a medicentre by now. I'm following Keritrek. From what I can see, she's on a direct course to Dronin.'

'I cancelled the medicraft. What is it with you lot? Are you trying to keep all the glory for yourselves?' Max laughed.

'Can't have you upstaging the boss, can we?' Luc added.

'Exactly, Luc. I can see you'll go far as an enforcer,' Simo replied.

'Hey, how did this become a Max roasting time?'

'Simple, Max. You're an easy target,' Simo chuckled.

'Not that easy, thank you. I've caught up with Luc already.'

'Hey, look guys, it's less Maxoraxin and more Maxoroastin,' Luc laughed as he welcomed his colleague with a hug.

'I'll remember that comment, young Luc, and revenge will be mine,' Max chuckled. 'Hey, look, Dronin is over there heading towards someone.'

'This is it, guys. I can see Keritrek approaching someone as well, so be careful where you're shooting as we're at opposite ends of this meeting,' Simo said as he signalled his enforcers to fan out and around the sides of Keritrek.

The storm's remnants had returned as a lazy wind, whipping debris around in swirls as the two groups of enforcers closed in on the pair of Shadowers they had been trailing. As they moved forward, Max noticed a large luxury landcraft partially hidden by the storm debris.

'Simo, can you see anyone in that Elite landcraft?'

'The only landcraft I can see appears to have been trashed by the storm, Max.'

'It would be on your left about fifteen to twenty paces back from the person Dronin is meeting. I know I only met her once, but it only looks like Keritrek's build if she's got taller and broader.'

'That bash on your head is affecting you. The only landcraft is that trashed one upside down on my right. But now you mention it, has Dronin been injured? He's walking very slowly.'

'Not that we've noticed, he's been moving quite quickly. You must see that landcraft. Another tall Shadower has got out and is opening the rear door.'

'I don't know what you're looking at, but I'll turn the communicator round so you can see what I'm seeing.'

'Okay, I can see the back of Keritrek, but that's not Dronin she's meeting that's—'

'Zymraxin,' Simo interrupted. 'Why is your brother here?'

'I have no idea. He's going to have some explaining to do. But it's clear you are not where we are, look,' Max said, turning his communicator around.

Simo studied the image and then blinked in disbelief as he saw the landcraft, 'Max, you need to proceed with extreme caution.'

'I always do, Simo. But is there any particular reason you're saying that?'

'That is one of the two new armed landcraft. They took delivery of them today, especially for the Migration Lottery. There's one for the Supreme Leader and the other for the Deputy Supreme Leader, and since the DSL is with Jeric heading towards Lin and Juli, that must be...'

'Luc, tell the rest of the team we may have a diplomatic incident. They are to proceed with extreme caution, and nobody fires without my say-so.'

'Yes, Max. By the way, I saw that landcraft this evening. There were two of them. It's identical to—'

'The Supreme Leader's, yes I know. Enforcers, fan out and move in on my mark. We are on our own. Simo has followed his suspect to a different location. Simo, I'll leave you to sort out Keritrek and Zym. I'm going in.'

The enforcers formed a semi-circle around Dronin, and on Max's instruction, they charged forward.

'Stay where you are. You are all under arrest on suspicion of treason against the planet,' Max shouted as he aimed his depletor towards Dronin.

The Shadower by the landcraft started to close the rear door.

'Leave it open enforcer. I'm confident Dronin will be joining us shortly. In the meantime, let's see what the armoury is like on this thing.'

'But, Sir—'

'Just sit back and relax. I'm not going to seriously injure them. We'll just confuse them a bit.'

Dronin turned with a depletor in his hand. 'Hello, Max. It's been a very long time since I heard your name. How's Zym?'

'Don't mess around, Dronin. I know you met Zym recently. Drop your weapon and lie on the floor.'

'Lie down amongst all this rubbish? I've got one of my best outfits on, so I'll pass if you don't mind.'

'Do it now, Dronin. I will shoot if I have to.'

'Oh, Max. I can see your parent's passion in you. Don't make the same mistakes they did.'

'What the heck do you mean by that? They died fighting corruption,' Max snarled, levelling his depletor at Dronin.

'They died fighting against the inevitable, not corruption.'

Max, followed by Luc, walked towards Dronin, 'This is your final warn—'

Explosions erupted around them as the luxury landcraft launched smoke canisters towards the enforcers. Max lunged towards Dronin, firing his depletor at the same time. His shot missed, but he collided with Dronin, and they both rolled across the ground. Dronin quickly jumped to his feet and tried to work out his bearings through the thickening smoke. He heard a voice shout his name and headed in that direction before an enforcer blocked his path. All around them, flashes went off as depletors were being fired with what would turn out to be marksmen-like accuracy.

'Hands over your head and on your knees now, Dronin or I will open fire,' Luc said.

'Can't blame a Shadower for trying,' Dronin smiled, as he initially started to raise his hands but then stopped and lowered them again. 'You know what, I don't think I will surrender, but you can if you want.'

'Max, over here, I've got Dronin,' Luc shouted. With his depletor aimed at Dronin, he said, 'Now do as you're told. I'll give you until the count of three. One, tw—' Luc crumpled to the floor as a flash hit him squarely in his back.

'Dronin, will you stop messing around and get in the landcraft now? We don't take risks; we manage or neutralise them.'

Max emerged through the smoke to see Luc on the floor and heard Dronin ahead of him saying, 'Oh, you Elites are so uptight.'

Max ran toward the voice and fired his depletor repeatedly. He was sure at least one shot connected, as he heard a curse just before a door slammed shut. Suddenly, the smoke was a blaze of light, and before he could move, he was sent spiralling into the air as the landcraft ploughed into him.

The last thought that went through Max's mind before he blacked out was, 'Must save Luc.'

6
THE END?

'I'm sorry, Linaxani, but I've just been told that several enforcers were caught in a rebel trap and killed,' Nicoeyel said.

'Is Max okay?' Lin asked desperately.

'Max was hit by a landcraft at speed, and we believe he died instantly,' Jericesen replied. 'I wish it weren't true. He was one of my best enforcers.'

Juli rushed to Lin's side, expecting to comfort her, but Lin stood silently, looking from Nicoeyel to Jericesen as if she was nailed to the spot.

'Lin, say something,' Juli said.

Lin turned towards Juli but appeared to look straight through her, 'Hmm.'

'Did you hear what they said? Max is dead.'

'Yeah. But it's not true. I'd know if Max was dead. Take me to him,' Lin said, staring at Jeric.

'I'm so sorry, Lin, but the report was clear: Max and his team were killed,' Jeric replied.

'No, it's not true. He's alive. I need to see him.'

Nicoeyel put his arm around Lin, 'I wish it wasn't true. You and Juli feel like family to me, but it seems that rebel Dronin will do anything to spread his hate. Jeric tells me his team has captured one of Dronin's team, and another managed to escape but was identified.'

'I want to see them. I have to see them. I want to know who they are and why they did this,' Lin replied.

'There's no easy way to say this, but they are both former enforcers. The one who escaped is Keritrek,' Jeric sighed.

'And who's the one you captured?' Lin asked.

'It's...' Jeric paused, then said, 'I'm afraid it's Zymraxin.'

Lin looked and felt empty as if her entire being had been torn away. Nothing made sense, and nothing was real, 'Zym would never be involved in killing Max. Zym and I rarely agreed on anything, but we both love Max.'

'Max tracked Zym meeting Dronin. We can only assume Zym had to make a choice, and Max paid the price for that choice,' Jeric replied.

'Is there any trace of Max?' Juli asked.

'You know there isn't Juli. Since we became energy souls when we die, we dissipate, leaving no remains,' Jeric said.

'Did anyone survive?' Lin asked.

'I'm sorry. From what I've seen, all of Max's team were killed in an ambush,' Jeric replied.

'Then I want to see Zym.'

'He's being interrogated, Lin. I'm afraid you can't see him,' Jeric replied.

'You seem to think I was asking. It's not negotiable. If I don't see him, I quit.'

'Don't be silly, Lin. You and Max are on the Elite Exodus list; if you quit now, you'll be taken off it,' Jeric said.

Lin turned on Jeric, 'You've just told me Max has been killed. Do you really think I care about your Exodus programme? Maybe I should tell everyone about your Alpha 5 Daxson plan?'

Nico glowered at Jeric and indicated for him to leave the room. 'Lin, I'm sorry about Jericesen. His years as an enforcer sometimes make him put procedure above the important things in life. I will personally arrange for you to see where Max was...well, where he died. Then, if you want to see Zym, we can sort that too.'

'Thank you, Nico. I didn't mean it about Alph—'

Nico interrupted, 'Don't even give it a second thought. I'm sure I'd be lashing out just as much if I had a partner who had been hit by a landcraft and killed.'

'When can we go to see where Max was and see Zym too?'

'I'll need to find out where he's being held, but I'll make sure Jeric sorts it out so you can go tomorrow. Will you trust me to sort this out for you?'

Nico's reassurances drained the adrenaline feeding Lin's emotions, and she collapsed back onto a chair. Juli crouched down to console her sister as Gran looked across the room at them. He struggled to empathise with others, a trait that often left him feeling perplexed and distant when faced with their emotions.

'I need to go and get everything ready for Lin. I'll be back in the morning. Take care of her tonight, and if you need anything, ask one of the enforcers outside. Argo provide Linaxani, Julirani and...' Nico looked at Gran.

'Granxili, sir.'

'Argo provide Linaxani, Julirani and Granxili with anything they want, including communication with me. Security code DSL4CRS.'

'Of course, esteemed Nicoeyel.'

Nico left Juli and Gran to look after Lin and joined Jeric by the chutes.

'What the hell were you doing in there, Jeric?'

'We need to make sure Zym tells us what he knows and how much of a danger he is?'

'Obviously, but the Project Leader refuses to follow the Daxson process, so we need Linaxani.'

Simo sat opposite Zym and studied him carefully. The enforcer interrogation room was stark, with whitewashed walls, a functional table and chairs, and cameras recording from all angles.

'We know Keritrek is part of Dronin's team, so why were you meeting her!' Simo asked, leaning back in his chair.

'Because she knows the truth,' Zym replied.

'The truth is she helped Dronin interrupt the Migration Lottery and spread unnecessary panic,' Simo replied.

'You don't have a clue, do you?'

'Why don't you educate me then?'

'Because you don't want to know. You're part of the Elite Establishment. If it doesn't follow your narrative, it's a lie.'

'Zym, help me here. I want to get to the truth, but I need to understand what's going on.'

'Dronin is a lot more dangerous than he seems.'

'Dronin is an enemy of the planet. How much worse could he be?'

'He's taking orders from someone in the Elite Council,' Zym sighed.

'That's a very serious allegation. I hope you've got evidence to back that up,' Simo insisted, leaning forward.

'That's why I was meeting Keritrek. When you told me about Dronin, I did some digging, and she arranged for me to see him.'

'You realise you've just confessed to colluding with an enemy of the planet.'

'I think you'll find I've confessed to following up on a lead, which enabled a serving enforcer to track Dronin down. Just ask Max.'

'Max hasn't reported in yet. He was trailing Dronin from the other direction. We assumed Dronin was meeting Keritrek.'

'What do they teach you at Enforcer College nowadays? Never assume. Get him on your communicator, NOW.'

'I'm giving out the orders, Zym.'

'We're talking about my brother and your friend—stuff semantics about who is doing what. Keritrek has been investigating Dronin for a long time, and she said he's ruthless. Get hold of Max.'

Simo opened his communicator and tried to reach Max unsuccessfully. He checked his enforcer device, and his face dropped.

'What's wrong?' Zym asked, his face etched with concern.

'Max, Luc and their entire squad have been reported as killed in an ambush organised by Dronin.'

'Get me to a medicentre now!'

'Are you feeling ill?' Simo asked.

'No, I'm feeling angry. I'm going through transition tonight, and then we are hunting down Dronin.'

'Are you forgetting you're in custody?'

'Are you forgetting we are talking about Max? Besides, you reinstated me based on my transitioning. So if I transition tonight, my actions today count as the actions of an enforcer and trust me, when I catch up with Dronin, I will either be an enforcer carrying out his duties or a civilian killing a terrorist.'

'There's a medicentre on the way to Max's last known location. I'll get one of my team to get them on standby for you. I'll also send a team to Max's last known location,' Simo said.

'Release Keritrek, too. She's got a lot of information on Dronin and his bases,' Zym ordered.

'That I can't do. She escaped when we were capturing you.'

'I'm beginning to think you need me more and more. Let's get going,' Zym stood slowly like a mountain growing from two tectonic plates inexorably rising.

A short while later, Simo's communicator burst into life. 'There's no sign of Maxoraxin, Lucraxin or two other enforcers, Sir.'

'And the others?' Simo challenged as he rushed to the medicentre with Zym.

'Their uniforms and weapons are here, so they've been killed.'

'Search the area. There must be clues to where the others are and what happened,' Simo ordered.

The enforcer landcraft screeched to a halt outside the medicentre, and the medistaff rushed out to meet them.

'I can walk. I don't need a chair,' Zym growled.

'Please, Zymraxin, let us do our job,' the medinurse pleaded.

Zym was wheeled through reception into a private room where a medidoc was waiting.

'Do you understan—'

'Just get on with the transition,' Zym snapped.

'We need you to sign thi—'

'There, come on, I'm in a hurry.'

'And you realise there's a one in five million risk y—'

'I may not survive the transition. Yes, get on with it.'

'We need to know your next of kin.'

'Maxoraxin.'

Simo coughed, 'Zym, you need to name someone aliv—'

'Maxoraxin,' Zym repeated, glaring at Simo.

'You will feel a tearing sensation as we separate your energy soul from your physical body, and I won't lie, it will hurt,' the medidoc said.

Zym was wheeled into a small room with a glass chamber in the corner.

'You need to stand in there without your support cage. Do you think you can do that?' the medidoc asked.

Zym stood up, turned off the support cage, and almost collapsed under the atmospheric pressure, 'Wow, I have got weak.'

The medistaff helped Zym into the chamber and closed the door.

'Zymraxin, we are legally obliged to ask you one final time, do you consent—'

'Yes, do it.'

The transition machine started to hum, and the chamber was filled with light. Zym felt the first pull on his body, like somebody tugging at his arms, legs, and body.

He thought, 'I don't understand why they make so much...'

Zym fell to the floor in unbearable pain. He felt like he was being torn apart limb by limb. He knew he was going to die, and this wasn't going to work. He was going to be the one in five million that didn't...

The transition machine slowed and then stopped. In the chamber, Zym's body lay curled up on the floor and above it stood a glowing, slim duplicate of Zym.

'How do you feel, Zymraxin?' the medidoc asked.

'Exhausted but better than I've felt in a long time.'

'You'll need to stay here for a day or two to recuperate, but then—'

'Not a chance. I'm leaving.'

'But Zymraxin, you're not ready. You'll be weak for the first day or so,' the medidoc protested.

'So give me some energy snacks. Simo, come on, we need to find Max,' Zym replied.

The medistaff helped Zym out of the chamber and sat him down in front of an energy meal and drink.

'This tastes terrible. Is it one of those energy Zingles meals?' Zym asked.

'No, Sir. That's junk energy. This is a carefully developed high-energy meal,' the medidoc replied.

'Oh, great. There's still awful healthy food to offset the decent stuff,' Zym replied sarcastically. 'Any news on Max?'

'It's been confirmed. Everyone is dead apart from four enforcers who are missing. From the uniforms and ID found, Max and Luc are amongst those missing,' Simo replied.

Zym stood, staggered, and then gathered himself, feeling slightly better after the energy meal. 'Let's get going. We need to find Max,' he said.

'Zym, we've been up most of the night, and the medidoc said you need to rest,' Simo said.

'I've been resting for years. It's time I paid Max back for all the years he's helped me. I'm not arguing with you, Simo. We're going.'

'Fine, but I'm giving the orders. Let's go before the trail gets cold.'

'Dronin said we need to take them to the Deserted Zone medicentre,' Keritrek ordered.

'But I thought he said tonight was the start of the revolution. How is saving enforcers part of a fightback?' Blar challenged.

'Because these are on our side,' Keri replied. 'We knew Dronin had help from some of the Elite and also amongst enforcers.'

'Where is Dronin?' Blar asked.

'He's working with his Elite insider,' Keri replied. 'Come on, we need to get these some help. They're in a bad way.'

Blar stared at Keri, 'I don't believe you. Dronin told me about you and —'

Keri turned her depletor on Blar and fired. He dissipated instantly, 'Anyone else want to argue about what we need to do?'

Cal opened his mouth and closed it as the others loaded the enforcers into a landcraft.

'Cal? Are you okay?' Keri asked.

'Yes, Keri, I'm fine.'

'We can't waste time arguing about what needs to be done, can we?'

'No, Keri. Dronin used to say the same.'

'Dronin says the same, you mean. He'll be back as soon as he's finished preparing the next phase. Now let's get these enforcers to our medicentre,' Keri replied.

'I know you're right, Keri, but please be careful. We know why we're doing this, but some are fiercely loyal to Dronin,' Cal whispered.

A while later, a medidoc finished examining the four enforcers. 'I'm not sure this one will make it. He's taken a blast to his back. The pack he had on spread the depletor impact, but every part of him is struggling to stay together.'

'What about the others?' Keri asked.

'They should be fine, especially this one. His injuries appear to be caused by a collision rather than a depletor. He just needs time to restructure,' the medidoc replied.

***

Zym looked around at the devastation caused by the storm. He picked up and studied a smoke canister before throwing it back down. He paced around the area, looking at the ground and other debris near the empty enforcer uniforms before studying the uniforms closely.

'This was a well-planned and expensive ambush,' Zym said.

'It looks like professional terminators. Have you noticed how few stray shot burns there are? Almost every shot hit its target,' Simo agreed.

'I agree, and those smoke canisters are Dolan Threes. Only a well-funded military can afford those. They make it almost impossible to see at ground level, but it's invisible from above. These enforcers never stood a chance,' Zym sighed.

'We need to search the tops of those buildings,' Simo said, ordering some of his team to search the surrounding buildings.

'Don't waste your time. Have you not noticed how many buildings have blown out windows from that storm? Even if anyone is still there, you'd never find them,' Zym replied.

'Guys, cancel my last order. Cogi, based on the cluster pattern of the smoke canisters, where were they fired from?' Simo asked.

'There is a ninety-three point six percent probability of the launch point being twelve paces to your left, Simohal,' Cogi replied.

Zym and Simo walked over to the point identified by Cogi.

'Cogi, when Maxoraxin made his last communication to me, show where he was in relation to where we are,' Simo said.

Simo's enforcer device showed an overhead image of the area with Zym and Simo marked and Max's location indicated.

'Where we are matches where Max told me there was an Elite landcraft,' Simo said.

Zym bent down and picked up a small pin, 'Any idea what this is?'

'That's a crystal migration pin. The Supreme Leader handed one tonight to Bobmaton or Bobevrin, whatever he is now,' Simo replied.

'Was Bob's the only one?' Zym asked.

'I'm sure there would be spares. But Bob's was the only one I saw issued,' Simo replied.

'Sir, we've found something,' an enforcer said, handing over a card on a lanyard.

'I was right, look, it's Keritrek's. She's as deep as Dronin,' Simo snarled.

'You're wrong, Simo. Keri hates Dronin. He shopped her partner to save his skin.' Zym replied.

'You seem convinced Dronin is the only bad guy? He can't be doing this alone.'

'He's not alone, but I think he is definitely nastier than most. What kind of guy sees his partner and child get killed and still helps those involved in killing them?' Zym challenged.

'What are you on about? I've researched Dronin's file, and he's never had a partner or a child.'

Zym stopped and thought about what Simo said. 'Keri was right then. Dronin will lie about anything. We need to find her. Where did you find this card?'

'Just to your left, Sir.'

'Cogi, what do you have on Keritrek's last movements?' Simo asked.

'Keritrek was last seen heading into the deserted zone, Simohal.'

'Cogi, was Keritrek in this location between the end of the Migration Lottery and now?' Zym asked.

'Yes, Zymraxin. Keritrek was here assisting Maxoraxin, Lucraxin and two other enforcers into a landcraft,' Cogi replied.

'Cogi, why didn't you tell me that?' Simo challenged.

'Because you did not ask me that, Simohal.'

'Maxoraxin and Lucraxin are reported as dead? But you've said Keri helped them into a landcraft,' Simo replied.

'That is correct, Simohal. Maxoraxin and Lucraxin have been reported dead, and Keritrek did help them into a landcraft.'

'So they're alive?' Zym asked.

'The four enforcers were alive when Keritrek helped them into a landcraft, and they have been reported as dead, Zymraxin,' Cogi replied.

'Cogi, ignoring the report of their death, are they flipping alive or dead?' Zym snarled.

'Their communicators were still connected to the respective enforcers when they entered the deserted zone, indicating they were alive. But they are reported as dead, Zymraxin,' Cogi responded.

'I swear if Cogi were a Shadower, I'd have given him a pasting by now,' Zym snarled.

'Zymraxin, I must inform you that damaging a Cogi is a criminal offence punishable by life imprisonment,' Cogi replied.

'Thank you, Cogi, for reminding me of the penalty for trying to prevent our every movement and conversation from being monitored,' Zym sneered.

'You are most welcome, Zymraxin.'

Zym turned to Simo, 'I guess they don't get sarcasm.'

Simo rolled his eyes. 'Cogi, are their communicators still active?'

There was a pause before Cogi replied, 'I'm sorry, Simohal. I do not understand your question. Whose communicators are you asking about?'

'The Supreme Leader's, you flipping electronic overlord, whose do you think we mean? We want to know about Maxoraxin and Lucraxin, of course,' Zym bellowed.

'The Supreme Leader's communicator is heading to his compound, Zymraxin. Maxoraxin's and Lucraxin's went offline shortly after entering the deserted zone,' Cogi replied.

'Cogi, show me where their communicators went offline,' Simo demanded.

'That's near the base where I met Dronin. Cogi, are there any former medicentres near that location?' Zym asked, tapping the screen, indicating the building where he'd met Dronin.

'That location was a major medicentre until the evacuation, Zymraxin.'

'Max is there. I know it,' Zym said defiantly.

'I'll let Jeric know we've tracked Max and the others.' Simo pulled out his communicator, but Zym put his hand on it.

'Let's wait until we've found them first. We wouldn't want anyone getting excited, would we,' Zym smiled.

'Do you think Jeric is involved?' Simo questioned.

'I'm not sure. Someone knew there were enforcers after Dronin and had the power and money to organise this ambush and...' Zym paused.

'Are you okay?'

'I've just joined some dots, and the image appearing is serious,' Zym replied.

'How serious?' Simo looked puzzled.

'Serious enough that I can't say with a C-O-G-I present,' Zym whispered.

'Zymraxin, I am fully capable of spelling and withholding evidence of a serious offence from the State is a crime.' Cogi said.

Simo nodded at Zym and said, 'Let's go and find Max and Luc.'

'Aaargh, what's happening,' Sabrath screamed.

Claudurath pushed her sibling forward into a nearby body.

'Quid agitur?'

'Claudu, where are we?' Sabrath asked.

'Quis Es?'

'Just relax and take control of the body you're in,' Claudu replied.

'I'm trying, but I don't understand what they're saying,' Sab replied.

'They are asking what's happening and who you are,' Claudu replied.

'Esne spiritus malus?'

'No, I'm not a malevolent spirit. I'm as confused as you are,' Sab replied.

'See, you're getting there. You can understand their language already,' Claudu replied.

'Me necabisne tu?'

'No, I'm not going to kill you,' Sab replied. 'Claudu, what's going on?'

'We're on a planet with a light atmosphere. We need to live inside these alien bodies until we can create versions of them,' Claudu replied.

'Quid est alien?'

'You're the alien. Although this is your planet, so we are the aliens, I suppose,' Claudu replied.

'But erm, I still don't understand what you mean, our planet?'

'We are not spirits, and we are not going to kill you. We were sent here from our planet against our will, and now we have to stay inside you for some time until we can work out how to escape,' Claudu sighed.

'Am I going mad? I can hear you but can't see you, and my friend Claudia seems infected, too.'

'She's called Claudia? That's my name, well almost,' Claudu replied. 'What is your name?'

'I am Valeria, widow of Lucius Cornelius Sulla. Claudia is my friend and confidant.'

'Claudu, help me. This thing is resisting me,' Sab wailed.

'Sab, calm down. You are sharing a body with Claudia, and I think she's as scared as you are,' Claudu said.

'Valeria, we are going mad. We are afflicted,' Claudia wailed.

'Claudia, I'm as confused as you are, but I seem to be able to understand everything this alien, or whatever they are, inside us, wants. They seem as scared and confused as us,' Valeria said, trying to reassure her friend.

'We are possessed. We are suffering from the wandering womb,' Claudia replied.

'I'm not possessing you,' Sab protested. 'I don't want to be inside you any more than you want me here. Claudu, how can we go back?'

'If you mean back to Zephyrion, we can't. But that cute Medidoc I used to look after told me about these light-atmosphere planets. Apparently, we can live inside animals from a light-atmosphere planet and build replica bodies that we can eventually move into,' Claudu replied.

'We are not animals!' Valeria protested.

'All living things are animals,' Claudu replied. 'I just mean we can survive inside any living thing on this planet and create a replica to live inside.'

'See, they are the manifestation of the wandering womb. I've heard tales of women in Greece who suffered with it, and they became hysterical,' Claudia cried.

Sab sighed, 'These...Roman things are so backward. Have you seen what they think this wandering womb thingy is?'

'Yes, I can see it in this Valeria one. They think bits of their internal organs can become dislodged and float around inside them, causing madness,' Claudu replied.

Sab laughed, 'I dread to think what they would think if they could read our—'

'This is madness. I can see flying, enclosed chariots and buildings that touch the sky. Claudia, you're right we are becoming hysterical,' Valeria screamed.

Claudu scowled. 'I've had enough of this. According to my lovely medidoc, we can force these alien souls back and take full control of their bodies until we separate.'

'But I don't know how to push this one back,' Sab replied.

'He said to imagine pushing them into a room and locking the door. It's working for me.'

'Hmm, I'm trying, but she's fighting,' Sab replied, frowning with concentration.

'That's it, you can do it,' Claudu said encouragingly.

'She's banging on the door inside my head. I can't go on like this.'

'Sorry, I should have said make it a soft room. I imagine mine is made from Fluffy Puff,' Claudu chuckled.

'As in that sweet fluffy stuff we ate as kids?' Sab queried.

'Yeah, that's the stuff. Imagine the walls and door are made from it.'

'Oh, wow, that's much better. I can still hear her whining, but I can put up with that,' Sab replied with a smile. 'So how do we start this replica body building thing?'

'From what I can remember, we just need to imagine separating from the animal, and it triggers the process automatically,' Claudu said.

'Well, that sounds easy enough. How long does it take, and how do we separate?'

'He said the timescale varies from planet to planet and also on the complexity of the animal,' Claudu answered.

'What about the separation process?' Sab asked.

'I don't think we discussed that,' Claudu replied coyly.

'What are you not telling me?' Sab challenged.

'Nothing. It's just we never got as far as discussing that.'

'Why not?' Sab asked.

'Do I need to spell it out? We got distracted,' Claudu blushed.

'Oh, Claudu, you're impossible,' Sab laughed.

'You're a fine one to talk,' Claudu chuckled. 'Come on, from what I've already learnt from this Valeria, we're in for a fun time in this Rome place.'

7
THE COLLAPSE

'That doesn't look like your average mediwarder by the entrance,' Simo whispered.

'That's Cal. He's one of Dronin's security team,' Zym replied, rubbing his head.

'Are you okay, Zym?'

'Yeah, I'm fine. I'm just a little dizzy. Come on, we need to get in there.'

'Cogi, how many people are inside that medicentre?'

'I'm s... Simoh... acces... desert... one,' Cogi crackled.

'Before your time, Simo, but Cogis were abandoned in the deserted zone during the evacuation. You're only getting the faint signal now because the enforcer landcraft is boosting its city signal,' Zym replied. 'Some days, it'll work perfectly, but you'll usually just get static.'

'Excuse me, old timer, but this isn't my first journey into the zone. I was hoping it might have some functionality as we are close to the city,' Simo said.

'Well, we aren't achieving much by crouching here. How about I lead half the team around the back of the building, and we coordinate our strike,' Zym suggested.

'That's a good idea, but you come with me,' Simo replied. Turning to his side, Simo said, 'Enforcer, take half the team to the rear of the medicentre. If you see any side entrances, station some enforcers there. Let me know when you're in position.'

The enforcer team crept out and around the right-hand side of the building.

'What about that crumbling skyscraper attached to the left of the medicentre?' Zym asked.

'I can't see anyone trying to escape that way. It looks close to collapse. I think that the storm earlier took its toll on it,'

'That's my fear. I think the storm we had earlier has pushed it to its limit. I wish Max was here in times like this,' Zym said.

'Hopefully, he is in that medicentre,' Simo replied.

'No, I mean out here. He trained as an engineer before becoming a raxin. He'd be able to tell you how safe it was just by the look of it.'

'I've worked with Max for years, and while I knew he was good with his hands, he never mentioned he was a trained engineer. Why did he become an enforcer?'

'To avenge our parents. When he found out they had been investigating corruption, he convinced himself that it was linked to their death and joined so he could investigate. When I had my accident, he was certain both accidents were connected,' Zym sighed.

'But he brought down those responsible for your accident,' Simo replied.

'But neither of us managed to identify who killed our parents,' Zym said.

'But I thought they died in a spacecraft accident?'

'That's what I believed, but Max was convinced there was more to it, and Dronin said something that made me doubt everything about their death,' Zym sighed.

'What did he say?' Simo asked.

'Just that it seems like whenever anyone gets close to corruption—did you hear that?' Zym asked.

There was a loud rumble, followed by a crack like a powerful rifle being fired.

'I'm not sure what you heard before, but I heard that one. Is somebody shooting a weapon?' Simo whispered, looking around.

'It's worse than that, look,' Zym replied, pointing up at the skyscraper. 'It's swaying like crazy.'

'We need to get in there,' Simo said urgently. He lifted his communicator and said, 'Enter the rear of the building now and proceed with haste. The building next door looks close to collapse.'

Zym, Simo and the other enforcers stormed the building. 'Cal, it's me, Zym, don't move; you're outnumbered. We're only here to help Max, Luc and the other enforcers; we're not interested in you, Keri or the others,'

Cal looked at the swarm of enforcers heading towards him and raised his hands. 'Zym? Is that really you?'

'Yes, I transitioned. Now tell me where they are keeping Max, and then surrender to one of my enforcers,' Zym shouted.

There was another crack as a metal beam fell from the neighbouring skyscraper and impaled a nearby abandoned landcraft, pinning it to the ground.

Cal looked up in shock. 'It'll take too long to explain Zym. I'll take you to him.'

'We can't trust him,' Simo shouted as the enforcers reached the medicentre entrance.

A shattering sound from above resulted in glass raining down like an almighty storm as the last few enforcers outside the entrance dived for cover.

Zym looked around quickly to ensure nobody was seriously injured. 'We don't have a choice. Enforcers follow Cal, but be on full alert.'

Simo considered arguing but then said, 'You heard Zym, move it.'

Cal headed down a corridor, followed by Zym, Simo and the rest of the enforcers. At the junction with another passage, they heard a shout.

'Armed enforcer, stand still with your arms raised.' A shot whistled past Cal and hit the wall behind him, sending bits of the wall flying.

'Enforcer, it's Simohal. He's friendly. Rejoin the group and follow us,' Simo shouted.

There was a crash as the enforcers regrouped and set off behind Cal. Zym and Simo turned to see the corridor they had been standing in collapse.

'Cal, speed up; the place is disintegrating around us,' Zym shouted.

'It's just down here on—' Cal dived for cover as the room to the right collapsed, spraying them with glass from the internal window.

The lights started flickering as Zym and the others scrambled to their feet. Water sprayed around them as bare electrical wires popped and snapped like a crackling fire, and electricity arced and danced across surrounding objects. Clouds of dust billowed behind them as parts of the skyscraper fell onto the entrance area, crushing it.

'Transitioning didn't kill me, but I think this might,' Zym thought as they all scurried after Cal.

Cal stopped at a doorway and battered it with his fist. 'Keri, let me in. It's Cal, and I've got help.'

Several door bolts clattered back, and the door creaked open. Keri ran into Cal's arms, and they hugged tightly.

'When I heard the building collapsing, I was sure you were dead,' Keri cried.

'I would have been if it wasn't for Zym turning up to rescue Max,' Cal replied.

'Zym? How the heck is he coping with this in that support cage?'

Zym stepped out from behind Cal. 'Hi Keri. Surprise!'

Keri paused and then smiled broadly. 'Wow, Zym. You look amazing.'

'Of course I do. But we need to get moving,' Zym replied.

With a timely reminder, there was a rumble followed by a crash as more of the building yielded under falling parts of the skyscraper.

'Where are Max and the other enforcers?' Zym asked.

'They're next door. I've ordered them all to be put on trolleys so we can wheel them out,' Keri replied.

'We need another exit. Everything that way,' Simo said, pointing back towards the main entrance, 'is crushed.'

'Then we're trapped. The rear exit is that way, too,' Keri replied.

'Dronin had a secret exit in the basement. It led under the road to a landcraft park,' Cal said. 'Let's get them and get out of here.'

Keri led them to the other room, where three hospital trolleys were loaded with patients, with a fourth patient in a wheelchair.

The enforcer in the chair saw Simo and tried to stand. 'Simohal, sir. I'm ready to report for duty.'

'Easy, enforcer. You need to sit back and enjoy the ride,' Simo reassured her.

Zym spotted Max and rushed over. 'Max, it's Zym, how do you feel?'

'He's unconscious, Zym. The doctor said he should survive, but he needs to restructure after the collision,' Keri said.

'What collision?' Zym challenged. 'I assumed he was hit by depletors like the others.'

'We don't know what happened, but a collision caused Max's injuries. We found him unconscious like the others, but he was the only one not hit by depletors. Paulie was caught by a glancing shot, but she's well on the mend. Kendra is stable, as is Max, but they're both still out of it.' Keri said.

'What about Luc?' Simo asked.

'I'm not sure if he'll make it,' the medidoc said from behind Keri. 'His backpack took the brunt of the depletor, but it also spread the shot across his body.'

Cal interrupted the discussion, 'Can we do this another time? When that skyscraper collapses, this place is dust.'

'Lead the way, Cal. I've got Paulie. The rest of you grab a trolley, and let's move it,' Simo shouted, pushing the wheelchair.

Cal set off through a second door and down another corridor, followed by Paulie, being pushed in her chair by Simo and the other enforcers pushing the three other trollies, with Zym at the rear pushing Max. The sound of the building straining under the battering of the collapsing skyscraper raining metal beams down on it was deafening. Lights flashed as water pipes burst, spraying everyone and everything. They reached a bank of medical chutes, but the glass tubes were shattered.

'We can't use them, which means we have two flights of stairs down to the basement tunnel,' Cal shouted above the roar of the collapsing building.

'Two enforcers at each end of the trollies now,' Simo shouted as Cal pushed open a stairwell door.

Simo led the way with Paulie in the wheelchair, but the stream of water made him slip and slide down the stairs.

'Cal, this is hopeless. Even Simo is struggling. We'll never get these trollies around the stair corners,' Zym shouted from the doorway.

'Unclip the bed from the wheels. We'll have to carry them down,' Cal replied.

There was a deathly scream from the back, and Zym turned to see a loose electrical cable lashing around with a crumpled enforcer uniform lying on the wet floor. 'What happened?'

'We've lost one of our team. That electrical cable hit him, and he vaporised,' an enforcer replied.

'Damn, I forgot we're by an old transition room. Some of the wires will be ultra-high voltage,' Cal said. 'Keep clear of any loose ones. We can't be sure which are standard voltage and which are the UH ones.'

Simo reached the bottom of the stairs. 'There's a locked steel door. We're trapped.'

'There's a keypad on the wall to your left,' Keri said as she reached the bottom of the stairwell, helping to carry Kendra.

'What's the code?'

'Ah, I don't know,' Keri shrugged. She turned to see Cal, who was helping to carry Luc, 'Cal. We need the code.'

'Three, eighteen, fifteen, fourteen, nine and nineteen,' Cal replied.

The keypad flashed red, and the door remained locked.

Simo wiped the keypad dry with his sleeve and tried again, but the keypad flashed red again.

Keri pushed Simo to one side. 'Simo, grab the door, and as soon as I hit the last number, pull it hard.'

Simo grabbed the door handle as Keri entered the code. As she hit the final number, she shouted, 'Now.'

The keypad flickered green but then returned to red, and whilst Simo felt the door give slightly, it remained firmly shut.

'What's going on down there?' Zym yelled down the stairs.

'The door won't open,' Simo replied.

'Well, that's our only way out. The building has collapsed onto the stairwell door,' Zym replied, as the water and dust combined, making the atmosphere increasingly inhospitable.

Cal got an enforcer to grab his part of Luc's stretcher and pushed past Kendra's to reach Simo and Keri.

'Try again, Keri. Simo, come on, we can do this,' Cal said, grabbing the handle with Simo.

'Cal, are you sure it's the right code?' Keri asked.

'Definitely. But the collapsing building is frying the electrics,' Cal replied. 'Get on with it. We're wasting time.'

Keri entered the code, and the keypad flickered green again, then returned to red. In that split second, Simo and Cal yanked open the door.

'We're through,' Keri shouted up the stairs. 'Let's get moving.'

They piled through the doorway and into the tunnel. As Zym reached the bottom stair, he fell forward, losing his grip on Max's stretcher and falling into the pool of water at the bottom of the stairwell.

'Simo, Zym's down,' an enforcer shouted, grabbing the end of Max's stretcher.

'Keep going, Simo. I'll go back and get him,' Cal said, running back towards the tunnel entrance.

'I'm fine, Cal. Get Max and the rest of them out of here,' Zym grumbled as Cal helped him to stand.

'You're far from flipping fine. You look drained. Jump on my back, and I'll carry you.'

'I've only just got rid of that support cage. There's no way I'm not doing this under my own power,' Zym snapped.

'Fine, but eat this energy bar. It's junk food, but it'll give you some energy. And I don't care what you say; we're getting out of here together,' Cal replied as he half dragged Zym into the tunnel.

'This tastes like cheap, overly sweetened rubbish,' Zym replied.

'I'm sorry it's not fine dining, but the head chef has gone home,' Cal laughed, hurrying Zym forward.

'I'm not complaining. Junk food is very underrated in the right circumstances,' Zym laughed, starting to feel the food's benefits.

'How's it going back there,' Keri's voice said from far ahead.

'We're on the way, just keep going. This grumpy git seems to be on the mend,' Cal shouted back.

Simo reached another door and pushed down the lock bar. The door opened into a landcraft park, and Simo and the rest rushed through just as it sounded like the gates of hell were opening behind them. He looked back to see parts of the tunnel collapsing behind Cal and Zym.

'Enforcers, help Paulie up and pass me her chair, NOW!' Simo barked.

He ran down the tunnel with the chair and reached Cal and Zym.

'Get in the chair now,' Simo shouted as more of the tunnel collapsed behind them, covering them with dust and plunging them into darkness.

'I can—,' Zym started to say.

'I'm not arguing, Zym. It's an order, or we will die down here,' Simo barked.

Zym sat in the chair as Cal and Simo raced him towards the growing light of the landcraft park.

'I can see you guys. Almost here,' Keri shouted from the doorway in encouragement as a rumbling sound turned into a screeching roar.

The tunnel walls vibrated like a cacophonic orchestra, followed by a snapping and grinding sound. For a split second, there was silence and then a massive crash as Cal, Simo and Zym disappeared in a cloud of debris and smoke.

'Cal,' Keri screamed as Zym and his chair shot into view. An enforcer rushed forward and grabbed the chair, pushing Zym into the landcraft park.

Keri tried to race into the tunnel, but another enforcer held her back. 'It's too dangerous,' he said.

Keri fought free, walloping the enforcer in the face with her elbow.

'Oi, hitting one of my enforcers is a serious crime.'

Keri looked up and saw Simo and Cal emerging through the dust cloud.

'In the circumstances, I think we can overlook it this time,' Simo continued as they reached the doorway.

Keri threw her arms around Cal, 'I thought I'd lost you.'

'You almost did, but Simo shoved Zym's chair forward and dragged me free,' Cal replied.

'I don't know how I can ever repay you, Simo,' Keri replied.

'Well, to start with, how's Zym? And then I need to know what you know about Dronin,' Simo replied as they staggered into the parking zone.

'I can answer the first one,' Zym replied, leaning against a parked landcraft. 'But I suggest we get out of here first?'

'We've got one of our medicraft over there for two patients,' Keri said, pointing towards it.

'It's a shame we can't get into that parcel landcraft and the peoplecraft. Between these and the medicraft, we'd get us all out,' Zym sighed.

'Who said we can't?' Simo said, pulling up his enforcer device. He pressed a few buttons, and the doors of the two vehicles Zym mentioned sprung open.

'How...' Zym started to say.

'Welcome to modern enforcement, Zym. Our hal devices enable us to open any craft or dwelling,' Simo smiled.

'Not quite any,' Cal said, unlocking the medicraft by pressing his hand against the doorplate.

'Okay, we've got the transport, but where are we going?' Zym asked.

'I know Dronin had senior staff at the medicentre by the Palace Compound on his side. We could try there,' Cal suggested.

'That's where they took me after my accident,' Zym replied. 'I think that's a big no-no.'

'I agree. The enforcer medicentre is the best option. We can book them in anonymously, and I can post my men there as protection,' Simo replied. 'Then we can crash at mine. We need to sleep.'

Cal pulled the medicraft out of the parking zone and whistled. 'The skyscraper has crumbled, crushing the medicentre. Anyone left in there is a goner.'

'You can even see where the tunnel was. Look, the road has collapsed into it,' Zym added.

8

I'M BACK

'Morning, Zym. Or should I say good afternoon,' Simo smiled, lounging in a chair.

'Why didn't you wake me? We've got a lot to do,' Zym yawned.

'And it's getting done. Cal and Keri have gone with two enforcers to check on Max, Luc and the others. We've got a meeting scheduled later with Jeric. Well, I have to be precise, but I need you there with me, and I've ordered some food for you in the kitchen,' Simo said.

'What about Dronin?' Zym asked as he went to get some food.

Simo got up and followed him. 'The only link we've got is Max telling me he saw the Supreme Leader's landcraft where they were ambushed.'

'Hang on. You never said it was the SL's. You just said it was an Elite one,' Zym snapped. 'We need to question him now.'

'That's why I didn't tell you. We can't just go hauling in members of the Elite,' Simo replied.

'But if he's killed en...' Zym paused and looked around. 'Where's your C O G I?' he whispered.

'Another hal privilege. We can stand them down in case they interfere with an ongoing investigation. Or, in this case, because I didn't want anyone to know we were here,' Simo replied.

'I need to be a hal,' Zym laughed. 'What did Jeric say when you told him about the Supreme Leader?'

'I haven't told him yet,' Simo replied, snacking on some food and leaning against a worktop, watching Zym dive into the bags of food.

'Wow, this stuff tastes amazing,' Zym said, eating the food straight from the containers.

'I had a feeling you'd be hungry. I remember what I was like after transitioning, and I didn't go on a manhunt straight after,' Simo laughed.

After devouring the food, Zym leaned against the wall, glugging an energy drink. 'I've not felt so full and satisfied in years. So what gives with Jeric? Why haven't you told him yet?'

'Blame your little brother,' Simo replied.

'Huh? Why Max?'

'Max believes in the Elite Council. He is convinced they want the best for us all.'

'That's one of his few flaws. His partner Lin is the same, although Max hates government bureaucracy more than she does. But what's that got to do with Jeric?'

Simo ate more food, not because he was hungry, but because it gave him time to think. He considered mentioning Jeric's comments about Max, Zym and their parents but decided against it. 'A couple of times since Dronin interrupted the lottery, Max has been evasive around Jeric.'

'In what way?' Zym asked.

'First, he waited until Jeric was out of the viewing gallery before confirming Keritrek was working with Dronin. Then, when Jeric asked if Max had tracked down Dronin's base in the

Deserted Zone, he said he had tracked him down to an area,' Sim said.

'Why is that evasive? Max admitted he had tracked Dronin down,' Zym queried.

'I saw that look, Zym. You know perfectly well that Max didn't just know the area. He knew the exact location. He took Luc and my enforcers straight to it.'

'Well, that's because of the tracker he put on my energy cage,' Zym smiled.

'You knew? He thought he'd planted and removed it without you knowing,' Simo chuckled.

'Sometimes it's good to give the lad a little victory. Don't you dare tell him,' Zym laughed.

'My lips are sealed. Max is lucky to have a big brother like you,' Simo sighed.

'What about you, Simo? Don't you have any family?'

'I never knew my father. It was just my mum and me,' Simo replied.

'Where's your mum now?' Zym asked.

'She was killed when I was still young. She was a Psiorite, and the Elite Council thought her psychic and telepathic abilities would enable her to communicate with Daxson,' Simo said, fighting back his emotions.

'I'm sorry to hear that, Simo. I've heard of Psiorites, but I always thought they were like the animal whisperers, the Gaianids, who were pretty much wiped out hundreds of years ago. I've only heard of one other Psiorite, and she was partnered with Zephyrion's first Supreme Leader.'

'I'm not surprised. Mum told me that they hid their skills and went into hiding. They blended in because so many were exploited by unscrupulous Shadowers and deceived into abusive slavery. Performing tricks for their masters,' Simo replied. 'They were the ones who started calling crooks Deceivers and Deceptors. I'm amazed that one partnered with the Supreme Leader and also that they let it be known they were a Psiorite.'

'It wasn't public knowledge. Only a few enforcers knew, like my parents. But if the others like your Mum hid their skills, how did the Council know about your Mum?'

'She was seeing a junior member of the Elite Council and confessed to him she was a Psiorite. He persuaded her to help him on a Daxson project, but after she was killed, I was dumped into the system. I don't even know who he was. It was so long ago, and she never let me meet him.' Simo grabbed some more food to stop himself from crying.

'If your Mum was a Psiorite, does that make you one too?' Zym asked.

'No. Well, at least not with telepathic or psychic skills. They only pass down through female family members,' Simo replied.

'So if you have any daughters, they'll have those skills?' Zym asked.

'I guess, but since Mum died, I've had to fend for myself, and I'm not sure I want the responsibility of having anyone else to care for.' Simo sat down, avoiding Zym's look. 'I'm better on my own.'

Zym walked over to Simo and put his hand on his shoulder. 'Simo, I know Max looks up to you, and the more I get to know you properly, the more I see why. You are as much a brother to us as anyone could be. Don't ever feel you're on your own again.'

'Thanks, Zym,' Simo replied, still staring at the floor.

'Now come on—no more of this soppy stuff. I've got a tough guy image to uphold. We need to get our arse into gear,' Zym said with a laugh and a gentle squeeze of Simo's shoulder.

Simo stood up, wiped his eyes, smiled at Zym and lifted a communicator.

'That's not an enforcer issue,' Zym challenged.

'Keri gave me it. We had a long chat this morning, and I'm questioning who is on whose side,' Simo replied. 'Let's see how she and Cal are getting on at the enforcer medicentre.'

'Hi Simo. We've got good news. Paulie has been discharged, and Kendra is awake and eating. Oh, hang on, someone else wants to speak to you,' Keri said.

'Simo, how's it going? I hear you got my grumpy brother to transition,' Max said croakily.

Zym grabbed the communicator off Simo, 'Max, you idiot. You've had me scared to death. Are you okay?'

'Hang on, Zym, you can't insult me and ask if I'm okay in the same breath,' Max laughed and then started coughing.

'Says the Shadower, whose opening comment was to call me grumpy,' Zym replied with a smile. 'What is it with this grumpy thing anyway? Cal called me it yesterday, too. Anyone would think I'm always moaning.'

'You are!' Max and Simo replied in unison before bursting into laughter.

'Oi, where's the respect for your elders and seniors?' Zym replied with a laugh.

'Excuse me, but you've barely been an enforcer for a day, so less of the senior, newbie,' Max chuckled.

'We're coming to see you, so sit tight. I'll soon teach you who's a newbie,' Zym replied.

'Not yet, Zym. We have to go and see Jeric first,' Simo interrupted.

'He can do one. Max comes first,' Zym snapped back.

'Easy, brother. Simo knows what he's doing. I'm not going anywhere. Go and see what Jeric wants, and then come over. Besides, the medidoc reckons I'll be ready to be discharged soon,' Max insisted between coughing fits. 'Simo, find out how Lin and Juli are.'

'Of course I will. How's Luc doing?' Simo asked.

Max looked at Keri, and she grabbed the communicator. 'He's still out of it, but the medidoc said he's over the worst. They can't be sure if there'll be any lasting neurological damage, though.'

'Zym, are you okay?' Simo asked, noticing the puzzled look on his face.

'I thought once we transitioned, it meant we didn't have to worry about physical injuries anymore. That transitioning to energy souls meant we lived forever, well, unless your energy is drained beyond recovery,' Zym said. 'I've got my leg back, so if this Luc lad is past the worst, surely he'll fully recover?'

'It's not that simple, Zym. If an energy soul's brain is too starved of energy, it can never fully restore itself,' Keri replied.

'If it's the last thing I do, I swear Dronin will pay for this,' Zym snarled.

'It's Cal here, Zym. Don't you worry. Between us, we will bring him down.'

'I don't want to bring him down. I want to put him down,' Zym replied.

'That's going to have to wait, Zym. We need to see Jeric. See you guys soon.'

A short while later, Simo and Zym were sat outside the office of the High Counsellor of Enforcers. Whilst they couldn't hear what Jeric was saying, there was no doubt he was angry with whoever he was talking to.

'I remember when the Chief Enforcer, as they were called when I first joined, was in a regular office, with a battered desk, old chair and a fire-breathing demon secretary guarding the door against unwanted visitors,' Zym said, looking around at the luxurious outer office decorated in mirrors, crystals and expensive metals with elaborate wooden doors and furniture.

Simo smiled at the young Shadower, who sat at the ornate wooden desk by the door to Jeric's office and received a glower in return. 'Looks like the fire-breathing demon is still here.'

'Except she's getting younger,' Zym laughed. 'There's more wood in here than is left on Zephyrion.'

Suddenly, the heavy, ornate wooden door to Jeric's office flew open.

Jeric stormed out and barked, 'Simo, get in... who the hell is that?'

'Zymraxin reporting for duty, Jericesen,' Zym said, standing to attention, albeit somewhat begrudgingly.

Jeric would have looked like snow if an energy soul could turn white. 'Both of you get in here. Erzsi.'

'Yes, Jericesen,' Simo's fire-breathing demon secretary Erzsi replied.

'Get me a glass of Energy Brackles and a Zingles energy burger,' Jeric growled.

'Yes, Sir. What about your guests?' Erzsi asked.

'They're not guests, they're enforcers, well one is. If they want something, they can get it themselves after I've finished with them,' Jeric shot back before slamming his office door shut behind him.

'Yes, your mighty uptight wazzack. Would you like me to polish your bottom while I'm at it?' Erzsi half whispered under her breath at the slammed door.

'You've got some explaining to do, Simo. And what the heck is Zym doing here?' Jeric demanded.

'I'm ba—' Zym started to say.

'I'm not talking to you, Zym,' Jeric snarled.

'Zym has been reinstated as an enforcer according to Section 13c of the enforcer's guide of conduct covering officers of the state injured in action and updated for the laws of transition,' Simo replied.

Jeric tapped his screen and said, 'Cogi, can an enforcer be reinstated according to Section 13c of the enforcer's guide after transitioning to full health?'

'No, Jericesen. That section of the enforcer's guide of conduct covering officers of the state injured in action and updated for the laws of transition has been repealed,' Cogi replied.

'Sorry, Zym. It seems you've been misled. You can leave us now. By the way, you're looking good,' Jeric smiled.

Zym went to stand, but Simo reached across and pushed his arm down.

'Cogi, when was that section repealed? And who was the last enforcer reinstated before that repeal?' Simo asked.

'It was repealed immediately after the reappointment of Zymraxin, Simohal,' Cogi replied.

'Looks like you're stuck with me, Jeric,' Zym smirked.

'That's High Counsellor Jericesen to you, Zymraxin,' Jeric sneered.

'Whatever you say, Sir,' Zym smiled.

Jeric blanked Zym and tapped his screen to deactivate Cogi. 'What's the situation regarding Dronin?'

Zym went to speak, but Simo kicked him.

'We believe he is being helped by a member of the Elite Council, Jeric,' Simo replied.

'That's a serious accusation, Simo. Do you have any evidence?' Jeric asked.

'We know he was using an Elite Council vehicle, and we found this at the site where Max and his team were ambushed,' Simo replied, handing over the crystal migration pin.

'This is Bobmaton's,' Jeric said.

'Yes, Sir. Either Bobmaton was involved or potentially the Supreme Leader if he had spares,' Simo replied.

'Excellent work, Simo,' Jeric said, leaning back in his chair. 'It's such a shame that Max, Luc and the others died at the hands of those Deceptors. The DSL and I took Lin and Juli to the ambush site this morning but found nothing.'

'We lost a lot of the team there, Sir. But luckily, Max and some other enforcers survived,' Simo replied.

'He did?' Jeric paused and then said, 'That's good news. How is he, and where is he?'

'He's on the mend, Sir. He's not fit for action yet, but he's improving daily,' Simo replied, studying Jeric's face. 'We found him in an enforcer medicentre as an unknown injured enforcer.'

'I think a hero like Max deserves better than that. Arrange for him to be moved to the medicentre by the Palace Compound,' Jeric replied, looking at Zym.

'I think he's hoping to join Lin, actually,' Zym said.

'I'm sure that can be arranged, once he's recovered in the Palace medicentre' Jeric replied.

'There's no need for that. The medidoc says he'll be okay to discharge,' Zym insisted.

'How are Lin and Juli, Sir?' Simo asked, trying to change the subject.

'They are working hard to get the Grand Exodus machine ready,' Jeric replied, and added, 'but obviously worried about Max.'

'So can we arrange for Max to be moved to where Lin is being held, I mean staying?' Simo said.

Jeric tapped furiously on his screen and replied, 'Yes, of course, Simo. Make the arrangements. I'll make sure it goes smoothly.'

There was a knock at the door, and Erzsi entered. 'Your Energy Brackles and burger, Sir.'

'A Brackles?' Zym queried.

'All of the taste of the real thing, but none of the alcohol,' Jeric replied.

'I must try one,' Zym smiled.

'Thank you, Erzsi. But what about my guests?' Jeric replied.

Erzsi scowled and said, 'But—'

'It's okay, Jeric. We'd already told Erzsi we weren't hungry or thirsty,' Zym said, winking at Erzsi.

'Okay, Erzsi, scram,' Jeric replied.

Erzsi smiled at Zym and said, 'Thank you, Jericesen.' Then she left the room, closing the door behind her.

'Well, you need to sort out Max's transfer to the DSL's edge of the city residence and welcome back Zym. I need to make some calls, so you can go. Keep up the good work, Simo. I knew

I could rely on you,' Jeric said, standing and opening his office door.

Zym and Simo left Jeric's office, and the door slammed behind them.

Zym noticed Erzsi slumped at her deck. 'Why do you put up with him?'

'I need the credits. My partner was injured in an Elite Council project, and I'm all he's got,' Erzsi replied.

'Well, let me know if you need any help. I've not got much, but nobody deserves to be treated like he treats you,' Zym said.

'Thank you, Sir. But I think you have enough troubles of your own. Look after your brother and his family,' Erzsi replied.

Simo and Zym left Jeric's office and headed towards Simo's landcraft.

'I don't think Jeric was pleased to see me,' Zym laughed.

'Really? I never picked up anything,' Simo chuckled.

'That Erzsi seems decent. She doesn't deserve a boss like Jeric.'

'Hang on, you were calling her a fire-breathing demon not long ago,' Simo challenged.

'No, I didn't, you did,' Zym replied. 'Admittedly, I agreed with you, but I might have been wrong.'

'Hang on, let me call the news stations. Zymraxin admits he was wrong, and enforcers break down in disbelief,' Simo said in mock surprise.

'I guess Bobmaton doesn't have to worry about you taking his comedy crown,' Zym replied.

'Who needs a crown? Anyway, let's get Max and Lin back together, and then we need to sort out Luc,' Simo replied.

'Ma'am, are you sure you should be here?' Gran asked.

'Life moves on Gran. Nicoeyel took me to where Max was ambushed, but they didn't have his uniform or any of his belongings, so I know he's alive. I'm just waiting for him to be well enough to get in touch,' Lin replied.

Juli looked at her sister with a mixture of love and sympathy. 'What's happened with those cleaners, Gran?'

'The data shows they arrived on KLT3.4e9.3 alive and well,' Gran replied.

'Excellent news. The Elite Council will be so pleased. How many do you think we can send at once?' Lin asked.

'We need to do more tests, but sending those two matched all our algorithms. Extrapolating that to the point before errors creep in, we could send thirty at a time safely over that distance and double that to Astral 5,' Gran replied.

'I'll let the Project Leader know we can proceed with the Grand Gathering in a few weeks. Send the final calculations to the other One World Research Centres,' Lin demanded. 'We need to make sure all the Grand Exodus machines are calibrated the same.'

'Of course, and we'll start the larger group tests in the next week or two,' Gran replied.

'Good idea, but make it in the next day or two,' Lin replied as her communicator rang. 'Excuse me, I need to take this.'

Gran looked at Juli with despair.

'Sorry, Gran. We need to accelerate the process due to the climate change. Get going as quickly as possible on your tests and safety checks. The Grand Gathering can't be delayed—'

Lin screamed.

'Lin, what is it?' Juli asked, rushing to her.

'It's Max,' Lin replied.

'Oh no, I'm so sorry Lin. Have they found his remains?'

'No, Juli. He's alive. Once the medidoc agrees to discharge him, they're arranging for him to be moved to the DSL's apartment. I need to be there to meet him,' Lin cried joyfully.

'Of course you do. I'll stay with Gran to get everything sorted for the Grand Gathering. Get going and give Max my love,' Juli replied as Lin left the Grand Exodus Room.

9

I'M ALIVE

'How come the Elite have stunning hi-tech offices and homes, but they can't even manage to keep a medicentre dedicated to injured enforcers clean and tidy,' Zym sighed, looking at the rubbish scattered down the corridor and the peeling paintwork. Even the strong disinfectant smell failed to mask the musky scent of dusty mould.

'What was the one you were in by the Palace Compound like?' Simo asked as he looked for someone to ask for directions.

'Not much better from what I can remember. Except I once got a glimpse into the VIP wing, which was sheer luxury,' Zym grumbled.

'Is there anyone even working here? The place has less staff than the one in the Deserted Zone. Oh, never mind, there's Cal,' Simo said.

'Hey guys, good to see you again,' Cal said. 'Keri is with Max. Straight down the corridor and the last door on the left. I'm just fetching some drinks. Do you want anything?'

'I'm fine, thanks,' Simo replied. 'Actually, I've changed my mind. I will have a drink. Anything will do.'

'I could do with something to eat, even if it's just an energy bar,' Zym said. 'I think my transitioning hasn't worked properly. I'm constantly hungry.'

Cal and Simo laughed.

'That's perfectly normal, Zym. It can take a few weeks for your appetite to settle,' Simo replied.

'I'll grab you something,' Cal replied, heading in the opposite direction.

As they approached the door to Max's room, Zym glanced through the window into the room and saw him talking animatedly to Keri, and he smiled.

'Max,' Simo said, walking into the room, 'it's so good to see you back with us.'

'It's good to be back,' Max replied. 'Zym, is that you?'

'Hi, Max. Yep, I took the plunge and transitioned. I decided you and Simo were struggling and needed my help,' Zym replied with a smile.

'That's very generous of you. I don't know how we coped without you,' Max laughed.

'To be honest, nor do I after recent events,' Zym chuckled.

'Oh, will you two behave and hug each other? We can all see how pleased you are to see each other,' Keri said.

Zym walked over to the bed and thrust out his hand, which Max shook.

'For crying out loud, why are you both so uptight,' Keri laughed, shaking her head.

The door opened, and Cal came in carrying some food and drinks.

'Two Zingles super-sized energy burger meals for Max and Zym and Ruby Glow energy drinks for us,' Cal said, handing drinks to Keri and Simo and the meals to Max and Zym.

'I love Ruby Glow. It's so fruity, like drinking real berry juice,' Keri said excitedly.

Max was ploughing through his meal but managed to mumble, 'So what did Jeric want to see you for?'

'He just wanted an update on Dronin, and we told him you were alive,' Simo replied.

'He was a bit upset to see me back. But it seems Simo needs to be renamed Simodevious for outwitting Cogi,' Zym laughed.

'Zymraxin, please explain how Simohal outwitted Cogi. The deliberate deception of a state device is an offence,' Cogi asserted from a speaker on the wall.

Zym scowled, 'I don't mean Simo delib—'

'Cogi, Zymraxin was talking metaphorically regarding his reappointment before the legislation was changed. No offence has been committed,' Simo said.

'Understood, Simohal. The record will show you acknowledge the event and deemed no offence as being committed,' Cogi replied.

'Thank you, Cogi. Security code S, arn, lit, orc, nelo, elt, 4E,' Simo said.

Cal frowned, 'What's that all about?'

'It's my code for deactivating Cogi if I believe it may interfere with an investigation. It lasts around an hour unless I reset it,' Simo replied.

'Dronin used to say something similar. Well, he'd start by saying "security code," but the rest would be different,' Cal said.

Keri nodded, 'You're right, Cal. I remember him saying it. I tried it myself, but it kept saying I wasn't authorised.'

Simo nodded, 'Cogi overrides are user-specific. It matches the code to the voice, but why would Dronin have an override code?'

'Maybe he hacked the system?' Max suggested.

'Possibly, but the list of override users is reviewed regularly by Jeric and the Supreme Leader, so he would have shown up,' Simo replied.

The door opened, and a medidoc entered. 'I'm sorry to interrupt, but I need to check Maxoraxin.'

'Sorry Doc, do you need us to leave?' Zym asked.

'No, it's fine. I'm very pleased with his progress. How are you feeling, Maxoraxin? I see your appetite has returned.'

'Please call me Max. Yes, I'm feeling a lot better.'

'Well, Max, I think we can discharge you, but you're on restricted service. You still need a lot of rest and no physical exertion. Is that clear?'

'Yes, Doc, absolutely. So can I leave now?'

'I need to know where you're going and who will look after you first.'

'Of course, I'm going home and my brother—'

Simo interrupted, 'He's going to the Deputy Supreme Leader's dwelling, where his partner will look after him.'

Max looked at Simo, stunned.

'Well, such exalted care and location sounds perfect, Max. I see no reason for keeping you here any longer.'

Max went to throw back his bedcovers, but Simo pushed him back. 'Easy, buddy. I think you've got time to finish your meal first. Besides, you can't get changed yet; ladies are present.'

Cal laughed, 'I wouldn't worry about that, Simo. When we got Max to the Deserted Zone medicentre, it was Keri—'

'That'll do, Cal. Let's give Max some space to get changed,' Keri replied, dragging Cal into the hallway. Looking back, she shouted, 'Have a nice time in your swanky new dwelling. Let us know when you're settled, and we'll pop round.'

'Don't worry about Luc and Kendra. We'll go and freshen up and get some food, then come back to keep an eye on them,' Cal shouted as the door closed.

***

'Excuse me, Ma'am. I've been told to inform you that Maxoraxin is just being added to Argo in the lobby and will be here shortly.'

'Thank you, enforcer,' Lin replied. 'Can I go down and meet him?'

'Sorry, Ma'am, but it's best to meet him up here.'

Eighty-nine floors lower, Zym snarled, 'Get out of my way, enforcer. Max is my brother, and you will not stop me from going up with him.'

'I understand, Zymraxin, but—'

'Don't but me, lad. I've been enforcing since before you were a spark in your Daddy's—'

Simo moved in front of Zym. 'Enforcer, I'm Simohal, and I'm ordering you to let Zym pass.'

'Sorry, Simohal, but these orders come from Jericesen to protect the residents in the Deputy Supreme Leader's dwelling. You are on the clearance list, but not Zymraxin.'

'Zym, lower your fists. There'll be no violence; we're doing this properly. I'll contact Jeric,' Simo said, lifting his communicator and walking away from the others.

'Excuse me, enforcer,' Max said.

'Yes, Maxoraxin, sir.'

'As someone invited by the Deputy Supreme Leader to live in his dwelling, am I permitted to have guests?' Max said calmly.

'Yes, of course, Maxoraxin. But you need to inform Argo at least one hour in advance so the appropriate checks can be made, and if approved, they can visit you.'

Across the lobby, Simo was raising his voice. 'Jeric, this is ridiculous...' his voice trailed off as he turned away.

'What about medistaff? Do I need to give advance notice for them? I'm just concerned in case I need emergency care.' Max enquired.

'You'll need to enter your medistaff into Argo, but they can attend without prior notice, Sir,' the enforcer replied.

'Jeric, I know it's normally the DSL's dwelling, but come on,' Simo shouted into his communicator.

Max walked away, lifted the Argo wristband he had been given, and started talking quietly into it.

A minute later, Max walked back towards the chutes, pausing halfway. 'Simo, come on, it's sorted. Say hi to Jeric for me, and hurry up.'

Simo looked at Max and said, 'It's okay, Jeric. It seems someone understands how to look after people.'

'Argo, please send a chute for three,' Max said.

A large glass-walled chute rose through the floor and opened behind the enforcer.

'Come on, Zym, Simo, our carriage awaits,' Max said.

'I'm sorry, Maxoraxin, but I've—'

Max raised his hand, 'Enforcer, please check the approved list. I think you'll find Zym is now approved.'

The enforcer checked his device and then waved them through.

As the chute door closed behind them and they sped upwards, Simo turned to Max, 'Who did you contact to give Zym clearance?'

'Nobody. I just made him my medicare assistant,' Max laughed.

'Well, I've been clearing up your mess since you were a kid,' Zym sniggered.

They were still laughing as they approached the door to the DSL's dwelling. The door opened, and Lin came running out and hugged Max.

'I was scared I'd lost you,' Lin said emotionally.

'Not a chance. I just needed a little lie-down. Zym's moaning had worn me out,' Max replied, winking at his brother.

'Come on, luvvies, do we get to see how the great and the mighty live?' Zym laughed.

'Where's the proper kitchen?' Simo asked after Lin gave them a tour of the dwelling.

'Apparently, the DSL always orders in for his food, or eats in the on-site gourmet restaurant,' Lin replied.

'I've never been a fan of the Elite, but it's good of the DSL to let you stay here. I bet he or his people are checking in on you regularly to ensure you're not trashing the place,' Zym said.

Lin laughed, 'Actually, apart from when we first moved in, we've not seen him or anyone except the enforcers protecting us.'

'Max, are you okay?' Zym asked, noticing Max frowning.

'Yeah, I'm fine, but this dwelling is wrong,' Max replied as he started pacing around the dwelling.

'Yeah, it's beyond repulsively ostentatious,' Simo added.

Max looked towards the stairs and started mentally pacing across the room. 'Hmm, bedroom there...'

'Oh no, he's gone into Max mode,' Zym laughed.

'That's the bed,' Max muttered, looking at the floor and then up at the ceiling.

'What's Max mode?' Simo asked.

'There's the wardrobe, and then the next bedroom, but that means...' Max mumbled.

'He starts talking to himself and pacing around,' Zym explained.

'It's very annoying, isn't it,' Lin said.

'I've seen him mutter to himself before, but I just assumed it was an occasional thing,' Simo replied.

'I wish it were only occasionally,' Lin said.

Zym glanced at Simo and frowned before turning to Max. 'What's up? Is there something wrong with the furniture?'

'It's not that, it's the footprint, it's wrong. Are there any rooms you haven't shown us, Lin?' Max asked.

'No, you've seen it all,' Lin replied.

'Any hidden doors or strange draughts or slits of light?' Max challenged.

'Hmm, now you mention it, there is something in the wardrobe in our room,' Lin said, leading them back to their bedroom.

'What's the code?' Max asked, looking at the alphanumeric keypad.

'I have no idea. I even tried Argo, but it didn't recognise there was a door here,' Lin replied.

'Let me try,' Simo said, lifting his enforcer device. 'Hmm, according to Cogi, we are stood in a field with no doors or walls near us.'

'Another Elite thing we know nothing about and have no control over,' Max replied. 'It's like they live in a different world without the rules the rest of us have to follow.'

'What do you mean, "another thing"?' Simo challenged.

'Dronin was driving an Elite landcraft,' Max said.

'Yeah, I remember you saying,' Simo replied. 'But what's that got to do with what's happening here?'

'We could only pick up the Elite landcraft from visuals and basic Cogi tracking. We couldn't shut it down or even stop it refuelling,' Max scowled.

'I understand not being able to take control of an Elite vehicle, as that would expose them to hacking and kidnap, but why couldn't you block Dronin's refuelling card?' Zym challenged.

'Because it wasn't Dronin's, he was using an Elite's card,' Max replied.

'You never told me that,' Simo protested. 'Where's the card now?'

'I don't know. I was going to search the vehicle when the sign knocked me out,' Max shrugged.

'You got knocked out by a sign and then run over by a landcraft? I thought you youngsters filled out safety assessment forms before putting your shoes on nowadays,' Zym laughed.

'I didn't exactly volunteer to get injured twice in one night, you know,' Max huffed.

'Will you two shut up for a minute? I'm sure I asked Luc to check the vehicle before he left you and went after Dronin,' Simo said, trying to remember that night's events.

'You ordered this Luc person to leave Max unconscious?' Lin snapped.

'Not like that,' Simo replied. 'I ordered Luc to leave enforcers with Max, get him some medicare, and then go after Dronin. Yes, yes, I did tell him to search the landcraft. I wonder if he found anything.'

'We won't know until he wakes up,' Zym said.

'Unless it's amongst his belongings. Are you alright if I go? I need to check Luc and see if I can find anything,' Simo replied.

'Simo, I've got an idea about that locked door. What was the code for that tunnel door in the medicentre?' Zym asked.

Simo started tapping an invisible keypad in the air. 'Three, eighteen, fifteen, uh fourteen, nine, oh hang on no, it was eight, I think, then nineteen. I need to go, but let me know if you find anything.'

Zym, Max and Lin saw Simo leave and walked back to the door inside the wardrobe.

'What have you got in mind, Zym?' Max asked. 'This pad only goes from zero to nine, so it can't be the same numbers.'

'Let's add the digits together for numbers above nine,' Zym said.

'Okay, so three, one plus eight is nine, then one plus five is six, then uh five, then eight, and finally one plus nine, maybe zero,' Max said as Zym tapped in the numbers.

'Nope. Say them again,' Zym said.

Two more failed attempts caused Zym to shrug. 'It looks like we won't be getting in there anytime soon.'

'Does Cronhs mean anything?' Lin asked.

Max and Zym looked at each other, then shook their heads, 'Nope, why?'

'Well, if you say each number is a letter of the alphabet, it is C R O N H S,' Lin said, showing them what she had written down.

Max stared at Lin's writing, then at Zym, 'Could it be?'

'Only one way to find out, and Simo did stumble over the fifth number. What if it was nine?' Zym replied.

'That makes the h an i. What's Cronis?' Lin asked with a puzzled look.

Zym hurriedly tapped the code into the keypad, and the door clicked open. He looked at Max and Lin, then pulled open the door.

'Cronis means we are in the middle of something huge and potentially dangerous,' Max said.

Zym walked into the room, followed by Lin and Max.

'It's empty. Where is everything?' Max asked.

'Argo, when was this room emptied?' Lin asked.

'It seems like even the Elite's device doesn't operate in here,' Max replied in response to the silence.

'That's worth remembering,' Zym said.

'There's a big computer bank over there,' Lin said, pointing to a large cabinet with a screen and lights flashing from various circuits.

Max walked over to the cabinet whilst looking around at the floor and walls. He tapped the screen a few times before turning around. 'It's just the control bank for the dwelling's systems like heating, visuals and sound. But look at the dust patterns and marks on the walls.'

'I was just thinking the same,' Zym replied, trying to pull something stuck between the floor and the wall.

'What are you both on about?' Lin asked.

'There were a lot of things moved out of here very recently. You can see where dust gathered up to the edge of whatever was on the floor around the room, but nothing underneath where the things were,' Max replied. 'By the looks of the scuffs on the wall near the door, I'd say it was emptied in a hurry, too.'

Zym stood up and looked at what he had found.

'What have you got there?' Max asked, watching his brother studying his hand.

'It's part of an old enforcer identity card,' Zym replied.

'I didn't know Nicoeyel was a former enforcer,' Max said.

'He wasn't,' Lin replied. 'I've had plenty of meetings with the DSL, and he's told me a few times about how he worked his way up from a tough upbringing as a child to be the Head of Zephyrion's House of Finance before being made the Deputy Supreme Leader.'

Zym looked at the card one last time before flicking it over to Max, 'It's not Nicoeyel's card. It's our Mother's.'

10
IT CAN'T BE

Lin looked at Zym and then Max, 'But your Mum died years ago. Why would her enforcer card be here?'

'That's an excellent question. I wish I had an equally excellent answer,' Max replied. 'Zym, who was in charge when our parents died?'

'That was about nine years after the Grand Formation when Zephyrion was unified. Timezel was elected the first Deputy Supreme Leader, and the first Supreme Leader was Zyrenev.'

'Oh, I've heard of him when I was younger. Wasn't he called Zyrenev the Wise?' Lin asked.

'Yes, although it was his wife, Kazi, who was the wise one. She was a Psiorite and his Chief Counsellor,' Zym replied.

'Why are you smiling, Zym?' Max asked.

'It's just that I haven't heard anyone mention Psiorites for years, and now I've had two conversations in one day.'

'I've never even heard of Psiorites. What are they?' Max asked.

'Oh, Max, you're hopeless if it's not something that interests you,' Lin laughed. 'They were a bit like seers or fortune tellers.'

'Something like that, yeah,' Zym agreed.

'What happened to Zyrenev and Kazi?' Max asked.

'Zyrenev volunteered to be one of the first to transition to show it was safe, but unfortunately, it went wrong, and he died,' Zym replied.

'I never heard anything about that,' Lin said.

'The Elite covered it up, and the official line was he died in a spacecraft accident after thirteen years as our SL,' Zym explained.

'What about Kazi?' Lin asked.

'From what I know, she had a breakdown and was provided with a dwelling inside the Palace Compound and died a few years later,' Zym replied. 'They say she refused to transition, and to be honest, that was what always made me reluctant to do it, too.'

'But this still doesn't explain how Mum's ID card ended up here,' Max said. 'Has anyone else lived here besides Nicoeyel?'

'Timezel would have had this as one of his dwellings originally,' Zym replied. 'But it was still quite a new building when he took over as SL. If I remember right, the election for a new DSL took half a year, so this dwelling would have been empty until Nicoeyel won.'

'So all we can be certain of is a few years after your parents died, your Mum's ID card found its way into this secured room in a dwelling that was Timezel's and then Nicoeyel's,' Lin said.

'Yep, either way, I don't like this one bit,' Zym growled.

'Maybe the card caught up with other reports,' Lin suggested.

'That's a good point. After all, when an enforcer is killed in action, the Supreme or Deputy Supreme Leader normally issues a personal message,' Max agreed.

'You mean they sign a pre-produced message,' Zym grumbled.

'Even so, they would be given the message to sign, so maybe they get it with the report of their death, and the card was in there and fell out,' Max said.

'I hear what you're both saying, but my raxin senses are telling me there's more to this than it simply dropping out of a file,' Zym replied.

'Maybe,' Max agreed. 'I can't see anything else in here. Can you?'

Lin shook her head, and Zym replied, 'Nor me. Let's get out of here.'

'I've got a better idea,' Lin replied. 'Why don't we move some furniture in here? If neither Cogi nor Argo are in here, we have somewhere we can talk openly.'

'Blimey, Max. How did you manage to get a partner who's so smart?' Zym laughed. 'She's more cunning than me.'

'My irresistible charm, of course,' Max replied.

'Will you two pack it up,' Lin said.

'Yes, Deputy Project Leader, ma'am,' Max laughed.

'As you two are fond of saying to each other, I can slap you, you know,' Lin smiled.

'Lin's right, Maxo. Behave yourself,' Zym replied.

'Oi, nobody calls me Maxo, except Mum when I was in trouble,' Max protested.

'Sorry, Maxo,' Zym said with a wink. 'But Lin has a good point. This room means we can discuss anything free of sanction or arrest. Let's use it to review everything we know about our parent's death.'

'We need to go back to our dwelling and get everything we have about their deaths and the Cronis files, too,' Max said before stumbling forward.

Lin jumped to support him. 'The only place you are going is to bed. Simo told me the medidoc said you had to get plenty of rest and no physical exertion.'

'But Zym might be right. We need to review everything,' Max argued.

'I'm sure Zym is more than capable of going home and bringing everything back,' Lin replied. 'In the meantime, you are going to bed.'

'Lin's right, Max. You rest up. I'll go and get everything, and if I need it, I'll get Simo, Keri and Cal to help,' Zym replied.

'But,' Max protested weakly.

'Bed now, my lad, or no supper later,' Zym replied with a wink.

As Max headed towards the bedroom, Lin escorted Zym to the front door. 'He will be okay, won't he?'

'Yes, the medidoc wasn't even slightly concerned with his health. Max just needs to rest,' Zym replied.

'Luc? Can you hear me?' Cal asked as Luc started to groan and twitch.

'I'll go and find a medidoc,' Keri said, heading for the door.

'D-D-Dronin, one, t-t-two...' Luc mumbled.

'Luc, you're safe and in a medicentre,' Cal said.

'I-I-I'll sho...' Luc went to sit but then slumped back.

The door flew open as a medidoc entered with an assistant and Keri in tow.

The medidoc started checking Luc over when Luc sat bolt upright and pointed an invisible depletor towards Keri. 'Don't m-m-move Keri, or I-I'll shoot.'

'Luc, it's Cal and Keri. They brought you here,' the medidoc said, trying to ease Luc into lying down but meeting stubborn resistance.

Luc turned his head, trying to keep an eye on Keri whilst also trying to look at the medidoc. 'Who are you? Get your hands off me. I'm an e-e-enforcer, and you're interfering in m-m-my arrest.'

'I'm your medidoc, Luc. You were shot and badly injured. If it weren't for Keri and Cal, you'd have died,' the medidoc said soothingly.

'Get back,' Luc shouted, scrambling out of the opposite side of the bed and collapsing to the floor.

Cal and the medidoc's assistant moved to help, but Luc grabbed the side of the bed and scrambled to his feet. He swung his nonexistent depletor towards them. 'Get back. W-w-where's Dronin and Max?'

'What the heck is all this commotion?' Simo asked, walking into the room.

'S-S-Simohal, sir. I've got them c-c-covered, b-b-but they won't say where D-Dr-Dronin or Max is,' Luc stammered.

Simo looked at the medidoc and the others. 'Well done, Luc. Why don't you get back into bed? I've got this covered now, and you look so tired.'

'I am tired, b-b-but I need to give you my r-r-repo...' Luc collapsed onto the floor again.

When Cal and the medidoc assistant rushed to help Luc this time, they met with no resistance. They lifted him back into bed and made him comfortable.

'What just happened?' Simo asked.

'He's only just woken up, so he's very disorientated,' the medidoc replied.

'But I've just left Kendra, and I was with Max earlier, and neither of them were like this,' Simo said.

The medidoc said, 'I'm afraid Luc was in a much worse state than Kendra or Max.'

'But he's imagining things and stuttering. Will that go away with rest?' Simo asked.

'Being honest, I don't know. The last scan Luc had showed his brain patterns were badly jumbled, but they looked like they were reforming. At this stage, we don't know.'

'Where's Mum?' Luc asked, looking straight up to the ceiling.

'She's on her way, Luc,' Simo replied.

'I'd better wash the dishes,' Luc said without moving.

'I've done them, Luc. You relax,' Keri replied.

'Yes, ma'am. I need my Mum. Will Mum be here soon?' Luc replied before closing his eyes.

'She'll be here as soon as possible, Luc,' Simo said.

'Have you found his family?' Keri asked.

'The enforcer file address he gave for them was in the Deserted Zone, but it was destroyed by one of the tectonic plate shifts,' Simo replied.

'Didn't he update his record after it happened?' the medidoc asked.

'That's the weird bit. It was destroyed three years before Luc became an enforcer,' Simo said.

'What about Cogi's historical records of births and deaths? Don't they give details of his parents and their addresses since?' Cal asked.

'They record his parents living in the same address as he put in his enforcer file from the date of his birth until the building was destroyed,' Simo replied.

'But where does Cogi say they moved to when their dwelling was destroyed?' Keri asked.

'It doesn't. According to Cogi, they disappeared,' Simo replied. 'Luc was recorded as being enrolled in a residential computer academy at the time, but he left after his family dwelling was destroyed. The next record Cogi has of Luc is him enrolling as a traffic enforcer.'

'So he's an orphan?' Keri said.

Simo started to say, 'We don't—'

'Shupreme Leader, Sir,' Luc said, turning his head and looking at Simo.

'What do you want, Luc?' Simo asked.

'M-M-My pocket, Shir,' Luc mumbled, then blacked out again.

'His stutter is coming and going. That must be good, surely?" Keri asked.

'His brain patterns are reforming links. All we can hope is that they make the right connections,' the medidoc replied.

'Where's his enforcer uniform?' Simo asked.

'In that locker,' the medidoc said. 'We had to cut him out of it, so it's pretty messed up.'

'We never had time to make them more comfortable,' Keri replied, trying to explain why they hadn't removed it previously.

'It's a good job you didn't, or I wouldn't have found these,' Simo said, holding up a card and payment disc.

'What are they?' Keri asked.

Simo scanned the items with his enforcer device, 'Well, the card is the Supreme Leader's all-access card, giving the holder access to enter anywhere on the planet.'

'And the payment disc?' Cal asked.

'That's also the SL's,' Simo replied. 'I assume Luc must have found them in Dronin's parcel landcraft when they chased him.'

'I knew it was someone high up,' Keri said. 'Dronin knew too much about everything.'

'He knew, S-S-S-Sir-r-r,' Luc said, sitting upright suddenly. 'I-I-I m-m-m...'

'Isn't there anything you can do to help him relax?' Simo asked.

'We could use an immobiliser on him. It'll lockdown his body and relax his brain patterns,' the medidoc said. 'But it also means that as he becomes more lucid, he'll be more aware that he's immobilised.'

'How long does it last?'

'We can set it for as long as we want, but the default is around an hour. It's a short-term suppressant normally,' the medidoc replied. 'Just designed to calm a patient down and stop them hurting themselves or anyone around them,'

'Then I think we have to use it,' Simo said.

'Who are you?' Luc replied, looking at the medidoc and trying to get out of bed.

'I'm your medidoc, Luc. Try to—'

'G-G-Get a-away from me, Dronin. I-I-I am arrest...' Luc said before passing out again.

'I think you're right,' the medidoc said, pulling out a small metal tube. He held the tube against Luc and pressed the end of it. Luc's eyes widened briefly before his body visibly relaxed.

'Can I see that?' Simo asked.

'Of course, you can have it if you want. I've got plenty,' the medidoc replied.

'How does it work? Has it got its own power supply or something?' Simo asked, inspecting the device.

'It's a very simple piece of equipment,' the medidoc replied. 'It uses our energy souls to zap the other Zephyrion and disrupt their energy souls. Very effective and totally harmless.'

'So their energy soul takes an hour to clear the disruption, and until then, they're immobilised?' Simo asked.

'Yep, unless you turn that disc to extend the time, but as it's using our energy souls, it can drain us if you set it too high,' the medidoc replied.

Simo's communicator went off. 'Zym, hi, yeah, I'm still at the medicentre. Luc is waking up, but he's still a mess. Yes, of course, I can give you a hand. I'll come over now.'

'Is everything okay?' Keri asked.

'Yeah, it's just Zym. They're going through some old cases and need a hand carrying some boxes.'

'Can we help?' Cal asked.

'Just keep an eye on Luc. I think we're all he's got,' Simo said. 'If you need me, use the communicator you gave me.'

'Simohal, based on your recent conversation, are you harbouring an illegal communication device?' Cogi demanded.

'No, Cogi. I was referring to my official communicator, which Keri handed to me. I'd dropped it on the floor,' Simo replied. 'Cogi. Security code S, arn, lit, orc, nelo, elt, 4E.'

Remembering that Cogi had been shut down for a while, Cal asked, 'So do you think the SL is behind all this?'

'We know somebody with a lot of power is helping Dronin, and Luc finding these in Dronin's landcraft is pretty conclusive,' Simo replied.

'So, are you going to arrest the SL?' Cal asked.

'Are you kidding? This is beyond career-limiting. It's life-limiting,' Simo laughed. 'I'm not even going to Jeric with this until I know something for sure.'

11

THE TRIPLE CROWN

'You do realise we have technology that will upload this lot and let you view it on a screen?' Simo asked, heaving a box into his landcraft.

'And if it had been, I guarantee the files would have been corrupted,' Zym replied, loading another into his vehicle.

'Who authorised you to have a parcel landcraft?' Simo challenged.

'You did. You should have an approval request on your device,' Zym laughed.

'You know you're supposed to wait for the approval before taking it?' Simo replied, opening his hal device and approving the request.

'Well, you've approved it, so what's the problem!' Zym said.

'That's not the point. What if I didn't approve it?' Simo asked.

'Were you likely to reject it?'

'No.'

'There you go then. No problem. Now, get a shift on. We've got a few more to load yet,' Zym replied, heading back to the cargo chute, which was still a quarter full of boxes.

A short while later, Zym and Simo pulled up outside the Elite Skyscraper where Max and Lin were staying.

'Enforcer, call a parcel chute, and you two come with me. We have some medical equipment and a few home furnishings for the DSL's guests,' Simo said with authority.

The enforcers complied, and soon the boxes were piled up in the DSL's living area.

'What are we looking for?' Simo asked, opening the first box.

'Not here; we've got something to show you,' Zym said.

Lin stood in front of Zym, 'We can't yet. Max is—'

'Max is wide awake and fed up with playing the support act,' Max said, walking into the room.

'Hey, little brother. How are you feeling?' Zym asked.

'Like I've been lied to once too often,' Max replied. 'Let's get them boxes shifted and find out how our parents are involved.'

'Your parents?' Simo frowned.

An hour passed as they shifted the boxes into the secure room and told Simo about finding their mother's enforcer card.

'You said your parents died before transitioning started?' Simo queried.

Lin stuck a self-adhesive white sheet to a wall and drew a timeline. 'So your parents died thirty-four years ago.'

'Deputy Project Leader born and bred,' Max laughed.

Lin ignored Max and looked at Zym, 'When did Timezel become Supreme Leader?'

'That was thirty years ago when Zyrenev died as one of the first to transition,' Zym replied. 'Nicoeyel became the DSL about half a year later.'

'And your parents were investigating voting fraud?' Simo asked.

'Yeah, when the Grand Formation happened forty-three years ago, they had reason to believe some of the voting was rigged,' Max said.

'Do you know who they were investigating?' Lin asked.

Zym started to say, 'Hopefully, we'll find out—'

'The results of the Supreme Leader, Deputy Supreme Leader and the Head of the House of Finance,' Max said.

Zym looked at Max with surprise. 'How are you so certain?'

'Because I went through their files when you were injured. I was sure the DSL was involved in the corruption you were investigating, and I hoped their investigation might have helped me link him to it,' Max replied.

'Don't be silly, Max. The DSL is an honest and kind person. Besides, look at the timeline. Timezel was living here as the DSL when your parents died,' Lin replied firmly.

'There's something else that points toward Timezel, too,' Simo said, pulling out the SL's all-access card and payment disc. Luc found these in Dronin's parcel landcraft, and they belong to the Supreme Leader.'

'Looks like you three are about to bring down our Supreme Leader,' Lin stated.

Lin's communicator went off. She looked at it and said, 'Sorry, it's Juli. I won't be long.'

After waiting for Lin to leave the room and hearing her start talking, Simo looked at Max. 'Is Lin always like that?'

'Like what?' Max asked.

'Yes, she is Simo,' Zym replied.

'She is what? What are you both on about?' Max asked.

'She seemed very dismissive of you and even ignored you at one point,' Simo replied.

'Oh, that's just her way,' Max replied.

Zym looked at Simo and discreetly shrugged.

'Sorry about that. Juli has been told the Elite Council want to see the Grand Exodus machine, and they've asked me to be there,' Lin said, wafting back into the room.

'When are they coming?' Max asked.

'Now. I need to go. Please don't overdo it, Max. You two look after him,' Lin replied, heading off.

'Will do,' Simo shouted after her.

The next few hours passed as Simo, Zym, and Max went through the old evidence boxes.

'According to this note by Mum, Zyrenev's son was promoted within the House of Finance without a vote,' Max said.

'I didn't know Zyrenev had any children,' Zym replied. 'Did you Simo?'

'You're asking the wrong person. I was still young when my Mum died, and the state brought me up. Every morning, it was "All praise our Supreme Leader Zyrenev," which changed to "All praise our Supreme Leader, Timezel," after Zyrenev died. We weren't told anything about the families of the Elite,' Simo sighed.

'What does your hal device say about Zyrenev and his family?' Max asked.

Simo picked up his device and started searching, 'Usual stuff, the first Supreme Leader of the unified Zephyrion and elected during the Grand Formation elections. Nickname Zyrenev the Wise due to his ability to understand others' points of view. Served for thirteen years, four months and two days. Died in a spacecraft accident on a scheduled flight to Astral 5.'

'Anything about his family?' Zym asked.

'Daughter, unnamed and died at birth. Son, Zeryn, died in the same spacecraft accident as his father. Wife, hmm,' Simo mused.

'What is it, Simo?' Max asked.

'Zyrenev's wife's file is classified. It doesn't even show her name,' Simo replied.

'Why would they hide her name? She was a public figure, the wife of our first Supreme Leader, and we all knew she was called Kazi,' Zym said.

'I know they classify files for anyone given a false identity. Maybe they did it to protect her after Zyrenev's death,' Max suggested.

'That would make sense. Perhaps hiding her from others in the Elite Council,' Simo agreed.

'Talking of which, there's a file here called Timezel,' Zym said, pulling out a dusty folder.

'I think I saw that when I was after the ones you were investigating for financial fraud before your accident,' Max replied. 'But I don't think there was anything relating to the House of Finance.'

'Maybe not, but look at this,' Zym said, holding up an image of a young Timezel with handwritten scrawls.

'Okay, I know this stuff goes back thirty to forty years, but that looks like another language,' Simo laughed.

'That's Dad's scrawl,' Max replied.

'Any idea what it says?' Simo asked.

'I can make out "Cronis," "SL out, RS in," and "digital vote." I can't read the next bit, but then it says "power grab" and "Double Crown," but the rest could say anything,' Max said. 'Hang on, that bit at the bottom "T tracked for SL," I think.'

'Is it "tracked" or "tricked"?' Simo challenged.

'It could be either, I reckon,' Zym replied. 'Hang on, Simo. Did you say it mentioned Zyrenev's son?'

'Yeah, Zeryn, but he died in the same spacecraft accident as his dad,' Simo replied.

'But there wasn't a spacecraft accident. Zyrenev died in a transitioning accident,' Zym insisted.

'So what happened to Zeryn?' Max asked.

'But it says here in the official record there was a spacecraft accident,' Simo protested.

'Do you really believe all enforcer records are accurate?' Zym smiled. 'Besides, I was an enforcer then, and we were given strict instructions about what to say.'

'But...' Simo started to say but trailed off in thought.

'Are you okay, Simo?' Max asked.

'Well, if that record is false…no, forget it. She'd have found a way to get to me,' Simo said.

'Who would have?' Max asked as Zym kicked him. 'Oww.'

'It's okay, Zym. Max knows about my Mum. I was just wondering if there's a record about her,' Simo said.

'Haven't you looked?' Max asked.

'We can't use enforcer equipment for personal use,' Simo replied.

'Hmm,' Zym mused. 'What was your mum called?'

'Shazonrani,' Simo replied.

'She was a rani, an engineer like Lin's sister Julirani,' Zym replied, writing something on the back of an old file he was holding.

'Juli's not a full engineer; she's still a technician, but she has passed enough exams to officially start calling herself a rani,' Max explained. 'So your mother was one too?'

'Yeah, I wish I'd known her as an adult,' Simo sighed.

'Well, there's a name in this file you need to check,' Zym said, holding up a sheet of paper.

'You've just written that,' Simo protested.

'I think you'll find that's our dad's writing. Don't you think so, Max?' Zym said.

'Absolutely, Zym. I'd recognise his scrawl anywhere. You need to see if that name is relevant to our investigation, Simo,' Max replied.

'Thank you,' Simo replied, typing the name into his device. Simo frowned and tried again.

'Well, don't keep us waiting,' Zym said.

'It says, "For senior Elite review only." I've never seen that before. I never knew there was a senior Elite level,' Simo replied.

'Didn't you say your mum was seeing a member of the Elite?' Zym asked. 'Perhaps whoever that was is senior enough to withhold data like this. Are you sure you can't remember anything about them?'

'Nothing. I remember Mum saying she was seeing her important friend and leaving me with our neighbour, which happened a lot. But one day, she never came home,' Simo replied.

'What happened to you?' Max asked.

'An Elite Family Unit team arrived. They told my neighbours my mum had been killed, and they took me to a home where I spent the rest of my childhood,' Simo replied, choking back his emotions.

'Don't you mean the Council Family Unit? The EFU is reserved for issues relating to Elite family members only,' Max said.

'I thought that, but when I queried it as I got older, they said my mum's Elite friend insisted I was cared for through the EFU,' Simo replied.

'Are you sure you're not related to any Elite members?' Zym laughed.

'If I am, I want a refund,' Simo replied, laughing.

Max held up another piece of paper, 'Look, another reference to the Double Crown and "T, rigged election." Our parents were sure Timezel rigged the election, but what is the Double Crown?'

'Dronin mentioned a Triple Crown, but not a Double Crown,' Zym replied.

Max carried on reading and then said, 'It says Astral 5 is to be the planet for the Elite, industry experts and key workers, with a secondary planet for all others, including all Daxson.'

'Does it say anything more about the plan for the second planet?' Zym asked.

'This report is quite detailed. The Zephyrions sent to the second planet will build a new civilisation from scratch. What they won't know is that they will be a future backup planet should Astral 5 suffer the same climate catastrophe as Zephyrion. It also says if the backup planet has descended into criminal chaos, the Daxson will be released to wipe out the population, leaving the infrastructure for evacuees from Astral 5,' Max replied.

'But I thought you went through all these files when you investigated my case?' Zym said.

'Only where it seemed to be related to financial irregularities. I'd still be reading them if I'd read everything,' Max protested. 'Populating planets wasn't a priority at the time.'

'I'm still confused,' Zym said.

'I thought transitioning would have fixed that,' Max laughed.

'You're heading into slapping territory,' Zym replied, smiling. 'Seriously though, how have we gone from a Double Crown to a Triple Crown?'

'If they've decided to add a second backup planet, you have the Triple Crown,' Simo suggested.

'Hmm, that would be a nice simple explanation,' Max replied, frowning.

'Here we go. Max always makes that face just before a but,' Zym said.

'Yeah, I've noticed it too,' Simo laughed.

'It's not a but; I just don't like simple explanations,' Max replied. 'Why do they want a third planet? If Timezel rigged the vote, why was he tricked about the Supreme Leader role? Also, I presume SL out RS in means the Supreme Leader out, so who is the RS being brought in?'

'Not who, what,' Zym replied. 'Dronin told me there is a plan to replace the Supreme Leader with a hereditary Regent Supreme. It looks like they would have ultimate rule of all three planets.'

'Effectively a Triple Crown,' Simo said.

'But Timezel is the Supreme Leader, so why would he want to replace himself with a Regent?' Zym challenged.

Max started to say, 'Maybe it's just the title—'

'Are you three still in here?' Lin smiled as she entered the room a few hours later.

Max smiled. 'Hiya. Yeah, we've found out quite a bit about—'

'I've got some exciting news,' Lin interrupted Max. 'The remnants of the Project Leader were found in his dwelling this morning. They think the storm on Lottery Night damaged the building's power supply, and a power surge vaporised him.'

'That sounds more tragic than exciting,' Zym said.

'That is sad, but the exciting bit is they've appointed me as the new Operation Exodus Project Leader, and the Deputy Supreme Leader has said we can stay here as our permanent dwelling until our Exodus. I am now Lineklis,' Lin said excitedly. 'Look, Nico gave me this bracelet to symbolise my authority.'

Max jumped up and threw his arms around Lin, 'I'm so pleased for you, my love. Or do I have to call you ma'am now?'

'Lin is acceptable for now,' Lin laughed.

'Congratulations, Lin. You've pushed hard to get to the top,' Zym replied.

'Yeah, well done, Lin. Not many get to become an Elite,' Simo added.

'Thanks, Simo. I almost forgot I ran into someone in the foyer looking for you,' Lin said. 'I got her a glass of water and left her in the living area.'

'Who is it?' Simo asked.

'I can't remember her name, but she said she was from Jericesen's office,' Lin replied.

Simo entered the living area, where someone stood looking out a window.

'It's a surreal view, isn't it,' Simo said, breaking the viewer's thoughts and making her turn.

'Simohal, I'm pleased to see you. Seeing such a wasteland of dead plants and animals out there, with such extravagant luxury in here, mirrors the difference between those who have and those who have not,' Erzsi replied.

Simo instantly recognised Jeric's downtrodden personal assistant. 'Hello, Erzsi. What are you doing here?'

'Jericesen insisted I come and find you. He said you'd either be at the medicentre with Luc or here,' Erzsi said.

'What does he want?' Simo asked.

'He wants you to head up the enforcers at the Grand Gathering,' Erzsi replied.

'But why not just contact me via my communicator or assign me on the system?' Simo asked.

'Because I've got to tell you his rules, and he doesn't want any record of them,' Erzsi replied.

'So his instructions are totally off the record?' Simo said.

'Yes, Simohal. The first two are obvious. Max and Luc are not to be given any duties. He wants them to rest even if they have received medical clearance for duty. It's planned for them both to be guests of honour,' Erzsi said.

'That's fine with me. What are his other rules?' Simo asked.

'There is only one more. Zym is not to be assigned to any duties inside the One World Research Centre,' Erzsi said.

'You're kidding?' Simo snapped.

'I'm sorry, Simo. Jeric was adamant about it,' Erzsi said.

'I need to see him,' Simo replied.

'He said you'd say that, and he told me to say it is not negotiable,' Erzsi replied. 'Of course, this conversation is off the record.'

'I don't care if it's on or...oh, I see what you mean. Okay, thank you, Erzsi,' Simo said.

'I need to go, but can I say one more thing confidentially?' Erzsi asked.

'Go right ahead.'

'If you try to access any files relating to Elite family members, a report gets sent directly to Jericesen. This includes files relating to your own family,' Erzsi whispered.

'Oh, I guess I can expect a Jeric roasting soon,' Simo sighed.

'No, and I'd appreciate you never mentioning anything to Jericesen. I intercepted the report and buried it under office administration,' Erzsi replied. 'Jeric hates admin, so it'll never be seen.'

'Why would you do that?' Simo asked.

'Because sometimes the good guys need a bit of luck,' Erzsi replied. 'Good luck, Simo. I'm sure we'll see each other soon.'

Simo watched Erzsi leave and close the door behind her. He wandered across the living area and noticed a glass by the window. He picked it up and saw a small envelope beside it. On the front was scrawled,

"Only open these files if you're prepared for your life to change forever."

Simo looked inside the envelope and saw a computer chip. He closed the envelope and stuffed it into his pocket.

12
THE REHEARSAL

'Come on, Max. We need to attend the rehearsal,' Lin shouted.

'Give Max a break, Lin. It's only been a couple of weeks since he came home,' Juli said, trying to calm her sister.

'He's always the last one ready. Gran, are you sure you've triple-checked everything?' Lin replied.

'Yes, Dep...I mean Project Leader, ma'am,' Gran replied.

'That's good. Whilst I'm not expecting the Elite Council to ask, can we send someone to another planet if they ask?' Lin asked.

'Yes, ma'am,' Gran answered.

Lin heard a noise and turned. 'Oh, at last, Max.'

'Sorry I took so long. I was helping Luc with his uniform,' Max replied.

'I-I-I'm s-sorry,' Luc stuttered. 'My hands still shake a b-b-bit when I'm n-n-nervous.'

'Don't be silly, Luc. You take all the time you need,' Lin replied, hugging him.

'B-B-But you've b-been so kind to let me stay here. I d-don't want to cause an argument,' Luc said.

Juli walked over to Luc and lightly kissed him on the cheek. 'Don't worry, Luc. Lin and Max are always like this. If anything, you being here is making them behave.'

'Juli, why don't you and Gran help Luc down to the foyer? Max and I will be down straight after you,' Lin said.

'Come on, Luc, let's get going. Gran, open the door, please,' Juli said.

As soon as the door closed, Lin turned to Max. 'How much longer is Luc staying here?'

'He's only been here a few days, and Simo said it looks like he's got no family,' Max replied.

'Well, that's not our fault. Why can't he stay with Simo?' Lin snapped.

'Because Simo has a one-bedroom dwelling, whereas we have this huge place with more bedrooms than we could ever need and enforcers on guard to help with anything we want,' Max replied firmly.

'That's because our lives were in danger,' Lin insisted.

'Luc was almost killed. I'm not turning my back on someone in need,' Max shouted.

Lin was taken aback by Max as he rarely got angry. 'Fine, but he moves out as soon as he's able. We're an Elite family now, not a home for disabled enforcers.'

'I'm sorry. Perhaps Zym and I should move out until I'm fully fit. Oh, hang on. Zym's okay since he transitioned, so is it just Luc and me who should leave?' Max snarled.

'You're impossible when you get like this. Zym's not even living here. He's in our old dwelling. Nobody needs to leave. I'm just saying we have standards now,' Lin replied.

'And my standards mean helping those in need,' Max said.

Lin put her arm around Max. 'I know it does, my love, and that's why you're so special.'

'Hmm,' Max replied.

'Come on, let's go and show everyone Zephyrion's new Elite couple,' Lin said with a smile.

Max resisted Lin's pull on his arm for a split-second but then relented and walked towards the chutes with Lin's arm wrapped in his.

The journey to the One World Research Centre was quiet. As the side entrance to the centre came into view, they saw Jericesen and Simo waiting.

Jeric walked forward to greet them. 'Max, Luc, you're looking so well,' Jeric said. 'Lin, clearly becoming an Elite really suits you. You look stunning. As do you, Juli, and you err...'

'Gran, sir,' Gran replied.

'Follow me. The Supreme Leader is looking forward to meeting you all,' Jeric said.

'Go ahead. I'm feeling a little dizzy. I'll catch you up,' Max said.

'Are you sure, Max? We can wait for you,' Jeric asked.

'I'll wait with him, sir,' Simo replied.

'Okay, Simo. Don't be too long. We don't want to keep the SL waiting,' Jeric said.

As the group walked away, Simo turned to Max. 'Do you need to sit down?'

'Of course not. Where's Zym?' Max asked.

Simo pointed up at a camera, and it nodded back.

'I thought Jeric said Zym wasn't to be on duty?' Max asked.

'No, I heard an unofficial rumour he didn't want Zym assigned to any duties inside the centre. But there are no official orders, and the camera control hub is in the building annexe, so it's not strictly inside the centre,' Simo laughed.

'He's going to lose it if he finds out,' Max chuckled.

'I'm just doing my job,' Simo replied.

'Talking of doing things, have you looked at that chip Erzsi left you?'

'We don't know for certain that it was Erzsi, anyone could have left it there. But no, I'm not sure I can face having my life disrupted even more,' Simo sighed.

'What're you going to do?'

'I want to know, but I also don't want to,' Simo replied. 'Anyway, how's Luc? Has he remembered anything?'

'The truth can be hard to face,' Max agreed. 'Luc's stutter gets worse when he's nervous, but it goes if he's really stressed or totally relaxed. But he's still confused about everything. He won't discuss his family, and he can't remember finding the Supreme Leader's all-access card or payment disc.'

'Simo, where are you?' Jeric's voice said from Simo's communicator.

'On the way, Jeric,' Simo replied.

Max and Simo entered the Grand Exodus room to see a buzz of people moving around, checking lighting and cameras. Near the centre, they saw Gran excitedly waving his arms, so they headed over to him.

'Hey, Gran. Is everything okay?' Max asked.

'No, it's totally not okay. They insist they want a camera set up here to watch the Exodus Platform as we send Bobmaton to Astral 5,' Gran sighed.

'Don't you mean Bobevrin?' Max asked.

'No. The Supreme Leader was very careful. Bobmaton only becomes a member of the Elite when he arrives on Astral 5,' Simo replied.

'I don't care what he is called; I can't allow a camera and operators so close to the Exodus Platform.'

'What's the issue, Gran? Would they block the access or something?' Max said.

'Oh no, where they want to be is clear of the door into the platform.' Gran replied.

'So why can't they set up there?' Simo asked.

'Because, whilst the glass contains most of the Exodus energy within the chamber, there is some residual leakage we've never been able to prevent. That's why we have the safety zones,' Gran explained.

'Cone on, mate, we have a job to do. Give us a bit of slack,' one of the camera technicians replies. 'We've only got a week to get this all set up before the big night.'

'I'm more concerned with giving you a bit too much slack, to be honest,' Gran replied.

'What might happen if they do set themselves up here?' Max asked.

'Well, depending on what stage during the Exodus they may be affected, they could be overloaded with energy and vaporise, or else they could be drained and wiped out,' Gran replied.

'Blimey, guys, I don't like the sound of either of those situations. Are you sure it's worth the risk?' Max asked.

'Come on, mate. That's the worst case. We can always wear protective outfits,' the technician replied.

'Oh, dear me no. Those are the best cases,' Gran replied. 'As you will not be scanned by the machine and coded, you will just be erroneous energy sources. The worst case is it may merge you both or even discard parts of you into deep space.'

'But if we stay behind that line, we'll be safe,' the technician replied, abandoning all thoughts of positioning themselves closer.

'That would be perfect,' Gran replied with a smile.

'Okay, that's the broadcasting crisis averted. Do you know where Lin and the others are?' Max asked.

'They're in that side room over there,' Gran replied. 'It's been turned into some sort of ceremonial chamber. I don't understand why. We just need people sent through to us in groups of up to ten at a time, wearing energy suits and without any organic matter on them.'

'Unfortunately, that wouldn't make good entertainment,' Simo replied.

'But this is about space travel and survival, not entertainment,' Gran sighed.

'Everything is about entertainment nowadays. The Elite work on the principle of keeping the masses happy or scared, and they will comply,' Max grumbled.

'Thank you, Maxoraxin, the Supreme Leader of positive thinking,' Simo laughed.

'Simo, will you and Max hurry up,' Jeric bellowed through Simo's communicator.

'We're outside in the Grand Exodus room. We were asking where you were,' Simo lied. 'Good luck, Gran. See you soon.'

'About time,' Jeric snapped as Max and Simo entered the side room.

'How is this a side room when it's bigger than the main Grand Exodus room?' Max asked.

'It's normally our auditorium and conference room, but the broadcaster stripped the room out to make it a giant studio and ceremony chamber,' Juli said, hugging Max.

'Where's Lin and Luc?'

'Over there talking to the Deputy Supreme Leader,' Juli replied.

'And they're waiting for you, Max. If you can spare the DSL you're precious time,' Jeric sneered.

'I'm sorry to keep you waiting, Deputy Supreme Leader, sir,' Max said as he joined the DSL, Lin and Luc.

'Please, call me Nicoeyel or Nico, Max,' Nico replied, shaking Max's hand. 'After all, you're not just a hero like young Luc here, but you're a member of the Elite yourself now, thanks to your partner's promotion to Project Leader.'

'Thank you, Sir, erm Nico,' Max replied awkwardly.

'The Supreme Leader will be here shortly, but I just wanted to see you both first and offer my thanks. I know Dronin is still on the loose, but you both put your lives on the line to try to capture him,' Nico said.

'We were lucky. Plenty of enforcers lost their lives that night,' Max replied.

'Of course, Max. We are equally grateful for their sacrifices that night and for the other enforcers who risk their lives daily. Think of this event as a way to pay respect to all of them by honouring the two survivors of Dronin's ambush,' Nico said with a smile.

'B-B-But we weren't the only survivors, Sir,' Luc said as firmly as he could.

'Oh, Luc. I guess your injuries are still taking time to heal. Jeric told me that only two enforcers survived the ambush,' Nico said patiently.

'N-N-No. K-Kendra and P-P-Paulie did, too,' Luc replied firmly.

'You look surprised, Nico,' Max said.

'I was led to believe after the smoke mortars were fired that all the other enforcers were killed, and you both only managed to survive due to being too close to Dronin for his men to get a clear shot on either of you. Which is why we, I mean why we heard they ran you over, Max,' Nico replied.

'Max, dear. Let's avoid getting bogged down with minor details. This is a celebration of your and Luc's bravery and the start of our civilisation's brave adventure to new worlds,' Lin replied.

'I'm sorry, but I don't call my friends and colleagues who died that night "minor details." Luc is right. Paulie and Kendra should be here too,' Max snapped.

Lin smiled at Nico. 'Excuse Max, Nico. He's not been himself si—'

'I don't need you or anyone else apologising for me,' Max snapped.

'Quite right, Max. I don't think Lin meant any offence, but she has been your partner for so long that she is bound to try to protect you. I promise we will ensure Kendra and Paulie get the recognition they deserve. I'll speak to Jeric and get all the names of the other enforcers and ensure the broadcaster does a roll call of honour during the show,' Nico replied.

'Excuse me, Deputy Supreme Leader, but we need to take you through the running order for your part of the ceremony,' a member of the broadcasting crew said, escorting Nico away.

'I'm going to check on Gran,' Lin snapped before walking away.

'What the heck is up with Lin?' Simo asked as he joined Max. 'She's just stormed past me like a planet about to explode.'

'I think the stress of taking the top job may be getting a bit much,' Max replied.

'Excuse me, Max. I've been asked to come and fetch you,' Juli said.

'I'm not ready for another slanging match with Lin,' Max sighed.

'What's happened between you two? Actually, never mind, it's not Lin. Timezel has asked if you can join him,' Juli replied.

A few minutes later, Max, Luc, Juli, and Simo entered an office with a long table against one wall, laid out with food and drinks. At the far end, the Supreme Leader was deep in conversation with Jeric and Bobmaton.

'Here they are, the heroes of the Lottery night,' Timezel said, walking forward and shaking the hands of Max and Luc firmly. 'Can I say how sad I am to hear of the loss of so many of your colleagues that night, too.'

'Thank you, Sir,' Max and Luc said in unison.

'T-T-Two of our colleagues also survived that night, Sir,' Luc said.

'You never told me that, Jeric,' Timezel said, turning to look at Jeric.

'Well, they were, um, well, regular enforcers, Sir. These two heroes were in charge of the attempt to capture Dronin, and it almost cost them their lives,' Jeric spluttered.

'There is no such thing as a regular enforcer, Jericesen. Our brave enforcers keep us all safe, and I want everyone present that fateful night to be here for the Grand Gathering tomorrow. Do I make myself clear?' Timezel ordered.

'Yes, Sir,' Jeric replied. Simo, let me have their names so I can organise it.'

'Their names were included in the report I sent you when we found Max and Luc, Jeric. It's Paulie and Kendra,' Sim said.

'Well, I want Paulie and Kendra on stage with Max and Luc tomorrow, and they will be getting the same recognition,' Timezel said firmly. 'Now, were there any other enforcers with you that night?'

'There were, Sir. But unfortunately, the rest died in the ambush,' Max replied.

'Jeric, get a full list of names to the show's producer and ensure that after we have honoured Max, Luc, Paulie and Kendra, we have a minute's silence as the names of those who died are shown on screen,' Timezel demanded.

'But Timezel. Tomorrow is supposed to be a celebration of Zephyrions embarking on a new life on new planets,' Bobmaton protested.

'My dear Bob. You are right. Tomorrow is about celebrating our brave voyage into a new life on new worlds, but it is also a time of reflection.

'As every Zephyrion embarks on their Exodus journey, they bid farewell to all they have ever known. We must recognise and appreciate their profound commitment and acknowledge that their decision is fraught with trepidation and fear. But showing respect for those who've sacrificed their lives to bring us to this point is the least we can do,' Timezel said.

'Thank you, Sir. That means a lot,' Max replied.

'On a brighter note, I hope you didn't mind me recommending young Luc to your team, Simohal?' Timezel said.

'Please call me Simo, Sir?' Simo replied. 'I was a little surprised when I heard his experience was in traffic, but I can't argue about his commitment. I'm proud to have him in my team.'

Luc blushed with embarrassment.

'Well, Simo, from what I've heard, you were born to lead. I'm sure your family must be proud of you,' Timezel said, smiling. Timezel glanced at his communicator and said, 'But please excuse me. Bob, the DSL and the broadcasting team require our presence.'

'Jeric, can I...' Max's voice trailed off as Jeric stormed off, following Timezel and Bobmaton.

'What just happened?' Simo said.

'W-W-What d-d-do you mean, Sir?' Luc asked.

'Well, you gave us the evidence the SL was helping Dronin, and yet he comes across as so nice and caring,' Simo replied.

'What evidence, S-S-Si-i-i...' Luc stuttered.

'The SL's payment disc and all-access card in Dronin's landcraft,' Max interrupted.

Luc looked from Max to Simo with a confused look.

'You mentioned the SL and said to look in your pocket for them,' Simo replied.

'B-B-But he's n-not helping D-Dronin; he's investigating him. He thinks s-s-someone is helping Dronin,' Luc said.

'But Dronin had his card and disc,' Max protested.

'The card was mine, M-M-Max,' Luc replied.

'Sorry, Luc, but I scanned it, and it is definitely Timezel's,' Simo said.

'Yes, S-S-Simo. Timezel gave me his card as he thought I c-could use it to find out if he was right,' Luc replied.

'Right about what?' Max asked.

Luc looked down and didn't reply.

'Luc?' Max said.

'Please, Max. I love you and S-S-Simo so much since I've met you,' Luc replied.

'Luc, we've been around long enough for nothing to offend us,' Max said.

'But what I know will d-destroy everything you know,' Luc said.

'I'm getting fed up with others saying my life will be changed or destroyed,' Simo replied.

'Have you looked at what E-E-E,' Luc sighed, took a deep breath and then tried again. 'Erzsi's files?'

'How do you know about that?' Simo demanded.

'Erzsi works for T-T-T, the SL, as well,' Luc replied.

'So they're all in it together with Dronin?' Max snapped.

'No, M-Max. Dronin is a criminal. T-Timezel has been trying to b-bring them all down for years.'

'Who are *they*?' Max demanded.

'The ones who killed your parents and tried to kill Zym and us,' Luc said.

'That's Timezel, Luc. I'm sorry he's lied to you,' Max replied. 'We found the evidence in my parents' files. They were investigating Timezel.'

'Your p-parents were working for...' Luc paused, taking a deep breath, 'Timezel. They thought the voting at the G-Grand Formation was r-rigged, and he was helping them prove it,'

'What if that scribble in your parents' notes wasn't Timezel rigged the election, but Timezel thinks the election was rigged?' Simo suggested.

'We need to go through it again. Maybe we did jump to conclusions,' Max replied.

'But if Timezel was the one helping to investigate corruption, who were the corrupt ones?' Simo asked.

'Who was the corrupt one, you mean. The leader was your uncle,' Luc replied.

13
THE PREPARATION

'I don't have an uncle,' Simo replied. 'I was alone after Mum died.'

'You need to look at E-E-Erzsi's files,' Luc said.

'If I had an uncle, why would he have left me in the Family Unit system?' Simo protested.

'Well, you were in the Elite Family Unit, not the Council one,' Max said.

'T-T-Timezel is sure your uncle is, uh, Zeryn, and it was because of him that you ended up in the EFU,' Luc replied.

'But where is Zeryn?' Max asked.

'We d-don't know. Zeryn disappeared after Zyrenev's death,' Luc replied.

'But if he disappeared, how can he have ensured I was in the EFU?' Simo protested.

Luc replied, 'I said you ended up in there b-b-because of him, n-n-not that he ensured you were p-p-put in there. You need to read Erzsi's f-f-files and speak to Timezel.'

Max said, 'This is sounding like a conspiracy theory. The son of a former leader disappears, he helps a nephew, who never knew he existed, grow up in a privileged family care unit—'

'Privileged? Are you flipping kidding?' Simo snarled.

'I only mean compared to the Council route,' Max said. 'Plus, that missing Elite family member tried to kill Zym, me and you, Luc, as well as killing my parents because we were all investigating and chasing fraud or corruption.'

'Listening to you all, this does sound crazy,' Juli said.

'Exactly. It's a fantasy,' Simo replied. 'Besides, if this Zeryn is my uncle, that means my mum was the daughter of Zyrenev, but his daughter died at birth.'

'P-P-Please, check E-E-Erzsi's files. I'm trying to r-remember everything, but her files will explain it better,' Luc replied.

'But how does Simo's background tie into what happened to my parents and us?' Max demanded.

'I-I-I can't remember,' Luc replied in frustration. 'I know it's linked. Like S-S-Simo's family k-k-k-killed your parents, but I-I-I...'

Juli put her arm around Luc, who was visibly shaking. 'It's okay, Luc. You're doing a great job.'

'I'm sorry, Luc. I miss my parents so much. I have no right to be so demanding,' Max said.

'It's okay, M-M Max. I know what it's l-l-like to lose all your f-f-family. I wish I c-c-could see my M-Mum again,' Luc sighed as he wiped away his tears.

'Maxoraxin and Lucraxin, I'm Stevmachon, the Show Director. I'm ready for your piece with the Supreme Leader and Deputy Supreme Leader now,' the director shouted from the doorway.

'We are on the way. Just give us a few minutes,' Max replied.

'You do realise you've just told the two most senior Zephyrions on our planet to wait?' Simo asked.

'Look at Luc. I'd tell them to go to hell if it meant protecting someone I care about,' Max said.

'He means it too,' Zym said through Simo's communicator.

'I wish I had a sibling. You and Max are so lucky,' Simo replied into his communicator. 'I guess you and Lin are the same, Juli?'

Juli paused before saying, 'I guess all families are different, but yeah, I'd do everything I could to help Lin.'

The rest of the day saw Max and Luc pretend to receive their honours, followed by a ceremony explaining that Astral 5 had seen the development of a Zephyrion base over the last forty years and then a procession of the lottery winners to the Grand Exodus machine.

'We need to see the Grand Exodus machine working to know the light and sound levels,' Stevmachon said.

'That's a great idea. The lottery winners can see how the machine works,' Nicoeyel replied.

'Do you mean sending someone through it?' Lin asked.

'Even better, Project Leader,' Nico replied.

'Gran, we can do that, can't we?' Lin asked.

'Yes, of course, Dep—Project Leader. We just need a volunteer,' Gran replied excitedly.

'Jeric, we can provide a volunteer, can't we?' Nico replied.

'No problem, Sir. Erzsi, I'm sure you'd love to get to Astral 5 ahead of your partner so you can get your new home ready for him, wouldn't you?' Jeric asked.

'I guess so, Sir,' Erzsi replied, looking at her feet.

'I'm sorry, Jeric, but Erzsi is part of an ongoing enforcer investigation, and therefore, we cannot allow her to leave the planet,' Simo replied.

Jeric glowered at Simo. 'We can't obstruct the law. How about we send your partner first instead, Erzsi?'

'I'll go,' Max said, smiling at Erzsi.

'No way, Max,' Zym bellowed, entering the Grand Exodus room.

'It's fine, Zym. I think this needs to happen,' Max replied.

Jeric glowered at Zym, 'What are you doing h—'

'Jeric, you need to control that temper. I'm proud to see one of our enforcers stepping forward for the greater cause,' Nico smiled.

'I'm afraid I must intervene, my friends. It is very noble of Maxoraxin to offer himself, but I am concerned that he is only doing this out of duty to me. Therefore, I cannot allow him to go,' Timezel said.

'Erm,' Max said with a puzzled look.

'It's okay, Max. I know I said I'd let you tell Zym first, but I cannot keep secrets from my Deputy Supreme Leader,' Timezel said reassuringly. 'You see Nico, I asked Max earlier if he would become the new Chief Enforcer of the Supreme Leader.'

'But that role is ceremonial, and the Palace Compound team reports to me,' Jeric protested.

'Relax, Jeric. You still have control of the team. Max will be running special projects for me. With the Exodus taking up so much of your time, I wanted to take some pressure off you by having someone I can use to follow up on things,' Timezel smiled.

'Excellent idea, Timezel,' Nico replied quickly to stop Jeric from responding.

'So will you stay and serve as my Chief Enforcer, Maxohal?' Timezel asked. 'After all, you shouldn't still be a raxin after all your years of service.'

'Thank you, Sir. I did feel obliged to offer to Exodus, but I see you need me, so I'd be honoured to take up the role,' Max replied, still confused about what was happening.

'But what about the demonstration for the lottery winners?' Nico asked.

Jeric smiled the smile of the hunter with his prey in sight, 'This means Zy—'

Timezel noted Jeric's sickening smile and quickly interrupted, 'We already have one organised, Nico. Remember, Bobmaton will be the first to go as he starts his new life on Astral 5 as Bobevrin.'

'But I need to test my sound and light levels,' Stevmachon protested.

'I'm sure a director with your experience has directed enough live events to cope with whatever happens,' Timezel replied.

'But...' Nico started to say.

'Well, if we are all done, I think that's enough for today,' Timezel said. 'Come on, Maxohal. We need to discuss your new role. Oh, Jeric, may I borrow Erzsi? I need some documents prepared.'

Jeric looked at Nico, who nodded. 'Yes, of course, Timezel. Erzsi, I need you here early tomorrow morning,' Jeric replied.

'Yes, Jericesen,' Erzsi responded.

'Thank you, Jeric. Come on, Max and Erzsi. We have a busy evening ahead of us,' Timezel said.

'Yes, Sir,' Max replied as he looked at Zym and shrugged.

Lin stepped forward and kissed Max. 'Congratulations, my love. It seems we are both moving up in the world.'

'Well, we are certainly doing something,' Max replied as he followed Timezel and Erzsi.

'Do you need us for anything else, Deputy Supreme Leader or Jeric?' Zym asked.

Jeric turned to Zym and started to say, 'Did you know ab—'

But Nico interrupted him, 'No, Zym, it's fine. You can go. Why don't you take Luc and the others with you, too.'

'Thank you, Sir,' Zym replied.

'I hear Lin and Max have asked you to stay with them, Luc,' Nico said before Zym and Luc could move.

'Y-Y-Yes, S-S-Sir. It's v-very kind of them,' Luc stuttered, smiling at Lin.

'You have all made our planet proud, and any luxury you can enjoy in my dwelling during the little time left is well deserved,' Nico replied. 'Oh, listen to me droning on. I'm holding you up. Please go and enjoy the rest of the evening.'

'I just need to check a few final calibrations,' Gran replied before noticing Nico staring at him. 'But I'm sure I can do it in the morning. Wait for me.'

Nico waited for the others to leave and asked Jeric, 'What do you think Timezel is up to?'

'I don't know, but I do know I don't like it,' Jeric replied.

'Nor do I,' Stevmachon added.

Nico turned to see the Show Director behind him, 'I'm sorry, Stevmachon, but would you mind leaving us? We are discussing Elite Council business.'

Jeric smiled at Stevmachon, 'Yes, thank you, Mr Director. You're certainly showing a flair for putting on a bit of a spectacle over the last couple of Exodus events, but now is not the time.'

'Yes, of course, Jericesen,' Stevmachon said. He turned and walked away, mumbling, 'Elites are always so uptight.'

Max looked around the luxurious interior of the Elite landcraft. Subtle lighting illuminated every switch and surface, from the white glimmering starlights in the roof to the blues and, finally, purple lights in the footwells. 'Excuse me, Sir, but can I ask what is happening?'

'We are going back to the Palace Compound, Max. You can drop the formality and call me Tim.' Timezel said.

'Thank you, Tim. But why did you stop me from going through Exodus, and what is this new role all about?' Max asked.

'I'll explain everything when we get to the compound, but I couldn't risk you, Zym, Simo, Luc, or Erzsi leaving the planet,' Tim replied. 'Speaking of which, Erzsi, can you contact Luc using the special communicator and get them to join us?'

'Yes, Tim. I assume Max's partner Juli and her sister Lin are still with them, along with the scientist Granxili. Do I include them?' Erzsi asked.

'You're wrong, Erzsi. Lin is Max's partner, and Juli is her sister. Say it's an enforcer issue, but if they want to come, don't argue. I'm sure we can keep them entertained,' Tim replied.

'This vehicle is amazing,' Max said.

'It's a bit over the top, but I prefer it to the two new landcraft Nicoeyel got us for the Exodus lottery. They are more like luxury armed pursuit vehicles,' Tim replied.

'This isn't your new landcraft?' Max asked.

'No. Nico's driver crashed his new one, and he asked if he could borrow mine. I agreed as the new ones are even more extravagant. Not me at all,' Tim said. 'Erzsi, has that message gone?'

'Yes, Tim,' Erzsi replied.

'E-E-Excuse me, Simo, b-b-but we've been summoned to an enforcer meeting,' Luc said.

'I've not seen anything,' Simo said, checking his hal device.

'It's come through on my c-c-communicator for some reason, Sir. They are d-d-demanding the presence of Zym, me and you,' Luc said. 'They said we are to join them at the Palace Compound.'

'I've not been to the Palace Compound,' Lin replied. 'This is turning into an exciting day.'

'It's an enforcer issue, m-m-ma'am,' Luc said.

'Given Max's promotion, I'm sure they won't mind us coming along,' Lin said chirpily.

'Actually, I'm tired, and I'd rather go home,' Juli replied.

'Me too,' Gran added. 'I need to get to work early to check those calibrations.'

'Oh, you two are such boo buddies. Well, I want to go, so you two take the Elite landcraft, and I'll go with Simo, Zym and Luc,' Lin replied.

A short while later, the four of them were escorted through the formal entrance hall towards the Supreme Leader's office. The hall was a vast room of marble, mirrors and wood designed to impress and intimidate in equal measure.

'This is stunning,' Lin said, admiring the room as they passed through. 'Look at all those paintings and the mirrors.'

Simo looked at Luc and Zym but said nothing. Their mutual disinterest said more than any words.

'Look, that's an original Vordrych,' Lin said in admiration at a painting as they entered the outer waiting room to the Supreme Leader's office.

'S-S-Simo, have you seen that picture next to the one of Timezel?' Luc said.

'Simo, it's you,' Lin added.

'That's ridiculous. Why would they have a picture of me,' Simo replied.

'That's not Simo,' Timezel said, entering the room. 'That's Zyrenev, our first Supreme Leader.'

'But he looks like Simo,' Lin replied.

'No, he doesn't,' Simo snapped. 'Can we get on? Why are we here, Supreme Leader, Sir?'

'Of course, Simo. Can you, Zym and Luc please go through to my office? I need a quick word with Lineklis,' Timezel said.

As the door to Timezel's office closed, he sat down and invited Lin to sit. 'Lin, as you're now a member of the Elite, I need to bring you into my confidence.'

'Yes, Supreme Leader,' Lin replied.

'There are members of the Elite Council working to enrich themselves at the expense of others. I was pleased to hear you were joining the Elite Council as Max's family have served Zephyrion well, as have you, and I know I can trust you both to help me,' Timezel said.

'Of course, Supreme Leader. Just tell me what you need from me or us,' Lin replied.

'All I ask at this stage is your loyalty. If anyone asks you to do something you know is wrong, just let me know,' Timezel replied, 'and please, call me Tim.'

'Thank you, Tim. I'm sure it'll never happen, but you can trust me,' Lin smiled.

'That means so much, Lineklis. Is there anything I can do for you?'

'Well...'

'No need to be shy, just ask.'

'Well, could I have a palace tour, Tim?'

Timezel smiled. 'I'll get my assistant to collect you and show you the entire palace. Don't let him skip Zyrenev's games room; it'll make you feel like a youngster.'

'Thank you, Tim,' Lin beamed.

'Now, excuse me, but I must discuss Max's enforcer role. I know it's mainly ceremonial, but it's important it's done properly and with the support of other enforcers,' Timezel replied. 'If you wait here, my assistant will be with you shortly.'

'Of course, Tim, and thank you,' Lin said excitedly.

Timezel walked back into his office, closed the door and pressed a device on his wrist. 'Please collect Lineklis from my waiting room and give her a palace tour. The Operations Wing is out of bounds; do not mention it or go near it. You should keep our guest entertained for at least three hours.'

'What is this all about, Supreme Leader?' Zym asked.

'You're always straight to the point, Zym,' Timezel laughed. I was still a pushy young enforcer the last time we met in person.

'Not so young now, though,' Zym replied.

'Age comes to us all, and in my case, I hope it's also brought some humility,' Timezel replied. 'Looking back, I don't know why you didn't put me in my place.'

'I was tempted, Timezel,' Zym sneered.

Timezel laughed, adding, 'I wouldn't have blamed you, and everyone, please call me Tim. We are friends here.'

'Friends don't have secrets,' Simo replied.

'And nor shall we,' Tim countered. 'Have you finished reading the documents Erzsi left for you, Simo?'

'I've not even opened them. The past doesn't belong in the present,' Simo replied.

'Wise sentiments, but the past can unlock secrets of the present. Take young Luc here,' Tim replied, looking at Luc.

Luc looked down, nodding in approval.

'Thank you, Luc,' Tim replied. 'Luc grew up on the wrong side of the Deserted Zone. His entire family died when the building they lived in collapsed during seismic activity. He only survived because he was in the city carrying out a robbery.'

'But Deceptors are banned from being enforcers. Even being partnered to one means you are dishonourably discharged,' Zym replied.

'Indeed, Zym. But is that fair? Should being dealt a bad start in life limit your ability to better yourself?' Tim asked.

'But it is the law,' Max replied.

'It is, but should laws be limitive or betteritive? I believe the latter. If a law prevents one from becoming better, it's a false law,' Tim replied. 'I found Luc—'

'P-P-Please, T-T-Tim, n-n-no,' Luc interrupted.

'Don't worry, Luc. That is your story to tell, not mine. I was only going to say I found you in difficult circumstances. I could not let someone so clearly just wanting a better life be consigned to the life of Deceptorism,' Tim replied. 'So, I helped him rebuild a life free from that past, including putting a little lie about him being at a residential computer academy, and today, he is everything an enforcer should be. Should either of us be charged with law-breaking?'

'So that's how you knew how to get more cameras for the lottery,' Max smiled.

'W-Well, old h-habits die hard,' Luc laughed.

'But why did you stop me going through Exodus, and why did you make me a hal?' Max asked.

'Because you, Zym and your parents have come closer to helping me break the corruption in the Elite than any other enforcers,' Tim replied.

'Helping you?' Zym smirked.

'Yes, Zym. Why are you so cynical?' Tim asked, frowning.

Zym threw the remains of his mother's enforcer card to Tim. 'Because we found this in your old Elite dwelling.'

'And we found our parents' notes saying they linked you to election corruption,' Max added.

'I wasn't linked to it. I was trying to stop it. I asked your parents to investigate the election following the Grand Formation. Zyrenev becoming Supreme Leader wasn't a surprise as he had that celebrity charm, but his son Zeryn almost became Deputy Supreme Leader, which was crazy. He was too young to vote, yet he was on the brink of the second most senior role on our planet,' Tim replied.

'And Mother's card?' Zym snapped.

Tim laughed. 'Oh, the irony. We spent so long looking for that when she lost it during one of our briefings. All these years later, her sons find it. We searched the Peace Room for ages, but your Dad said it was pointless in the end, so we just made her another one using the security equipment there.'

'The Peace Room?' Max asked.

'That was your Mum's name for it,' Tim replied. 'I presume you found the card in the room behind the bedroom cupboard?'

'Yes, that's where we found it,' Max replied.

'Well, the Peace Room is one of the few places without Cogi or Argo. Your Mum said you could have total peace in there,' Tim said. 'The Cogi and Argo devices caused technical issues with the security equipment there, which is why they weren't installed.'

'There isn't any equipment in there,' Zym said.

'Although it looks like the room was emptied in a hurry,' Max added.

'That's strange. That room produces all the security cards, payment discs, etc., for this zone's senior Elite Council members. Only the DSL is entrusted to produce them. There is a backup facility here at the palace, but it's still under the DSL's control,' Tim mused.

'Perhaps he thought he should move the equipment as he is letting us stay there?' Max suggested.

'That makes sense, but any changes to the equipment or moving it requires the approval of three senior Elites and my signature,' Tim said.

'And have you approved any move?' Max asked.

'No. I wasn't even told the DSL was moving you in until after the event. He said the lottery hijack by Dronin created an emergency, so I let it slide at the time,' Tim replied.

'How did he get someone to remove everything with almost no notice?' Max asked.

'The DSL didn't, Max. Jericesen put the Elite moving team on standby two days before the lottery,' Erzsi said. 'He told me to arrange it just in case something happened.'

'That's either inspired planning or Jericesen knew Dronin's plans,' Max said.

'Talking of Dronin, he told me he carried on our parents' investigation. So, was he working for you after they died?' Zym asked.

'To start with, he pretended to work for me, but he found less evidence over the following years of investigation than your parents discovered in months. I also began to suspect he was leaking information to the ones I was trying to catch,' Tim replied. 'In the end, I decided to leak some false information to him, and sure enough, it came out.'

'What happened?' Max asked.

'I quickly proved the information was false, and Dronin was suddenly removed from office, but by then, he was wealthy. That's why I started the financial fraud investigation,' Tim replied.

'That was my investigation,' Zym said.

'Which I concluded,' Max added.

'Indeed, you were both involved. I made sure of it. Your parents always considered loyalty important, so I was sure their sons would too,' Tim said.

'Excuse me, Tim. But I've got a message saying Simo's grandmother is ready to receive him,' Erzsi interrupted.

'My what?'

14

THE GRAND GATHERING

'You haven't looked at Erzsi's files, have you?' Tim said.

'I was a child of the Elite Family Unit after my Mum died. What is the point of knowing anything more?' Simo replied sharply. 'I don't have any living family. I don't have an uncle, nor do I have a grandmother.'

'Come with me, Simo. You need to meet Kazi, your grandmother,' Tim said.

'I don't need to meet anyone. Even if I did have any living relatives, they deserted my Mum and me,' Simo protested.

'Everyone, can you leave us, please?' Tim said to the others.

'Max and Zym are the closest thing I have to family. You can say whatever you want to tell me in front of them,' Simo insisted.

'Okay. Luc told me he's explained to you about Zyrenev dying and Zeryn disappearing. He said he also told you that Zeryn is your uncle,' Tim replied.

Simo just sat with his arms folded.

'What you won't know unless you've read Erzsi's files is that Zeryn killed Zyrenev and almost killed Kazi,' Tim said.

'That's not what we were told,' Zym said.

'Of course it wasn't. We couldn't let the world know the son of our Supreme Leader was a psychopath,' Tim replied.

'But if Zyrenev didn't die transitioning, how did he die?' Max asked.

'He did die transitioning, but let me take you back a few years. Before the Grand Formation, Zyrenev was the leader of this region of the planet when Zeryn was born. Zeryn was a challenging child and a computer genius in equal measure. As he grew up, he became more unruly and, on several occasions, he assaulted Zyrenev's enforcer guards and even put both of his parents in hospital on separate occasions. He was out of control, so when Kazi was pregnant with Shazon, Zyrenev decided to send Kazi away to protect them.

'Zyrenev and Kazi decided it wasn't safe to bring Shazon home. The official line was that Shazon died during her birth, but a distant relative of Kazi raised her until she became an adult. Then, she was provided with a modest Elite dwelling where you were conceived, Simo. That was your childhood home,' Tim explained.

'But why didn't they visit me?' Simo asked.

'They did,' replied Tim. 'They made a lot of secret visits when you were very young, but that was their undoing.

'As I said, Zeryn was a computer genius, and we've found computer records showing that he used his skills to track his parents during one of their trips to see you both. As far as we know, he never made contact, but we can't be sure. We think he may have been involved in your mother's death, but as I said, we don't know, and we can't prove anything.'

'But he made sure I went through the Elite Family Unit,' Simo insisted, looking at Luc.

'I'm sorry, Simo. But I asked Luc not to mention your grandmother. Kazi was the one who ensured you were looked after by the EFU, not Zeryn. We just think that Zeryn may have killed your mother, which meant you had to go into the EFU,'

Tim replied. 'We swore an oath to Kazi to keep you anonymous and safe and only tell you when she was dying or when we knew Zeryn was dead.'

'But Zeryn knew about me, and presumably he or his supporters knew I was in the EFU?' Simo replied.

Tim shook his head, 'No, we created a false identity for you using only paper documentation claiming you were from an Elite family from a remote part of Zephyrion. Because it wasn't in electronic form, Zeryn couldn't use his computer skills to track you down. I never found out who helped him, but we kept those who knew to a tiny select team.

'I'm sure his helpers also got him on the ballot paper for Supreme Leader and Deputy Supreme Leader. Their help and his computer skills helped him hack the voting, but luckily, the hacking was uncovered and blocked, although nobody involved was traced.'

'And was that hacking what our parents were investigating when their spacecraft crashed?' Max asked.

'That's right. They had spent nine years investigating the vote rigging unofficially for me when the crash happened, and the report into the crash said it was a technical fault. But they had been to Astral 5 and had contacted me on their way back to say they finally had proof of which Elite members were involved,' Tim replied. 'I think that communication was intercepted, and as a result, a virus was sent to their craft, which caused it to crash,' Tim sighed.

'Was there an investigation?' Max asked.

'I can answer that,' Zym snarled. 'Yes, there was, and Dronin led it.'

'I'm sorry to say I trusted Dronin, but after years of investigation and several Elite inquiries, they concluded that there was no evidence that your parents discovered corruption and no signs of computer tampering with the spacecraft,' Tim replied. 'In fact, the only thing that happened was a lot of Shadowers got very rich from the inquiries.'

'That's when you involved me and then Max,' Zym said. 'But what happened to Zyrenev?'

'About four years after your parents died, the scientists cracked transitioning. Zyrenev, Kazi and the now-adult Zeryn were to be amongst the first. But as Zyrenev started transitioning with Kazi outside the chamber, Zeryn hit the emergency chamber door opener,' Tim paused.

'What happened?' Max asked.

'Zyrenev's energy soul exploded from the chamber, knocking Kazi unconscious,' Tim replied. 'Zyrenev's old body was slumped on the floor, dead, and Kazi never fully recovered.'

'In what way?' Simo asked.

'The energy leak from the transition machine changed the shape of her face, so she no longer looks the same, and her mind rambles like she's talking to herself,' Tim replied.

'What about Zeryn?' Simo demanded.

'He ran off and hasn't been seen since,' Tim replied. 'There was a special investigation, but he disappeared without a trace.'

'I'm sorry to interrupt, Tim, but the medidoc has said we either go now or else it'll have to wait until tomorrow as she's so tired,' Erzsi said.

'Are you ready, Simo?' Tim asked.

Simo nodded and stood up. Max and Zym also got to their feet, but Simo shook his head. 'Can you wait here, please? I need to do this.'

'Whatever you want, Simo. We'll be here if you need us,' Max replied.

As Tim and Simo left, Zym turned to Max. 'Maybe Timezel isn't quite as bad as I thought.'

'My brother, admitting he was wrong? Who are you, and what have you done with Zym?' Max laughed.

'You are heading to Slapsville,' Zym replied.

Tim led Simo out of the offices and across a courtyard towards a grand four-storey stone building covered with ornate impressive sculptures and carvings, which also hid the utilitarian functions of plumbing, etc. The courtyard was laid out with low-walled flower beds waiting to be filled with plants that would never appear as the collapsing climate had reduced any plants once present to dust.

'Simo, I should warn you that your grandmother is unlikely to make much sense. The medidocs don't think she has long to live, but she started insisting she had to see you,' Tim said.

'Can I ask why now?' Simo asked.

'When they put Shazon into hiding, they insisted her existence was never revealed until Zeryn was found and locked away or killed,' Tim said.

'What's changed then? Has Zeryn been found?' Simo asked.

'No, we are no closer to finding him now than we were back then,' Tim sighed. 'But Kazi has been demanding to see Shazon's saviour child.'

'What does that mean?' Simo asked as they reached a doorway.

'I don't have a clue, but you're Shazon's only child,' Tim replied, opening the door.

Tim and Simo walked down the corridor in silence. To their left, hazy light streamed through the windows, picking out the dust in the air as they passed one closed door after another.

'Are you ready?' Tim asked as they reached the door at the end of the corridor.

'I don't think I have a choice,' Simo replied, pressing down the old-fashioned lever handle and opening the door.

'We are here to see Kazi,' Tim replied as they entered the room.

The room felt old. The wood panelling contrasted with the modern machines bleeping around the large wooden bed, which dominated the centre of the room.

'She's resting but alert,' the medinurse replied. 'But I'm afraid she may not last the night. She's deteriorated badly in the last few hours.'

Simo walked towards the bed and looked down at the elderly female in the bed.

'Zyrenev?' Kazi said, opening her eyes and looking at Simo.

'No, Grandmother, I'm Simo, son of Shazon,' Simo said.

'Is it really you?' Kazi replied. 'Shazon's beautiful boy. I'm so sorry we couldn't be in your life more, but if Zeryn knew about you, he'd have killed you.'

'I wish you could have too, Grandmother,' Simo said.

'But Zyrenev, I know,' Kazi replied. 'Yes, it's him, and he's got Shazon with him.'

'My mum, Shazon, died,' Simo replied.

'I know she has, Simo. When she stopped coming to see us, I knew she had died. I said she died, didn't I, Zyrenev. I bet he killed her. No, don't argue. Zeryn did it. We know he did it. We...' Kazi trailed off.

'Zeryn did what, Grandmother?' Simo asked.

Kazi's voice changed and deepened, 'Zeryn was our son, and Shazon was our daughter. They would never hurt each—'

Kazi's voice changed back and replied, 'He killed you, so don't defend him. I love my son, but he is evil.'

'I'm sorry, she's delirious again,' Tim said.

'No, she's not,' Simo replied. 'Psiorites can communicate with the living and the dead and even let loved ones talk through them if they want to.'

'Let Shazon speak,' Kazi ordered, looking to the left of Simo.

Simo followed his grandmother's gaze, but nobody was there. Nobody spoke as Kazi stared to the side of Simo and just nodded or shook her head as if in deep conversation.

'And you've been watching over your beautiful boy ever since?' Kazi replied to the emptiness beside Simo.

Kazi's voice deepened, 'Once again, my soulmate, you have been proved correct. How did we spring forth such evil as Zeryn? He cannot bring forth the prophecy of the Psiorite dynasty.'

'I KNOW,' Kazi shouted in her normal voice. 'Only Shazon's son can produce our saviour.'

'What do you mean, Grandmother? I don't have any offspring, and what prophecy,' Simo replied.

'Shazon's grandchildren shall expose the corruption of the world, and you must stop Zeryn from becoming Regent,' Kazi said in her normal voice.

'I did warn you that she wouldn't make sense,' Tim replied.

Simo studied his grandmother and saw her face soften and grow younger. When Kazi spoke, Simo recognised the caring voice of his childhood. 'Simo, my dear sweet son.'

'Mother, is that really you?' Simo replied, kneeling by the bed and holding his grandmother's hand.

'I'm sorry I couldn't protect you more. When Zeryn first reached out to me, he pretended he was my long-lost older brother who wanted to learn about our history as Psiorites. My mother and father warned me against him, which is why I hid you, but to have a sibling who seemed to love me seemed to fill a void in my life,' Shazon explained.

'Why have you never communicated with me?' Simo pleaded.

'I tried so hard, but like most male Psiorites, you don't seem to have our mind skills,' Shazon replied. 'I almost made you aware of me. Do you remember when your toy called Oski appeared to jump off your bed one night?'

'I do. I screamed and ran out of the room,' Simo replied, wiping a tear away at the childhood memory. 'Was that you?'

'It was me. It seemed like that moment just before you fell asleep was when you were most receptive, but I could never do more.' Shazon sighed. 'I must go now. Mother is so weak.'

'Please, Mum, don't leave me again,' Simo begged.

'I have never, and will never leave you, my son. That little shadow or the flash of light in the corner of your eye is me, standing over you and trying to protect you. But beware of my brother. He's been studying the black art of Psiorite culture.

Given a chance, he will use it to lock you in your body and enslave you,' Shazon replied.

'What is the prophecy that Grandfather mentioned?' Simo asked.

'The prophecy of the Psiorite dynasty says that one day, a powerful Psiorite shall use the black art to control an eternity of misery for all kind,' Shazon replied. 'But your grandmother's time to rest has come. One day we shall speak again, my darling son.'

'No, Mum, please? I love you,' Simo wailed. 'Stay and tell me more, I need you.'

Kazi grasped Simo's hand. Her voice returned to normal as her complexion hardened again. 'Simo, you are the energy of our soul. Zeryn is us, but he cannot be. You and your friend must stop him. Remember the puzzle of Cronis, the pursuit of ultimate power. He isn't as he was like I am not what I was, just...'

'Just what, Grandmother,' Simo asked.

'Zeryn must never be Regent...' Kazi replied before passing her last breath.

'No, it's not fair! Grandmother, I've just met you and Mum, and I need you. Please,' Simo cried as he fell forward, clutching Kazi's hand.

Tim looked at the medinurse, who shook her head. 'I'm sorry, Timezel, she has passed.'

Tim sat in a chair in the corner of the room as Simo grieved.

'Please, medinurse, isn't there anything you can do?' Simo pleaded.

'I'm sorry, Sir. Your Grandmother has gone,' the medinurse replied.

Simo and Tim walked back across the courtyard in silence, leaving the old stone buildings behind as they headed towards the modern glass structure of the offices. As they rejoined the others, Simo looked at Max, and in that second, the recent events hit Simo, and he collapsed.

Max rushed over to his friend. 'Simo, are you okay?'

Tim said, 'I'm sorry to say Simo's grandmother has passed over.'

'S-S-Simo, S-S-Sir. I'm so sorry,' Luc said as Zym walked over to Simo and Max and held them tight.

'I've only just found her, but I've already lost her,' Simo said blankly.

'How can we help?' Zym asked.

'Grandmother said Zeryn is us but cannot be, and he's not as he was. She also said remember the puzzle of Cronis,' Simo replied.

***

'It's the Grand Gathering, my friends,' Bobmaton said into the camera.

The crowd in the Grand Exodus room cheered, electronically boosted by the millions watching online.

'Simo, are you sure you should be here?' Tim whispered. 'It's only been a few days since your grandmother died, and the funeral was only yesterday.'

'I'm fine, Sir. Max and Zym have been incredibly supportive,' Simo replied.

'I'm sorry your grandmother's funeral had to be so quick and without the ceremony she deserved,' Tim said. 'She was precise about how it should be.'

'It's okay, Sir,' Simo replied. 'At least I got to meet her briefly.'

'And now, please welcome our Supreme Leader,' Bobmaton's voice boomed.

'Good luck, Sir,' Max said to Timezel before stepping forward and putting a comforting hand on Simo's shoulder.

Timezel walked across the room to the Exodus platform, 'Thank you, Bobmaton. It's now time for you to be the start of the Exodus of Zephyrion. I bet you're so excited.'

'I'm honoured, Sir,' Bobmaton replied. 'I need to leave you now to change into my energy clothes, but I'll return shortly.'

'Fellow Zephyrions, show your support for Bobmaton,' Timezel said enthusiastically.

'Max, come here,' Zym whispered into his communicator.

'Where's here?' Max asked.

'By the side room next to the auditorium. I'm with Luc,' Zym replied.

Max left Simo watching the show and walked through the auditorium, where an audience laughed at a warm-up comedian. As he reached the far side of the auditorium, he saw Zym near a doorway.

'What is it, Zym?' Max asked.

'Nico and Jeric are in there,' Zym replied.

'And?' Max asked. 'They are both Elites, and Jeric reports to Nico, so what's the issue?'

'M-M-Max, I h-h-heard Nico mention K-K-Kazi,' Luc replied.

'Well, she has just died, and it was on Lin's Elite network,' Max said. 'All Elites would know about it.'

'B-B-But N-N-N...' Luc paused and took a deep breath, 'He s-s-said he should have b-b-been there as her son.'

'Nico said that?' Max asked.

'Y-Yes,' Luc replied.

Max frowned. 'But Zyrenev and Kazi only had one son and —'

'And that was Zeryn,' Zym interrupted. 'That's why I knew you'd want to be here.'

Max said, 'But that would mean Nico is...'

'Nico is Zeryn,' Zym said.

'P-P-Please, guys. I might b-be wrong, b-b-but I'm sure he said that,' Luc said.

'We need to do some digging. How can Nico be Zeryn when Nico was an upcoming House of Finance person while Zeryn was still around?' Max challenged.

'C-C-Could he have assumed Nico's identity and got rid of the real one?' Luc asked.

'That's an idea. I'm not sure it's a sound one, but it is an idea,' Max replied.

'Max, where are you and Luc? Tim is doing the awards piece,' Simo said through his communicator.

'Flip, I forgot. I'm on the way,' Max said, running back towards the Grand Exodus room.

'W-W-Wait for me,' Luc said, running after Max.

'Fellow Zephyrions. When we held the Migration Lottery, you'll remember a terrorist called Dronin hijacked the show's opening,' Timezel said solemnly. 'Following that event, a group of brave enforcers went out to arrest him, but they were lured into a brutal ambush.'

'It wasn't brutal,' Stevmachon said to the editor beside him as they watched from the production gallery.

'I am humbled to introduce Kendra, Luc, Paulie and Maxo, four noble enforcers who put their lives on the line day in and day out for our safety,' Tim said.

'Pish,' Stevmachon said. 'They were lucky to survive.'

Kendra, Luc, Paulie and Max walked out onto the raised area, where Tim shook their hands.

'We owe you our gratitude for keeping our planet safe,' Tim said.

'Thank you, Sir,' Kendra said.

'But can I point out that a lot of our colleagues died that night,' Paulie added.

'Of course you can,' Timezel replied. 'Zephyrions, can I ask those here and all of you watching to stand for a minute's silence for those friends we lost that night.'

Below the image of Timezel standing with his head bowed, the screen scrolled with the names of the enforcers who had died.

A bell tolled as the minute ended, and Tim looked up.

'The four heroes before us and those who gave their lives are awarded the medal of honour. The families of those who've passed will receive theirs shortly, but in the meantime, I am humbled to present these medals,' Tim said as he walked down the line of the four enforcers draping medals around their necks.

'Heroes? The heck they are,' Stevmachon muttered.

As Paulie, Kendra, Luc, and Max walked offstage, Tim leaned towards Max and said, 'Thank you, Max. Your team are exceptional.'

Max smiled and walked off stage as Bobmaton bounced back on the other side.

'Hello Zephyrions, I'm back, and it's great to see you all,' Bobmaton said.

'Bob, you're looking great,' Timezel smiled.

'Thank you, Supreme Leader,' Bobmaton replied. He looked towards the Exodus Machine's upper platform. 'Can we check that we are ready to start the Exodus?'

Lin was prepared for her cue, 'Yes, Bob, we are ready for you and the lottery winners.'

'Then let's get going,' Bobmaton said, walking into the Exodus deck.

Gran leaned forward and pressed the button to close the door.

'Bob, are you, are you ready?' Timezel asked.

'Yes, Supreme Leader,' Bobmaton replied.

'Exodus team, are you ready?' Timezel asked.

'Yes, Supreme Leader,' Lin replied.

'Then let's count down from five,' Timezel said. 'Five, four, three, two, one, go.'

Lin initiated the firing procedure, and the ceiling split in two, followed by a low grumbling noise as the barrel slowly moved into position and a siren sounded. The machine started to hum, and an electronic voice said, 'Target planet secured.'

'Permission to go, ma'am?' Gran asked.

Lin nodded, and Gran pressed the buttons on each screen, triggering the familiar rising electrical hum as the electronic voice counted down from ten before the Exodus Deck flooded with light, followed by a flash of white light shooting out of the upper end of the barrel. As the light subsided, the empty chamber was revealed, and the audience gasped on cue from a show producer standing off camera.

'Zephyrions, in just a few seconds, Bob will be on Astral 5 and ready to start his new life as Bobevrin,' Timezel said. 'Do we have video coverage yet?'

The giant screen to the side of Timezel flickered, and then Bobevrin appeared. Behind Bobevrin were lush green plants and a small crowd cheering and waving flags.

'Hello Zephyrion. Can you hear me?' Bob said into the camera.

'We can hear you loud and clear,' Tim replied. 'How was the journey?'

'Incredible,' Bob replied. 'You feel tingly, followed by a flash of light, and then just a minute later, you can feel the soft vegetation under your feet.'

'It looks amazing there, Bob,' Tim said.

'The air is so fresh and clean,' Bob replied. 'Let's turn the camera around, and you can see the founding city.'

The camera moved and revealed a small city of two-storey houses with gardens, and far behind them were a few taller office buildings.

'It looks stunning, Bob,' Tim said.

'Are our lottery winners ready to join me and become Astralians?' Bob asked.

The camera cut to the lottery winners in the auditorium next to the Grand Exodus room, and they cheered excitedly.

Bob smiled and said, 'I'm sorry, the signal must be weak. I couldn't hear anything. I asked if our lottery winners were ready to join me.'

This time, the winners roared with approval as a member of the broadcast production team waved his hands up in the air to indicate they should shout louder.

Bob laughed loudly. 'Well, come on then, let's start the Exodus.'

'That's my line, Bob,' Tim said with a smile. 'Let the Exodus begin.'

The camera followed the first ten winners from the auditorium to the Exodus platform. As the Exodus deck filled with light, the broadcast images flashed to other Exodus machines around the planet following the same process. Then, the images changed to show Zephyrions appearing on different parts of Astral 5.

Simo noticed Max wasn't watching the show and grabbed his communicator. 'Max, where are you, Luc and Zym?'

'By a side room on the far side of the auditorium,' Max replied.

A few minutes later, Simo spotted his three colleagues and walked over to them, 'You three look like those three brothers from those old comedy films. Hopeless, Hapless and Harmless.'

'Well, there's no hope for me, and Luc is harmless, so that must make Max Hapless,' Zym laughed.

'Seriously guys, what are you doing here?' Simo asked.

'Nico and Jeric are in there, and Luc heard Nico saying he should have been at your grandmother's funeral,' Max said.

'I guess as the Deputy Supreme Leader, he felt he should have paid his respects,' Simo said.

'N-N-No, S-S-Simo,' Luc said. 'He s-said son.'

'What?' Simo asked. 'What do you mean, son?"

'Luc is trying to say he heard Nico say he should have been there as Kazi's son,' Zym said.

15
THE TICKING CLOCK

'I'm going to confront him,' Simo snapped.

'And say what? Someone overheard the DSL claim he was the psychotic son of the former Supreme Leader, who murdered his father—a murder that the Elite Council covered up. But don't worry, you can trust the Council regarding Operation Exodus,' Max said.

'Don't forget he is also accused of making that claim to the High Counsellor of the Enforcers, who didn't do anything,' Zym added.

'And he d-d-doesn't even l-look l-like Zeryn,' Luc said.

'Who doesn't look like Zeryn?' a voice said behind Luc.

'Keritrek, what are you doing here?' Max asked.

'Surely you've noticed all the Zingle Burger branding,' Keri laughed.

'Now you mention it, even the lottery winner's Exodus gowns are in Zingle colours,' Zym agreed.

'So, who doesn't look like Zeryn?' Keri asked.

'N-N-Nicoeyel. I h-heard him claim to b-be Zyrenev's son, b-b-b...' Luc said.

'But he doesn't look like him?' Keri said, completing Luc's sentence.

'Yes,' Luc replied in frustration.

'Just let me ask him outright,' Simo demanded.

'You do know there is an underground network doing energy soul reconstructions?' Keri asked.

'C-C-Can it h-h-help me?' Luc asked.

'I'm sorry, Luc. It reconstructs the shape of an energy soul. It doesn't solve connection issues,' Keri replied, hugging Luc.

'How different does it make you look?' Max asked.

'Well, Cal and I volunteered to work here today because we are sure Dronin is here,' Keri replied.

'I've not seen him,' Zym snapped. 'After what he did to Max, Luc, Kendra and Paulie, I'd make his Exodus terminal.'

'That's the point. You wouldn't recognise him. We think he's the Show Director,' Keri replied.

'You mean Stevmachon?' Simo said.

'Yeah, that's him,' Keri replied. 'Actually, can I ask a favour? Can you do a background check on him with your hal device?'

'I can do that,' Max said, pulling out his device and typing Stevmachon's name.

'When did you become a hal?' Keri asked.

'Timezel promoted him,' Zym replied proudly.

'Simo, am I doing this right?' Max asked.

Simo looked at Max's device, 'Yep, that's right, but how can that be true?'

'What does it say?' Keri asked.

'That Stevmachon died in a car crash, but his injuries were treated, and he was released from hospital five days later,' Max said, frowning.

'Did you feel that?' Zym asked.

Simo shook his head, 'Feel wh—'

The ground shook violently, and parts of the ceiling fell to the floor. The crowd in the auditorium screamed as Nico and Jeric came running out of the side room.

Jeric spotted Max and the others and ran over to them. 'What's happening!'

'We don't know, Jeric. We're just heading to the Grand Exodus room to ensure they're okay,' Max replied.

In the Grand Exodus room, Lin leant forward and shouted above the growing roar of the shaking room and people screaming, 'Gran, is it safe to continue?'

'No, ma'am. These vibrations mean we could miss Astral 5 by hundreds of miles. They could end up in deep space,' Gran replied. 'The monitors are saying this is a global seismic tremor, but there is no information on when it might settle down.'

'We have to stop,' Juli said.

'Agreed. Stay here, and I'll let Timezel know,' Lin replied, running down the steps.

'Lin, what's the situation?' Tim shouted as more debris showered down on everyone.

'We have to stop Supreme Leader. We can't guarantee the accuracy of the Exodus machine. They could end up dying in space,' Lin replied.

Tim walked back across the stage erected in front of the Exodus platform and held his hands up, 'Zephyrions, please stay calm. We are experiencing a seismic tremor. We will restart the Exodus once it has calmed down.'

The Supreme Leader's words did little to calm the audience rushing towards the exits. Max pushed through the crowds, followed by his colleagues.

'Lin, Tim, are you okay?' Max asked.

Lin hugged Max tightly, 'Max, I love you.'

'I love you too, sweetheart,' Max replied. 'Does Gran know what's going on?'

'He said it's a global seismic tremor,' Lin said.

There was a violent shudder, and a wall at the back of the Grand Exodus room cracked and fell forward, stopping at an acute angle. Enforcers rushed forward and tried to move the crowd away from the wall before it collapsed.

'How long will it last?' Max asked.

'Gran said the monitors don't have any information about that,' Lin replied.

'I'll have a look,' Max said, running up the steps.

'What does Max know about climate change?' Simo asked.

'Nothing, but he trained as an engineer and specialised in seismic resistance,' Zym replied.

'I knew something about him starting as an engineer, but I didn't realise he had even started to specialise in certain areas,' Simo said.

'Max has this gift of not revealing just how clever he is,' Zym smiled.

'Gran, what's happening?' Max asked.

'Hey, Max. The monitors are showing intense ground movement and severe structural strain,' Gran replied.

'Is there any indication of it stopping?'

'The machines aren't predicting anything yet,' Gran replied as another violent tremor tore through the building, causing the back wall of the Grand Exodus room to finish its collapse.

Max tapped away on the screens, flicking from one monitor to another, grabbing the railings at various times to stop himself from falling.

'Max, come on, we need to get out of here,' Lin shouted up the steps.

'Is Juli there?' Max replied.

'Yes, I'm here, Max,' Juli shouted from behind Lin.

'Get up here. I need to check something,' Max replied. 'Gran, what frequency range does the Grand Exodus machine cover?'

Gran dodged a piece of falling ceiling and called up an image on one of the screens. 'There you go. You can power it as high or as low as you want.'

Max held his finger on the screen and turned down the frequency dial. 'Start here and increase it slowly until the tremors start slowing, then hold it there.'

'Max, what do you want?' Juli asked, clutching the railings.

'Can this machine point downwards?' Max asked as another tremor hit.

'If you mean straight down, then no. If we disengage the Exodus deck, it can get to around fifty to fifty-five degrees below horizontal,' Juli replied.

'We need closer to sixty. Get Zym to take Tim and Nico out of here. Don't let Simo or Jeric do it. Then, get Simo and Jeric to round up some enforcers and volunteers to take off the Exodus deck. How long will it take?' Max asked.

'Around thirty minutes,' Juli replied.

'I don't think we have that much time,' Max shouted.

Juli ran down the stairs, falling down the last couple of steps as another tremor reverberated through the building.

Juli scrambled to her feet. 'Zym, get the Supreme Leader and Deputy Supreme Leader out of here. Simo, Jeric, we need a team to help remove the Exodus platform and yank that stage out of the way.'

'I'll take Tim and Nico. Zym, you stop here and help,' Jeric volunteered.

'No, Max insisted Zym do it,' Juli replied.

Jeric said, 'But—'

But Tim interrupted, saying, 'Jeric, Max needs your authority and skill here. Come on, Zym, lead the way.'

Another significant tremor shook the room. Nico and Tim followed Zym, with Stevmachon close behind.

'No chance, Dron... Mister Director. We need your team's help to shift that stage,' Jeric said, grabbing Stevmachon's arm.

'Hello down there. Can you hurry up?' Max said as the upper platform swayed under another tremor.

Stevmachon got a team together, and they started pulling down the stage as Juli led another team unbolting the Exodus platform.

'Gran, can we turn off the energy beam and make it a pulse instead?' Max asked.

'If we remove the restriction filter from the discharge tube, it'll pulse instead of being a focussed beam,' Gran replied.

'Great, where is the filter?' Max asked.

'Right behind that central plate on the main Exodus barrel between the two Exodus turret pivots,' Gran replied, pointing to a section of the machine's main barrel around fifteen feet away.

'Oh great, what tools do I need?' Max asked.

'None to remove the plate. They've all got catches on. But you'll need a micro-screwdriver to undo the filter,' Gran said. 'Here, take mine.'

'Thanks,' Max said, climbing over the platform railings.

Stevmachon's team finished pulling the temporary stage out of the way and started helping to decouple the Exodus deck from the machine. Max glanced at the drop below before staggering across the thin connecting walkway to the Exodus machine as tremors rumbled. As he almost reached the nearest turret pivot of the Exodus machine, a huge tremor ripped through the building, and Max slipped off the walkway.

'Max,' Gran shouted, causing those below to look up.

Max grabbed the walkway as he fell and hung there for a moment or two before hauling himself back onto the platform. He sat on the narrow walkway, steadying his nerves as the worst of the latest tremor subsided and then stood up, walking the last few steps to the turret pivot. Below him, Simo was holding Lin, preventing her from running up to the control platform.

'He needs to know you're safe. Running up there will just distract him,' Simo said.

'But I need him,' Lin replied, 'and I love him.'

'He knows you do, Lin. The best way you can show him is to let him concentrate on whatever he is doing,' Simo said.

Max studied the curved casing of the turret pivots to see if there was a foothold or ladder to get across, but it seemed hopeless. He undid the catches on the turret's upper plate, which also covered the curved top of it.

'This might work,' Max thought as he threw the plate away from his friends below and stepped up onto the exposed edge of the turret casing. With the upper plate removed, he noted the gearing mechanism which controlled the movement of the barrel and saw a large lever.

'Gran, what's this control lever near my foot?' Max shouted above the noise of the tremors.

'It's not a control lever. It's a release lever for the main Exodus barrel,' Gran shouted.

Max nodded and studied the lever before stepping across the rest of the turret arm onto the main Exodus barrel.

'It's stuck on your side,' Juli shouted to Keritrek.

'I flipping know that. Would your psychic skills like to tell me where,' Keri shouted back.

'Have you released the pins underneath?' Juli replied.

'Dronin, get under here and check while we hold it up,' Keri shouted.

'Who's Dronin?' Stevmachon replied.

'Look, either argue that you're not Dronin as the planet gets ripped apart and we die or do it, and hopefully, we all live another day,' Keri snapped.

Stevmachon slid under the Exodus deck and edged towards the link to the main Exodus machine.

Max released the catches on his side and pushed the plate upwards, but it barely moved. 'The hinges have seized,' he shouted back to Gran.

'They're not hinged. There are catches on each side,' Gran replied.

'Oh, great,' Max thought. He studied the Exodus barrel and realised that the only option was to try to slide over.

'Gran, lower the angle to horizontal,' Max shouted.

'I can't until they've removed the platform,' Gran replied. 'If I move it while they are disconnecting it they may get crushed.'

'Well, tell them to hurry,' Max said.

'How much longer?' Gran shouted.

'A few more seconds,' Juli replied.

'Pull,' Stevmachon shouted.

Keri and the others tugged on the deck, and it slid out of the main Exodus machinery and dropped to the floor with a heavy thud.

'Okay, it's clear,' Juli shouted.

Gran pressed some buttons, and the Exodus barrel groaned into life and started to lower towards horizontal as Max straddled the barrel and started sliding across. He made it to the other side without a problem and then realised the turret pivot on that side was still complete, so he had nothing to stand on other than the curved plate covering the top of it. He turned and sat on the turret, reached back to the barrel and started to undo the clasps when another tremor hit. Max gripped the clasps tightly as the tremor looked set to dislodge him.

'They're getting worse,' Simo said.

'A lot worse. I hope Max knows what he's doing because this feels like the end,' Juli replied.

Max finished undoing the last clasp and threw the panel behind him. He climbed into the exposed workings of the Exodus barrel, looking for the restriction filter.

'What does the filter look like?' Max shouted.

'Like an inverted Y,' Gran replied.

Max spotted the filter and quickly used the micro-screwdriver to release it, 'Okay, it's free. Start lowering the barrel.'

Max slid off the barrel, over the pivot turret and stood on the narrow walkway as another tremor tore through the Grand Exodus room.

'Fifty-five degrees, fifty-six degrees, fifty-six point-five degrees,' Gran shouted as the Exodus machine groaned. 'I think that's it.'

Max sighed and looked at those below him. 'Gran, get ready to fire up the machine when I shout now.'

'Okay, Max,' Gran replied.

'I love you, Lin,' Max shouted as he kicked down on the barrel release lever, climbed onto the smooth barrel, and started edging towards the firing end. He silently counted to three. 'Now,' Max shouted as he jumped up and landed on the barrel of the Exodus machine with a heavy thud. There was a crack, and the front of the barrel twisted as the released catch gave way, and the front dropped lower.

As another tremor ripped through the building, Gran fired up the Exodus machine.

The machine pulsed, but the tremors increased, so Gran slowly turned the frequency dial on the screen. Wave after wave pounded into Zephyrion, and just as it seemed hopeless, the tremors slowed and then stopped. Gran powered down the machine and looked towards Max.

'Max, where are you?' Gran shouted.

'Max!' Lin screamed, running up the steps to the control platform, followed by Juli.

'Luc, get everyone down there looking for Max,' Simo shouted, running after Lin and Juli.

'Y-Y-You heard h-him, get going. K-Keri, you go that way, and I'll go this way and see you at the f-f-front of the machine,' Luc shouted.

Lin tried to climb over the railings, but Simo held her back. 'Lin, it's not safe. Look at the angle of the Exodus machine barrel.'

'But I can't cope without him,' Lin cried above the noise of parts of the ceiling and walls crumbling.

'Hello, is anyone there?' Max shouted.

Luc stepped over a mixture of ceiling debris and a large metal plate, 'Can anyone s-s-see an-n-anything?'

'I'm up here,' Max shouted, seeing Luc below him.

Luc heard a voice and looked around, 'Max, is that you?'

'Yes'

'Where are you?'

'I'm up here having a party.'

Luc looked up and spotted Max hanging from the barrel of the Exodus machine. 'Max, what are you doing up there?'

'I missed the gym this morning, so I thought I'd catch up while it was quiet,' Max replied. 'I slipped off the machine, you idiot. What do you think I'm doing?'

'Over here,' Luc shouted.

'They've found him,' Lin replied, running down the stairs followed by the others.

Before long, there was a group looking up at Max.

'Don't move, Max. That barrel looks precarious,' Simo shouted.

'Aww, that's a shame. I was thinking of doing some press-ups and a few star jumps,' Max replied.

'I'm detecting some tension,' Jeric said.

'I'm detecting my fingers going numb. Would you be so kind as to hurry up and get me down?' Max shouted.

'Is there a ladder or anything that would reach him?' Simo asked.

'No, Sir,' Gran replied.

'Max, can you swing yourself up onto the barrel?' Juli asked.

'Brilliant, why didn't I think of that instead of just clinging on,' Max replied.

'He's always testy when under pressure,' Lin said.

'W-W-What about c-c-climbing over the barrel and p-pulling him up?' Luc suggested.

'The barrel is too unstable. He opened the release lever on one side, so it's hanging by just the one lever now,' Gran replied.

'Can we get on the roof? The dome is open, so we could lower a rope down,' Simo suggested.

'Yes, there's a long one on the tarpaulin we use to cover the computers on the control deck,' Gran replied before running off to get it.

'How do we get up to the roof?' Simo asked.

'I'm not sure I can stay here much longer, and the alternative down there looks a bit hard,' Max shouted.

Gran returned with the tarpaulin and started to remove the rope.

'We don't have time for this,' Jeric said, pulling the tarpaulin from Gran and noticing it was stretchy. 'Why not use the tarpaulin as a net for Max to fall into instead?'

'Great idea. Everyone grab the edge and stretch it out,' Simo replied.

'Max, get ready to fall. We'll catch you in this tarpaulin,' Jeric shouted. 'One, two, three, jump.'

'Oh well, here goes,' Max thought as he let go.

Max hit the tarpaulin and felt it give under him, but thankfully, there was no thud.

'Can we not do that again?' Max laughed as they lowered him to the floor, and he stood up.

Lin ran over and threw her arms around him, 'Max, you made it.'

'Well, I considered the options and decided this was the best choice,' Max replied.

'You've just saved the planet, and yet you're cracking jokes,' Juli laughed.

'All I've done is stopped this wave of tremors, but there'll be more,' Max replied.

'But if frequency pulses can stop the tremors, can't they set up a machine to neutralise them each time?' Juli asked.

'It's not that simple. Those pulses stopped it this time, but next time, the tremors might be on a different frequency and constantly hitting the planet with opposing frequencies will weaken it even quicker,' Max replied.

'Where's Stevmachon?' Keri asked.

'He's probably done a runner while we were distracted,' Simo said. 'Also, where's Jeric?'

'I'm over here,' Jeric shouted by the Exodus deck. 'I've found Stevmachon.'

'Avoiding the hard work, are you Dronin,' Cal said as they walked towards Jeric.

Jeric looked at Cal and shook his head. 'You'll need to shout much louder than that. He's gone.'

'See, I said he'd run off,' Cal replied.

'I don't mean that sort of gone,' Jeric said. 'It looks like the Exodus deck crushed him. All that's left are his clothes.'

'The irony is that in the end, he lost his life helping to save the planet,' Keri said.

'But not for long,' Max said.

'How long will it take to get this machine fixed?' Jeric asked.

'A few weeks, Sir,' Gran said. 'Maybe longer fixing the room too.'

'Based on the readings for the tremors, I'm not sure we have that long,' Max replied.

'How long have we got?' Jeric asked.

'I don't have a clue. You need to ask an expert, but I wouldn't plan any holidays for next year,' Max replied.

16
CRONIS

'We need that Exodus machine working in the next few days.' Nico stated.

'That's not possible,' Gran replied.

'Gran, you don't seem to understand. I'm not asking if it can be done. I'm telling you,' Nico replied.

'Don't worry, Nico, we'll work day and night to get it ready,' Lin said.

'Perfect, and the first Exodus will be a Daxson to Astral 5 in accordance with Project Cronis,' Nico replied.

'Cronis, Sir?' Lin queried.

'Yes, Lineklis. All plans need a project name so we know what we are working towards,' Nico said.

'What does Cronis stand for, Deputy Supreme Leader?' Juli asked.

'Nothing in particular. Juli, isn't it?' Nico replied.

'Yes, Sir.' Juli said.

'Well, Juli. Cronis was just a nickname I used to have when I was younger. My parents said it meant ambitious one in Psiorite,' Nico replied.

'Oh, were your parents Psiorites then?' Juli asked.

'My mother and sister were,' Nico replied.

'Oh, I take it they're no longer with us then, Sir?' Juli said.

'My mother passed away recently, but my sister died years ago,' Nico replied.

'I'm so sorry,' Juli said.

'Life happens,' Nico replied coldly. 'Anyway, let's get this machine back up and running. I want a daily update, Project Leader.'

'Yes, Nico,' Lin replied.

Gran waited for Nico to leave and said, 'Ma'am, we can't do it.'

'Of course we can. We know where Max broke it, and we know the settings. Just get some cranes in to lift the barrel into place. Then recalibrate it, and it'll be fine. I'm off to a meeting now, but I know you and Juli can manage,' Lin replied before walking off.

'Juli, how are we going to do it? This is impossible in the time the DSL wants it done.' Gran said.

'I'm not sure, but we need to get a crane in quickly. It's not even been a day, and the barrel has dropped further,' Juli replied.

'Did somebody mention a crane?' Cal asked, walking towards them.

'Yeah, we're going to need a few,' Juli sighed. 'But what are you doing here, Cal?'

'Max messaged me to ask if I could help. I've got two cranes outside and a couple of long-reach lifts at your disposal,' Cal shouted.

'And some labour too,' Keri added. 'I think you know Kendra and Paulie; they've brought some friends, too.'

'Can we really do this?' Gran asked.

'I reckon with a few Zingles burgers and a bit of luck, we just might,' Juli replied.

'Can I pass on the burgers,' Kendra laughed.

'Tim, I'm so sorry I wrecked the Exodus machine,' Max said.

'Max, you're a hero. Why are you apologising?' Timezel laughed. 'The Exodus machines across the planet are still sending our people to safety. You had a little incident with one machine, that's all.'

'I know, Sir. But our machine was the most powerful on the planet,' Max replied. 'Lin told me it was created to enable the Exodus of the Daxson.'

The conversation was interrupted by someone hammering in the corner of the office.

'Sorry about this. The tremors caused some damage, but they've restored the security and wiring, and they're just finishing off,' Tim said. 'Excuse me, Danwhitren, wasn't it?'

'Yes, Supreme Leader,' the tradesman replied.

'Would you leave us for a while?' Tim asked.

'Of course, Sir,' he said, climbing down the ladder and leaving the room.

'Now, back to your comment about the Exodus machine being designed to Exodus Daxson. It's not something I was aware of, Max,' Tim replied. 'There's about a hundred Daxson left on the planet, and we were going to use a spacecraft to shift them. But that was only after saving the rest of the planet.'

'Maybe we should make some enquiries,' Zym suggested.

'Good idea, Zym—' Tim paused as there was a knock at the door. 'Enter.'

'Supreme Leader, Jeric sent me. The geologists have finished running their tests, and it's not good news,' Erzsi said.

'Max, you and Zym find out all you can about this Daxson story while I go with Erzsi to check these results,' Tim replied. 'Out of interest, did Lin say where she heard about a plan to Exodus Daxson?'

'She said the original specification from the previous Project Leader always required being able to Exodus Daxson,' Max replied.

'But it was never mentioned in any reports I saw,' Tim replied. 'Check the code marks of who authorised it.'

'Yes, Sir,' Max replied.

As Timezel and Erzsi headed off, Max looked at his brother. 'Do you trust Timezel?'

'You never ask those sorts of questions unless you don't,' Zym replied. 'Why're you asking?'

'I don't know. Someone is lying to us. Tim says he swore an oath not to tell Simo until his grandmother was dying and that he doesn't know about the Daxson Exodus. Erzsi and Luc agree with him. But we know Dronin had Tim's payment card, and Tim had to approve the Exodus machine plans,' Max said.

'But Luc said the card was his,' Zym replied.

'No, Luc said the all-access card was his from Tim, not the payment card,' Max insisted.

'True. But Nico was responsible for producing all Elite cards. So he could have made another one in Tim's name,' Zym said.

'Good point and Nico stripped the Peace room. Plus, Lin is always saying Nico said this or that as if he were running things,' Max said.

'If you don't trust Tim, why are you working for him?' Zym asked.

'Because I believe what Dronin said to you. He may be a Deceptor, but the best way to disguise a lie is to wrap the truth around it. Someone in the Elite killed our parents and tried to kill you and now me,' Max replied. 'The chance to work for Tim was too good an opportunity to refuse.'

'Come on, Cynical Sid. Let's go to the One World Research Centre and do some digging,' Zym said, heading toward the door.

'Ha, you've not called me that for years,' Max laughed as they left the Supreme Leader's office.

'That's because you became too trusting of the Elite. It's good to see my suspicious, cynical little brother back,' Zym replied as the door closed.

'Are you sure they won't find this new surveillance equipment? Whenever we've tried to bug the SL's office in the past, it got discovered very quickly.'

'It's the latest technology, Sir. Plus, the latest climate crisis will keep them distracted.'

'I hope you're right as this will be very useful. Look at them chattering in blissful ignorance.'

'They're getting very suspicious.'

'So I see, but Max is still unsure whether to blame the SL or the DSL.'

'Let's help him come to the right conclusion.'

'Do you mean the right one or the right one for you, Sir?'

'Unless you want to meet the same fate as their parents and my father, you know the right answer. And remember my motto.'

'Yes, Sir. Don't take risks. Manage or neutralise them.'

'Hold it right there,' Cal shouted from the basket attachment fitted to a long-reach lift to the crane operator. 'It's a bit of a tight squeeze in here, Gran.'

The harnesses stretched under the Exodus barrel were suspended from two cranes and groaned under the weight.

'Are you sure that catch is safe? Max did hit that release lever hard,' Cal asked.

'It looks good to me,' Gran replied.

There was a loud clattering from the far side.

'What's going on over there?' Cal shouted.

'Juli is making some minor technical adjustments with a whopping big hammer,' Keri replied with a laugh from a basket on the other long-reach lift.

'The catch got bent this side when the barrel twisted. It just needs tweaking a bit,' Juli said with one more hammer whack. 'Okay, I think it's spotling.'

Cal looked at Gran with a puzzled look. 'What does spotling mean?'

'It's a Juli phrase. It means it looks fine, or it'll do like it's about spot on,' Gran laughed.

'Okay. Well, it's spotling here too, so let's lift it into position,' Cal replied as the cranes slowly lifted the barrel, engaging the axle into the catches on each side. They snapped shut, locking the barrel in place.

'Looking good from here,' Max shouted as he walked into the Grand Exodus room with Zym.

'Oh, look, everyone. The vandal has turned up; now the hard work is done,' Keri shouted as the baskets were lowered.

Gran said, 'Excuse me, but we don't know if it works yet regarding movement, let alone calibration, alignment, and whether there has been any damage to the firing mechanism, the barrel—'

'Gran, Keri was only kidding,' Juli said.

'But it'll be days before we know it's safe,' Gran protested.

'It's okay, Gran. This is all my fault anyway,' Max said.

'Why are you and Zym here anyway? Don't you have enforcement work to do?' Juli asked.

'We're following up on a few loose ends for the Supreme Leader,' Zym said.

'How can we help officers? Do you need to lock us up?' Keri laughed.

'I think we'll leave locking you up to Cal,' Zym laughed.

'Juli, can we have a word with you in private?' Max asked.

'A lot of the side offices by the auditorium were wrecked, but I'm sure we can find some quiet area over there,' Juli replied as they headed off.

Juli led them into one of the few reasonably intact side offices. 'What's this about, then?'

'Do you know about the plan to Exodus Daxson?' Max asked.

'Not all of it, no,' Juli replied.

'But there is a plan to Exodus some of them?' Zym asked.

'I know about a plan to send one Daxson,' Juli replied, avoiding looking at Max.

'What is it, Juli?' Max asked.

'I was told this in confidence,' Juli replied, still avoiding looking at Max.

'Juli, we've been sent by the Supreme Leader. What is the Daxson plan?' Max asked firmly.

'This looks serious,' Lin said, walking into the room.

'Hi, Lin. We're just checking some facts about the Exodus machine,' Max said.

'I heard, Max. How come you didn't ask me?' Lin challenged.

'We've only just arrived, and we saw Juli first,' Max replied.

'Oh, just a coincidence then,' Lin said sarcastically.

'Yes, it was,' Max agreed.

'Juli, you can go back to Gran. I'll be able to tell Zym and Max everything they need to know,' Lin said.

'Actually Juli, can you stay here please,' Zym said firmly. 'We may have questions for you.'

Lin glowered at Zym. 'How can we help then?'

'It's about the Exodus of Daxson,' Zym said.

'What about it?' Lin replied.

'What's the plan?' Zym asked.

'That's classified,' Lin replied.

'Lin, we're here under the direct orders of the Supreme Leader,' Max said.

'Well, ask him then,' Lin replied defiantly.

'What does that mean?' Max asked.

'It means our Supreme Leader approved the plan himself,' Lin replied, holding up her tablet showing the Supreme Leader's code mark in the corner.

'But what is the plan?' Max asked.

'That's for Elites only,' Lin replied.

'But I am a member of the Elite,' Max protested.

'Only through partnership, my dear,' Lin replied. 'That doesn't count.'

'How about under the authority of the Supreme Leader Timezel?' Zym replied firmly.

'Just tell them, Lin,' Juli said.

'I don't understand why you're making such an issue of this,' Lin replied. 'The plan says we are supposed to send a Daxson to Astral 5 to ensure it works.'

'And if it does?' Max asked.

'Then we can rescue the others by sending them to a planet where they can live,' Lin replied.

Juli opened her mouth, but a glare from Lin made her shut it.

Max started to say 'Why—', but he was interrupted.

'The S-S-Supreme Leader and D-D-Deputy want you all n-n-now,' Luc said, rushing into the room.

'Where are they?' Lin asked.

'In the G-G-Grand Exodus r-r-room,' Luc replied, trying to hurry them along.

'Thank you for joining us,' Timezel said as Max and the others entered the Grand Exodus room.

'What we are about to tell you must stay within these walls,' Nico said.

Zym looked around the partly destroyed room. 'You mean within what's left of these walls,' Zym replied.

Tim laughed, then said, 'Indeed so, Zym. We've been reviewing the data from the geologists, and it's grave news.'

'How can we help, Supreme Leader?' Lin asked.

'The geologists have said those tremors are the start of Zephyrion collapsing,' Tim replied.

'How long have we got, Sir?' Max asked.

'The geologists say the total collapse could take four or five years, but within a year, the tremors will be constant,' Tim replied.

'Oh, that's plenty of time to Exodus the planet, Sir,' Lin said. 'I calculated about a year.'

'But we have a problem. Your timelines don't include not using the machines when we have tremors,' Tim replied.

'But Max showed how we can stop them,' Zym said.

'He did, and we are very grateful for that, but while it stops the tremors, it also increases the rate of collapse,' Tim replied. We can't be sure of the frequency of the tremors, but the geologists think using the Max solution to stop the tremors may give us between four and five months of stable Exodus time at the most.'

'Max, you've not given us time to save everyone,' Lin snapped.

Max looked down and said, 'I'm sorry, I thought it was for the best.'

'Well, yet again, you're wrong,' Lin replied.

'Actually, without Max's idea to use a machine to pulse inverse frequencies into the planet, the geologists think the tremors would have been milder but more frequent in a shorter timeframe, giving us the equivalent of only a couple of months when the planet was stable enough to Exodus,' Tim said. 'The tremors will soon be several times a day.'

'Excuse me, Sirs,' Gran said, raising his hand. 'What does it mean for us?'

'It means, Gran, we need that machine up and running as quickly as possible. All Exodus machines are running non-stop, but we need this machine's capacity,' Tim replied.

'What is the message to the population?' Simo asked.

'Radio silence,' Nico replied.

'But how can we keep this from everyone? They have a right to know,' Zym protested.

'Because if we tell them, there'll be panic. The Elite Council knows what's best for our citizens. If we keep this on a need-to-know basis, we can manage the Exodus in a civilised way and avoid civil unrest,' Jeric said.

'You mean lie to them and decide who escapes first,' Zym replied sarcastically.

'Zym, you are the consummate conspiracy theorist,' Jeric sneered.

Nico held up his hands. 'Jeric, don't be so harsh on Zym. He is right; our citizens have a right to know, but does anyone know how to handle the fallout and riots? We need to make sure we stay calm and save everyone.'

'We just tell them that we are accelerating the Exodus because the planet is collapsing,' Zym said.

'Are you going to stop them storming the place and demanding to be next?' Lin asked.

'If necessary,' Zym replied.

'Come on, Zym,' Simo said. 'There'll be riots at every Exodus machine location.'

'I'll do a broadcast and make a global announcement,' Tim said.

'But Supreme Leader, you'll cause global rioting and looting,' Jeric replied.

'I'll make it clear all Elites will be the last to Exodus, with anyone rioting or looting left to sort out their own Exodus,' Tim said.

Jeric looked shocked. 'But Supr—'

'Jeric, Tim knows what he is doing,' Nico said sharply.

'Get me that Show Director Stevmachon. He can organise my broadcast,' Tim insisted.

'Brilliant idea, Tim,' Nico replied.

'I'm afraid Stevmachon died helping Max save the planet,' Jeric said.

'You mean Dronin,' Keri replied.

'You only thought he might be Dronin,' Jeric replied.

'We all knew he was,' Cal insisted.

'That's not true,' Jeric replied.

'Please, we have far more pressing things to worry about,' Nico said forcefully. 'Lin, is the Exodus machine ready? I'm impressed with how quickly you've got it back in one piece.'

'It's almost ready. We've just got some final tests to do,' Lin replied.

'But ma'am,' Gran said.

'It's okay, Gran, I'm not taking all the credit. I couldn't have done this without all your hard work and help,' Lin said with a smile.

'Tim, may I make a suggestion?' Nico asked.

'Of course, Nico. What have you got in mind?' Tim replied.

'Let's split the two challenges. You, Max, Simo and Jeric sort out the speech to the planet, and I'll work with Lin, Zym and the team here to get the Exodus machine up and running,' Nico suggested.

'That's a good idea, Nico, having two Elite Council members on each task. You and Lin working on the machine, and Jeric and I preparing the communication,' Tim agreed. 'Lin, you said you just had some final tests to go, so when will the Exodus machine be working safely again?'

'By tomorrow afternoon, Supreme Leader,' Lin replied.

Gran went to protest, but a sharp look from Lin was enough to keep him quiet.

'Excellent work, all of you,' Tim said. 'We've got work to do if we are going to make this announcement tomorrow evening.'

'Tim, can I suggest you make your announcement the following morning?' Nico said. 'We need to be sure the machine is safe.'

'That's a sensible idea, Nico. Come on, Max, Simo and Jeric. Oh, Erzsi, can you join us too?'

Erzsi looked at Jeric, who nodded his approval. 'Of course, Tim.'

As Timezel and the others left, Nico said, 'Juli, can you and Gran take charge and get going? We need to be doing the first tests in the morning, so it will be a long night. Lin, can you come with me, please? We have some Elite business to discuss.'

'No problem, Nico. Those tests tomorrow are they for your Cronis plan?' Juli asked.

'The last one will be, and we must do it before Timezel returns. The stakes are too high to risk putting that machine back into operation without a full test,' Nico replied. 'Come on, Lin, we are wasting precious time.'

'Did you say Nico had a Cronis plan?' Zym asked when Nico and Lin were out of sight.

Juli handed a screwdriver to Gran. 'Yeah. He plans to send a Daxson through an Exodus machine. Lin mentioned it before we were summoned to see the Supreme Leader.'

'That's right, you were going to say something before Lin gave you that look,' Zym said.

'Juli, I need the radioactigram, please,' Gran growled in frustration.

Juli passed over the meter to Gran. 'I don't know what you're on about.'

'Juli, I've known you for years, ever since Max and your sister started dating at the education centre when they were fifteen,' Zym smiled. 'You can't fool me.'

'I said the radioactigram, not the frequency modulation monitor,' Gran grumbled.

'Sorry, Gran, here,' Juli replied, passing over another meter. 'Do we need to do this now, Zym? I'm a bit busy.'

'Okay, one last question. Where does Nico want the Daxson sent and why?' Zym asked.

'Gran, have you checked the stability scanners?'

'Not yet, Juli. I'm concentrating on the radiation transmitters at the moment, but don't let that stop you from checking them.' Gran answered without breaking his gaze from the monitors.

'Juli!' Zym said firmly.

'Fine! Nico wants to send a Daxson to Astral 5 to wipe out all the Deceptors on the planet,' Juli replied. 'But don't you dare let Lin know I told you. Now, can I get on, please?'

'Gran, if you were given precise coordinates, could you Exodus someone into something like a cage or a room on another planet?' Zym asked.

'In theory, but you risk them being reformed with the cage inside them or the Exodus signal being deformed by the room's building materials. It's always best to send them to an open area,' Gran said. 'Can someone give me a hand with these transmitters, please?'

Zym decided to look for Nico and Lin. He passed a young technician running up the steps to Gran on the Central Control platform.

Zym whistled to Luc. 'Come with me, Luc, I need your help.'

Luc ran across the Grand Exodus room and followed Zym. 'W-W-Where are we g-going?'

'Chasing some old investigations,' Zym replied.

Zym and Luc checked the offices on the far side of the auditorium, but there was no sign of them. They walked across to the chutes and headed back to the main One World Research Centre buildings.

Luc headed towards a security guard at the far end of the centre, who was minding the chutes to the central office superscraper.

'E-E-Excuse m-m-me, S-S-Sir.'

'Yes, officer, how can I help?' the guard said.

'M-M-My c-c-colleague and I have a m-m-meeting with the P-P-Project L-L-Leader and D-D-Dep-p-puty S-S-S-Sup—'

'The Deputy Supreme Leader?' the guard suggested helpfully.

'Y-Y-Yes, S-S-Sir.'

'They're in the Project Leader's new office on the eighty-second floor. Can I have your names to let them know?' the guard asked.

'I-I-It's L-L-L-L,' Luc sighed in apparent frustration. 'L-L-L-Lu—'

'Just introduce yourself when you arrive. Office 8213,' the guard interrupted before waving Luc through, who was quickly followed by Zym.

'Wow, Luc, your stutter is getting bad,' Zym said with concern.

Luc smiled, 'Yeah, it's f-f-funny how b-bad it can get at times. But most p-p-people are so k-kind and talk for me or just d-d-don't wait for an answer and move on.'

Zym paused for a minute and then burst out laughing. 'Now that is the cunning thinking of someone brought up on the wrong side of the tracks.'

'Tracks? W-What are t-t-tracks?' Luc asked.

'Sorry, Luc, I forget how much younger you are since I transitioned. We used to have vehicles that moved on rails or tracks. Someone brought up on the wrong side grew up in the rough area of a town. I guess you'd now say brought up on the wrong side of the solar dome,' Zym explained. 'Why are you laughing?'

'B-B-Because you're so easy to wind up. Of course, I know what t-tracks are,' Luc laughed. 'Our chutes are here. S-S-See you on the eighty-second floor.'

The door to the chute opened, and Zym saw Luc by a door.

'They're in h-here. I can hear them,' Luc said.

'I'm going to check the room on this side and see if I can hear any better. If anyone comes, hide in that cleaning trolley,' Zym said, pointing to a trolley behind Luc.

Zym tapped lightly on the door to office 8214, and when he didn't get a reply, he walked inside quietly and closed the door.

'What was that?' Nico said.

'What was what? Lin replied.

'Who's in that other room?'

'Nobody. When I replaced the previous Project Leader, they joined these two offices and made that my conference room.'

Nico crossed the room from the window and looked through the connecting door. 'Hello, anyone there!'

'The place has been almost deserted since the storm we had on Migration Lottery Day, and I think yesterday's tremors convinced the rest to work from home now,' Lin laughed. The only people still coming in regularly are the cleaners.'

'Well, we can't be too careful,' Nico said. 'You're clear on what needs to be done?'

'Yes, Nico. We get everything ready by lunchtime tomorrow at the latest and send a Daxson to Astral 5 before the Supreme Leader arrives,' Lin replied.

'If we can send two or three more over the next day or two, they should have wiped Astral 5 clear before the end of this week. This means we can adopt all the infrastructure without the existing bureaucracy and start our own colony, free of Deceptors and other unpleasantness,' Nico said, walking back to the window in Lin's office.

Lin paused for a minute and said, 'But we still keep sending people to the two other deserted planets?'

'Of course, Lin. They are our reserve planets, and I'll be the benevolent Regent Supreme of all three planets. The triple crown of Zephyrions as is my birthright.'

'Regent Supreme,' Lin laughed. 'So that's what the RS means in Cronis.'

'If anyone was going to work it out, I knew it would be you. You'll make an excellent Deputy Regent of Astral 5, Lin.'

'With my beloved Max by my side.'

'If you insist, but we can just as easily leave him and his half-wit brother behind and give you a new start.'

'Absolutely not. There's no way I'd leave Max or Juli behind, and as frustrating as Zym is, his heart is in the right place.'

'I suppose we'll need good enforcers, so maybe Max can be the new High Counsellor with Zym as his deputy,' Nico laughed.

'What about Jeric? I thought he'd be your High Counsellor on Astral 5.'

'He's a useless fool. I only supported him getting the job here because I knew he'd never be able to outwit Dronin.'

Zym felt his leg ache from hiding under the conference table and stretched out, kicking over a wastepaper basket.

'I definitely heard that,' Nico snapped.

Nico and Lin rushed into the conference room as the door opened. 'Cleaning services,' shouted a short cleaner with a cheery smile, pushing a trolley draped in a cloth.

'Is there anyone else in here?' Nico asked loudly.

'Nobody here but the three of us, my lovelies,' the cleaner replied with a grin.

Nico glanced around the room from where he was standing, and then, satisfied there was nobody else present, he turned back towards Lin. 'Let's go and see how Juli and the others are getting on.'

The door to Juli's office slammed shut, and Nico and Lin's voices trailed away.

The cloth over the trolley flipped back, and Luc clambered out. 'It's okay, Z-Zym, they've gone now.'

Zym crawled out from under the table and stood up, looking confused. 'What the...'

'Meet my Auntie Dee,' Luc said with a smile. 'Obviously, she's n-n-not my real Auntie, but she took care of me when m-m-my family died.'

'Pleased to meet you, my lovely. You'd best close your mouth before someone lands a spacecraft in it,' Dee laughed.

17
Face-Off

'Are you sure they plan to wipe out everyone on Astral 5?' Tim asked the following morning.

'Yes, Sir,' Zym replied.

'Do you think Max knows?'

'No, Sir. It seems like Nico has lured Lin with the prize of being the Deputy Supr... I mean Deputy Regent Supreme for Astral 5,' Zym said.

'Nico RS,' Erzsi said.

'Sorry, Erzsi, what are you on about?' Tim asked.

Erzsi grabbed a computer marker and started writing on a nearby screen. 'Cronis is an anagram of Nico RS.'

'Lin did say that was what the RS in Cronis was,' Zym agreed.

'But the Project Cronis covering vote rigging was masterminded by Zeryn,' Tim insisted.

'Although it did see Nico being elected as the Head of the House of Finance,' Zym said.

'No, Zym. When the elections happened during the Grand Formation, Nico was just a rising star in the House of Finance,'

Erzsi said, checking her records. 'He didn't become the Head of the House of Finance until a few years later, following the death of his predecessor, Pietr.'

'But I don't remember any elections,' Zym replied with a puzzled look.

'It was done quietly as his predecessor was killed in a freak Daxson accident,' Tim said.

'How do you have a freak Daxson accident?' Zym challenged.

'A Daxson escaped their facility on the Palace Compound and ended up by Zyrenev's office where Pietr was visiting the Supreme Leader,' Tim sighed. 'It was only by luck that Zyrenev and Zeryn weren't killed as well.'

'Sorry I'm late. Erzsi's message about this meeting only came through not long ago. But I've sorted a Show Director who said they can prepare everything for tomorrow,' Max said, entering the Supreme Leader's office. 'By the way, what do you mean "by luck" he wasn't killed? Is Zyrenev alive!'

'No, Tim was telling us about Nico's predecessor, Pietr, at the House of Finance being killed by a Daxson whilst visiting Zyrenev,' Simo explained.

Zym sat quietly, thinking before saying, 'You said it was lucky Zyrenev and Zeryn weren't killed as well. Why was Zeryn there?'

'It was Zeryn who warned his father that there was a Daxson outside his office. Zyrenev hit his panic button, but by the time the guards arrived, Pietr was already dead, and Zeryn and Zyrenev were cornered in the office. Zyrenev had been caught a glancing blow by the Daxson, but they both survived. A few seconds later, and it might have been a different story,' Tim replied.

'But that still doesn't explain why there weren't any elections,' Zym said.

'Zeryn refused to accept an award for gallantry for saving our Supreme Leader, but he said if we could promote his friend, Nico, that would be award enough. To be honest, at that stage,

Nico was the Elite Council's preferred candidate anyway,' Tim explained.

'Hang on, Nico and Zeryn were friends?' Max said.

'And we're sure Nico is behind Cronis,' Zym said. 'But now we know Nico is actually Zeryn.'

'Yes, Cronis is an anagram of Nico RS or Regent Supreme,' Erzsi said. 'But what do you mean Nico is Zeryn? Before Zeryn disappeared, Nico and Zeryn were separate people.'

'Zeryn organised the original vote-rigging under the codename Project Cronis,' Max said. 'So why would he use a codeword based on his friend's name? Unless...'

'Unless, what, Max?' Tim asked.

'It's no use talking to him when he enters Max mode,' Zym laughed.

'W-W-What m-mode?' Luc said.

'Unless...' Max said.

Zym held up his hand to quieten Luc and said, 'Any second now, he'll start moving and talking to—'

Max stood up, walked to the furthest corner from the main entrance, and inspected a small, locked door. 'Hmm, that's new.'

'That was installed after the Daxson incident to provide a second escape route from this office,' Tim said.

Max looked at the polished floor and noticed it was worn in front of the door. 'Was there a desk and chair here?'

'That's where this desk used to be with Zyrenev's chair roughly where you're standing. It was moved to allow free access to that new door,' Tim replied.

Max crouched as if sitting and then jumped up. 'We need to escape. Now.'

Everyone except Zym looked around in a panic.

'What is it, Max?' Simo asked. 'What are we escaping from?'

'Relax, it's just Max mode. He's not talking to us,' Zym replied.

'This way,' Max said, turning, unbolting the door and opening it whilst looking at the floor. Max slammed the door shut and turned, raising his arms.

'Zeryn wasn't warning Zyrenev and Pietr. He was trying to kill them,' Max said. 'Simo, didn't you say your mother and grandmother were Psio-somethings?'

'Psiorites, yeah,' Simo replied.

'Do they have the ability to communicate with Daxson?'

'I think some do, but only female descendants of Psiorites can be Psiorites,' Simo said.

'Not strictly true,' Erzsi said. 'There have been cases of males having some Psiorite skills. It's said in history that both males and females could have the abilities, but the males lost them over the generations.'

'What if Zeryn was one of those cases, and he communicated with one of the Daxson and lured it here to kill Zyrenev,' Max said.

'That's a leap of logic,' Simo replied.

'Look at that large picture of Zyrenev sitting at his desk. It always puzzled me that the bookcases behind him looked different to those behind Tim's desk,' Max said, walking over to it. 'See how that bookcase in the middle is narrower than the others. Plus, there are two vertical pieces of wood on either side of it.'

'I'm no carpenter, but isn't that how they make a bookcase? Two verticals, a top and bottom, and add the shelves? So two bookcases side by side means two verticals together,' Tim said.

'Not if they are made on-site. It wastes wood. Look at the others in the room. Each vertical piece of wood is the left side of one bookcase and the right side of the other,' Max said assuredly, walking back to the previously bolted door.

'M-M-Maybe t-they got their measurements wrong,' Luc suggested.

'Look at the floor here. You can see how Zyrenev moving his feet around over the years has scuffed it, and as you'd need to strip the entire floor and repolish it to remove the marks, you can still see them under subsequent years of cleaning and polishing. I bet if Tim looked under his desk, he'd see some similar marks,' Max explained.

Tim looked and nodded. 'Max is right.'

'But how does that lead you to say Zeryn tried to kill his father with a Daxson?' Simo asked.

'Because if Zyrenev was sitting at his desk here and heard a Daxson was outside that door, why didn't he escape with the others this way?' Max said, pointing at the door behind him.

'I've already explained that door wasn't there then,' Tim replied.

'That door wasn't, but the secret door behind that narrow bookcase in the picture was,' Max said. 'Those doors are heavy because of the bookcase, so they have wheels hidden behind the kickboard. If you look here, you can see how the wheel has left a curved scratch, which has a wider arc than the door installed to replace it.'

'Max is right. I've just checked the maintenance records from that period, and it confirms the order from Zyrenev was to replace the second office door, not install one,' Erzsi said.

'So, just in case something went wrong, Zeryn used Nico as a cover name for himself. That's why he used Cronis instead of, erm, Renzrys, Synrezr, or whatever,' Max replied. 'If anyone uncovered his plan, he could point the finger at Nico. That's the only thing that makes sense, I think.'

'But Zeryn disappeared around thirty years ago after Zyrenev's death, and yet we've had the Cronis financial fraud and now this triple crown Regent Supreme Cronis,' Zym said. 'Nico must be involved.'

'D-D-Does N-Nico have any family?' Luc asked.

'He had one brother who was the chief of internal controls at the House of Finance and the ringleader of the financial fraud that almost saw Zym killed and which I brought down,' Max replied. 'I did think Nico might have been involved, but he wasn't, and I tried hard to catch him. But he doesn't seem to bear any grudges as he has never mentioned it despite meeting him a lot since this all blew up.'

'Where is his b-brother now?' Luc queried.

'Like all traitors of Zephyrion, he was sentenced to death by Daxson,' Tim said.

'What are you thinking, Luc?' Simo challenged.

'R-R-Remember how your g-g-grandmother looked very d-different because of the transition accident?'

'Yeah,' Simo replied.

'Well, the underground n-n-network t-t-took that knowledge to create a way to change our energy s-soul's appearance,' Luc said.

'But it was only known about by a select few of us senior Elite members,' Tim protested.

'I assume Z-Z-Zeryn knew?'

'Yes, he would have known as Shazon changed before our eyes,' Tim agreed.

'S-S-So, w-w-what if Zeryn was the one who took that knowledge underground?' Luc said.

'And once it was perfected, he had his energy soul changed to match Nico. Then he killed and replaced him,' Max said.

'Exactly,' Luc replied. 'Remember how they t-t-turned D-Dronin into Stevmachon? What if Zeryn t-t-transformed into N-Nico, killed the real one, and, to avoid d-d-detection, framed Nico's brother? Zeryn would know he would be k-k-killed for t-treason, and that r-r-removed the only one who might have b-been able to prove he wasn't N-N-Nico.'

'But we all know Nico,' Tim protested. 'We know about his upbringing, his habits, and his behaviour. We'd have known if he had changed.'

'But his old best friend, Zeryn, would also know all that about him,' Simo said.

'Luc, I could kiss you,' Max said. 'That is the bit I couldn't reconcile in my mind. Why keep the Cronis codeword going?'

'M-M-Mind if I p-pass on that k-kiss, Max?' Luc laughed.

'Will everyone slow down just for a second? Are you saying Nico is my Uncle Zeryn?' Simo asked.

'That seems very likely, and it answers so many questions,' Max replied. 'I'm sorry, Simo.'

'So if certain members of the Elite hadn't been more concerned about their image, which is why they covered up Zeryn's actions, like killing his father, this wouldn't be happening now, and I'd have grown up with my mother, grandmother and grandfather,' Simo snarled.

'Simo is right, Tim. Your actions and those of other Elite members have allowed Zeryn to start again and become even more powerful,' Zym said.

'It's just politics,' Tim replied. 'It's not about protecting anyone's image.'

'You believe your own rhetoric, don't you?' Zym said. 'You and the other Elites are so remote from reality that you just think you can do what you want and claim it's for the wider good.'

'Simo put out an immediate arrest warrant for Nicoeyel for treason,' Tim ordered.

'Simo, cancel that order,' Max said. 'Tim, whilst naming Nico means his devices won't show up the warrant, Jeric's will and as High Counsellor and therefore the most senior enforcer on the planet, the warrant to arrest the DSL will be assigned to him.'

'Are you telling me Jeric is involved too?' Tim asked. 'What proof do you have to support that?'

'None, Sir. Except my gut feeling and instincts,' Max conceded.

'That's not enough to justify accusing him of being complicit in treason,' Tim replied.

'Please, Tim. You trusted our parents, and they gave up their lives trying to support you. I almost lost my life investigating that financial fraud, and even young Max almost died recently trying to capture Dronin,' Zym pleaded. 'If Max says his instincts are warning him, I'd trust him with my life.'

'Supreme Leader?' Simo asked.

'What if I put Jeric under investigation?' Tim said.

'That would stop Jeric from seeing any warrants for senior elites issued after he is placed under investigation. But if Jeric is involved, then he would have other enforcers helping him,' Max explained.

'Erzsi, invoke protocol SL9Echo3,' Tim said. 'Simo, I rescind my previous order for the arrest warrant for Nico.'

'S-S-Sir, what is that p-protocol?' Luc asked.

'Zephyrion is now officially under emergency measures. Only actions already authorised may continue, like the Exodus. I now have total authority, and all Elite Councils are suspended,' Tim replied. 'Nico and any of his cronies now have no authority. Only my emergency council, which is everyone in this room, and I can authorise changes to our planet's plans.'

Max said, 'But, Sir, you've just alerted the planet to a crisis.'

The room started to shudder and then shake violently. The books began to fall from the bookcases, and even the chairs being sat on started to dance across the room.

'I think the planet has just announced that itself,' Tim replied.

'Sir, I've just received a request to fire the Exodus machine stabiliser,' Erzsi said.

'Why are they asking? Permission granted,' Tim replied as the tremors worsened.

'They're asking because you've put us under emergency measures,' Simo said.

A few minutes later, the tremors started to subside.

'We need to get Nico. Erzsi, do you know where he is?' Tim asked.

'He's at the One World Research Centre, Sir,' Erzsi replied. 'And you've currently got 376, no 456, make that over 600 requests for an immediate call from Elite Council members around the planet.'

"Erzsi, organise calls with the regional leaders of each inhabited zone and their local Elite Council members,' Tim said.

'Starting when Tim?' Erzsi asked.

'In ten minutes,' Tim replied.

'But what about Nico?' Simo demanded.

'I don't have a choice. With the planet now under emergency measures, I have to follow protocol, which means briefing all suspended Elite Councils on why I have invoked these measures and the next steps,' Tim explained.

'Why did you invoke that protocol?' Zym asked. 'Impulsive behaviour is not your normal behaviour, Tim.'

'Because I've witnessed Zeryn's brutality first-hand,' Tim sighed. 'Everything I've heard today and my concerns about Nico mean I cannot allow him to be my deputy for one moment longer, and the emergency protocol is the only way to remove him.'

'But you've locked down the whole planet,' Simo said.

'No, he hasn't,' Max replied.

'Care to explain, Maxo?' Zym said.

Max ignored Zym's friendly name dig and said, 'Tim has just put the planet under an emergency Exodus protocol. The geologists have made it clear the amount of time Lin and her colleagues calculated to save everyone was too long compared to the planet's stability.'

'Exactly, Max. Zephyrion only has one business now: the urgent Exodus of everyone to one of the three identified planets of Astral 5, Noton 3 and Tascun 3. The fact that it removes Nico from office is a coincidental side effect,' Tim explained.

'But what about Nico?' Simo repeated.

Nico, Jeric, and Lin will be invited to the call for our region. In the meantime, take Max, Zym, and Luc to the One World Research Centre. Simo, you are the acting High Counsellor, and Max is the Head of Zephyrion defence. Whatever Nico is trying to make happen, stop him, and if you need to appoint or draft in anyone you trust, do it,' Tim said.

'Tim, Region One is waiting for you,' Erzsi said.

18
No Time to Mourn

'Lin, how are the tests going?' Nico asked.

'Far better than we could have hoped. We've sent energy meals across to Astral 5 and further planets without problems,' Lin replied.

'Excellent. We need to do the Daxson test now,' Nico said. 'I've arranged for one to be brought over right away.'

'Nico, can I have a word in private?' Jeric whispered.

'Now is not a good time.'

'You need to hear this as it's about to get far worse,' Jeric insisted.

Jeric and Nico walked towards the wrecked auditorium.

'Tim has done WHAT!' Nico bellowed.

'He's invoked the emergency protocol. It means—'

'I KNOW WHAT IT MEANS.'

'He's even had the nerve to use my assistant, Erzsi, to send out invites to our regional Council call.'

'Do you think I care about him stealing your staff? He's taken away all of my authority.'

'We'll have to stop the Daxson test,' Jeric said.

'No chance. It's Timezel that needs stopping. I should have let Dronin kill him when he wanted to.'

'But Lin will receive these messages too, so she won't agree to proceed with the test,' Jeric said.

'Good point. I'll make sure Lin does as I tell her, and you need to kill Timezel,' Nico said.

'I can't kill the Supreme Leader, Sir,' Jeric protested.

'Yes, you can. It's fairly easy, although it took me two attempts to get rid of my father,' Nico replied.

'But the emergency protocol means he'll be surrounded by armed guards,' Jeric protested.

'Do I have to do everything myself? Just lure him here and make sure he uses the new SL landcraft. After all, it is the most high-tech and attack-proof vehicle on the planet. Even the most powerful bombs can't penetrate its skin in either direction,' Nico smiled.

'But that'll make it even harder to kill him,' Jeric said.

Nico rolled his eyes. 'Maybe I want to make sure he gets here safely. Just do it and quickly. I need to get as many supportive council members here before our call as possible.'

'Yes, Sir,' Jeric replied before turning and running towards an exit.

'Lin, your Elite thingy is buzzing like crazy,' Juli shouted to the control platform.

'Oh, I forgot about that thing. I took it off when Gran had us clambering over the Exodus barrel. Can you bring it up here, please?' Lin shouted.

'I'll take it up to Lin, Juli. You've got more important things to do than be your sister's servant,' Nico laughed as he took Lin's Elite device off Juli.

'Thanks, Deputy Sup—'

'Just call me Nico. Our planet is in crisis, so I think we can park the formalities,' Nico smiled.

'Thank you, Nico,' Juli replied before heading towards the Exodus deck.

As Nico walked towards the steps leading to the control platform, he grabbed a small pointy tool from a bench and rammed it through the connection port at the bottom of the device. There was a short spark, and the device went blank. Nico dropped the tool on the floor and started walking up the stairs.

'Here you are, Lin,' Nico smiled.

'Thanks, Nico. Oh, it's dead,' Juli said.

'I swear these things eat their batteries,' Nico laughed.

'They probably do,' Juli smiled. 'I wonder why it was buzzing?'

'That would have been Timezel. He sent out a message to all members of the Elite updating them about what the geologists had told us,' Nico lied.

A deathly scream echoed around the room.

'What was that?' Gran asked, peering past Juli and Nico to see what was screaming.

'Oh, the Daxson has arrived,' Nico replied. Stay here, and I'll calm it down. Are we ready for the test?'

'Just about,' Lin replied.

Nico walked down the steps, making some soothing humming sounds. The Daxson stopped screaming and looked at Nico. Its anger seemed to subside as the intense glow of its energy soul dimmed from an almost sun-like burn, making the room unbearably bright, to just an intensely powerful light illuminating the immediate area around it.

Nico mumbled some words in a smooth, calming tone whilst gently stroking his hands down his arms.

'Are you seeing this, Lin?' Gran said, mesmerised by Nico's communication with the Daxson. 'He has a wonderful way with such a wild, uncontrollable beast.'

Nico looked up at the control platform, and in the loudest voice he thought he could risk with the Daxson, he said, 'Open the Exodus Deck door, please.'

Gran pushed a button, and the door to the deck opened.

Nico turned back to the Daxson and continued talking to it in the strange, calming rising and falling sounds and hums. 'Open the Daxson cage,' he ordered.

The guards by the cage looked at each other and ran out of the room.

'Why do people struggle to understand if you manage or neutralise the risk, you're not taking any?' Nico sighed as he stepped forward and unlocked the cage.

As everyone in the room backed themselves against the wall, Nico summoned the Daxson forward. The glow from its energy soul remained bright but steady as it looked around the room. It felt no anger or pain, just intrigue and a touch of confusion. It looked at Nico and let out a quiet, almost serene sound like the gentle touch of a finger across the strings of a harp.

Nico tilted his head and slowly pointed towards the Exodus Deck while letting out a soothing sound. The Daxson appeared to understand and walked cautiously towards the entrance to the Exodus Deck, followed by Nico. As it passed the stairs leading to the control platform, it paused and looked up at Lin and Gran, then back to Nico as it started to glow brighter.

Nico tilted his head again and hummed a soothing melodic tone, which seemed to calm the Daxson and its glow subsided. It looked back towards the control platform but then started moving towards the Exodus Deck as if Nico had satisfied the Daxson that it was safe.

As the Daxson reached the doorway, it stopped and curiously banged on the glass wall, making a noise almost as if it were laughing. Nico stood by the entrance to the Exodus Deck and motioned to the Daxson. As it entered, Nico hummed another melodic series of sounds as he slowly closed the door.

Nico quickly walked away from the Exodus Deck and ran to the control deck. 'Okay, Gran, send our friend to Astral 5.'

'Yes, Sir,' Gran replied. He checked the location devices of those working on the Exodus machine and then visually checked everyone's position before he initiated the firing process.

The ceiling split in two as the barrel slowly moved into position; the siren sounded, followed by the confirmation of, 'Target planet secured.'

'Permission to go, ma'am?'

Lin nodded, and Gran pressed the separate firing buttons. The electrical hum increased as the electronic countdown started, 'Ten, nine, eight...'

'Everyone stay where you are,' Simo shouted as he ran into the room with Max, Zym, Luc, and several other enforcers, all with their depletors drawn.

'Stop the Exodus machine, Gran,' Max shouted.

'I can't, Max. Once it starts glowing, it is already disassembling the energy soul to send it,' Gran replied. 'And please do not get closer than that circular line I've marked on the floor around the machine.'

'Gran, what's going on?' Lin said as the Exodus Deck started to glow far brighter than ever.

'...Three, two, one.'

An intense scream tore through the room.

'Gran, shut it down. You're killing the Daxson,' Lin ordered.

'I can't, Lin. Even if it were possible to stop the machine, the Daxson would be dead. According to the readings, it's been thirty percent disassembled and is being transmitted to Astral 5,' Gran said, examining the monitors.

The scream from the Exodus Deck reached such a level that almost everyone covered their ears. The Daxson's screech was haunting and tortuous in equal measure, like a thousand fingernails dragged down a board.

'Please make it stop,' Max cried.

As the deafening scream of the Daxson caused everyone else to crumple, Nico descended the stairs and retrieved a depletor from Zym's side, who was curled up on the floor in agony.

'Drop it, Zeryn,' Simo ordered.

Nico spun round to see Simo standing behind the steps with a depletor pointing towards him.

'Well, well, if it isn't my dear nephew. What an unpleasant surprise,' Nico sneered, curling his lip contemptuously. He started circling the stairs to keep them as a barrier between them.

'I'm not your nephew. I'm nothing to do with you,' Simo replied.

'I heard someone talking in Timezel's office about me being their uncle, and the fact you're the only person not crippled by the Daxson's screams proves you're the child of a Psiorite,' Nico said. 'My dear sister, Shazon, did so well to hide you. I didn't know you existed until I heard you talking earlier.'

'Don't you dare mention my mother's name,' Simo snapped.

'Simo, it is Simo, isn't it?' Nico smiled.

'That's my name,' Simo replied.

'You know your name means the one who listens in Psiorite?' Nico said.

'You're the one doing the listening. Drop that depletor and accept your defeat,' Simo snarled. 'You realise you'll be outnumbered once the Daxson stops screaming.'

Nico paused for a second before he started laughing. 'You're right, nephew. We do think so alike.'

'What do you mean?' Simo frowned.

Nico lowered his depletor and fired at almost point-blank range into the enforcer curled up on the floor near him, who evaporated. 'That's one less.'

'No-o-o...' Simo shouted, firing his depletor. Unfortunately, the stairs between them took the brunt of his shot.

'Nephew, calm down. Join me, and we can be the future for Zephyrion,' Nico said as he moved to keep the stairs between him and Simo. He glanced back and noticed Zym still at the foot of the stairs.

Simo noticed Nico glancing at Zym and snapped, 'Don't even think about it.'

Before Simo had the chance to block Zym, Nico took a shot. The blast ricocheted off the stairs and hit Zym, who started flickering. Simo dived in front of Zym and fired, but Nico quickly anticipated the move and dodged the shot.

'You don't have a future, Zeryn,' Simo replied. 'I'm going to do what my grandfather should have done.'

'Zeryn's future ended many years ago, nephew. I'm Nico now,' Nico smiled as he shot another enforcer curled up on the floor and continued to circle the stairs. 'It was a shame about the original Nico. He was a bright but naïve guy. I quite liked him.'

'I'm sure he felt so much better for that when you killed him and his brother,' Simo replied as he tried to move and shoot quickly. The depletor shot flew past Nico and hit the wall.

'I didn't kill his brother. Max proved he was the ringleader of the financial fraud, and the state sentenced him to death by Daxson,' Nico smiled.

'But he wasn't the head of that fraud, was he? You were, and you framed him. So you are responsible for his death,' Simo said, firing his depletor again.

Nico preempted the shot and moved quickly to his left as it flew past him. 'You can't blame me for Max's incompetence, nephew, and you shouldn't be trying to kill the last surviving member of your family,' Nico scowled. 'Talking of family, where's Zym's brother Max?'

'Don't even think about it,' Simo snarled, trying to avoid looking in Max's direction.

Nico noticed he was standing under the control platform and pointed the depletor straight up. 'Of course, I could take out his partner, but I need her to complete our Exodus.'

Simo considered shooting at the Exodus Deck to stop the screaming, but he remembered what Gran had said about being too close to it when it was firing.

Nico fired a few shots at others curled up on the floor. 'At this rate, it'll just be you and me, nephew.'

Simo glanced down and noticed Nico moving closer to Max. He started moving back in the opposite direction and saw a chance. He lowered his depletor and fired at Nico's foot, jutting out beyond the Exodus deck.

'Damn. That wasn't nice, nephew. It hurts,' Nico said, rubbing his foot before smiling. 'Well, it would have hurt without these metal and rubber shoes. You really should get a pair.'

The whole room was engulfed in an intense white light accompanied by a terrifying scream and then silence.

'Time's up, Zeryn,' Simo said.

'Yes, it is for your friends,' Nico replied, shooting indiscriminately around him.

Simo dived sideways to the floor and fired at Nico. His shot hit Nico's depletor, making it fly across the room.

'It's over, Zeryn,' Simo said as everyone started to move.

'Oh, nephew. You're as feeble as my father,' Nico said, pulling a device out of his pocket comprising two rings and a piece of silver wire holding them together. He slid the rings over his thumb and little finger and widened his palm, which was followed by a voice overhead saying, 'Device armed.'

Simo glanced upwards in the direction of the voice, but the control platform blocked his view.

'I've just armed this, and if the tension between these rings disappears, the device it's connected to will explode,' Nico smiled.

'Yeah, right,' Simo sneered. 'What mythical device is that?'

'Let me show you,' Nico replied, bringing his fingers closer together.

A computerised voice said, 'Firing in five, four, three...'

Simo looked up at the control platform again and saw a red glow on Lin's wrist.

Nico widened his palm, and the countdown stopped. 'Well done, nephew. You spotted it so quickly. That lovely bracelet I gave Lin to recognise her becoming a member of the Elite has a little extra surprise. If you try to kill me, Max's beloved Lin is history, along with anyone standing near her.'

'Give yourself up, Nico,' Timezel said, walking into the room surrounded by enforcers.

'Hello, Tim. I wasn't expecting to see you here. In fact, I wasn't expecting anyone ever to see you again,' Nico sneered.

'Oh, you mean that little device you planted inside my luxury landcraft? One of the two new landcraft that you insisted we have and for which you oversaw the design,' Tim replied. 'My driver noticed it doing his checks when you arranged for it to be returned this morning. I'm impressed that when it was detonated, the exterior looked untouched.'

'You know I've always taken pride in my work, Tim,' Nico sneered. 'But never mind, I've had time for a catch-up with my nephew Simo. Did you know all those years I was meeting my sister Shazon, she never once mentioned him? How devious is that?'

'I know you were the Elite Council member she was meeting,' Simo replied flatly. 'I even know you killed her.'

Nico smiled. 'I didn't kill her, nephew. But asking that Daxson to end her did us all a favour.'

Simo rushed towards Nico, 'You sick evil —'

Nico lifted his hand, 'Calm down, nephew. You wouldn't want dear Lin to die now, would you? My dear sister tried to humiliate me, saying she knew I'd lured the Daxson to kill our father but that I was unable to control it. So I had to prove I could control them.'

Around the standoff, those deafened by the Daxson started to stand and look around, trying to comprehend what had happened.

'Is everyone okay down there?' Gran shouted.

'We're all good, thank you, Gran. How's the Daxson?' Nico replied.

'I'm afraid it's dead, and its energy has all gone, and so is the Exodus machine. Trying to send it has drained the machine before it could complete the Exodus. It'll take several minutes to recharge the machine,' Gran replied.

'Where's the Daxson's remains?' Lin asked.

'There are no remains, ma'am. As the Exodus machine ran out of energy, it started using the Daxson's energy to keep going until both were depleted,' Gran replied.

'Give up now, Nico, and we may consider exiling you to your own planet,' Tim said. 'Refuse, and we will shoot you where you stand.'

Nico laughed. 'Why am I the only one who understands the concept of never taking risks? You manage and neutralise them. Nephew, you tell them why they shouldn't kill me.'

'If Nico dies, it triggers a bomb on Lin's wrist, Tim,' Simo sighed.

'WHAT!' Max shouted as he scrambled to his feet.

'Ah, there he is,' Nico smiled. 'Well done, nephew. If you hadn't shot at my foot and made me backtrack, Max would have been one of my next targets.'

A group of Elite Council members and their families entered the Grand Exodus room.

'Oh look, my friends are here,' Nico smiled. 'Esteemed friends. Our Supreme Leader seems to think we should be left on this dying planet until all his beloved Deceptors and other undesirables have been sent to safety, and he's invoked the emergency protocol to deliver it. Do you agree?'

The group mumbled their disapproval.

'That's not what I've said,' Tim protested.

'So you have no objections to these upstanding Zephyrions being sent now?' Nico asked.

Tim looked at the group of Elite members and said, 'If those present feel they deserve priority, I won't stand in their way.'

'Thank you, Supreme Leader,' Nico replied, turning to the Elite members and families. 'I know some of you want to go to Astral 5, and others would rather go to our own selected planet.

Can those going to Astral 5 stand over there, and the rest stay where you are.'

'Elite members, I should mention that after doing the first regional call to explain why I have invoked the emergency protocol, I was persuaded to come here first to prove it before doing anything more. Everything happening is being transmitted globally for all Elite Councils to see,' Tim said. 'Erzsi, is the uplink working?'

'Yes, Supreme Leader, they can all see and hear what is happening,' Erzsi confirmed.

'Zone 5 here, Supreme Leader. After what we've been told, heard and seen, you have our full backing.'

'Zone 17 here, and we agree with Zone 5.'

Each zone replied with similar messages of support, and slowly, the group going to Astral 5 either joined the others going to the other planet or dispersed.

'It seems none of your supporters want to go to a planet their fellow Zephyrions will be going to, Nico.' Tim said defiantly. Then, noting that a few had started to leave, he added, 'Some even appear to be changing their mind about supporting you.'

'They're the fools,' Nico said. 'Gran is the Exodus machine ready.'

Gran looked at Lin despairingly, but she just shook her head.

'Gran, tell me before I have to start taking action again,' Nico snapped.

Tim looked up at the control platform. 'It's okay, Lin and Gran. We don't want to stand in his way.'

'I do,' Max snarled, stepping forward and raising his depletor.

'Now, now, Max,' Nico said, bringing his fingers together.

The computerised voice said, 'Firing in five, four, three...'

Max lowered his depletor but kept staring at Nico.

'Wise decision,' Nico sneered.

'The Exodus machine has recharged enough to send twenty at a time,' Lin shouted, angrily glancing at the bracelet. She tried to slide it off, but since Nico had activated the device, it had tightened on her wrist.

'Remember, Lin. We agreed that it's that distant emergency planet. Don't try to change it, as I can see the planet's destination on the screens down here and the one inside the Exodus Deck,' Nico shouted back.

After the first six groups had been sent, only Nico and half a dozen others were left.

'It's such a shame that it's come to this. Zephyrions could have had such a wonderful future under my reign,' Nico said as he and the remaining stragglers entered the Exodus Deck.

'We are Shadowers and proud of it,' Max snarled.

'Oh, Max, your family were such a thorn in my side. None of you ever realised the world has moved on,' Nico smiled, holding up his hand as a reminder that he still had Lin's life in his hand.

Gran shouted that he was firing up the machine, and it confirmed the planet was targeted and started the countdown.

Nico turned to Max and Simo. 'At least you have each other; now everyone else is gone. It's bee—'

Max looked at Simo. 'What does he mean now everyone else —'

There was a clink as something dropped to the floor on the Exodus Deck. Max tried to see what it was as a computerised voice said, 'Firing in five, four, three, two, one.'

Lin screamed, 'Max, I love yo—' as an explosion went off on the control platform.

Max ran to the stairs and started to run up them, but Luc was already there and grabbed him.

'Let me go, Luc,' Max shouted.

'I'm sorry, Max, it's t-too late. Lin's gone,' Luc said.

'No, let me help her,' Max screamed, fighting against Luc's grasp with all his might.

Gran staggered down the steps, clearly injured and weak. He collapsed on the stairs just in front of Max and Luc and started sobbing. 'She's gone, Max. She fell onto her arm to minimise the risk to me. She's gone, and I couldn't help her.'

Max broke free of Luc, but hearing Gran, he collapsed into Gran's arms. 'Not Lin, please tell me it's not true.'

Gran looked awkwardly. He'd never had to deal with other people's emotions. Work was his normality; other people's happiness was fine, but he didn't know how to cope with such raw emotions, and he froze.

Juli ran over and hugged Max. She looked at Gran and whispered, 'It's okay, Gran. Max is just very sad.'

'Yes, Juli. It's so bad,' Gran replied stiffly as Juli lifted Max off him.

'Tim, I'm asking for your permission to take a team and pursue Zeryn. But I want to clarify: if you say no, I'll do it anyway,' Simo said.

'I won't stand in your way,' Tim replied. 'Nicoeyel's title as Deputy Supreme Leader is revoked with immediate effect, and you are authorised to use terminal force. Take anyone you need, but I think Max and Zym will be at the front of the queue.'

'Max will be, but Zeryn shot Zym,' Simo sighed.

'Zym! Where's Zym?' Max shouted from the stairs.

'He's over here,' Juli shouted. 'But I'm not sure he will be here much longer.'

19
No Turning Back

The following day, the group of volunteers Simo had organised to go after Zeryn were in the largest room of a suite of offices Tim authorised for their use in the One World Research Centre.

'Gran, can you send us to that planet with any weapons?' Simo asked.

Gran said, 'I'm sorry, Simo, but it's impossible. The Exodus machine can only send energy. We couldn't even send a Zephyrion—'

'Shadower,' Max growled. 'We are Shadowers. Zephyrions is a term the Elite came up with to make us feel inclusive. I'm a Shadower, Lin was a Shadower, Zym was a Shadower, and Simo is a Psiorite.'

'Sorry, Max. We couldn't even send a Shadower or Psiorite who hadn't transitioned,' Gran replied. 'That's why the device Nico was wearing dropped to the floor of the Exodus Deck.'

Simo looked at Max with concern. He noted the large black circles under his bloodshot eyes. Max's short hair looked dishevelled, and he wore the same uniform as yesterday. 'Have you been to sleep, Max?'

'He spent all night at the medicentre with Zym,' Juli replied.

'I'll sleep when Zeryn is dead,' Max replied. 'I've been reading everything I can about him and the planet he's gone to.'

'Talking of that planet, what do we know about KLT3.4e9.3?' Simo asked.

'Not a lot. It was eliminated as a potential Exodus location due to its existing civilisation,' Erzsi replied. 'It's a light—'

'It's a planet with a light atmosphere and a primitive but civilised population. We knew Deceptors were going there using an Exodus machine for some time, but it wasn't a priority problem according to Jeric,' Max said coldly.

'Well, it wasn't. We had so many issues here; losing a few Deceptors to a distant planet we had deselected as an Exodus target some time ago wasn't a priority,' Jeric protested.

'Except it was a priority as Nico or Zeryn or whatever had it as his getaway planet,' Max snapped.

'And how was I supposed to know that?' Jeric shouted back.

'Because you were thick as thieves with him. In fact, why are you here, Jeric?' Max snarled. 'You and Zeryn were inseparable.'

'I didn't know he was Zeryn. He was our DSL. I had to do what he told me to,' Jeric protested. 'Besides, I wasn't even there when he attacked all of you.'

'Will you two pack it in? We need to work together. Now, how light is the atmosphere?' Simo asked as a minor tremor vibrated around the room.

'We don't know. The decision to eliminate it from Operation Exodus early in the process means data isn't available. But, as a light atmosphere, we will need to inhabit locals for some time to develop an atmospheric-friendly shell based on their genetics. With the basic data I've got from Lin's notes, we are talking of anything between half a year and a year, Zephyrion time,' Max replied, glowering at Jeric.

'Excuse me, but you're talking nonsense speak to us,' Cal said.

'I agree with C-C-Cal. I hear what you're saying but don't know what it m-means,' Luc said.

'It means I'll need to train you to inhabit a local host, develop a shell and transmute. You'll also need emotional and behavioural coaxing training as your hosts will likely try hard to reject you,' Max said sharply.

'And you can do that?' Keri asked hesitantly.

'Yes, of course,' Max replied. 'You may also need to take full control and suppress them until you've finished your transmutation if they refuse to accept you.'

'B-B-But you said it could take some t-time to develop a shell,' Luc said.

'Yes, that's right. But if that's what it takes to get Nico, so be it. Do you have a problem with that?' Max replied sharply.

'N-N-No, M-M-Max,' Luc said.

'How soon before we can get going? We don't want Nico's trail going cold,' Cal asked.

'No, really? Did you ever go on one of those quiz shows? "Hi, my name is Cal, and my specialist subject is the flipping obvious," or what,' Max snapped.

Simo stood up. 'Max, can you come with me, please? I want to check something with you.'

Max followed Simo into the corridor, and they started walking towards the refreshment area of the Centre. Another more prominent tremor hit the building, causing dust to shower from the ceiling.

'Why are we here? I don't need anything to eat; I just need to get Nico,' Max grumbled.

'I did not bring you here to buy you lunch. I needed to get you away from everyone else,' Simo said.

'I knew it. One of them works for Nico, and I bet it's Jeric. Come on, he's got some questions to answer,' Max said, turning back towards the offices Timezel had provided them.

Simo grabbed Max's arm. 'Max, it's not that.'

'Well, if that's not the problem, why are we wasting time? As Cal said, the longer we wait, the colder Nico's trail is getting,' Max replied, trying to pull away.

'Max, stop. I know you hate Zeryn or Nico or whatever you want to call him, and so do I. You're also worried about Zym and grieving for Lin, but you can't take your grief out on your friends. They're doing everything they can.'

'I'm not, and if they don't want to be here, I'll do it alone,' Max growled.

'See, you're doing it again.'

'I'm not doing anything.'

'Yes, you are. You're pushing everyone away with your pain,' Simo said, grabbing a seat and sitting down, pulling Max down onto another chair.

'I don't know what to do, Simo. I've lost Lin and my parents, and they don't think Zym will survive because of Nico, and now he's on the other side of space,' Max replied, holding his head in his hands.

'I'm angry too, Max. My mum may have died a long time ago, but I've only just found out Zeryn did it, and even worse, I'm related to him.'

'I hate him, Zym, sorry Simo. I mean, I hate him, Simo. I hate Nico with every ounce of my soul.'

'It's okay, Max. Zym is a big part of all our lives, and we hope he pulls through.'

'I know Lin could be challenging for some, and she and Zym didn't like each other, but they were my family, and now one is gone, and the other is struggling to stay alive.'

'As Zym once said to me, you are as much a brother to me as anyone could be, and as for Zym and Lin, well, Zym heard Lin talking to Nico in secret. According to Zym, Nico offered to make Lin the Deputy Regent Supreme and said she could leave you all behind, but she refused and said you, Juli and Zym had to go with her,' Simo explained.

'She insisted Zym came with us too?' Max said, looking up.

'Yep, Zym said he felt so proud of her,' Simo replied.

Max looked at Simo and smiled. 'Thank you.'

'You've nothing to thank me for, but I have a favour to ask,' Simo said.

'Yeah, sure, what is it?'

'Help me get that lot ready to go to that planet, find Zeryn and teach him what we do to Deceptors,' Simo smiled.

'I think I can manage that, Simo. On one condition,' Max said.

'Which is?'

'We've both lost virtually everything, but we never lose each other,' Max replied.

'Of course, but you've still got Zym. We'll all understand if you help with the training, but stay here to look after him,' Simo said.

'Are you joking? Zym would be insufferable if I stayed here instead of pursuing Zeryn,' Max laughed. 'He'd accuse me of being scared!'

'You're probably right. Come on, I want us on that planet within two days. If we can't take weapons with us, we will have to work out how to use theirs and get used to their landcraft and communicators,' Simo said.

'You do remember me saying it was a primitive civilisation, don't you?' Max asked.

'Yeah, I assume that means they're still using fossil fuels and having to pass electricity through wires rather than it just being in the atmosphere,' Simo replied.

'I think you may need a bit of training too. From what I've read, it's a little more rustic than that,' Max laughed. 'Come on, let's get Ni... no, let's get Zeryn. Poor Nico was another of Zeryn's victims and doesn't deserve his name dragged into this.'

Another tremor struck as Max and Simo started walking back to the others.

'I hope the Exodus programme is going well, or we'll all be victims soon,' Max said.

'Gran and Juli were telling me they're all pushing the Exodus machines to maximum and doubling the number of people sent per exit,' Simo replied.

'Is that safe?' Max asked as another tremor caused them both to steady themselves against the wall.

'Safer than staying on Zephyrion.'

As Max opened the office door, he heard Luc talking.

'S-So according to this site, you n-need to think about separating to s-start the t-t-tra-a-a...'

'The transmutation process,' Max said, walking back into the room with Simo.

'That's right, M-Max,' Luc replied nervously.

Max shut the door and turned slowly, giving himself time to consider and reconsider what to say. 'I'm sorry I've been a nightmare. Cal, I had no right to speak to you like that, nor to you, Luc. Juli, you're suffering every bit as much as me, and yet I was the one behaving like the only one grieving. If anyone wants to pull out of going after Zeryn, I will support their decision.'

Juli and Keri walked over to Max and hugged him.

'If you think for one second I'm letting you get that nasty piece of work without me, you're in for a shock, Max,' Juli said with a smile.

'And the same for me, too. Anyone who can speak to my Cal like you did without him slapping them deserves our support,' Keri replied.

Max looked around the room as Luc, Paulie, Kendra, and the others nodded in agreement. 'I don't deserve you lot.'

'Shut up and get on with it,' Erzsi said with a smile. 'I've told Tim we'll go in the next few days.'

Max paused and turned to Gran. 'Yeah, about that. Gran, how long will it take to build an Exodus machine to bring us back once we get Zeryn? Oh, and from now on, we never call him Nico. Nico was another of Zeryn's victims.'

'I've examined the planet's geology, and the spectroscopic reading confirmed the presence of both novasium and luminae.

Novasium seems widespread in small pockets, but luminae is rare. However, there is a seam near the landing site Ni...Zeryn was sent to,' Gran replied.

'Which means?' Max asked.

'Building the machine and obtaining adequate quantities of both should take maybe half a year,' Gran replied.

'What power and other technology will we need?' Simo asked.

'Just the normal computers and electricity like we have here in the atmosphere,' Gran said. 'Nothing special.'

'Assuming it takes half a year to track him down, we should be back in about a year then?' Kendra said.

'Not too bad,' Paulie replied, doodling on her pad.

'Woah. Don't get carried away, everyone. Gran, assume computers don't exist, and there is no electricity,' Max said.

Everyone started laughing and shaking their heads.

'Max, electricity exists naturally in the upper atmosphere, and we just draw on it. How can anything exist without computers?' Gran said.

'It may do here, but Lin's notes and my research when tracking the Deceptors going there before Jeric dismissed it showed the planet was very primitive, with no computers or electricity. Apparently, they rely on animals to pull their landcraft, and they have no technology,' Max replied.

'Without computers or electricity, there is no way back,' Gran said.

'That's what I thought you'd say. This is effectively a one-way trip then,' Max said.

'I don't care. If it means I can end Zeryn, I'm going,' Juli said. 'Besides, knowing there's novasium and luminae there means we can eventually return to Astral 5 or one of the other planets. It's just going to be a while.'

'I'm going too,' Gran said. 'That planet may not be ready for us to build an Exodus machine, but I'll do anything to help catch the Project Leader's killer.'

'So we have a scientist, and I'm a technician and junior engineer, but we need a senior engineer,' Juli said.

'Why?' Jeric asked.

'As a scientist, Gran knows how it should work. As a technician, I know how to make it work, but we need an engineer to build it to the right tolerances. In theory, any of us could make it, but together, we can do it quicker and make it work better,' Juli explained.

'Fion is a great engineer. I'm sure she'd be willing to come along,' Gran suggested. 'I'll message her now.'

'Okay, Gran. Ask her. But, as it's a one-way journey, or at least it could be a long time to get back, does anyone need to drop out?' Max asked.

'Max, my partner's disabilities would make it hard on such a planet. I can't come yet. But I'll do everything I can to help,' Erzsi replied.

'Erzsi, you've done so much already. Take care of him,' Max replied.

'But I feel guilty for not going with you,' Erzsi said emotionally.

Max walked over to Erzsi, and they hugged. 'I've got an even more important job for you if you don't mind.'

'Anything, Max.'

'Take care of Zym for me, and when he recovers, make sure he doesn't do anything stupid,' Max replied.

'It will be my honour,' Erzsi said with a smile.

'M-M-Max, I've got a question,' Luc said.

'Yes, Luc,' Max replied.

'I've r-read the theory on t-t-t-transmutation about how we need to b-b-build a shell over a p-p-period of time, but what if we get killed t-t-transmuting?' Luc asked.

'We are energy souls, so we can't be killed unless our energy is depleted or exposed to a light atmosphere and dissipates. Whether we are in a host building the shell or even after transmuting into the shell if we are attacked, we can repair the shell, or if the injuries are too bad, we can jump into another local body as long as there isn't already a Shadower in it, of course. One host, one Shadower, you can't get into a host if a Shadower is already inside.' Max explained.

'But that means we can't kill Zeryn,' Simo said.

'Thanks to you, we can,' Max said. 'That immobiliser you got from the medidoc got me thinking. If we immobilise the host or shell first, it traps the energy soul. If we kill that host or shell, the energy soul will float out and dissipate in the light atmosphere.'

Gran scowled. 'I've already said only energy can be sent through the Exodus machine. This immobiliser thing can't be sent.'

'It's okay, Gran. We don't need you to. The technology relies on our energy. When we get to the planet, we can build our own, immobilise Zeryn and then kill his shell, which will kill him,' Max said.

'That's flipping genius,' Simo said.

Erzsi's communicator rang, 'Hi Tim. Yes, they're all here. Oh, okay, let me connect you to a holoscreen.'

Erzsi tapped her device, and a life-size hologram showed Tim in a room surrounded by computer screens and four scientific-looking people.

'How's the training going?' Tim asked.

'We're making good progress. We should be ready after another full training day,' Simo replied.

'I was worried you'd say that?' Tim said.

'Why?' Juli asked.

'You may have noticed we've had a few tremors today,' Tim said as another slight tremor shook the room.

'We did. Is it going to stop the Exodus programme?' Juli asked.

'That's why I need to speak to you. The geologists tell me we're heading into a brief period of high-tremor activity, and it would be better to ride it out than try to use an Exodus machine to halt them,' Tim said.

'What timescale are we talking about?' Max asked.

'They think you have a few hours left before the tremors will be too frequent to risk sending anyone much further than Astral 5, and a day or so later, not even that will be safe,' Tim said. 'It'll then be two or three weeks before it settles down.'

'But if they can still go to Astral 5, why is it a problem for us?' Cal asked.

'Because the further away the target planet is, the wider the landing area will be if there are vibrations at this end. Meaning the Exodus beam could even miss the planet,' Gran explained. 'Think of it like shining a light. Point it at a wall near you, and your natural shake will make it move a bit, but point it at a wall further away and shaking the same will make the beam move across a wider area.'

'What is their recommendation for us leaving?' Max asked.

'To be honest, they say in the next hour,' Tim replied.

'In which case, Tim, thank you for your support and good luck to you, our home planet and its citizens,' Max said.

'B-B-But w-we're n-not ready,' Luc said.

'We've got one hour to answer any questions and tell you everything you need to know about arriving on the planet, getting a host, persuading them to accept you and start transmuting,' Simo said. 'Everything else we can explain when we're there.'

Over the next hour, Fion joined them as Max, Simo, Jeric, and some of the more experienced enforcers imparted their knowledge about light atmosphere planets.

'I'm sorry, I'm a bit late to this, but how can we be sure there'll be hosts where we land?' Fion asked.

'I can't guarantee it, but using the data we have from our scans, we have identified areas where there are only a few buildings but where there seem to be gatherings of the planet's inhabitants,' Gran said. 'So I'll try to get us there.'

'Won't that cause a scene if we suddenly appear amongst them?' Cal asked.

'There's a strong likelihood that some of you may land directly inside them. But if I aim for the outer edge of their gathering sites, it may be safer,' Gran replied.

'If one of us goes first, we could try to get hosts into more isolated places. Plus, if we send smaller groups, they'll be less likely to draw attention,' Jeric suggested.

'Good idea, Jeric,' Simo agreed as another tremor vibrated through the room.

'I think that was our alarm call, folks,' Max said. 'Let's go.'

A few minutes later, they were in the Grand Exodus room.

'Nerin is very experienced using the Exodus machine as she's been one of the three in charge of the mass Exodus from here,' Gran explained. 'She knows where to send us, and there's nobody I would trust more with my life.'

'It's a good job, as Nerin will have your life in her hands,' Keri joked.

'Well, this is it, my friends. The next time we are together, we will be on a new planet,' Max said.

'This is for our friends and family. Zeryn, we are coming for you,' Simo said.

Jeric approached the Exodus Deck and waved to Nerin before turning round. 'See you there.'

Nerin fired up the Exodus machine as everyone else stood in the safe zones.

The machine started to hum, and an electronic voice said, 'Target planet secured.'

The electrical hum increased, and the Exit Deck filled with a bright light. The electronic voice started the countdown, 'Ten, nine, eight, seven, six, five, four, three, two, one.'

A flash of white light shot out of the barrel's upper end towards the stars.

'Ready for the next group,' Nerin shouted.

'Gran, you and Fion are only going next if you have a couple of enforcers with you,' Max said.

Over several minutes, the rest of the group were sent on their way.

In reality, the journey had taken a few days, but to those sent, it felt like minutes before they were arriving on a new planet.

When Jeric opened his eyes, the bright, clear light was almost blinding. He spotted a burly alien nearby and dived into him.

'Quid agitur?' the man asked.

Jeric paused momentarily, reading the man's mind, 'I'll tell you what's happening, my friend. It's your worst nightmare. But look on the bright side; I'll probably let you live, unlike the clowns about to arrive. And Zeryn, you may think you manage or neutralise risks? Well, how about this for neutralising them?'

20
VENI, VIDI, MERCATUM FECI

Gran and Fion appeared simultaneously but couldn't see the two enforcers sent with them.

'Look, there's some aliens over there. We need to get to them,' Gran said, grabbing Fion's hand.

'Gran, Fion, I'm Jeric,' a tall male said to them. 'Quickly, this way, I've got you some hosts.'

'But, Jeric, there's some there,' Gran protested.

'I'm feeling strange,' Fion said.

'They've got Shadowers in already. Quick, come on before it's too late,' Jeric said.

Fion staggered and said, 'But, I don't think I...'

With a quick flash, her energy soul dissipated as she tried to scream.

'Fion!' Gran cried. 'Jeric, help m...'

'Two down,' Jeric thought out loud as Gran dissipated into the atmosphere. He glanced towards the crowd and noticed two people talking to each other and glancing around in a confused state. 'They must have landed in two hosts. Never mind, there's plenty of time to get them.'

Luc appeared a few feet from Jeric and ran towards him. When he bounced off the man's body, he looked confused.

'Luc, it's me, Jeric. Come this way. I've got some hosts over here,' Jeric said reassuringly as he grabbed Luc's arm.

'N-N-No, there's some right there,' Luc said, trying to break free.

'Relax, Luc, this won't take long,' Jeric replied. 'It'll soo—'

Jeric crashed to the floor with a thud.

'Come on,' Max shouted, grabbing Luc. 'This atmosphere is incredibly light.'

They reached the edge of a small group of people, and Max pushed Luc into one host before diving into another.

'Quid es?' the boy asked.

'There's no time to explain who or what I am,' Max said, grabbing the girl he had pushed Luc into and running back to where they'd left Jeric, but he had disappeared.

'Max, is that you?' Luc said, struggling to control his host's body.

'Yes, it's me. Remember what I taught you about suppressing your host. It's not for long. Once the rest are here, we can explain to them,' Max replied as Simo, Cal, and others arrived.

Over the next few minutes, Max and Luc raced against time to get everyone into hosts, but the lighter-than-expected atmosphere meant they lost several colleagues as they dissipated faster than anticipated.

After Paulie arrived and confirmed she was the last one, Max led them away from the people who appeared to be milling around stalls selling things.

'*Is it this way?*' Max asked.

'*Rogō, nōn noceās mihi,*' the boy pleaded.

'*I'm not going to hurt you. I need your help.*' Max thought. '*You don't need to speak. Just think what you want to say to me.*'

'*Esne umbra?*' the boy said.

'*No, I'm not a ghost, and I am friendly. My name is Max.*'

'*My name is Gaius,*' the boy replied.

Max sighed with relief. It was much easier when the host started understanding and speaking the same language. '*Hello, Gaius. I promise we just need your help. Will you help me take your friends and mine to somewhere quiet, and we will explain why we need your help.*'

'*I don't know most of these citizens, Sir, except for my sister, Livia. Please, you won't hurt her, will you?*' Gaius pleaded.

'*I swear we will not harm any of you. Please help us,*' Max replied.

'*Very well. Head towards those old buildings. Nobody uses them now,*' Gaius said. '*Why can't I control my body?*'

'*Because I have taken control. I'm sorry, and I swear I'll let you have control back, but I need to speak to everyone first,*' Max replied.

'*If that is true, let me control myself, and I'll take you to the buildings so you can speak to your friends,*' Gaius said.

'*Sorry, Gaius, but I can already read your mind, and I know you're asking so you can try to run,*' Max said.

'*But how is that possible?*' Gaius asked.

'*Think about your question?*' Max suggested.

'*But I'm asking you. I don't know how... oh, I see. We can see what each other is thinking and see each other's memories. What hell is that place?*' Gaius thought, alarmed at the images.

'*That is where I am from, Zephyrion,*' Max explained.

'*But those tall things. Do you really live in them?*' Gaius asked.

Max sighed. It is always challenging on any planet when you first go into a host. There are so many questions that they can answer themselves.

'*That's rude, Sir. How am I supposed to know I can answer questions by thinking? I've never been inhabited by a... Shadower before,*' Gaius protested.

'*I'm sorry, Gaius. You're right, and I'm sorry. I've had a difficult few days,*' Max thought.

'*Well, my day isn't exactly what I planned, Sir,*' Gaius replied defiantly.

They arrived at the abandoned buildings and gathered inside. The air was heavy, mixing damp earth, old stone, and decay. As they ran into the building, the dust stirred up, dancing across the beams of light shining through the cracks in the ceiling and walls.

Max stood at the front of the group and called out the names of those who came with him to the planet. 'It looks like we've lost seven colleagues, including Gran and Fion. Juli, did I hear you say you were here?'

A man stood up and said, 'I'm here, Max. This is Cornelius Felix of Pompeii.'

'Wow, Juli, you're a man. Well, we still have our technician, but we've lost our scientist and engineer,' Max said.

'*You don't seem very sad about losing your friends,*' Gaius thought.

'*I am sad, but I've lost so much. It is what it is now,*' Max replied.

'*Oh, your uxor, Lin, was killed by this Zeryn, and he's badly injured your frater, Zym,*' Gaius exclaimed. '*I would want him killed too.*'

'*We don't have wives. We have partners, and yes, Lin was mine, and Zym is my brother,*' Max answered.

A small but wealthy-looking woman stood up and said, 'Max, I'm Kendra. Bobi and I were sent straight into a host. The Exodus disoriented us, but we saw someone grabbing Fion and Gran.'

'That was Jeric. I managed to stop him from doing the same to Luc,' Max replied.

A young girl stood up and said, 'Max, I'm Luc, and thank you for saving me. This is Livia, the younger sister of Gaius, who I think you are in.'

'Yes, Luc. I can feel Gaius's love for you,' Max replied.

'*I don't understand this love thing you talk of, but she is my soror or sister as you call them, and I will do anything to save her,*' Gaius said.

'*That is love*,' Max replied. '*Or at least one type of it*.'

'*Ah. Love is like amor*,' Gaius replied.

'Can you or Gaius help me? Livia is scared, and I need help making her realise I mean no harm,' Luc said.

'Of course, Luc. It seems we'll be spending a lot of time together in the, uh, food preparation areas for someone called Dominus Caesar,' Max replied. 'I'm sure the three of us can help Livia.'

'Luc, you're not stuttering,' a man said behind him.

Luc turned and looked confused, 'Who are you?'

'I am Decimus Junius Brutus Albinus,' the man said.

'Okay, Decimus, Luc was asking me, not you. It's me, Simo.'

'Well, how am I supposed to know he's not talking to me but the thing inside me?' Decimus challenged.

'I'm not a thing. I'm a Psiorite,' Simo protested.

'Blimey, Simo, you're so tall,' Luc said, interrupting the argument.

'No, Luc, you're just a young girl,' Simo laughed.

'I'm fifteen, thank you,' Livia retorted.

'And a feisty fifteen by the sound of it,' Simo replied.

'But you're right, my stutter has gone,' Luc said. 'Livia has cured me.'

'I'm fifteen, too. I'm Cal, and this is Appius,' Cal laughed, although, to the others, he was a scruffy-looking boy.

'Cal, is that you?' an elegant female in her early twenties asked. 'It's me, Keri, and this is Tullia Flavus.'

'Okay, you've got time to get used to your new selves later. There's fifteen of us left, so we must concentrate on the target,' Max said.

'Do you mean Zeryn or Jeric?' Luc asked.

'Zeryn is our priority,' Max replied.

'We need to understand what tracking devices they have on this planet. I don't think they'll have anything like Cogi, but we need communicators and some way to divide the city into zones,' Simo said.

'Is it just me? When I think of Cogi, I'm just getting a blank response,' Paulie said. 'It's like they don't have any home or work assistant devices.'

'I'm getting a blank response, too,' Keri said. 'Also, Tullia is saying they use tabellerii, which seems to be people running or riding big four-legged animals called horses, to communicate. It's like our couriers except instead of delivering packages, they deliver messages.'

'Do they not have ways to contact each other directly? What if they need to discuss something?' Cal asked.

'Decimus says they meet in the Forum, or one invites the other to their domus, which seems to mean their dwelling,' Simo said.

'Gaius says that's where a lot of discussions happen over wine and food,' Max replied.

'So the only way to communicate is by talking face to face or by messengers?' Keri said. 'This seems ancient.'

'We'll need to use their landcraft to get around the city quickly if we want to find Zeryn,' Paulie said.

'Erm, according to Cornelius, they get around by horseback or carpentum, which is some sort of horse-pulled landcraft or carriage,' Juli said. 'That's if the journey was too far to walk.'

'So communicating is in person and travel is by foot or by using an animal?' Max said.

'This is going to be impossible,' Simo said. 'How can we find Zeryn in such a backward place?'

'We know Zeryn is power-mad, so he'll be linked to somewhere called the Senate,' Max replied.

'I'm a Senator,' Decimus said proudly.

Simo added, 'It's true. I can see Decimus is an influential person in this place.'

'Can Decimus help us try to find Zeryn?' Max asked.

'If anyone behaves out of character, he says he'll know,' Simo replied. 'But he asked, what do you mean about food preparation for Dominus Caesar?'

'We work with our mother. We are responsible for preparing the food and drink for the Dominus and his guests. That's why we were at the market today,' Livia said proudly.

'But Caesar as in the former proconsul of Gaul, Julius Caesar?' Decimus asked.

'Yes, Sir,' Gaius said. 'It is good to be back in Rome. Gaul was fine, but Rome is where life is.'

Max watched as everyone started talking to each other, a crazy mix of Shadower's expectations against Roman reality.

'Gaius, have you had time to read my thoughts and understand that I mean you no harm?' Max thought.

'Dominus Max, I not only understand you, but I feel sorry for your pain. I cannot imagine what I would do if someone killed Livia in the same way Lin was killed,' Gaius thought.

'I need to build a device that traps Deceptors like Zeryn. Do you have conductive materials like antrium?' Max asked.

'Yes, Dominus Max, many homes have atriums,' Gaius replied.

'You don't need to call me Dominus, although I appreciate the respect. But I'm not referring to an open space in your dwellings. I mean the metal that conducts electricity,' Max said.

'Electricity? What is that?'

'It's the thing that powers computers, communicators, landcraft, and a lot of our lives,' Max replied.

'Images flash through my mind as you say those words, but I don't understand what they are or what they have to do with atriums.'

'They've nothing to do with atriums, Gaius. Those images are things we have on my home planet.'

'I can see them, but they make no sense. You talk into a box, and someone can hear you and reply from...sorry, but from anywhere on your planet? Is that like speaking to someone in Northern Gaul from Rome?'

'Yes, that is what it means,' Max replied.

'*But if you can talk over such great distances and have such amazing technology, why are things so bad? Why would this Zeryn want to give up such a perfect life?*' Gaius asked, confused by what he could see.

Max sighed. '*Because the better things are, the more people want. As for our amazing technology, it enabled us to escape our planet, which is on the brink of collapsing. We came to your planet to capture Zeryn. He was trying to overthrow our government and become the Regent Supreme, the leader of the whole planet.*'

'*And he killed your family and even his own. Oh, do I understand correctly that Decimus Brutus is related to him?*'

'*Not Decimus, but Simo inside Decimus is Zeryn's nephew.*'

'*Then surely you want death for Simo, too? But you don't. You think of him like your frater, sorry, I mean brother. But why?*'

'*The more you can read my thoughts, the more you'll understand why. Simo only found out recently that Zeryn was his uncle and that Zeryn killed Simo's mum and grandfather,*' Max replied. '*Now, what about that metal?*'

'*I think I understand about the metal you seek. We have lodestone or ferrum that may have the qualities you need.*'

'*Ah, yes, ferrum seems to be like antrium. We need some thin wires or strips of it. Do you have any?*' Max replied.

'*I have an acus,*' Gaius replied, pulling a needle from his pocket.

Max studied the needle Gaius held up. '*That's perfect. We need a few other things, but having antrium, or ferrum as you call it, is the main thing.*'

'Please listen,' Max shouted. 'We have what we need to create the immobilisers. I'll try to build one, and if it works, I'll tell you what you need. In the meantime, we need to keep a low profile. Try to blend in with your host's life and see if you can find out about any Shadowers or Deceptors here. Let's explore this Rome place and meet back in a few days.'

'How will we know if we find Zeryn, Jeric or any of the more than one hundred Elite Council members and families who came here?' Keri asked.

'Hi Keri, it's me, Paulie, and this is Atia. I forgot to introduce her earlier,' Paulie said, standing up as a slim, tall, elegant Mediterranean woman dressed in fine silks. 'Atia tried to see me in her speculum, and we made a discovery.'

Paulie handed Keri the speculum, a small, highly polished metal disc in a frame.

'It's like a mirror,' Keri said, looking at it. 'Oh, my word, Tullia, you are stunning—with your long black hair and deep brown eyes.'

'Never mind admiring your host. What else do you see?' Paulie said in frustration.

'Could you give me a clue?' Keri said, moving the speculum around as she admired Tullia's looks.

'Oh, for goodness sake. Is there an aura, like a glowing light around you?' Paulie replied.

'Oh yeah,' Keri said before turning the speculum to examine others' reflections. 'Look, Cal, you've got an aura too, and you Juli.'

As they all took turns looking in the speculum, Cal asked, 'If these Romans all have auras, how will that help?'

'Because these Romans don't have auras, it's our auras we can see,' Paulie answered. 'Atia said she never had an aura before I arrived.'

'Great work, Paulie,' Max said. 'We all need to have one to check others for auras. But it also means we need to be careful. If our hosts can see them, the other Romans may be able to.'

'There is a stall on the market selling them,' Kendra said. 'My brother runs it. Oh, I mean Fabia's brother. It's so confusing having our host's thoughts and ours together.'

'*I don't have pecunia or money as you call it,*' Appius moaned.

'I'm afraid my host can't buy one as he lacks money,' Cal said.

'I'm not surprised he is but a pauper,' Tullia sneered.

'Tullia, that's awful,' Keri snapped back at herself.

'But it's true. I bet he doesn't even have a home,' Tullia protested.

'It's true,' Cal said. 'Appius says he lives on the streets.'

'Not anymore,' Paulie replied. I've asked Atia, and she's agreed he can stay in our servant's quarters.'

'Over my dead body,' Tullia said indignantly. 'My brother will never allow it.'

'Your brother is my husband, and that is the end of the discussion. We let you stay, and I feel Appius has far better manners,' Atia retorted.

'*Thank you, Atia,*' Paulie thought.

'*There's no need to thank me,*' Atia replied. '*Anything that annoys Tullia is fun. She's so full of herself.*'

'Kendra, can you show us where Fabia's brother's stall is so we can all get some of these mirror things?' Max asked.

'Of course, but can I suggest you come to the stall in small groups to avoid suspicion,' Kendra said.

'*Max, we need to go. We haven't got the food we need for Dominus Caesar's meal,*' Gaius said.

'Good idea, Kendra,' Max replied. 'Luc and I will go first, and don't forget to be back here in three days.'

Kendra told Max and Luc to give her time to return to the stall and talk to her brother before they arrived.

When they arrived, Max picked up a small mirror, pretending to admire it but scanning the reflections of people around him.

'It's a fine piece of craftsmanship, young man,' Kendra said.

'It'll cost you two denarii,' the man beside Kendra said.

'Gaius, that's Dominus Caesar's money. We can't spend it,' Livia protested.

'Did you hear that, Manius? This is for the house of Julius Caesar,' Kendra said.

'Then he can afford to pay double,' Manius replied.

'Please, Sir. How about one as?' Max asked.

'Make that one sestertius, and I might agree,' Manius said, folding his arms.

'But that's four as, Sir,' Max answered.

'And it's one-quarter of a denarius. So I think that's fair, boy,' Manius replied.

'We'll let you take two for one sestertius,' Kendra replied with a wink.

'Thank you,' Max replied as Livia picked up a more ornately framed mirror.

Manius shouted, 'Hey, that's for one —'

'My brother means that's one for you and one for your sister,' Kendra said firmly.

'But...' Manius started to say.

Kendra ignored him and leant forward, whispering to Max, 'They can't see our auras either. I asked Manius if he could see a glow around me as I pretended it might be a fault, but he checked several, and only I could see it.'

'Great, let the others know,' Max whispered before he turned and left with Livia.

'What did you say to him?' Manius demanded.

'I just said make sure Caesar knows it's from Manius Albinus, the finest speculum maker in Rome,' Kendra replied with a smile.

'Hmmm, sometimes, sister. I'm not sure if you're clever at business or just clever at playing me,' Manius laughed.

'Come on,' Livia said, pulling her brother by the arm.

'What's the rush?' Max asked. 'We've got the speculums.'

'Because we need to get Dominus Caesar's food, and the stalls are running out of the freshest,' Gaius replied.

Livia screeched to a halt and looked at her brother. 'What was that?'

'What?' Gaius asked.

'Your voice. You said two things, but your voice sounded different as you asked a question and then answered it,' Livia replied with a puzzled look.

'Oh, can you tell us apart?' Max asked.

'I thought you sounded a bit different, but hearing you both talking one after the other was weird,' Livia said.

'Do we sound different too?' Luc asked.

'Well, maybe it's best you never talk in front of anyone who knows Livia,' Max laughed.

'Can we get on, please!' Gaius said. 'We can't serve the Dominus rotting food.'

After travelling around the stalls, Gaius and Livia were getting increasingly frustrated.

'All the quality cuts of meat have gone, and these vegetables are so limp,' Livia groaned. 'We can't serve the Dominus these.'

'He'll be expecting platters of food to choose from,' Gaius sighed.

'Don't worry, I'm quite good in the kitchen,' Max said.

'The kitchen?' Gaius queried. 'Ah, you mean a culina.'

'We are also very good in a culina,' Livia replied indignantly.

'I'm good with bread,' Luc said, trying to be helpful.

'First things first, we need plenty of eggs,' Max said.

'Eggs? Oh, you mean ova. You can't just cook ius in ovis coctis,' Gaius protested.

'I think you'll find they're a lot more than sauce with cooked eggs,' Max replied. 'Where I come from, we call them frittatas.'

'I don't think that stupid name will ever be popular,' Livia said, folding her arms.

'Come on, we need to get a lot more ingredients. Let's grab those vegetables and some herbs and go to that cooked meats place over there,' Max said.

'Do you have any flour in your dwelling?' Luc asked.

'Yes, there is flour, but it's too late to make bread,' Livia replied.

'Not the sort I'm making, and we'll need cheese too,' Luc said.

21
JUST AN OMELETTE

'Where is the fresh meat?'

'It didn't look very good quality, Mater,' Gaius lied.

'You went out early to make sure you got the best cuts,' Gaius's mother, Marcia, insisted.

'We did try, Mater. Gaius asked the carnifex if he had any more, but he said he'd had a lot of customers buying in bulk,' Livia said.

'*Carnifex?*' Luc thought. '*Ah, a butcher. Your language is so strange.*'

'*I've got someone from another planet inside me, and you've got the nerve to say our language is strange?*' Livia replied.

'*I guess you've got a point there,*' Luc laughed.

'You know how much the Dominus loves meat,' Marcia said.

'We've got cooked meats and cheeses,' Max said.

'You say that like I should be impressed, Gaius. And drop that strange voice; it's not impressing anyone. I'll go and see what I can find. In the meantime, prepare those sorry-looking vegetables,' Marcia said, storming out of the kitchen.

'What are you doing?' Livia demanded.

'I'm making wrapees,' Luc said.

'But we don't have time for bread to rise,' Livia replied.

'These don't need to rise. Just a short time to rest and then two or three minutes to cook,' Luc said.

'You can't bake bread that quickly,' Livia protested.

'Wrapees aren't like bread in that way; they're more like libum. They're ideal for encasing other ingredients,' Luc said. 'Flour, water, salt and some things like these herbs, onions and even a bit of cheese.'

'Sounds dreadful,' Livia replied. 'Libum wrapped around things? It's all dough.'

'Just wait and see,' Luc replied.

'Why are you cracking open so many ova?' Gaius asked.

'Because eggs are the base for our frittatas,' Max replied. 'Besides, these eggs are tiny. Ours are twice the size of these with green shells.'

'Green?' Gaius cringed. 'They sound disgusting.'

'Says someone from a planet where the centre is yellow instead of pink.'

'Pink? I'm so pleased you didn't bring yours here,' Gaius replied. 'To think I was going to say cooked ova are boring.'

'Not the way I do them,' Max answered.

An hour later, Marcia walked back into the kitchen to see platters full of different foods, from frittatas filled with various fillings, including cheeses, hams, sausages, and vegetables with herbs, to wrapees encasing fried and charred vegetables, cheese, and meat. Alongside were dips made from olive oil, garlic, leeks, and honey.

'What is this?' Marcia demanded. 'Those look like ova dishes, but I've never done them like these different ones. What are those things like filled parchment?'

'Try them, Mater,' Livia said proudly. 'We've made lots of different wrapees.'

'And taste the frittatas. They are like the food of Gods,' Gaius added.

'Hmm,' Marcia said, trying a wrapee. 'Oh my word, this is good, and those fritties are incredible.'

'Frittatas,' Gaius corrected.

'How did the pair of you learn to cook like this?' Marcia said.

Livia said, 'We had help from —'

'From the people in the market,' Gaius said. 'They knew we were from the domus of Caesar.'

'I don't know how you've done it, but you've made these lamb and chicken dishes boring compared to those vegetable frit things and wrapees,' Marcia said. 'Come on, the Dominus will be expecting his food soon.'

Gaius, Livia and Marcia carried the food to the dining room or triclinium as the Romans called it. A while later, they were summoned to a meeting with Dominus Julius Caesar.

'By what God does this food match my expectations?' Caesar asked.

'I'm sorry, my lord, we had problems at the market,' Marcia replied.

'Well, I can only be grateful you did,' Caesar said. 'Those flatbread things are great, but what are those yellow things? They must be ova, but I've never tasted anything so incredible.'

'They are my son, Gaius's invention, Dominus. He calls them frittatatas,' Marcia said.

'My mater means frittatas, Sir,' Max replied.

'Well, whatever you call them, young Gaius, I want them at my banquet tomorrow and as a regular treat,' Caesar said with a smile.

Across Rome, Decimus and Cornelius came across a rowdy bar and decided to enter.

'Are you sure about this?' Simo asked.

'I have to find out what happened to those cleaners,' Juli replied. 'Besides, they will never recognise you as Decimus or me as Cornelius.'

'Why are you making me come here?' Decimus demanded. 'I'm a senator, and this area is full of raucous cauponae or bars as you call them, where citizens of my standing don't belong. Oh, is that Marcellus Cassius?'

'Decimus, we don't normally see you down here,' Marcellus said, hugging Decimus. 'Who is your friend?'

'This is Cornelius Felix of Pompeii. He's a friend of my...I mean a friend of mine,' Decimus said.

'A pleasure to meet you, Cornelius. I've been considering investing in Naples or Pompeii,' Marcellus replied.

'Don't go for Naples. Pompeii is the place to be. It has a prosperous urban economy and exports many local products. Its future is secure, but Naples is waning,' Cornelius said.

'Wise words, my friend. Why have you brought your friend down here, Decimus?' Marcellus asked.

'I thought I'd see what I'm missing out on,' Decimus replied nervously.

'You're in for a treat. This is Claudia and Sabina's favourite place,' Marcellus replied.

'Who?' Decimus asked.

'A strange couple. Claudia used to be known as Valeria, widow of Lucius Sulla, and Sabina used to be known as Claudia, Valeria's friend,' Marcellus laughed, slapping Decimus on his back. 'But enough of them, let's have some wine and fun.'

'Why are they strange?' Simo asked.

'Decimus, my friend, just wait until you meet them. They talk of a world with tall buildings and carriages without horses,' Marcellus replied.

They ordered a jug of wine and moved to the side of the bar.

'To friendship and good times,' Decimus said, raising his glass.

'*I thought citizens of your standing didn't come down here?*' Simo thought.

'*It's more civilised in this bar than others*,' Decimus replied. '*Besides, have you not heard of the phrase, when in Rome do as the Romans do*,'

'*As I've only been on your planet less than a day, no, I've not heard that phrase*,' Simo said.

'Let the wine flow!' Cornelius said, raising a glass.

'*This tastes like alcohol*,' Juli thought as Cornelius took a large swig of red wine.

'*I know not what you mean by alcohol, but it is vinum or wine*,' Cornelius replied, taking another swig.

'*But I don't drink alcohol*,' Juli said as she already started to feel light-headed.

Several shared jugs of wine later, two vibrant noble women entered the bar, bringing a buzz of contagious energy.

'Well, look at the crowd in here tonight. There's a lot of handsome citizens,' Claudia said with a swagger.

Sabina glanced around the bar and nudged her sister, 'Claudia, look, Marcellus is here.'

The women approached the table, smiling at Marcellus and his friends.

'Marcellus, you saucy Senator. What a delight to see you,' Claudia said.

'Claudia, the pleasure is mine. Will you and Sabina join us for some wine and revelry?' Marcellus asked.

'Marcellus, you are so naughty. The old Valeria in me would never let me drink with a group of strangers,' Claudia laughed.

'Where are my manners,' Marcellus replied. 'Claudia and Sabina, let me introduce my fellow senator Decimus Albinus and his friend Cornelius um...'

'Cornelius Felix of Pompeii,' Cornelius said.

'A delight to meet you all,' Claudia smiled. 'So what must a lady do to get a drink?'

'Allow me,' Decimus said, going to get another flagon of wine and two more goblets.

Cornelius pulled out the mirror he had bought earlier in the market and pretended to look at himself while trying to check Claudia and Sabina.

'You know only we can see the auras,' Claudia whispered.

'Are you from Zephyrion?' Juli replied.

'So you're not really Cornelius then?' Claudia said.

'No, I'm Julirani. I was involved in Operation Exodus, sending the first Zephyrions here,' Juli replied.

'Nice to meet you, Juli. I'm Claudu. I was a cleaner on Zephyrion until my sister Sab and I were tricked and sent here by an evil woman,' Claudia said.

'Oh, you were the cleaners Lin and Gran sent,' Juli said.

'You know them?' Claudia snarled. 'They sent us to this backward hole without any choice. Where are they? Is that Decimus one of them?'

'No, he is Simo, an enforcer,' Juli replied. 'Lin and Gran were killed by Nicoeyel and Jericesen.'

'Nicoeyel and Jericesen? As in the Deputy Supreme Leader and the enforcer's High Counsellor?' Claudia replied. 'Did they have them sentenced to death by Daxson for what they did to us?'

'Nicoeyel is evil. His real name is Zeryn, the son of Zyrenev, the first Supreme Leader. He killed his father and sister and, I'm sure, many others before killing my sister Lin, the one who tricked you and sent you here. He killed her before escaping to this planet,' Juli replied. 'I may be wrong, but I think Jericesen is one of Zeryn's cronies.'

'Oh, she was your sister,' Claudia said. 'Well, I'm sorry for you, but I'm not sorry to hear her and that mad scientist are gone.'

'I understand why you feel like that, but Zephyrion is on the brink of collapse. Since you left, it's got so bad there are tremors all the time as the planet crumbles. An emergency mass Exodus is in progress to get everyone to another planet before it's too late. Ironically, sending you here may have saved your life,' Juli said.

'If you're asking me to forgive her, I can't. But I'm also sad to hear our home is dying,' Claudia replied.

'Wine for our new friends,' Decimus said, pouring two goblets for Claudia and Sabina.

'It's Claudu and Sabina, the cleaners Lin sent from Zephyrion,' Juli whispered.

'Do they know where Zeryn is?' Simo asked.

'Hello, I am here, you know, and my hearing in this body is amazing. I didn't know our first Supreme Leader's son was here, although there were a lot of Zephyrions already here when we arrived, and a lot more have come in the last day or so,' Claudia replied.

'I'm sorry for being rude, but I have to find Zeryn,' Simo said. 'I think he would have looked for someone of power to inhabit.'

'I've not heard of anyone in any positions of power behaving strangely,' Claudia replied.

'Although there was that servant of Quintus Caepio Brutus who killed himself in front of his Dominus,' Sabina said, breaking from her conversation with Marcellus.

Claudia paused and said, 'That's true, that was a bit strange.'

'*Quintus Caepio Brutus is one of Dominus Caesar's best friends,*' Decimus thought. '*He used to be known as Marcus Junius Brutus until he was adopted.*'

'*Is Caesar powerful?*' Simo replied.

'*Most think he will be made dictator perpetuo, or dictator in perpetuity, after his successes in battle,*' Decimus replied.

'That sounds exactly like someone who Zeryn would connect to. We need to find this Brutus and Caesar,' Simo said.

'Max and Luc are inside servants of Caesar,' Juli replied.

'Luc?' Sabina queried. 'You don't mean Lucraxin, the traffic enforcer, do you?'

'Yes,' Simo said. 'Do you know him?'

'I knew his mother. It was so sad when they were killed when the building was demolished while they were still inside,' Sabina replied.

'Demolished? A tremor destroyed it,' Simo stated.

'Who told you that?' Sabina asked. 'The Elite ordered its destruction as part of their failed attempt to recover the deserted zone.'

'But if that were true, they'd have evacuated the building before demolishing it,' Simo replied.

'You enforcers are so gullible,' Claudia said. 'Sabina is right. It was demolished without any attempt to save anyone inside. The Elite has never cared about anyone but themselves.'

'We can't tell Luc this,' Juli said. 'It'll break him.'

'We have to tell him. I've spent my life not knowing Zeryn is my uncle and that he killed my mother and grandfather,' Simo snapped. 'That deception eats you up.'

'Friends, what's with all this serious talk?' Marcellus challenged. 'Let's get merry.'

'Marcellus is right,' Claudia replied. 'We need more wine.'

'I want to have some fun. How about you Decimus?' Sabina asked.

'I'll have another drink,' Decimus replied.

'*I thought this wasn't your sort of place?*' Simo thought.

'*It's more appealing than I had thought,*' Decimus said.

'I think we'll leave you to it,' Juli said.

'*I agree. However, tonight has given me a business idea to take back to Pompeii,*' Cornelius thought.

'Really?' Juli replied. '*What could you possibly learn here?*'

'*Somewhere where people can come for a few days, relax and enjoy good wine and company,*' Cornelius said.

'*You mean like a holiday?*' Juli replied.

'*Oh, that's a great idea. Doing special relaxation periods around religious or holy days, like the festivals of Quinquatria and Floralia,*' Cornelius said.

'*No, not holy days, holi... Never mind,*' Juli sighed.

22
Accidents Not Allowed

'Gaius, Livia, get up. The market opens soon,' Marcia shouted.

'Mater, it's so early. It's still dark,' Livia groaned.

'And the Dominus is having a banquet for Rome's noble leaders,' Marcia replied. 'So get up. You two need to get to the market to get the best quality food while I prepare everything. Gaius, I know you heard me, so stop pretending to be asleep.'

'I am asleep,' Gaius answered.

'Nice try, fili,' Marcia replied.

'*Fili*?' Max said. '*Ah, fili means son.*'

'*Yes, now let me go back to sleep,*' Gaius grumbled.

'Gaius, I'm not going to ask again. You can either get up or stay there and get very wet,' Marcia said, holding a jug of water.

'Okay, I'm getting up,' Gaius replied, closing his eyes again because every second of sleep counts.

'Gaius!' Marcia shouted.

'Alright,' Gaius snapped, throwing back his blanket and sitting up dramatically.

'Here's a list of what we need,' Marcia replied, handing Gaius a wax tablet.

Gaius glanced at the tablet as he rubbed his eyes. 'Why so many eggs? I mean ova.'

'Because the Dominus has insisted on a variety of your different frittatas and those wrapees too, Livia,' Marcia said.

'Okay, Mater. I've been thinking of some spicy wrapees mixed with peppers and cheese,' Livia said.

'We need to ensure the Dominus and his guests are impressed, and if you're going to experiment, I want to taste them first,' Marcia replied.

As Gaius and Livia headed towards the market, the sound of clicking coins, vendors shouting their wares and people haggling over prices grew in intensity. The other thing which became more powerful was the odours.

'I don't know if the smell in this Rome place makes me crave food or want to be sick,' Max said.

'I know what you mean. The aroma of fresh bread, sizzling meat and spices makes my stomach rumble,' Luc replied.

'And then you get the smell of sweaty stale tunics and body odour from the crowds, which is overpowering,' Max added.

'I can smell the food, but I don't know what you mean about body odours,' Gaius said.

'Nor me,' Livia added. 'Come on, let's get the food, and then we can eat.'

They started ordering everything their mother had written on the tablet while adding a few more items at Max and Luc's suggestion.

'Hello, you two,' a voice said from behind them.

They turned and were greeted by Fabia's warm smile. 'How are you finding life as servants to the most famous person in Rome?'

'Kendra, it's great to see you,' Max replied. 'We've not seen much of him. It's mainly been cooking and cleaning all day. How are you and Fabia?'

'Very well, surprisingly. I thought I'd miss all our gadgets, but it's nice to talk about anything and not have Cogi threatening us with fines. I'm also teaching Fabia about using fabrics to make more elaborate clothing,' Kendra laughed. 'Fabia says she loves having an extra mind to argue with her brother. She calls him stubborn, but I know she loves him.'

'Talking of gadgets, I've finished making an immobiliser, using two ferrum needles inside a tube and a lever,' Max said, holding up a small thin metal tube with a cork and a rounded piece of metal on top.

'How does it work?' Kendra asked.

Max put his thumb on the metal and cork top and pressed down, revealing two metal points at the other end. 'You push it against the Deceptor and press down so those points hit the skin of the host or shell, and it sends a burst of our energy into them, disrupting their energy soul and immobilising them.'

There was a scream from across the marketplace.

'How long for?' Kendra asked, glancing towards the noise.

'I remember the medidoc said you can adjust the setting to make it as long or short as you want,' Luc replied.

'Well, yes, on the ones back on Zephyrion, but the technology isn't that advanced here,' Max said. 'The best I could do is the longer you hold it down on them, the more it'll immobilise them.'

More shouts wafted over from the direction of the earlier scream.

'Does it work?' Kendra asked.

'Only one way to find out,' Max replied. 'Are you or Luc volunteering?'

'Don't you dare come near me with that,' Livia said with a scowl.

Several people ran past them, with one shouting, 'Don't go that way. There's some crazy woman attacking people.'

Max started running towards the commotion, followed by Luc and Kendra, and after pushing through a crowd, they saw a woman waving a sword.

Max pulled out his mirror and angled it to see the woman in it. 'She has an aura.'

'Where are all the brave men? I'm Dantrek from Zephyrion and I never asked to be a woman. Zeryn promised us we would rule this world,' Dantrek shouted.

'He's a trek, so he's someone in catering. How did he end up as one of Zeryn's cronies?' Kendra asked.

'Because when you don't have much, the promise of power and wealth is compelling,' Luc replied.

'And when you've got both, they become even more compelling for some,' Max added before walking towards Dantrek. 'Drop the knife, Dantrek. It's not fair on the Roman you're inhabiting.'

'Stay back, boy. Actually, no, come closer. If you kill me, I can move into you,' Dantrek replied.

'Sorry, but this fine lad is already hosting me. I'm Maxoraxin, and it's one energy soul per host.'

'You! Zeryn mentioned you and your family. He's been sending us here over the last year or so and said if you or your brother Zymraxin ever came here, we're to kill you,' Dantrek sneered, waving the sword back and forth.

Hearing Zym's name made Max pause briefly before moving closer to Dantrek. 'Drop the sword, Dantrek. The woman you're inside doesn't deserve to die.'

'She's already dead. Zeryn said I was one of his leaders when he sent me here in one of the first groups. As soon as I separated from her, I killed her,' Dantrek replied.

'But if you're now free, why are you behaving like this?' Max asked, moving even closer.

'Because I've heard we are immortal on this planet and can choose our form. If you kill this shell, I'll be free to move into a male body, which is what I want,' Dantrek snapped.

'But why terrorise others?' Max asked.

'Because I can't do it myself. Look,' Dantrek replied, running his hand down the blade and holding it up. 'See, once we learn how to build their shells, we know how to repair their bodies, and if it gets injured, it starts to repair itself.'

The crowd gasped as Dantrek's slashed hand stopped bleeding and started to heal.

'She's possessed,' someone shouted.

'She's a witch. She must be killed,' another screamed.

'Please, Max. I'm scared. I don't want to die,' Gaius thought.

'I promise you won't get hurt,' Max replied reassuringly. *'I've dealt with these situations so many times before.'*

'Get the witch,' the crowd shouted.

'Put your hand down,' Max ordered. 'I've been to light atmosphere planets before. You don't have to heal the body; in most cases, you shouldn't. As you can hear, it creates fear and anger.'

The crowd's rage was a mix of terror of this sword-waving witch and determination that she should be punished. As their wrath grew, they started to push forward, encircling Dantrek.

Dantrek waved the sword wildly to keep them back. A young man tried to grab Dantrek's arm from behind, but Dantrek was too quick and grabbed the man, spinning him around and holding the sword up to his throat.

'If anyone gets any closer, this male will die,' Dantrek bellowed.

'Dantrek, let me help you. I'll kill you, and then you can move into this innocent man's body,' Max said reassuringly, taking another step closer.

'How can I trust you?' Dantrek challenged.

'Because I know where Zeryn is, and I can take you to him,' Max said calmly.

'Zeryn is here?' Dantrek said, widening his eyes and looking around.

'Not in this marketplace, but yes, he is in Rome. We followed him here,' Max said, edging further forward as he tightened his grip on his handmade immobiliser.

'Take me to him,' Dantrek demanded, tightening the sword against the man's throat.

Max looked around at the crowd, who were still shouting witchcraft and calling for the witch to be stoned to death.

'Look at this mob. They're never going to let you go. Let me stab you, and then you can move into this man called...' Max paused and looked at the man being held.

The man looked at Max with fear in his eyes. 'I'm Publius.'

'So you move into Publius, and we can take you to Zeryn while the crowd get your dead shell,' Max replied.

'Max, what are you doing? He's crazy. You can't let him occupy Publius,' Gaius pleaded.

'Trust me,' Max replied.

'Is Zeryn ready to take control?' Dantrek asked.

'Of course. He's convinced us that we should work together,' Max replied, edging forward.

'So you and Zymraxin are with us now?' Dantrek asked excitedly.

'Absolutely,' Max replied, fighting back the emotions of using his brother's name to placate this Deceptor.

'But...' Gaius started to say.

'Trust me,' Max thought again.

'Okay. Come close so you can kill this shell, but I'm holding onto Publius so I can move into him quickly,' Dantrek said.

Max moved close to Dantrek. The waft of stale body odour overpowered the cheap perfumed oils Dantrek had used, causing Max to gag. He lifted his arm, revealing the immobiliser.

'What is that?' Dantrek asked, flinching backwards.

'It's a new weapon,' Max replied, pushing the metal and cork top to reveal the two pointed ends.

'Is that enough to kill this shell?' Dantrek asked.

'A quick jab, and it'll all be over,' Max replied with a smile.

'Okay, do it,' Dantrek said.

Max quickly moved his arm and held it against Dantrek's neck, pressing the metal and cork top. Dantrek looked at Max in shock. His eyes widened, and he crumpled to the floor as his sword fell from his hand.

As the crowd rushed forward, Max turned and walked in the opposite direction of Luc and Kendra.

'What about me?' Publius asked, running after him.

'Do you feel any different?' Max asked, observing the crowd throwing stones at Dantrek's body.

'Different in what way?' Publius asked in confusion.

'What's a Cogi?' Max asked.

'A what?' Publius replied.

'A Citizen Observation and Government Intelligence device,' Max said, walking away.

'I've never heard of it,' Publius answered.

'Then go back to your life. You're normal,' Max said coldly.

Publius scratched his head, looking confused by what had just happened. He looked back towards Dantrek and saw the crowd throwing stones.

'What's happening?' he asked.

'I think they're killing Dantrek,' Kendra replied as she and Luc ran past towards Max.

'Max, you're scaring me,' Luc said. 'It's like you don't care. They're killing Dantrek.'

There was a flash followed by a scream.

'It is what it is,' Max replied, still walking.

'You risked my fratris's life,' Livia protested.

'I would never risk a host's life, especially your brother's,' Max replied without breaking his stride.

Kendra grabbed Max's arm, forcing him to stop walking. 'Max, when did you become so cold? I remember when you used to say shoot to disable, never to kill.'

'Where's the Max who was so kind to me when he realised I wasn't some experienced security enforcer, just a traffic one,' Luc asked.

Max turned slowly and looked at Kendra and then Luc. 'Ask Simo how he feels about Zeryn and his followers. Then, ask Lin and Zym. Oh, sorry, you can't ask them, can you?'

'Max, neither Zym nor Lin would want you to be like this,' Kendra insisted.

'Kendra, we've worked together for years and are friends, but don't you dare tell me what you think my brother and partner would think,' Max snapped. 'Zeryn killed Lin and, for all I know, did the same to Zym, and I will never rest until he and his cronies are wiped out.'

'You scare me,' Gaius said.

'Me too,' Livia added.

'I'm sorry,' Max replied. 'But my life is empty. I promise I will never risk your life, Gaius, nor yours, Livia, but until Zeryn dies, I don't have a future.'

'This is so confusing. I can see my frater, sorry brother, but I can hear Max, a torn and broken man,' Livia replied, wiping a tear from her face. 'I can see from Luc's memories what happened before they came here, but those images are nothing compared to the shell I see before me, Max.'

'Please, don't show me pity,' Max replied. 'My life is about avenging the death of my partner and brother. I deserve nothing.'

'Max, you're incredible. You deserve so much more than you think,' Luc replied. 'I will stand by your side no matter what.'

Max choked back his feelings. He no longer mattered in his mind, so such an outpouring of love was hard to accept. 'Just help me get Zeryn. Beyond that, nothing matters.'

'You matter, Max,' Kendra stated. 'You don't know it, but you can make a difference. Your passion for doing the right thing is what makes you special.'

'We need to buy food for the banquet,' Max replied, changing the subject.

Kendra hugged Max. 'Go and get what you need. But remember, we are here for you.'

Max looked down at the immobiliser in his hand. 'Could Manius make copies of this for all of us? There must be a connection of ferrum from top to bottom in all of them except one.'

'That won't be a problem for my Manius,' Fabia replied.

'Can you make one extra one with a wooden breaker so there isn't a full connection?' Max asked.

'Of course, but will it work without the ferrum going through it?' Kendra queried.

'That's the idea. Think of it like a non-working demonstration model,' Max replied.

'Leave it with me and Fabia. We'll get them made for you,' Kendra replied. 'We'll make the demonstrator look virtually the same, but just different enough that you can spot it.'

'Come on, Luc and Livia, we've got some shopping to do,' Max said. 'Thank you, Kendra and Fabia.'

Gaius and Livia headed into the market crowd. Kendra looked down at the immobiliser, turning it over in her hand. *'Can Manius do this?'*

'My brother is an annoying and arrogant man but also a craftsman. He can make these with his eyes closed,' Fabia replied.

'Hail, the saviour of the day,' a small crowd chanted as Gaius and Livia walked through the crowds to a vegetable stall.

Gaius spoke to the stall holder, explaining what he wanted.

'I was keeping these for myself, but you deserve only the best, young man,' the stallholder said, pulling out the best examples of fresh vegetables Gaius had seen in a long time.

This pattern of gracious stallholders continued until they finally came to the butcher with the final part of their shopping list.

'Is this really for Julius Caesar?' the butcher asked.

'Yes, Sir,' Gaius replied.

'Then your bravery deserves only the best cuts of pork and lamb,' the butcher said.

'But we only have a fixed budget from our mater, Sir,' Gaius answered.

'Your Dominus shall eat well, but because of your bravery today, you shall eat better,' the butcher replied. 'I shall deliver your meat and eels this afternoon with payment on delivery like normal, but this beef steak is for you and your young lady and at my cost.'

'I'm not his lady. I'm his sister, I mean soror,' Livia protested. *'I can't even remember which language to use.'*

'I know what you mean,' Luc thought in reply.

23
BANQUET TIME

'Decimus, how wonderful to see you in my humble domus,' Caesar said. 'Your support means so much. I am pleased you could come.'

'Julius, how could I refuse the champion of Thapsus,' Decimus replied.

'*What was Thapsus?*' Simo asked.

'*A decisive battle which heralds a new future for Rome,*' Decimus thought.

'Who is your friend?' Caesar asked.

'This is Cornelius Felix of Pompeii,' Decimus said.

'I'm humbled to meet the noble Julius Caesar. The mightiest soldier of our age,' Cornelius added.

'I am merely your servant, Cornelius. Without the support of such noblemen as you, I would be nothing,' Caesar said.

'Your humility makes you a great leader,' Cornelius said.

'I trust the spread is to both of your liking. It's a celebration of our successes,' Caesar said. 'I recommend the frittatas. They are sublime.'

'The spread is impressive, and I've already heard rumours of your slave Gaius's frittatas,' Decimus replied.

'*Slave?*' Simo thought. '*You mean Gaius and Livia are Caesar's property?*'

'Yes, of course,' Decimus said. '*But he looks after them well.*'

'Let's raise a toast to the future of Rome and the bonds that unite us,' Caesar said, handing goblets of wine to Decimus and Cornelius.

'To Rome. Your vision for our future is an inspiration,' Decimus replied, raising his goblet.

'*A vision where everyone is free,*' Simo said.

'*You may have had so much technology, yet you're so backwards,*' Decimus thought. '*If it weren't for masters like Caesar, there would be many more homeless citizens.*'

'*Backwards? You have no idea,*' Simo snapped. '*On Zephyrion, we were all free, and nobody owned anyone else.*'

'*Free? You forget I can read your memories. I know your childhood was controlled and ruined by your uncle to gain power. As for your citizens, you had monitoring devices in their homes, workplaces, and even on the roads. Your government controlled what they did, where they went, and even what they said,*' Decimus said. '*You were more slaves than the ones we have.*'

Simo was about to reply, but then he paused, mulling over Decimus's words. '*Okay, you're right; we weren't free, but I still don't like the principle of owning people.*'

'Enjoy yourself, my friends,' Caesar said to Decimus and Cornelius. 'Please excuse me while I greet my new guests.'

'Simo, Juli, is it you?' a voice behind them whispered.

They turned and saw a young serving girl with a platter of nibbles.

Juli smiled. 'Luc and, err..'

'Livia, Sir,' Livia replied.

'Sir?' Juli queried.

'Well, I am a man,' Cornelius replied.

'*Oh, sorry, I keep forgetting I'm inside your body,*' Juli laughed.

'Livia, you mustn't bother the Dominus's guests,' Gaius whispered.

'It's Juli and Simo,' Luc replied.

Gaius looked up and recognised Cornelius and Decimus. 'Please take some food off our platters, or Mater will scold us.'

'I'll have one of those, thank you,' a voice said as a hand took a frittata off Gaius's platter.

The small group turned, and Juli said, 'Paulie, is that you?'

'It certainly is,' Paulie replied, adding, 'Wow, these egg things are incredible. Gaius is very talented.'

'Excuse me. Whilst Gaius is talented, those frittatas are my speciality,' Max insisted.

'Max has always been famous amongst his family and friends for his skill with eggs,' Simo laughed.

'It was his bravery against a Deceptor in the market today that made him famous on this planet,' Luc said.

'I heard about that, but I didn't realise it was Max,' Paulie said.

'Please, keep eating,' Gaius said, holding forward his platter.

Cornelius took a wrapee off Livia's platter. 'These are pretty special, too. The fillings are good, and that flatbread is so thin and light.'

'Never mind the food. Has anyone got a lead on Zeryn,' Max asked.

'We thought we might have, but it turned out to be Claudia and Sabina,' Juli replied.

'Who?' Max said.

'The two cleaners Lin and Gran sent here in that Dronin video during the Migration Lottery,' Juli said. 'They are a bit crazy, but I wouldn't call them Deceptors.'

'I agree. I'd say they're just a bit wild and looking for a good time,' Simo said.

'Has anyone heard from the others?' Juli asked.

'We saw Kendra earlier, and she hadn't heard of anyone. Even the Deceptor Max killed didn't know Zeryn was here,' Luc replied.

'I didn't kill him. The crowd did. I just immobilised him in his shell,' Max said flatly.

'Paulie, what about Keri and Cal? Have they seen anything?' Juli asked.

'Talking of which, where are they? I suppose Cal wouldn't look right in this environment as Appius, but Keri would fit in,' Simo said.

'Keri seems to have worked her magic on Tullia. She has taken Appius as her personal servant and decided they'd rather enjoy some time at home without us,' Paulie laughed. 'But none of us have come across any Deceptors.'

Marcia walked behind Decimus, deliberately passing in front of Gaius's eyeline. She lifted her finger and circled it around in the air, making it clear that Gaius and Livia should circulate with their platters and not stay in one place.

'We need to go, but please keep looking,' Max said. 'Even finding Jeric would help, as I'm sure he'll lead us to Zeryn.'

'Don't worry. If I see Zeryn first, you'll hear his screams across Rome,' Simo replied.

The evening wore on without any unexpected events. Max and Luc had polished their platters to an almost mirror-like finish to spot Deceptors, but aside from their friends, they saw no auras.

'Caesar, I'm sorry I'm late,' Marcus Tamphilus said. 'There was a late senate vote.'

'Worry not, my friend,' Caesar said warmly. 'There is still plenty of wine and food, and the entertainment has barely begun.'

'Quintus, fetch me some food and wine,' Marcus snapped to the teenage boy by his side.

'Yes, Sir,' Quintus replied.

Marcus slapped Quintus. 'I've told you before, just do what I say. I don't need to hear your voice.'

Caesar looked at Marcus and frowned.

Marcus smiled back. 'I know what you're thinking, and I agree. Servants nowadays are so above themselves. They seem to forget that without our generosity, they would be begging on the streets.'

'Actually, I never hit my servants. They respect me, and I respect them,' Caesar replied. 'Maybe I've been lucky, or perhaps my actions make me lucky, but Marcia and her children are incredible, and her son has a talent with food. You must try his frittatas. Now excuse me while I mingle.'

'Are you okay?' Max asked the awkward, pale, thin boy before him. Max thought the boy was around his age, well, the age of his host Gaius, although the boy's thin, drawn face, lean body and above-average height made him look several years older.

'Yes, I'm fine. I need to get my Dominus some food and wine,' Quintus replied.

'Did he hit you?' Max asked, noticing the redness on the boy's face.

'Of course not,' Quintus snapped. 'What is the best food? My Dominus only eats the finest.'

'Your Dominus sounds very unpleasant. Who is he?' Max asked.

'He is Marcus Tamphilus, senator of Rome and a fine man,' Quintus replied, pointing in Marcus's direction. 'Now, which food should I pick?'

'I recommend the frittatas and the wrapees,' Max said. 'But if he is more traditional, the roast pork and the beef steak strips are delicious.

Quintus smiled weakly, 'Thank you...'

'Gaius,' Max said quickly.

'*You were about to say, Max,*' Gaius laughed.

'Maybe,' Max thought. '*I'm not perfect, you know. I'm only human.*'

Gaius let out an audible laugh. '*I think you'll find I'm the human, and you're the Shadower.*'

'*Okay, you got me there,*' Max replied.

'What's funny?' Quintus asked.

Max thought quickly and replied, 'Sorry, I just saw my sister, Livia, by someone she said was obnoxious, and she pulled a funny face.'

'What is your Dominus Caesar like?' Quintus asked. 'Oh, I forgot to say I'm Quintus.'

'I'm pleased to meet you, Quintus. Caesar is a kind and giving master. He made my uncle a free man last year after he saved his life in battle,' Gaius replied. 'One of my Dominus's friends is Quintus Brutus, although he also used Marcus Brutus. Were you named after him?'

'*I hadn't seen that in your memories before. He is quite a kind man for such a successful military leader,*' Max thought.

'*He knows how to destroy his enemies but reward his friends,*' Gaius replied.

'I don't know how I was named. I should take this food to my Dominus before he gets angry,' Quintus said. 'Where can I get him some wine?'

'Take the food over and say you've ordered his wine,' Max replied.

'Thank you, Gaius,' Quintus replied, hurrying towards his master.

'*What do you think?*' Gaius asked, watching Quintus manoeuvre with the small food platter through the crowds.

'*About what?*' Max asked.

'*Could Quintus's Dominus be the Deceptor you're looking for,*' Gaius said.

'*He seems unpleasant enough to be,*' Max said. '*Let's grab some wine and take it over after I've polished this platter clean.*'

As Gaius approached Marcus Tamphilus carrying the polished tray with a few goblets and a jug of wine, he was stopped several times to give guests refills.

'*He's talking to Paulie and Atia, and I assume that's Atia's partner*,' Max muttered.

'You boy. About time. My servant said you were bringing my wine ages ago,' Marcus snapped, grabbing a goblet off Gaius's tray as Quintus cowered behind the far side of Marcus.

'I'm sorry, Sir. I needed to dilute some more wine as we ran low,' Gaius replied.

'Did I ask you to speak to me, boy? I'll be raising your rudeness with Caesar,' Marcus snapped, grabbing the wine and taking a large sip.

'Thank you, Gaius,' Atia said, holding her goblet for a refill.

Gaius smiled and turned back towards Marcus, angling the tray to see if he could spot an aura.

Marcus spat out his wine and swung his arm and the goblet, sending Gaius's tray flying and knocking him to the floor. 'Are you trying to poison us? This is almost pure wine.'

Gaius scrambled to his knees and started to stand. 'I'm so sorry, Sir. I'll—'

Gaius's sentence was cut short as Marcus hit him again, sending him sprawling across the floor.

'You need teaching some manners, boy,' Marcus growled, walking towards him with a menacing glare.

Max's mind raced for ideas on defending his and Gaius's body from Marcus's next attack. He spotted the tray he'd been carrying and grabbed it, intending to use it as a shield.

'That isn't going to save you from learning some respect, boy,' Marcus snarled.

'Maybe not, but I certainly intend to,' Paulie said, stepping between Marcus and Gaius.

Marcus turned towards Atia's husband, 'Sir, I suggest you remind your wife of her place.'

Paulie took a step towards Marcus, forcing him to step back. 'And I suggest you start respecting people.'

Marcus smiled sarcastically, 'As a mulier, I wouldn't expect you to understand how we men must train these boys. But fear not. It is our job to make your lives safer.'

Paulie visibly bristled with anger. 'My dear senator. As you said, I may be a mere woman or mulier, but my family have been responsible for the careers of many senators and even a few consuls. Including your career, I might add. We helped fund our host's recent foray in Hispania, and we'll do all we can to ensure he becomes dictator perpetuo.'

'And your noble contribution is appreciated so much. But there are times—'

'Yes, there are times when you need to know what is acceptable,' Paulie snapped.

Caesar walked over to find out what was causing the disturbance. He had a hushed conversation with Gaius and then approached Marcus. 'Atia, Tamphilus, tonight is a night of celebration, not one of debate. Let's drink and be merry,' he said, holding out two goblets of wine passed to him by Gaius.

'Caesar, my friend, you are so right. Tonight is not the time to discuss meaningless politics,' Marcus replied smarmily.

'I don't call attacking servants meaningless,' Paulie replied. 'However, this is your night, Caesar, so as long as there is no more abuse, let's not dwell on it.'

Caesar escorted Atia and her husband away, ensuring Gaius was with them.

'Gaius, keep a careful watch on our guest Tamphilus. If he steps out of line again, I want to know,' Caesar whispered.

'Yes, Dominus,' Gaius replied.

'Oh, that felt so thrilling,' Atia thought.

'What was?' Paulie replied.

'Arguing with that awful senator,' Atia said.

'Don't you ever argue with anyone?'

'With Tullia and my husband all the time, but never with a man not in my family.'

'Why not?'

'*Because I'm a woman. We never argue with men as they are superior.*'

'*Things will have to change on this planet, and I don't care how long it takes. We are all equal,*' Paulie replied.

'*Even servants?*'

'*Everyone!*' Paulie said sharply.

Caesar headed towards another senator, leaving Atia and her husband by Decimus.

'What was going on over there?' Simo asked.

'An altercation with an arrogant and bullying senator,' Paulie replied.

'I think he's more than just a senator. I'm not sure if he's Zeryn, but I definitely caught a glimpse of an aura off my tray,' Max said.

'He has an aura?' Paulie asked.

'I only caught a glimpse, but yes, there was part of an aura from my quick look,' Max confirmed.

'If it's Zeryn, he's not leaving here alive,' Simo said. 'I'm going to find out.'

'Going where?' Luc said as he and Livia approached the group.

'To see Marcus Tamphilus,' Simo replied.

'You'll need to run. He's just left, dragging Quintus behind him,' Livia said.

'Which direction did he go?' Simo demanded.

'I heard him mutter about the Temple of Saturn,' Livia replied.

'That means heading towards the Forum Romanum,' Gaius added. 'It's so busy around there you'll never find him.'

'But if he's going to the Temple of Saturn, I can get him there,' Simo said.

'I'm sorry, but we are not fighting with anyone inside there,' Decimus replied insistently.

'Keep your voices down,' Max said in a hushed voice. 'You sound quite different even though you're sharing one body.'

'I'm not fighting in the home of Rome's history and laws,' Decimus said.

'I didn't say I would fight him,' Simo answered.

'You seem to forget I know everything you're thinking, Simo. You don't just want to fight him; you want to kill him,' Decimus said.

'Will you two think your argument, please,' Max said. 'Someone arguing with themselves in different voices will cause problems.'

'If you're going to confront Marcus to see if he is Zeryn, then I'm coming too,' Juli said.

'Why are you trying to follow him?' Gaius asked.

'Because he's responsible for my mother's death as well as the deaths of my grandfather and Max's partner,' Simo replied. 'I'd have thought you could have seen that in Max's memories. Now come on, or we'll lose him.'

'I can see all that, and I understand why you want him dead, but why do you need to follow him?' Gaius said.

'So we know where he lives,' Simo said. 'Plus, if I can get him alone, I can kill him.'

'But he's a senator, so he's around the Forum most days, and his dwelling is on the Vicus Jugarius, the street that leads past the Temple of Saturn,' Paulie said.

'How do you know that?' Simo asked.

'Because he's been a customer of Atia's husband for years,' Paulie replied.

'But that means you've risked their business,' Max said. 'The first rule of enforcers is we never deliberately interfere with innocent inhabitants of other planets.'

'It is fine, Max. Marcus Tamphilus needs my family's patronage far more than we need his business,' Atia replied. 'Besides, with Paulie inside me, I've not enjoyed myself as much as this for years.'

'If we know where he lives, then we can monitor his behaviour, confirm he's Zeryn and then kill him,' Max said.

'Why wait?' Simo demanded.

'Because if we kill Marcus now, Zeryn will move into another person,' Max explained.

'But you've got an immobiliser. You used it earlier on that Deceptor,' Simo said.

'And if we immobilise Zeryn inside Marcus, we won't just kill Zeryn. Marcus will die too,' Max said.

'I don't think Rome will miss such a horrible man,' Juli replied.

'That may be so, but let's ensure we do this right and minimise the impact on others,' Max said. 'Luc and I will befriend Quintus and make sure he is safe before we move on Marcus and Zeryn.'

'Perhaps Cal can help as Appius is a similar age to the three of you,' Paulie replied.

24
THE WAITING GAME

The following morning, Livia was doing the usual food shopping with Gaius tagging along when they spotted a familiar tall, thin male.

'Quintus, what are you doing in the marketplace?' Gaius asked.

'My Dominus wanted some fresh fish and vegetables for lunch, and the coquus is ill, so I've been sent to get them,' Quintus replied.

'*Coquus*?' Max thought. '*Ah, the cook. Our languages have some similarities.*'

'*The more I see of your mind, the more similarities I see,*' Gaius said. '*Your world has many magical things like your transport and communication, and yet the basics of life are the same.*'

'Are you shopping too?' Quintus asked meekly.

'Livia is, but my mother has said I can have a couple of hours of free time as a thank you from my Dominus,' Gaius replied. 'I'm meeting Appius, a friend of a friend.'

'Free time? What does that mean?' Quintus queried. 'Do you normally have to pay to spend time outside?'

Gaius laughed, 'No, it means I have a little time to do what I want. It doesn't happen very often.'

'But what about your chores? Won't your Dominus be angry if they're not done?' Quintus asked.

'Of course not. He said I deserved some free time because of how your Dominus hit me, and Livia and my mother will do my chores,' Gaius replied.

'That's what you think,' Livia protested. 'They'll be waiting for your return.'

'She means it too,' Luc added.

Quintus frowned. 'Why did you change your voice and refer to yourself like that?'

'What do you mean?' Livia asked.

'See, you've done it again. Going back to your other voice,' Quintus challenged.

'*What do we do?*' Gaius thought.

'*Nothing. Hopefully, Luc or Livia will pretend they were putting on a voice for effect,*' Max replied.

'Because, umm,' Livia paused, screwing up her face in thought.

'Because it's funny,' Luc replied.

'*Please tell me they didn't just say and do that?*' Max sighed.

'*I'm afraid they did,*' Gaius thought in reply.

'Livia, go and finish the shopping. Quintus, can I speak to you a minute,' Max said, grabbing Quintus's arm and moving away from Livia.

'*I'm not sure what I'm going to say, but I can't let Livia and Luc make it any worse,*' Max thought to Gaius.

'Have I done something wrong?' Quintus quivered. 'You're not going to hit me, are you?'

'Why would I hit you?' Max asked.

'Because I always get hit for doing wrong,' Quintus replied.

'I would never hit you, and neither should your Dominus,' Max said.

'He only does it when I do wrong. It makes me remember not to do it again,' Quintus explained.

'But hitting you isn't right,' Max said.

'No, it's fine. My Dominus gives me food and shelter. I'm grateful as he could have taken anyone on, but he chose me. If he hadn't, I'd be on the streets,' Quintus replied.

'There are worse places to be,' a voice said behind them. 'I've lived on the streets of Rome, and it's tough, but you can get some help here, unlike in other places.'

Max turned and smiled. 'Cal, I mean Appius, I was worried you couldn't make it.'

'There, again. It's like two people. Is he Cal or Appius? It's like Livia having two voices,' Quintus said.

'I'm Appius Calinarus, but my friends call me Cal or Appius,' Cal explained.

'Calinarus isn't Roman,' Quintus said.

'I'm Galli,' Cal replied quickly.

'Oh. Gaul seems so exotic,' Quintus said.

'It's only the land to the north of us,' Max answered.

'But I've never been outside of Rome,' Quintus said.

'Never?' Max questioned.

'No, why would I? Rome is the centre of the world,' Quintus replied.

'Don't you want to explore your world and see what you're missing?' Cal asked.

'What makes you think I'm missing anything?' Quintus said. 'After all, you're just a vagabundi.'

'I may have been a vagabond, but I've travelled further than you'll ever imagine,' Cal replied sharply.

'I'm sorry if I've insulted you,' Quintus said nervously. 'Please forgive me. I never meant to. Please don't punish me.'

Cal looked at Max and frowned. Max shrugged but tried to convey his concern for this timid young Roman.

'It's okay, Quintus. You've not insulted me, and I'd never punish you. Why would I?' Cal asked.

'Because I challenged your motives,' Quintus replied. 'I'm sorry, I try not to, but I also like to understand why people do things.'

'Quintus, you don't need to apologise. Any friend of Max—Gaius is a friend of mine,' Cal said.

'What's going on? You've done it now, Cal or is it Appius? Is it any friend of Gaius or Max, Maximus, Maximilianus, or Maxentius?' Quintus challenged.

'I'm just Gaius,' Max replied.

'I was saying, any friend of m'amicus Gaius is a friend of mine,' Cal said.

'So, who is Max?' Quintus demanded.

'I didn't say Max, I said m'amicus. It's Galli slang for meus amicus or my friend, as you would say,' Cal explained.

Quintus looked at Gaius and then Appius. 'Gallice loquor.'

Appius's face blanched, and he looked nervously at Max.

'Did you just say you speak Gaul?' Gaius asked. 'I speak a little, too. I presume you learnt as I did from your Dominus entertaining foreign guests.'

'Thank you, Gaius. I'm still finding things in your mind that surprise me,' Max thought.

'It shouldn't be surprising. Our Dominus, Caesar, was the proconsul of Gaul,' Gaius replied. *'I can speak it fluently.'*

'As you only speak a little Gallice, Gaius, let's stick to Latin,' Cal said.

'Thank you, Appius,' Max replied.

'Appius? I thought it was Cal. In fact, whilst the difference between Cal's voices and Livia's voices are quite distinct, even your voice changes a little, Gaius,' Quintus said with a scowl.

'Is that Marcus Tamphilus?' Gaius asked, pointing towards the crowd.

'Oh no. I need to go. If he sees me idling, he'll have to punish me again,' Quintus replied.

'He'll have to get past me first,' Cal said, puffing out his chest and standing upright to his full height of five foot four inches.

Max started laughing. 'You forget, my friend. You're not tall on this planet. Even I'm two uncia taller than you.'

Quintus was too busy trying to spot his Dominus to notice Max's comment. 'Did either of you see which way he went?'

'He was near the Temple of Concord. If you go round the Temple of Castor, you should miss him,' Gaius suggested.

'You really shouldn't be in fear of your Dominus,' Cal said. 'If we can help, just ask.'

'I'm not in fear of him. I don't want to disappoint him, so he has to teach me another lesson,' Quintus said. 'Did you say this way?'

Max nodded. 'Yes, go around the back of Castor, and you'll be fine. If you'd like to be friends and let us help you, we'd like that.'

'Thank you. I'd like that too,' Quintus said, looking increasingly scared. 'Now I've got to go.'

Quintus started hurrying away but stopped and turned. 'Gaius, did you mean it when you said you'd help me?'

'Yes, of course, Quintus,' Max replied.

'Could you please ask your Dominus if I could work in his domus?' Quintus asked, wiping a tear away from his eye.

'I don't have the right to ask such a thing, but I'll try,' Max replied.

Quintus lifted his face, showing the tears of fear running down his face. 'You promise?'

'I promise. Now go before Tamphilus sees you,' Max replied.

They watched Quintus scurry away into the crowds.

'I've always respected your ability to achieve what seems impossible, but do you really think you can persuade the most powerful man in the empire to take on an extra servant?' Cal asked.

'It's going to be a challenge, but you saw how scared he is of Marcus Tamphilus,' Max said.

'Paulie said you saw an aura around Tamphilus at Caesar's banquet,' Cal said. 'Do you think he is Zeryn?'

'I can't be certain, but there was an aura, and he is nasty enough, plus Tamphilus is a senator. Just the sort of position of power Zeryn likes,' Max replied.

'Why don't we just kill him then?' Cal asked.

'Simo said the same thing, and you'll get the same answer. Killing Zeryn while he's in Marcus Tamphilus would mean killing Tamphilus, too,' Max explained.

'He's a nasty piece of work, so would anyone mourn him going?' Cal replied.

'That's pretty much what Juli said,' Max sighed. 'What if Tamphilus is kind, and Zeryn is just making him behave like that?'

Cal frowned and said, 'But what if Zeryn completes his trans...thingy.'

'Transmutation,' Max replied.

'Yes, exactly. If he finishes his transmutation, he could disappear,' Cal said.

'That is a risk, but I think it's unlikely. Zeryn needs power like we need food,' Max said. 'The biggest risk of Zeryn transmuting isn't him running away, it's him killing Marcus and trying to seize power.'

'So what do we do?' Cal asked.

'We need someone working in his household to spy on him and report back to us,' Max said.

'Hold your chickens, buddy. I will not work for that nasty piece of work,' Cal protested.

'I don't mean you. I'm referring to Quintus,' Max laughed.

'That's okay then. Well, it's not okay for Quintus, but I think that's a good idea,' Cal replied.

'I'm so pleased you agree,' Max said. 'And where did "hold your chickens" come from?'

'I thought your Gaius and Appius were about the same age?' Cal replied.

'I'm sixteen,' Gaius stated firmly.

'I'm almost sixteen,' Appius protested. 'And everyone says hold your chickens nowadays.'

'No, they don't,' Gaius insisted. 'It doesn't even make sense.'

'Yes, it does. It means stop what you're doing or hold on a minute,' Appius said.

'Obviously only amongst the street dwellers,' Gaius replied pompously.

'*That's rude, Gaius,*' Max thought.

'*But he is a street dweller, or he was until your friend came along,*' Gaius responded.

'*Clearly, you've learnt none of Caesar's manners when treating people of a lower status than you,*' Max sighed. '*I'm disappointed in you.*'

'*Fine, okay,*' Gaius replied. 'I'm sorry, Appius. I was rude saying that.'

'Yes, you were. We all die the same; it's just a twist of fortune that decides how we are born and live,' Appius said firmly.

'*Appius, be the better person,*' Cal thought.

'*I am the better person,*' Appius protested.

'*Then prove it,*' Cal replied.

'Thank you for your apology, and I'm sorry if I offended you,' Appius replied.

'Right, now what do we do?' Cal asked.

'We need to befriend Quintus and get him to tell us what Marcus and Zeryn are up to,' Max said. 'Then, as soon as he transmutes, we must get him quickly.'

'But how can we stop Zeryn killing Marcus and assuming his position in Rome?' Cal asked.

'That's a very good question. I wish I had an equally good answer,' Max replied.

'*What about your immobiliser?*' Gaius asked.

'*What do you mean?*' Max replied.

'*If you give Quintus one, he could use it on that Zeryn person as soon as he transmutes,*' Gaius said.

'*Why didn't I think of that?*' Max thought.

'*As we are in one body, which is my body, I might add, you technically did think it,*' Gaius laughed.

'Come on. I've had an idea,' Max said.

'Where are we going?' Cal asked.

'To see Kendra,' Max replied.

A few minutes later, Max and Cal arrived at Manius's stall.

'Excuse me, Sir. Is Fabia here today?' Gaius asked.

'She should be back soon. She needed to go to the ornatores because getting her hair done every week is a necessity,' Manius said in frustration. 'Meanwhile, I must mind the stall and produce the stock.'

'*What's an ornatores?*' Cal thought.

'*I think you call them hairdressers,*' Appius replied.

'Can we help?' Max asked.

'You look familiar. Do I know you?' Manius queried.

'I bought a speculum from you recently, Sir,' Max said. 'I work in the domus of Julius Caesar.'

'Good grief, yes. You're the servant that the bullying senator attacked. Fabia's new friend Atia told us about it,' Manius replied. 'How are you? I'm sorry I've forgotten your name even though Fabia told me.'

'I'm Gaius, Sir, and I'm okay. Atia's kind intervention saved me from a more severe attack, although I fear his servant, Quintus, receives far worse at his hands,' Max replied.

'Gaius? Do you have a friend called Max?' Manius asked.

'Yes, I do why?' Gaius asked nervously.

'Then I have something for you,' Manius replied, rummaging in a box behind him and pulling out more than a dozen polished silver tubes, which he placed on the counter.

Max picked one up and turned it over, inspecting the craftsmanship.

'This looks incredible,' Max said as he put his thumb on the metal button on the top and pressed down, revealing the two small prongs. 'The mechanism is so smooth.'

'I hope you don't mind, but I adapted your recoil mechanism. The one you had was cleverly engineered, but you would see it wear and jam after regular usage. I've created a simpler but more reliable one,' Manius proudly said.

'Oh, what about the ferrum—'

'Yes, when you press the button, there is still a ferrum connection from the top to the bottom. Atia made it clear that was important,' Manius smiled.

'They look incredible,' Cal said, picking up an immobiliser.

'I hope you'll excuse me for exercising my artistic side with the engraving,' Manius smiled proudly.

'Not at all. They're amazing,' Max replied.

'May I enquire what they are used for?' Manius asked.

Max looked blankly at Manius. 'You want to know what we use them for?'

'Only if you don't mind telling me. They're just so unusual in their design with those two prongs. I wondered if it was some form of eating device, but the prongs don't extend far enough to stab safely into food,' Manius said with a frown as he studied one.

'It's for needlework, Sir. You can punch two holes into the material and then pass a thread through them to pull it tighter,' Gaius replied.

'*Thank you, Gaius. My mind just went blank,*' Max thought.

'*I hope not. There's two minds inside my head at the moment,*' Gaius laughed.

'Hmm, I would have thought a wider gap between the prongs would work better, but I can see how this is very portable,' Manius said. 'Do you mind if I develop some products like it?'

Max paused as Cal whispered, 'You don't want Deceptors getting hold of these.'

Max nodded and said, 'Of course you can, but can you not use ferrum for all the internal mechanisms, please.'

'That reminds me, why did you want the one with wood inside instead of ferrum all the way through?' Manius queried.

Max thought and then said, 'It's my demonstration model. Having wood inside will make it feel a little lighter.'

'I can see the logic in that. I was planning to use gold and silver. I can see this being a useful device for noble folk to pick up food if I make the prongs longer,' Manius replied.

'What are you dreaming up now for noble people,' a voice said.

'Fabia, my dear. The ornatores have worked wonders on your hair,' Manius said with a cheery smile.

'You say that every week, Manius,' Fabia laughed. 'and it's a good job you do. Gaius, Appius, I'm so pleased I didn't miss you.'

'Never mind catching up with friends. Can you take over the stall? I need a break,' Manius said.

'I've not been gone long. Can't your business wait until I've chatted with these two?' Fabia protested.

'I can, but I'll be producing a new aqueduct,' Manius said with a strained look.

'Oh, fine. I'll manage,' Fabia replied in mock disgust.

As Manius ran toward the nearest public toilets, Fabia walked behind the counter and picked up one of the immobilisers. 'Manius loved working on this. I even caught him whistling as he worked on it, which is a sign of a happy Manius.'

'He has made them look incredible,' Max replied.

'So we've come from landcraft, communicators and depletors to walking, people running around with messages and a pointy forked stick,' Cal groaned.

'A beautiful, pointy forked stick,' Kendra replied.

'Even so. This place feels like the tales I used to hear as a child of people going to live in the wilderness before things started to go wrong with Zephyrion,' Cal said. 'Except our tools are a mirror and this jabber.'

'I know what you mean, but I'm happy swapping all that we had for the fresh, clean air, freedom to do what we want and the sight and taste of fresh green vegetation,' Kendra smiled, taking a deep breath.

'What's the plan then, Max?' Cal asked.

'We can't do much while Zeryn is inside Tamphilus. You know the enforcer code is never to harm aliens on their planet unless they are dangerous to us,' Max replied.

'But we've seen how dangerous and violent Tamphilus is to Quintus,' Cal challenged.

'That's why we'll help Quintus, but Tamphilus is a problem for Rome's authorities, not us,' Max said. 'We have to wait for Zeryn to transmute from Tamphilus. We'll give Quintus an immobiliser and tell him to use it on Zeryn when he separates, and then he'll come and fetch us to finish Zeryn off.'

Kendra looked at Max and said, 'Aren't you forgetting a small but significant detail?'

'I don't think so. I'd love to give Quintus a depletor, but they don't have the technology here to make them,' Max said.

'That's my point. How is Quintus going to make the immobiliser work?' Kendra asked.

'That's easy. He holds this against Zeryn, ideally a bare arm or neck and presses down on the button,' Max replied.

'And then?' Kendra challenged.

'Then a small amount of his energy soul zaps into Marcus...' Max paused. 'Oh.'

'Exactly, Quintus doesn't have an energy soul, does he?' Kendra replied.

'So how will Quintus use it!' Cal asked.

'He can't, but I know someone who could,' Max said, looking at Cal.

Cal looked at Max with a frown, which slowly turned into a terrifying realisation. 'No, no, *no*. I'm not setting foot inside that domus as a slave.'

'But I can't go, as I'm already a servant of Caesar, like Luc. Kendra is the sister of a successful merchant, and Paulie is married to a businessman. Keri is the sister of Paulie's husband,

Simo is a senator, and Juli is a wealthy man from Pompeii,' Max said.

'But I'm Tullia's personal servant now,' Cal protested.

'I'm sure Keri can persuade Tullia to let you go,' Max replied.

'But I don't want to go,' Cal argued.

'I wouldn't ask if you weren't the only one I could trust,' Max said.

'How about if I befriend Quintus? I can visit him regularly and see how Marcus is behaving,' Cal suggested.

'*That's what you wanted him to suggest,*' Gaius thought.

'*Maybe, but I haven't forced him to do it. It was Cal's idea,*' Max replied.

'*Only because the alternative was worse,*' Gaius replied.

'*Isn't that the normal choice? It's not what we want to do, but what is the least worst option,*' Max said.

'That sounds like a good idea,' Kendra said.

'I guess that could work,' Max replied.

Cal and Quintus became good friends over the following four months. Quintus often fell under the ire of his Dominus, but he remained in good spirits thanks to his new friend Appius.

As Quintus learned to trust his new friends, they, in turn, started to tell him a little about who they were. They warned him about Zeryn and explained the transmutation process.

'I wish I could transmute into some wealthy free citizen,' Quintus mused.

'You'd need to be a Shadower,' Cal laughed.

'I think I'd have enjoyed living in your world,' Quintus smiled.

'I doubt it. Unless you were a member of the Elite Council, we had little freedom,' Cal replied.

'But I bet those in power did,' Quintus said.

'Yeah, they had what we were denied,' Cal shrugged.

25
Gladiators

'Quintus, where is my ientaculum?' Marcus Tamphilus shouted.

'Sorry, Appius. I'll be back shortly,' Quintus said, carrying a tray of bread, cheese, and olives as he hurried away.

'*Is ientaculum a regular thing?*' Cal thought.

'*Yes, you call it, erm, breakfast. That's it, breakfast, your first meal in the morning,*' Appius replied.

'*But breakfast is hearty, filling food that gives you a good start to the day. That platter looks more like a snack,*' Cal replied.

Appius laughed. '*Your eating habits are so strange, although I wish I could try those Zingle burgers I can see in your memory.*'

'*What I'd give for a Zingl—*' Cal was cut short by a loud crash and a scream.

'*That sounds like Quintus,*' Appius said.

Appius ran towards the scream and found Quintus kneeling beside Marcus. 'What happened?'

'He went to hit me, but then he went pale and grabbed his chest before passing out. Could this be the transmitting you told me about?' Quintus asked.

'You mean transmuting. Yes, it's possible,' Cal replied. 'Go and fetch Gaius and Decimus. I'll watch over Marcus.'

A while later, Decimus ran into the room, followed by Gaius and Appius.

'Where is he?' Simo demanded.

'I've put him to bed. He woke up but looked so weak, and he was breathing heavily. He also seemed confused,' Cal said.

'So he is transmuting,' Simo replied. 'Zeryn, you will soon be mine.'

'Hold on, Simo. I'm not so sure. I've done a lot of light atmosphere enforcing, and those symptoms don't sound right,' Max said. 'I think we need a medicus.'

'But if we get a medicus, we can't immobilise him,' Simo protested, holding his immobiliser.

'What is that?' Quintus asked.

'It traps the Deceptor in the body so when we kill him, he can't escape into another host,' Simo explained.

'So it stops that Zeryn from being immortal?' Quintus queried.

'Yes, it does,' Simo replied, 'and I'm looking forward to ending my uncle's life.'

'Your uncle?' Quintus queried. 'So you're...'

'I'm Simohal, the son of Shazonrani and grandson of Zyrenev and Kazi,' Simo said proudly.

'And you're inside, Senator Decimus?' Quintus queried. 'Like Cal is inside Appius.'

'That's right,' Simo replied.

'I don't understand how that works,' Quintus said.

'We are Shadowers from another planet with a much denser atmosphere,' Simo explained. 'To survive on your planet, we have to live inside your race, so you're a host, and we build our version of your body, which we can use as a shell to protect our energy souls and separate to live independently.'

'So all we have to do is wait until he's in that shell, and then we can kill him?' Quintus asked. 'But why can't we just kill the host?'

'If we kill them inside the host, then the host dies, and the Deceptor can move into a new host,' Max said. 'It's the same if we kill them once they're in a shell, they can just find a new host and start again.'

'But that imboliser thing stops that?' Quintus queried.

'Immobiliser, you mean. Yes, it does. They can't escape the shell or the host, whichever they're in, so they die when the shell or host does. It's like they're paralysed,' Simo replied.

'Can I have a look?' Quintus asked.

Simo handed over the immobiliser. 'If you push down on the top bit, you'll see two small prongs emerge from the bottom.'

'So, do you stab the person with the prongs?' Quintus queried.

'Not quite. You hold it against them, then push down so the prongs go into them a little, and your energy soul zaps theirs,' Simo explained. 'That's how Max described it to me. But it won't work for you as you're a human, not an energy soul.'

'No, of course not,' Quintus replied. 'Look, Appius is back with the medicus.'

As Simo met the doctor, Quintus looked at the immobiliser and held it against his lower arm before pressing the button. 'Ow, that hurt.'

Max came out of the room where Marcus was resting and saw Quintus using the immobiliser. 'Of course, it hurts. It is stabbing you, even if it's just two small holes,' he said, laughing.

'But it's not doing anything,' Quintus moaned.

'You can't immobilise yourself,' Max laughed. 'The person using it has to have a different energy soul, so the frequencies are different.'

'Can I try it on you?' Quintus asked.

'You're not a Shadower, so you don't have an energy soul to zap anyone with,' Max said, taking the immobiliser off Quintus. 'We'd better give this back to Simo in case he needs it.'

'But how does the energy soul from you travel into the shell of the other Zephyrion?' Quintus said with a puzzled frown.

'That's the ferrum connection all the way through, and the two prongs pass a shot of our energy soul between them and through the Deceptor,' Max explained before turning to Simo and the doctor. 'Simo, this is yours.'

'Where is the aegrotus?' the medicus asked.

'The patient is through here,' Max replied, escorting the doctor into Marcus's room.

The medicus sat on the edge of the bed, studying the senator's laboured breathing and pale complexion. 'Tamphilus, my friend. What ails you?'

Marcus, his face twisted in agony, gasped, 'It feels like a mighty weight crushes my chest as if the fires of Pluto rage within me. The pain... it consumes me like the fury of Vulcan himself.'

After checking Marcus's pulse and placing his hand on his forehead, the medicus reached into his bag and pulled out a small bottle. 'I think your humours are not aligned. A small sip of this and...'

The medicus paused mid-sentence before saying, 'As I was saying, drink a little of this, and we'll let our leech friends do some bloodletting. You'll soon be up again.'

After removing the stopper, he held the bottle to Marcus's lips, who took a large sip. The medicus then stoppered the bottle and placed it back in his bag. Then he pulled out a larger jar, removed the lid, and reached inside. Suddenly, he stopped and quickly withdrew his empty hand.

'Is there a problem?' Max asked.

'You! What are you doing here, boy? You're Caesar's disobedient slave,' Marcus shouted before grabbing his chest.

'Tamphilus, you must not exert yourself. This boy and his friend are why I am here,' the medicus said soothingly.

'But—' Marcus started to say.

'No buts. Lie back and let me apply these leeches,' the medicus said.

Max watched as the medicus lowered his hand into the jar but turned his head away. He pulled out a leech and placed it onto Marcus's chest before repeating the process five more times.

'*This is very odd,*' Gaius thought.

'*What's odd? I'd be squirming about those creepy things,*' Max replied.

'*So would I, but he is an experienced medicus. My Dominus has even used him, and that medicus is fond of applying leeches,*' Gaius said.

'*But if that's true, why is he acting so squeamishly?*' Max asked. He paused briefly and added, '*Unless he is being controlled by someone else inside him.*'

'*You think he's got a Shadower inside him?*' Gaius replied.

'*Only one way to be sure,*' Max said, checking for his mirror.

'Don't worry, Tamphilus. These leeches will sort you out. They'll manage and neutralise your humours,' the medicus said.

'*Did you hear that? Actually, never mind, where's your mirror?*' Max thought.

'*Oh, sorry, I forgot to pick it up,*' Gaius replied.

Max ran into the outer room, 'Simo, give me your mirror.'

'What?' Simo asked, turning from his conversation with Appius and Quintus about the excitement of gladiator battles.

'Your mirror. Pass it to me quickly,' Max said urgently.

'Yeah, sure,' Simo said, passing it over.

'He'll need the leeches left on until they fall off in about an hour,' the medicus said, walking into the room. 'I'll call back later to check on Tamphilus. Please put my leeches in a bowl.'

Max spun around and angled the mirror towards the medicus.

'Don't pull them o—,' the medicus looked down and saw Gaius' reflection in the mirror with a bright aura around him. He realised that meant the young boy may be looking at him similarly.

'Well, is there an aura Max?' Simo asked.

'Simo,' Max snapped, giving a glower that said be quiet.

'Max, Simo?' the medicus said in shock. 'Erm, I thought you said your names were Appius and...'

'Gaius,' Max replied. 'But that's not what surprised you, is it, Jeric?'

'Uh, who?' the medicus said.

'I'd recognise that phrase you use anywhere, no matter how you looked,' Max snarled.

'What did he say?' Simo asked.

'That thing about managing and neutralising things,' Max replied, not breaking his gaze from the medicus.

'You killed Fion and Gran,' Simo said, moving towards the medicus.

'Senator Decimus, forgive me, but this lad's words are mere folly. You know me well. I attended to your wife during her pregnancy,' the medicus insisted.

Simo looked at Max. 'Hand me that mirror.'

Max held it out for Simo, but the medicus immediately dashed towards the exit.

'It is him,' Cal said, sticking out his foot and causing the medicus to sprawl across the floor.

The medicus scrambled to his feet, protesting, 'I'm not Jericesen.'

'Who mentioned Jericesen? I called you Jeric,' Max replied.

'No, you said Jericesen,' the medicus said, backing towards the exit.

Max walked towards Jeric. 'It's over, Jeric. We know you killed Fion and Gran, which means you've been helping Zeryn.'

'Who the heck is Zeryn?' Jeric replied. 'The only Zeryn I know was the son of Zyrenev, and he disappeared years ago.'

'That's him, but he's been pretending to be Nicoeyel,' Max said.

'Nicoeyel isn't Zeryn,' Jeric protested.

'Yes, he is,' Max answered. 'Stop denying it.'

Simo edged towards Jeric and slowly raised his immobiliser.

'Simo, only immobilise him. The medicus is innocent in this,' Max said.

There was a loud crash behind Max, and everyone turned to see Quintus sprawled across the floor, surrounded by goblets and a tray. Max, Cal and Simo ran over to him.

'Quintus, are you alright?' Max asked, helping Quintus to his feet.

'I'm sorry. I went to check on my Dominus, and when I came back in, I tripped and knocked a tray over,' Quintus replied.

As Max released Quintus's hand, he noticed something. 'What happened to your arm?'

Quintus shrugged. 'Nothing, it's fine.'

'That's what I don't understand. I saw you use an immobiliser on yourself, but there are no puncture marks now,' Max challenged.

Quintus frowned but then replied, 'Oh yes, but it hurt, so I never stabbed myself fully with it. It just left two small red marks, which are gone now.'

Max also noticed a bruise growing on Quintus's face. 'Did you hit your face falling, or did Marcus hit you?'

'Uh, no, no, my Dominus never touched me,' Quintus said unconvincingly.

'Max, even when he's ill, Zeryn attacks people, and Tamphilus isn't someone Rome will miss,' Simo said.

'I agree with Simo. We can rid this world of two bad people in one go,' Cal agreed.

'Please, Max. If anything happens to my Dominus, I think I'll be on the streets,' Quintus pleaded. 'Unless Caesar agrees to take me in.'

'Nobody is killing Marcus,' Max said firmly. 'He is Rome's problem, not ours. We have no right to intervene.'

'Maxohal, as I was promoted before you, I am your superior, and if I decide Marcus has to die for the success of this mission, then so be it,' Simo said firmly.

'Of course, Simohal, but you'll have to go through me to do it,' Max replied.

'Max, Simo, come on, you guys have been friends for years. You fighting is what Zeryn wants,' Cal said, putting himself between them.

'Zeryn needs to die. He killed my family and made me an orphan,' Simo snarled.

'I know that Simo and he also killed my partner and possibly my brother. Don't you think I want him to pay as much as you do?' Max replied calmly.

'So stop protecting him. Zeryn deserves to die,' Simo snapped.

'I'm not protecting anyone. I'm only saying Zeryn must pay, but we have no right to kill Tamphilus,' Max said.

'But you've said Tamphilus's treatment of Quintus is wrong,' Simo protested.

'Yes, it is, but—where's Jeric?' Max said, looking around.

'He was here a second ago,' Cal insisted.

Max ran to the doorway and saw the crowd being bustled by someone running through them. 'Come on, he's running away.'

Max ran after Jeric with Cal and Simo in pursuit.

Of all the people he could have encountered, why did it have to be Max and Simo? Jeric cursed. As he passed the Temple of Hope and the vegetable market, Jeric glanced over his shoulder and saw the distinctive sign of people being pushed aside by others running through the crowd. He was sure he could lose Max and Simo if he could reach the Temple of Saturn and the Forum.

'Stop that doctor, he's a killer!' Max shouted.

Jeric turned and saw the three of them closing in. He turned back and clattered into someone, sending them sprawling. He saw a sword on the floor and grabbed it as he got to his feet.

'Stop him, he killed our friend,' Simo screamed.

Jeric turned, swinging the sword before him.

'Drop my sword,' the gladiator said, standing up.

'Stay back,' Jeric shouted, waving the sword wildly.

'You heard my friend, Titus,' a deep and powerful voice said from behind Jeric. 'Drop his sword.'

Jeric spun around, and his sword clashed against another, almost dislodging his own in the encounter. 'Drop your sword, or I'll shoot.'

'Give up, Jeric,' Max said. 'That's a sword, not a depletor. You're not shooting anyone.'

'Maybe not, but I can still kill anyone who comes near me,' Jeric replied as he caught a nearby man across his arm, drawing blood.

'Drop that sword before you injure anyone else, and I have to stop you,' the gladiator with the sword said.

'I'm not scared of you,' Jeric snarled.

'Hey, Cassius, did you hear that? He's not frightened of you,' Titus laughed. 'My sword is making him feel powerful.'

'It's a good job it was your sword and not mine he picked up, or he'd be calling himself our leader,' Cassius laughed as he swung his sword against the one in Jeric's hand, causing it to vibrate.

Jeric grabbed the sword with both hands to steady it, then swung it towards Titus, catching him on his chin.

'Oww, that's not very nice,' Titus said with sarcasm and a smile.

'Looks like he gave you a shaving cut, Titus,' Cassius laughed.

'Jeric, drop your sword and come with us before these gentlemen kill you,' Max said, trying to defuse the situation.

'Is that so you can kill me instead? No thanks,' Jeric replied, continuing to wave his sword from side to side.

Max turned his back on Jeric and whispered, 'Cal, go round to the left, and Simo to the right. We need to bring him down alive. Use your immobilisers on him.'

'We should just let those gladiators kill him,' Cal replied.

'If we do that, his energy soul can move into any of these hundreds of people, and we'll never find him,' Max explained.

Jeric kept waving his sword from side to side, trying to keep Cassius and Titus back, but he noticed Simo and Cal starting to circle him and realised he'd soon be surrounded.

'Now come on, you've had your fun. Now hand back my sword before I get annoyed,' Titus said.

'Never,' Jeric snarled, jabbing the sword towards Titus's stomach.

'Do that again, and it'll be your last act,' Titus said with a scowl.

'No, don't kill him,' Max pleaded.

'You said he was a killer and killed your friends,' Cassius challenged.

'Well, yes, but he needs to face the law,' Max replied.

'If someone attacks me or my friends, I am the law,' Cassius said, prodding his sword towards Jeric.

Jeric used his sword to swipe Cassius's sword away, then noticed Simo moving towards him, and in that instant, he decided.

'Titus, if you want your sword back, then have it,' Jeric screamed, swinging the sword above his head and arcing it downward towards Titus's neck and shoulder.

Cassius saw Jeric move, and as he swung his sword upwards, Cassius drove his sword straight through Jeric's exposed side, making him crumble to the floor. There was a brief flash and then nothing.

'Noooo,' Max screamed, running towards Jeric's dead body.

Titus bent and picked up his sword. 'That'll teach him to mess with a gladiator.'

'Well said,' Cassius laughed. 'I don't know about you, but that's worked up an appetite. Let's eat.'

Max looked around, trying to understand where Jeric had gone.

'Is he dead?' Simo asked.

'The medicus is, but Jeric could be anywhere in this crowd,' Max replied angrily.

'We'd better get back to Zeryn before Tamphilus dies and Zeryn disappears too,' Cal said.

'I told you I wasn't scared of you, didn't I?' Jeric thought.

'What in the gods?' Cassius shouted.

'Cassius, my friend, are you alright?' Titus asked.

'I'm fine. Sorry, something hit me in the eye,' Jeric replied, using his best attempt at Cassius's voice.

'It sounds like it hurt your throat, too,' Titus laughed. 'You need some food and drink. That looks like a good place to eat.'

'You need to realise that I am in charge now. I can make you say and do anything I want, and if you try to disobey me, I can make your existence very uncomfortable,' Jeric snarled. *'From now on, if you want to talk to me, think your words; if you try to shout out, there will be consequences. Now let's go and eat. This strong body needs food.'*

26
HELP ME

'Gaius, Appius, Decimus, please help. I think my Dominus is getting worse,' Quintus pleaded as they walked back into the domus of Marcus Tamphilus.

'What happened?' Max asked.

'The leeches started to drop off, and he said he was hungry. So I made him some soft cheese and bread. He ate some, but the rest is on the table by his bed,' Quintus said.

'Did he become ill straight away?' Max asked, glancing at the fire hearth, where some breadcrumbs were.

'No,' Quintus replied, watching Max. 'He ate a little, then threw some at me, saying it was disgusting, and accused me of poisoning him.'

Max picked up the platter and was about to sniff the plate when Quintus grabbed a chunk of bread and cheese.

'See, it's fine,' Quintus said, eating the food.

'Help me,' Tamphilus said, gasping for air.

'He's very sweaty and pale,' Simo said. 'He's almost blue.'

'We need that medicus again,' Quintus said.

'I'm afraid that medicus was a Deceptor,' Max replied.

'A what?' Quintus asked.

'A Deceptor, it's what we call a criminal on Zephyrion,' Simo explained.

'So, you've killed him?' Quintus asked.

'No, two gladiators killed his host. We don't know where he's gone,' Max said.

'I cannot move,' Tamphilus said. 'Curse those who betrayed me...'

'If my Dominus is dying, does that mean that man, Zeryn, will die too?' Quintus asked.

'Quintus has a point. If Tamphilus dies, then Zeryn can escape,' Simo said.

'We have to immobilise Zeryn now,' Cal said.

'But we have no right to hurt Tamphilus,' Max insisted.

'But if my Dominus is dying anyway, all you're doing is stopping Zeryn's escape,' Quintus insisted.

'He's right, Max,' Cal said. 'We've just lost Jeric; we don't want to lose Zeryn, too.'

'Zeryn's going nowhere,' Simo said, jabbing his immobiliser into Tamphilus's neck.

Tamphilus's eyes widened, and then his body relaxed.

'Is he dead?' Quintus asked.

Max felt Tamphilus's pulse. 'It's very fast, but he's still alive.'

'Look, he's twitching. Zeryn is trying to fight and escape,' Cal said.

'That isn't possible. Once he's immobilised, he can't move,' Max insisted.

'Well, he doesn't seem to know that. He's fighting hard,' Cal replied.

Tamphilus twitched violently and then collapsed.

Max checked his pulse. 'He's dead.'

'Finally, that nasty piece of work has got what he deserved,' Simo snarled.

'But where do I go now?' Quintus cried.

'You'll be busy supporting your Domina now her husband has died,' Gaius explained.

'Can't I come with you to serve Caesar?' Quintus asked.

'Your Domina needs you,' Gaius replied. 'My Dominus would never allow her to be left short.'

'I understand, Gaius. I'm just so worried. I've never lived on the street with the beggars and ruffians,' Quintus said.

'You'll be fine,' Gaius replied. 'We'll help you, won't we, Decimus and Appius?'

'Quintus, if your Domina cannot keep you, I'll take care of you,' Decimus said.

'Where is your Domina?' Gaius asked.

'She's visiting her sister on the other side of Rome,' Quintus said.

'Appius, get the address off Quintus and run to inform her of Tamphilus's death,' Decimus said.

'Shouldn't Quintus do that?' Cal asked.

'Absolutely not. Quintus needs to stay here to prepare Tamphilus's body,' Decimus replied.

'What do you mean, prepare his body?' Quintus asked nervously.

'You need to wash and dress his body, anoint it with perfumed oils and make him dignified for viewing by his family and mourners,' Decimus said.

'Eww,' Quintus replied squeamishly.

'Okay, I'll go and tell her,' Cal said, needing no further explanation.

'Gaius, run back to your domus and inform Caesar of Tamphilus's death,' Decimus ordered.

'Yes, sir,' Gaius said before running off.

A few hours later, Tamphilus's home was teeming with family, friends, and other well-wishers.

'My condolences, Aurelia. Tamphilus was a big character in the senate,' Caesar said.

'He was fine this morning. My house servant said he had some form of attack and called the medicus, but the medicus couldn't make him well, and he died soon after,' Aurelia replied.

'I was passing when the servant rushed out seeking aid,' Decimus said. 'Despite our efforts, fate deemed it was time for Tamphilus to depart this world and join the gods.'

'You're a good man, Decimus,' Caesar said.

'Aurelia, I'm so sorry we meet again under such sad circumstances,' Atia said.

'Atia, thank you for coming,' Aurelia replied. 'Please excuse me, but I must leave you awhile.'

'You need offer no apology. We shall remain at your disposal whenever you require us,' Caesar stated.

'Aurelia, whilst my family funded Tamphilus's career for political gains, I supported it because you and I are friends. If I can help, just ask,' Atia said.

'Thank you, Atia,' Aurelia replied. 'I just need to lie down for a while. I'll be back shortly.'

As Aurelia left the room, Quintus saw an opportunity to approach Caesar.

'Pardon me, esteemed Caesar. Might I have the honour of offering you a refreshment?' Quintus proffered, carrying a tray of wine goblets.

'You're the one who tried to get Tamphilus help, aren't you?' Caesar asked.

'Yes, Sir,' Quintus replied. 'Quintus at your service, Sir.'

'Your Dominus was lucky to have such a dedicated servant. I, too, have servants like that with Marcia and her children Gaius and Livia,' Caesar said.

'Yes, Sir. I know Gaius and Livia. They say working for you is a privilege. I hope I have such an opportunity,' Quintus stated.

'I clearly treat them too well,' Caesar laughed before walking off.

Quintus headed back towards the culina, where more food and drinks were being prepared. He noticed Max inspecting some flowers on the far side of the room and rushed over to him.

'Max, what are you doing?' Quintus asked.

'I was admiring this lovely plant. I've never seen anything like it with blue flowers,' Max said. 'Plants have died out on my planet, so it's nice to see this looking almost majestic, with its tall stems and those flowers almost like an army helmet.'

'Don't touch it,' Quintus shouted.

'Why not?' Max asked.

'Um, it's delicate. If you touch it, the flowers die as humans are poisonous to it,' Quintus replied.

Max looked at the plant sadly and turned away. 'It seems both our species are poisonous to plants, but in different ways.'

'Let's get these refreshments to our guests,' Quintus said, moving Max towards some loaded platters and carrying them back into the main rooms.

Across the central atrium, Simo spotted Paulie alone and wandered over to her. 'Paulie, lovely to see you. Is Keri and Cal with you?'

'Yes, Tullia and Appius are almost inseparable,' Paulie replied. 'I have to keep reminding Keri and Cal they're not a couple on this planet.'

'Hello, both of you,' Kendra said, acknowledging Paulie and Simo. 'It seems everyone is mourning the passing of Tamphilus.'

Paulie scoffed. 'I'm not mourning him. He was a most unpleasant man. Atia's family only supported him for political reasons. I'm here for his widow's sake. Aurelia and Atia have been friends since childhood.'

'I heard you recently had an altercation with him at Caesar's banquet,' Kendra said.

'He was hitting Max, well Max inside that sweet boy Gaius,' Paulie replied.

'Well, that's the end of that bully Tamphilus and Zeryn,' Kendra said. 'I'm sure there's no tears for Zeryn's passing.'

'Pardon me, esteemed guests, but may I offer you some refreshments?' Livia asked.

'Livia, Luc, why are you serving?' Kendra asked.

'Caesar offered Gaius and me to help because Tamphilus's death was so sudden the family had made no preparations,' Livia explained.

'Livia, you don't have time to chat,' Quintus snapped.

'Sorry, Quintus,' Livia replied.

'He's very bossy,' Kendra said. 'Is he normally like this?'

'He's a strange one,' Cal said, joining the group with Keri. 'I've known him for nearly five months now, and sometimes he's timid and nervous; other times, he can be aggressive and challenging.'

'You should see my Cal sometimes when he returns after spending a day with Quintus,' Keri said, hugging Cal. 'He's worn out.'

'Tullia and Keri, do I need to remind you that Appius is your servant boy? Such public behaviour is not acceptable,' Atia said sternly.

'Sorry, Atia,' Tullia replied with an impish grin.

'May I offer you some refreshments?' Gaius asked.

'Your sister just beat you to it,' Paulie said.

'What's next, Max?' Keri asked.

'The family have announced a week of mourning with a procession on the seventh day, followed by a service and internment in the family mausoleum,' Max replied.

'Max, you're adorable,' Kendra laughed.

'What did I say?' Max frowned.

'It's that you're always about the moment,' Kendra chuckled. 'I think Keri meant what's next for all of us?'

'Yes, I did,' Keri laughed.

'Kendra has a point, Max,' Simo said. 'Now that Zeryn has gone, do we stay here and hunt for Jeric, or do we build an Exodus machine and head home?'

'How can we build an Exodus machine?' Max challenged. 'We've got no computers or electricity, and thanks to Jeric, we've lost our scientist and engineer.'

'Poor Gran and Fion,' Paulie said.

'I miss Gran's quirky ways,' Luc added. 'But we still have one engineer.'

'Who?' Keri asked. 'Oh, you mean Juli. Where is she anyway?'

'Cornelius said he had to return to Pompeii, but he promised to return with Juli soon,' Simo said.

'Juli's a technician and a junior engineer. Fion was a senior engineer,' Max replied.

'But you're an engineer, Max,' Luc said.

'No, I'm not. I'm just a simple enforcer,' Max insisted.

'Zym told us what an incredible engineer you were until you gave it up to become an enforcer to investigate who tried to kill him,' Simo replied.

'My brother is just living in the past,' Max replied, looking away.

Kendra drew her finger from her eye and down her cheek, indicating to the others that she could see Max was crying.

Simo moved in front of Max and put his hands on Gaius's shoulders. 'Your brother is an incredible man who loves you so much.'

'If he loves me, why did he have to get fatally injured?' Max asked, looking down at his feet. 'Everyone leaves me; for all I know, he's gone too.'

'He hasn't left you, Max. I bet he's getting better and planning to join us to find Zeryn and get revenge,' Simo replied as the others gathered around Max in a protective circle.

'But I don't want revenge, I just want Zym, Lin and my parents b...' Max's voice trailed off as he collapsed to the floor.

'We need a medicus,' Decimus shouted as more people gathered around the body of Max curled up on the floor.

Caesar heard the commotion and came to investigate. 'What's happened to Gaius?'

Decimus was crouched on the floor, checking Gaius's pulse and temperature. 'He was talking, and then he suddenly collapsed.'

'Is he still alive?' Caesar asked.

'Yes, Caesar. His pulse is weak but steady,' Decimus replied.

'Quintus!' Caesar shouted.

Quintus came running. 'Yes, Caesar, sir.'

'Go and fetch a cart to take Gaius to my domus,' Caesar ordered. 'Livia!'

'I'm here, sir,' Livia replied.

'Run and fetch my physician; we'll meet you at my domus,' Caesar instructed.

A short while later, Gaius's weak body, laid on a simple stretcher, was lifted off the cart by Decimus and Appius and carried into the domus of Julius Caesar.

'Gaius, my son! Thank the gods you were there, Caesar, sir,' Marcia said, fussing around Gaius on the stretcher. 'What's happened?'

'We don't yet know what ails him, Marcia. He collapsed for no reason,' Caesar replied. 'I've called for my physician.'

'This way,' Marcia said, waving towards the servants' quarters.

'Nonsense, Marcia,' Caesar said. 'Decimus, go this way to one of my guest rooms.'

Marcia looked shocked. 'But—'

'No buts, Marcia. Besides, I can't have my physician going into servant quarters,' Caesar said.

A short while later, the physician finished examining Gaius. 'I don't think bloodletting will help, but we need to boost his pulse. I recommend rest for three days, plenty of fresh food and a massage of lavender oils twice daily.'

'I'll prepare the oils right away,' Marcia said, hurrying away.

As Caesar escorted the physician out, Decimus and Appius stayed with Gaius.

'Max, can you hear us?' Cal asked.

Max opened his eyes and closed them again.

'Max, it's Simo. How are you feeling?'

'Qui…' Max muttered before passing out again.

'Quick, what?' Cal asked.

'How is he?' Luc asked, rushing into the room. 'I've just been talking to Marcia, and she's so worried.'

'I'm not sure,' Cal said. 'Could he have been poisoned? Maybe what killed Tamphilus is in that house, and now it's got Max.'

'But we've all been there, and we're…' Livia fell to the floor as Marcia entered the room.

'No, no, no. My beautiful children, what have I done to anger the gods?' Marcia screamed.

Caesar was bidding farewell to the physician when they heard Marcia's scream and ran back to the guest room.

'That bed is plenty big enough for both of them. Help me get Livia into the other side of the bed,' Caesar instructed the physician.

After a quick examination, the physician confirmed that Livia was suffering from the same mystery ailment as Gaius.

'Should we ban citizens from attending the domus of Tamphilus?' Caesar asked.

'No. If there is anything there, then it's too late anyway after today's gathering,' the physician said. 'I'll just spread the word about treatment in case anyone else falls ill.'

Caesar escorted the physician out and then headed back towards the guest room. Marcia had left to prepare more oils, leaving Decimus and Appius to look after Livia and Gaius.

'Marcia, come quickly,' Caesar bellowed as soon as he entered the room.

'Yes, Caesar, sir,' Marcia replied before rushing into the room and stopping short. 'What the gods!'

'We need two more beds,' Caesar said, looking at the collapsed bodies of Decimus and Appius.

A few hours later, after putting two more temporary beds into the large guest room, the house settled for the evening as Caesar and his family retired to bed. Marcia wandered into the guest room and checked on Appius and Decimus, rubbing lavender oil onto their limbs before repeating the process on Livia and Gaius.

'My babies, please don't leave me,' Marcia pleaded as she stroked Gaius's hair back from his eyes.

Livia groaned, and Marcia walked over to her and looked down at her daughter. 'How can I have produced something as special as you and your brother? May the gods hear me and let me go so you can survive, my precious children.'

'Marcia, you need to sleep,' Caesar said.

'Oh, Lord Caesar. I didn't hear you enter. I didn't disturb you, did I?' Marcia said.

'No, Marcia,' Caesar replied. 'I was just worried about our patients and wanted to check on them.'

'They all seem to be in a deep sleep,' Marcia said.

After a quick check on each of them, Ceasar headed towards the door. 'I realise you will probably ignore me, and I have no issue with that for once, but please get some rest. We will all need to be strong over the coming days.'

'Yes, Sir. I will try,' Marcia replied as Caesar headed off.

The following morning, Caesar was up early and wandered into the guest room to check on his unexpected guests. He walked over to Marcia, asleep in a chair in the corner of the room, and gently shook her.

'Marcia, you need to go and rest. Nothing can be gained from wearing yourself into the ground,' Caesar said quietly.

'Oh, my word, Caesar, Dominus, sir. I must have drifted off. I need to get on. I've not cleaned or even started to prepare your ientaculum,' Marcia said in a fluster.

'I will get something to eat at the Forum, and Calpurnia is going to see her brother Lucius and won't be back until tomorrow evening, so all you have to do today is rest and take care of these sleeping guests,' Caesar replied.

'But I need—'

'You need to rest, Marcia. These young ones, plus Decimus, need you fit and healthy, and so do I,' Caesar said. 'Now, has there been any change in their symptoms overnight?'

'Not really, Sir. Although they've been shouting some strange things in their sleep,' Marcia replied. 'I've heard several mentions of Exodus and Zeryn plus Decimus called out to his mother. But the strangest thing was...'

'Was, what, Marcia?'

'My boy shouted out for someone called Zym, calling him his brother,' Marcia replied, frowning. 'Then he mentioned a Lin, saying he'll love her forever, but he's never been with a woman.'

'It's probably delirium caused by this illness,' Caesar replied. 'I'll see if there is any news at the Forum. Now go and get some rest.'

'Yes, Sir,' Marcia replied. 'I just need to give them their lavender oil massages first.'

'And then to bed with you. The domus needs a head of house who is gladiator fit,' Caesar insisted. 'That means well rested and fed.'

'Yes, Sir. I swear I will after their massages,' Marcia replied.

Caesar headed off as Marcia went off to prepare the oils.

As he walked towards the Forum, Caesar called into his favourite thermopolium.

'Some cheese, olives and bread, please, and my usual drink,' Caesar requested.

'We have some especially roasted chicken, Caesar,' the thermopolarius said.

'You have tempted me; I'll have some,' Caesar replied.

Caesar sat listening to those around him as he consumed his food and drink.

'I hear Tamphilus died from a contagious illness,' someone said.

'Indeed, several servants have succumbed to it. They're calling it the deep sleep,' another said.

'Not just servants. Senator Decimus has fallen foul of it and several noblewomen.'

'It's not even restricted to Rome. A tradesman told me his contact in Pompeii also went into the deep sleep.

'Are you still attending the funeral procession of Tamphilus?'

'I'll make sure I'm busy.'

'Me too.'

'Well, I'll be attending,' Caesar said, interrupting the gossip.

'Caesar, are you sure that's wise?'

'Why wouldn't I?' Caesar replied.

'But all those people getting ill, and the death of Tamphilus.'

'I understand your concerns, but we must pay our respects to Senator Tamphilus and his family,' Caesar responded. 'Besides, Decimus and several affected staff are at my domus, and I'm unaffected.'

'I wish I had your confidence. Just be careful, Caesar,' one of them said.

Caesar smiled reassuringly before rising from his seat.

'Thank you for your counsel, my friends,' he said. 'I shall heed your words and welcome your company.'

Caesar left the thermopolium and wandered towards the Forum, his mind full of the last twenty-four hours. His head told him to be cautious, but his heart said he knew Decimus, Gaius, and Livia, and what he saw was not a deadly illness. He didn't know what ailed them, but he felt it wasn't what killed Tamphilus.

'Please, Sir. Spare a denarius.'

Caesar started to walk past the beggar, but the familiarity of the voice made him stop and look. 'Haven't I seen you at the domus of Tamphilus?'

'I was, Sir. But my Domina said the scandal of the Tamphilus virus meant she could no longer afford to keep me and several other servants,' Quintus replied.

'I have a temporary need of servants. Come to my domus in three hours,' Caesar said.

'Yes, Caesar. Anything to be of service to you,' Quintus replied.

27

THE AWAKENING

Marcia had spent almost every night sleeping in a chair, watching over Gaius, Livia, and the others, but with so little change in their condition and fatigue ravaging her, she decided to spend one night in her bed. This made being disturbed by a noise in the middle of the night even more frustrating, but she had to investigate.

As Marcia entered the central atrium, she spotted the shadowy outline of a man's back on the far side. Creeping, she closed the gap until she could see him. Her gasp caught his attention, causing him to turn.

'Oh my word, Gaius. What are you doing out of bed, and why are you naked?' Marcia said.

'Uh, who? What?' he replied.

'You need to get back to bed, but first, let's get you a tunic. What would our Domina or Dominus have said seeing you wandering about like this with your tunic tassel swinging around?' Marcia scowled, grabbing him by the arm.

A few minutes later, Marcia pulled a grey tunic over Gaius's head and hugged him. 'My boy, I've been so worried about you.

I thank the gods for bringing my Gaius back to me. Now let's get you back to bed.'

'Yes, Mater, but first, I need to attend to a private matter,' he replied as the fog slowly cleared from his brain, and he started to understand his circumstances.

'Well, you know where it is. I'll check the rest of the domus, and then I'll come and look in on you and the others,' Marcia said before heading towards the front entrance to check the doors.

'I need to get back to the others quickly,' he thought. 'Tonight could become very difficult.'

After confirming that the domus was secure, Marcia entered the guest bedroom. After checking on Decimus and Appius, she wandered over to Livia and kissed her gently on the forehead. 'Your frater has returned to me; now it's your turn, my beautiful.'

Livia moaned gently, which Marcia interpreted as a positive sign, before she went to check on Gaius. 'Gaius, are you still awake?'

Gaius snored quietly, and Marcia smiled. 'Just like your father used to,' she said. Marcia went to pull the sheet over him but stopped short. 'I'm sure I put a grey tunic on you, not a white one. Oh dear, did you have a little spraying accident and have to change? Never mind, I won't tell anyone.'

As Marcia returned to bed, a figure stealthily crept into the guest bedroom. He looked around the room, noting Livia, Appius, and Decimus. 'This is worse than I thought,' he said.

He walked over to Gaius's bed and shook him gently. 'Gaius, wake up.'

Gaius grumbled, 'I'm asleep. Besides, it's not my turn.'

'Not your turn for what? Actually, that doesn't matter; wake up. It's me, Max.'

'You can't be Max. I can feel you shaking me, but Max is inside me, so you can't be Max,' Gaius replied, keeping his eyes shut. 'Now go away.'

'Gaius, you need to wake up. I am Max. I've transmuted,' Max replied, shaking Gaius more vigorously.

Gaius opened one eye and looked up at the person shaking him. Then he opened his other eye, and they both widened before he let out a scream, 'Wha—'

Max quickly put his hand over Gaius's mouth, 'Shh, you'll wake everyone up.'

'B-but, you're me.'

'No, I just look like you,' Max said. 'We separated tonight after my transmutation finished. I wandered off, all confused and dazed, until Marcia found me.'

'At least my Mater found you. That's okay then,' Gaius replied, closing his eyes again.

'Gaius, it's not okay. Now two people are walking around looking like her son,' Max said.

'So, she's got twins now. Two for one. Now, can I go back to sleep?'

Max sighed and shook Gaius again. 'In the next few hours, she will see two Livias, two Appius and two Decimus.'

'Whaat?' Gaius exclaimed.

'If I've transmuted, so will everyone who came with me. Including the three in this room,' Max replied.

'What three?' Gaius asked, begrudgingly sitting up and looking around. 'What the gods?'

'It seems like the others collapsed not long after we did,' Max said.

As Gaius looked around the room, there was a thud from the other side of his large bed. 'What was that?'

'I think Luc may have just left Livia,' Max replied. 'Are there any tunics in this room?'

'Over on those shelves. Why do you want one? You're already wearing one,' Gaius replied in a sleepy haze.

'Do you want to see your sister naked?' Max asked.

'Eww, no, thank you.'

'Then let me get a tunic,' Max replied as he grabbed one before heading to Livia's side of the bed.

'W-w-where am I?' a voice said from the floor beside the bed.

'You're in Rome and just finished transmuting from Livia. Now put this on,' Max replied, handing over a tunic.

'I'm w-w-where, and who's L-Livia?' Luc replied.

'Livia is my soror; what's wrong with your speech?' Gaius asked, sitting up as curiosity beat his desire to sleep.

'W-W-Why is everyone calling me L-Livia?' Luc asked, pulling the tunic over his head. He started to pull it down and then gasped. 'Why is my chest swollen?'

'It's not swollen, Luc. You're a girl. They're breasts,' Max replied.

'I'm a g-g-girl?' Luc challenged.

'Whoa, hang on. Max, you look like me, and you're saying that's not Livia; it's Luc who looks exactly like her?' Gaius said, getting out of bed. 'Will all of you look identical to your hosts?'

'Yes, Gaius. That's how this works. We build a shell identical to yours so we can transmute from you into it,' Max explained.

'But, Max, can't you change bits so you look a little different?' Gaius asked.

'Changing anything might make the shell unstable because we don't know the impact of changing a cell here or there. So we have to make an exact copy,' Max replied.

Luc looked at Gaius and then turned to Max. 'You're M-Max? As in M-M-Maxoraxin?'

'Maxohal, actually, but don't worry, Luc, the confusion wears off quite quickly,' Max said.

'Where's Keri?' asked Cal, sitting up.

'The whole house is going to wake up at this rate,' Max sighed, rushing over to Cal. 'Put this on,' Max said, handing over another tunic.

'Why would I wear that?' Cal asked before looking down. 'I'm naked, and who is this boy in my bed?'

'That's Appius. He was your host,' Max replied.

'Who are you?' Cal demanded, putting the tunic on.

'It's M-M-Max,' Luc said.

'Max? But he's about ten years or more older than that boy,' Cal stated. 'Actually, who are you?'

'I'm L-L-Luc.'

'But you're female, and Luc is male,' Cal snapped. 'Where are we?'

'M-Max!' Luc exclaimed.

'Yes, Luc. Do you want something?' Max asked.

'Yes, no, I m-mean, I remember. We're on KLT3.4e9.3,' Luc said.

'Well, yes, I think that's the planet, but we are definitely in Rome,' Max replied.

'Where's Jeric and Z-Z-Zeryn?' Luc asked.

'Zeryn is dead, but Jeric escaped, and we don't know where he is now,' Max replied.

'Zeryn! Yes, I remember now. We came here to find and kill him,' Cal replied.

There was another thud, and Max groaned.

Simo stood up, looking around in a daze.

'Blimey,' Gaius said, looking at Simo standing there naked.

'Oh, for the love of gods,' Max said, grabbing another tunic and rushing to Simo. 'Put this on, Simo.'

'Who is Simo? Oh, yeah, that's me.'

'Just put the tunic on, and can you lower your voice, please,' Max said in frustration.

'Who are you?' Simo asked.

'I'm Maxohal.'

'But Max is—'

'Yes, Max is older than I look now, but we've come to a new planet with a light atmosphere, and we've had to use local inhabitants to transmute into a shell,' Max said. 'Now we've all caught up, can we be quiet?'

'Where's Jeric? He could help us find Zeryn?' Simo said.

Max visibly sagged his shoulders like someone who had been progressively worn down. 'Zeryn is dead, and Jeric has escaped and could be anywhere.'

'Zeryn's dead? I wanted to kill him,' Simo growled.

'You did,' Max said. 'Or at least you immobilised him inside Marcus Tamphilus, so he died with Tamphilus.'

'I did?' Simo asked, and then the confusion started to lift. He added, 'I did. I remember now. He was trying to escape, and I immobilised him.'

'Yes, I remember that,' Cal said.

'I d-d-don't r-remember that,' Luc replied with a puzzled look.

'You weren't there,' Max said. 'Quintus came for Gaius and Decimus when his Dominus took ill. Mater wouldn't let you come as well.'

'M-M-Mater? Oh, you m-m-mean Livia's m-m-mother,' Luc replied.

'And mine,' Gaius added. 'But I'm confused.'

'About what?' Max asked.

'How come Luc looks like Livia but has that stutter?' Gaius said.

'Yeah, w-w-why am I s-s-s-stuttering again? I thought I was cured.' Luc grumbled.

'I'm no medicus, but I'd guess your stutter is part of you, but when you're in a host, their mind suppresses it,' Max replied.

'S-So I'm stuck like this f-f-f-f, until all time,' Luc sighed.

'Not forever, hopefully. Over time, you might learn how to control it,' Max said.

'I've heard singing or speaking in a rhythm can help with stuttering,' Gaius suggested.

'W-W-What do you m-mean,' Luc asked.

'Well, think of a poem or say a speech that rhymes,' Gaius suggested.

'I d-don't know any poems,' Luc said.

'Well, make one up,' Simo said.

Luc frowned and said, 'My name is Luc, and I make people puke.'

Simo looked at Max, who looked at Gaius, and he looked at Cal before they started laughing.

'W-what? I d-didn't s-stutter,' Luc protested.

'Oh, Luc, only you could do a poem to insult yourself,' Max laughed, wiping the tears from his eyes.

'Come on, Luc. Pretend you're my soror, sorry, my sister, Livia. Give it some style,' Gaius laughed.

'Like w-w-what?' Luc asked.

'You've been inside her for a few months; use her attitude to say something,' Gaius replied.

Luc looked around the room as his brain spun with ideas, and then he put his hand on his hip and started to sashay across the room.

'My name is Lucius Livia,
In Rome, I strut like a diva!
A teenage girl with sass and sheen,
In sandals, I reign as the Roman queen.'

As he finished the poem, Luc turned dramatically to see Gaius, Max, Cal and Simo in hysterical laughter. 'Now what?'

'Nothing,' Max replied, fighting back his tears.

'That was perfect,' Simo cried.

'I can't breathe,' Gaius said, holding his sides. 'That was more Livia than Livia.'

'And you didn't stutter,' Max said, still wiping his eyes.

'I know, b-b-but I can't talk in p-p-poems all the time,' Luc replied.

'What in the gods is going on here?'

The fear of being discovered had come to fruition as they all turned towards the voice.

'Quintus, you scared us to death,' Max sighed with relief.

Quintus scanned the room, noting Gaius and Max. 'So, you've transmitted then.'

'Transmuted, yes,' Max said.

'Where are Appius, Decimus and Livia?' Quintus asked.

'They're still asleep,' Simo said.

'Well, you can't be here when the Dominus and Domina awaken,' Quintus stated.

'What do you mean?' Cal asked.

'How would you explain two of each of you?' Quintus said.

'Quintus is right, but where can we go?' Max asked.

'We could go to the domus of Decimus,' Simo suggested.

'How would you explain it to Decimus's family when he wakes up here?' Quintus said.

'We need an empty safe house,' Max said.

'What about the domus of Marcus Tamphilus?' Quintus suggested.

'But isn't your Domina there?' Max asked.

'She has gone to her parents until the day of Marcus's funeral in two days due to the deep sleep disease,' Quintus said. There's a hidden chamber under the building you could hide in.'

'If she's gone away, why are you here and not with her?' Max asked.

'Caesar asked for help because Gaius and Livia were struck down, and she agreed to lend me to him,' Quintus replied.

'Tamphilus's domus sounds like a good option,' Simo said.

'I don't think we have any choice,' Cal added.

'My Mater and Dominus can't see duplicates of us,' Gaius confirmed.

'I'll take you there and show you the hidden chamber,' Quintus said.

'What about Appius, Decimus and Livia?' Simo asked.

'I'll tell them what happened,' Gaius replied. 'We can meet up once things have settled down.'

A short while later, Quintus moved a large, heavy seat in Tamphilus's home to reveal a trapdoor. He put his finger into a hole and slid it backwards, releasing a bolt before grabbing the rough hessian handle and pulling it upward to reveal a ladder into the basement.

'Quick, hide down here. I've already put some jugs of wine and water mix down there, just in case you get thirsty, and I'll bring some food later this morning,' Quintus said.

'Thank you, Quintus. How can we ever repay you?' Cal asked.

'Just keep quiet is all I ask,' Quintus replied.

Max, Cal, Simo, and Luc climbed down the ladder into the underground room and looked around using the candle Quintus had given them. Above them, they heard the trapdoor close, followed by the bolt sliding and the scraping sound of the seating being pulled back into position.

'What's that smell?' Cal asked.

'It's coming from over there,' Simo said, pointing towards an area blocked by some crates.

Max walked towards the crates and started to retch. 'The smell is dreadful as you get closer to the crates, and the flies are increasing too.'

'Let me look,' Simo said, marching over to the crates and looking behind them. 'There's nothing there, but the smell is awful.'

'I think there's rotting food in these crates,' Max replied. 'Help me get them down and open them.'

They started lifting the crates down and opening them to reveal military equipment, cutlery, and other tableware. After a fifth box of tableware, military tunics and clothing, Max said, 'Could the smell be from these? There is blood on some of them like they were used in battle.'

Simo glanced down at the crate he had just opened. 'Max, you need to see this.'

28
THERE CAN BE ONLY ONE

'B-B-But that's not possible,' Luc said.

'I'm afraid we're proof that it is possible,' Max replied.

The four of them looked down into the contents of the crate.

'So, if that is Quintus, then the Quintus who showed us down here is?' Cal said, looking at the face exposed above the surrounding salt.

'It must be Jeric,' Simo replied. 'Or another of Zeryn's cronies.'

'But Quintus was with Tamphilus when we chased Jeric to the Forum, and that gladiator killed Jeric's host,' Max stated. 'So, it can't be Jeric inside Quintus.'

'Are we overthinking this?' Cal said.

'What do you mean?' Max asked.

'We know Zeryn is dead, and Jeric escaped in the Forum, so surely Simo is right. The Quintus who brought us down here is one of Zeryn's cronies,' Cal replied. 'Besides, even if Jeric had managed to get from the Forum to Quintus before dissipating, he hasn't had time to transmute. It's taken us months.'

Max looked at Cal and frowned, 'Possibly, unless...'

'Unless w-w-what?' Cal asked.

Max started pacing the room, 'Well, if Quintus is dead, then Quintus cannot be Quintus and must be… but that's impossible. Therefore, Quintus is, no, he can't be him either. So…'

'What's he doing?' Cal asked.

'He's in M-M-Max mode,' Luc said.

'What?' Cal said.

'When Max starts to think about things, he wanders around talking to himself,' Simo replied. He only does it when confused or stressed.'

Max walked back to the crate containing Quintus. 'Hmm, several days, possibly a week. But there's a lot of salt in there…'

Simo walked back to the ladder they had used to enter the basement. He climbed up and tried to move the trapdoor, but it wouldn't budge. 'Luc, Cal, give me a hand.'

Luc climbed the ladder beside Simo as Cal pulled a crate over and stood on it. The three pushed against the trapdoor, causing dust to rain down on them as they banged and heaved against the hatch, but it wouldn't move.

'We're trapped,' Simo said.

'But there were breadcrumbs in the fireplace…' Max mused.

'Max, we need your help to open the trapdoor,' Cal said.

'What plants are humans poisonous to?' Max thought.

'L-L-Lots of p-plants are p-poisonous to humans,' Luc said.

'I know, but I mean the other way round. What plants are humans poisonous to?' Max replied.

'What are you on about, Max?' Simo said. 'Plants can poison humans, but humans don't poison plants. We can kill them in many ways, but humans are not poisonous to them.'

'Exactly,' Max replied with a smile.

'Exactly what?' Cal asked.

'Does anyone remember that lovely blue flowering plant in Tamphilus's culina?' Max asked.

'I d-do,' Luc replied. 'Livia called it the p-p-poisonous hood of monks or s-s-something like that.'

'That's right. Appius called it monkshood and aconite,' Cal confirmed.

'Aconite?' Simo challenged. 'But that causes nausea and weakness and can be fatal from what I can remember from Decimus's memory. He'd often joke about people he hated needing a good dose of aconite.'

'Hmm, why would you keep a poisonous plant in a kitchen?' Max pondered.

'Well, I'm no enforcer, but at a guess, I'd say to poison people,' Cal replied.

'Exactly,' Max said.

'What's with all the 'exactlys'?' Cal asked.

'What if Tamphilus wasn't Zeryn?' Max challenged.

'But we saw it was him, and we saw him die,' Simo protested.

'Did we?' Max replied. 'What if he was just a nasty person who was poisoned and died?'

'But I immobilised him, and he fought against it until Tamphilus died,' Simo argued.

'Luc, you were immobilised on Zephyrion; how did you feel?' Max asked.

'T-T-To start with, I just felt at ease, and then I r-r-realised I couldn't m-m-move, which stressed m-m-me, but then I felt like I was d-d-dreaming, so I relaxed again,' Luc replied.

'So, you couldn't fight back?' Max said.

'I d-d-didn't want to. It was so p-p-peaceful,' Luc answered.

'So, an immobilised Shadower is relaxed and can't resist,' Max said.

'But you saw his aura,' Cal insisted.

'I saw a glimpse of an aura, but it could have come from someone behind Tamphilus,' Max replied.

'S-S-Someone like Q-Quintus!' Luc exclaimed. 'He was the other side of Tamphilus when the senator hit the tray out of your hand.'

'Exactly,' Max said.

'But we saw Zeryn die!' Simo argued. 'And will you stop saying exactly? It's getting on my nerves.'

'We saw Tamphilus die, but where was the flash as Zeryn left the body and dissipated as Dantrek did?' Max insisted. 'Also, what is the one thing Zeryn craves the most?'

'P-P-Power?' Luc suggested.

'Exact...um, you're spot on. Ever since Quintus knew Gaius was Caesar's servant, he's wanted to work in the same household, and where is he now?' Max asked.

'Oh no, Livia, Marcia and Gaius are at risk,' Luc replied.

'And so is Caesar,' Max agreed. 'I see you didn't stutter under stress, Luc.'

'Do you think he'll kill Caesar?' Simo asked.

'No, I think it's far worse than that,' Max said.

'W-W-What could be worse than Caesar being k-killed?' Luc said with a puzzled look.

'Quintus killing himself and moving into Caesar,' Max said. 'Come on, we need to get out of here.'

'I need a drink first. We dislodged a lot of dust trying to open that trapdoor,' Cal said, walking over to the jugs of wine and water. He poured himself a cup of the mix. 'Anyone else want some?'

'No,' Max shouted, running across the room and knocking the cup out of Cal's hand.

'Whoa. Why did you do that, just because you don't want one?' Cal asked in annoyance.

'How did Quintus know we would need to hide down here and leave jugs of drink for us?' Max challenged.

Simo picked up a jug and sniffed it. 'This smells like soil, really strong soil. I'd recognise that smell anywhere; it's mandragora.'

'What does it do?' Max asked.

'It's used for all sorts of things, like pain relief, to help with digestion and as a sedative, but Decimus said it was very toxic.

He fired one member of his staff for bringing it into his domus,'
Simo explained.

'As a sedative?' Max mused. 'Would it be enough to render
them unconscious?'

'In the right quantities. At lower doses, it would cause
drowsiness, dizziness and possibly hallucinations, and too
much could be fatal,' Simo replied.

Max started smashing the jugs.

'What are you doing?' Cal protested. 'It may not be that good
for you, but it's all we have to drink.'

'And that's why I'm doing this, because the longer we're
down here, the more tempted we would be to drink it,' Max
said.

Luc picked up a jug and smashed it into the floor. 'M-M-Max
is r-right. Quintus knows that even if we d-d-detected the
poison, as we got thirstier, we'd be increasingly t-tempted to
drink it.'

Simo walked over to the crates and started opening more of
them.

'What are you looking for?' Cal asked.

'Some more salt to cover Quintus to mask the smell and
hopefully some swords to prise open that trapdoor,' Simo
replied.

Twenty minutes later, Simo sighed. 'How can anyone have so
many crates of military things but no swords?'

'I've f-f-found some m-more salt in this small crate,' Luc said.

'Let's tip it over, Quintus's deceased body, to try to stop
the smell,' Simo said as he and Cal lifted it and tipped it over
Quintus's head. As the last of the salt poured out, a clunk of
metal hit the stone floor.

Luc bent down and picked up a large key on a ring. 'Why
would you hide a key in some salt?'

'Presumably to conceal the key to a door,' Max said. 'Check
all the walls to see if there's a hidden door down here.

A short while later, the friends slumped to the floor after pulling everything away from the walls.

'There's no hidden door down here,' Simo sighed.

'Hmm,' Max mumbled, lying on his back and staring at the ceiling.

'I said there's no hidden door down here,' Simo said.

'We've checked behind every crate and shelving,' Cal said.

'I even checked the f-f-floor,' Luc added.

'Hmm,' Max replied, tilting his head but still looking up.

'Are you listening to us?' Simo asked.

'What's that board up there with the hooks in?' Max said, looking straight above him.

'It looks like somewhere just to hang tools, etc. To keep them out of the way,' Cal replied, looking in the same direction as Max.

'But why is it held in place by grooved tracks, like it can slide?' Max pondered.

Cal got up, dragged a crate underneath the board, and stood on the crate. He grabbed one of the hooks and pulled hard, and the board slid along the grooves, revealing another trapdoor with a keyhole. 'Luc, pass me that key.'

Cal slid the key into the lock and tried to turn it. 'It won't open.'

Simo climbed up beside Cal. 'Let me try. I'm a lot bigger than you.'

Simo used all his strength, and the lock started to give with a groan and a creak. With one final twist, the lock cracked, the trapdoor swung down, and a rug fell through.

'What can you see?' Max asked.

'It looks like Tamphilus's bedroom,' Simo replied, brushing aside the dust that fell on him from the rug.

Simo clasped his hands together. 'Step on my hands, Cal and I'll lift you up.'

Cal clambered into the bedroom and looked down. 'Yes, it's his bedroom. Come on, there's nobody here.'

Decimus helped Max and Luc clamber into the bedroom and climbed up with their help.

'We need to get back to Caesar's domus,' Max said urgently.

'Okay, but can we get a drink from the culina first?' Cal asked.

'Y-Y-Yes, p-p-please,' Luc said.

'Come on then, but we need to be quick,' Max insisted.

'Do you want some mulsum?' Cal asked as they entered the kitchen, and he found and opened a sealed amphora.

'T-T-This is posca n, not m-m-mulsum,' Luc insisted after sniffing it first to ensure it didn't have the earthy smell of mandragora.

'What's the difference?' Cal said, pouring some into goblets.

'Mulsum is a mix of wine, honey, and water, but posca is a soldier's drink of wine, water, vinegar, and sometimes herbs,' Simo replied.

As the others were getting drinks, Max looked around the kitchen. 'Where's the plant gone?'

'What plant?' Simo asked, glugging the posca.

'The aconite?' Max said.

'If Quintus has taken it with him, then he intends to use it again,' Cal replied, dropping his goblet as they all left in a hurry.

They rushed out of the domus of Tamphilus and headed back towards the domus of Caesar. As they passed the Temple of Saturn, Luc tripped and sprawled across the cobbles. Max heard the clatter and turned.

'Luc, are you okay?' Max asked with concern.

Grimacing, Luc struggled to his feet, his hands throbbing with pain from the impact. He inspected his raw, bleeding palms. 'I-I'm fine, keep going,' he stuttered.

Simo was well ahead of the other three as Decimus's older and longer legs powered him through the crowd.

'Come on guys, we need to stop Quintus before he hurts Livia or Gaius,' Cal shouted urgently, sprinting after Simo.

'If Quintus has laid a hand on Livia or Gaius, I will hurt him in ways he can't imagine,' Max replied with resolute determination.

They raced through the streets, driven by their urgency; their hearts pounded as they ran towards Caesar's domus, each second feeling like an eternity. Finally, breathless and adrenaline-fuelled, they burst through the doors of Caesar's domus, desperate to confront Quintus before it was too late.

'Where is everyone?' Max asked.

'Gaius, what are you doing back here?' Marcia demanded.

Max turned to see Gaius and Livia's mother standing in a doorway. 'Sorry, I needed to attend to something personal.'

'They have latrinae by the Forum. Why didn't you go there?' Marcia challenged. 'Livia, I told you to clean the Dominus's private quarters.'

'Sorry, M-M-Mater. I just heard voices and c-c-came to investigate,' Luc lied.

Turning to Decimus, Marcia said, 'I apologise, Senator. How may we help you and young Appius?'

'We're looking for Quintus. I need to check some of Tamphilus's funeral arrangements with him,' Decimus said.

'Decimus, my dear friend. I thought I heard your voice,' Caesar said. 'You look much better than you did this morning when you left.'

Simo turned and paused before replying. 'Caesar, erm, yes. A hearty meal and some rest made such a difference. I just wanted to come and thank you in person and check with Quintus on some funeral details for Tamphilus.'

'Your gratitude is noted and gratefully accepted, even if unnecessary. As for Quintus, I'm afraid Aurelia let him go, so I've offered him service in my home. But it means he's unlikely to know of any funeral arrangements,' Caesar replied.

'Oh, I thought Aurelia had lent him to you because Livia and Gaius were ill, and she was visiting her parents until the funeral,' Decimus said.

'No, I found him begging on the streets. Aurelia couldn't afford him after Tamphilus died,' Caesar explained.

'Quintus is, or should I say was with Gaius,' Marcia snapped, giving Gaius the mother stare.

'Erm, I left him near the Forum,' Max lied nervously. 'I need to go back to him.'

'Yes, you do,' Marcia said. 'Do you still have the list of what I need?'

'Yes, well no, I left it with Quintus,' Max replied hesitantly.

'I need to go. I bid you farewell, Caesar. I'm sure we'll see each other again before Tamphilus's funeral,' Decimus said.

'Indeed, my dear friend,' Caesar replied as Decimus left, followed by Max, Simo, Cal and Luc.

As Caesar wandered off, Marcia demanded, 'Livia, where are you going?'

'W-W-With M-M, Gaius,' Luc said.

'Get back to cleaning out Dominus's quarters,' Marcia instructed.

Luc looked at Max, who shrugged in defeat. 'Y-Y-Yes, M-Mater.'

Luc headed towards Caesar's private quarters but kept looking back. When he was sure Marcia had returned to her duties, he rushed out of the domus after Max and the others.

Even though it wasn't the first time they had been there, as Max and the others entered the Roman Forum, they couldn't help but be in awe of the grandeur of the gleaming marble columns.

Max looked around at the bustling crowds, soaking in the atmosphere as the Forum teemed with life. Senators wandered past, draped in richly embroidered togas and followed by their entourage like a bride's train, as merchants clamoured to draw the attention of passersby to the beauty of their wares.

As street musicians brought life to the streets and children ran and played, Max spotted Kendra and Fabia and ran over to them.

'How are you both here?' Max asked.

'I collapsed in front of Manius, and when the transmutation finished, he said two sisters were better than one,' Fabia said.

'It wasn't quite as simple as Fabia said,' Kendra laughed. 'He was shocked, then horrified, and finally accepting. He also insisted that I use my dressmaking skills to make us look different.'

'Only because he knew that was another professional service to sell,' Fabia laughed.

'Max, we don't have time for this. We need to find Zeryn before he kills anyone else,' Simo insisted.

'Zeryn?' Kendra replied. 'But I thought you said Tamphilus was Zeryn?'

Max asked, 'We thought he was, but Zeryn deceived us. Have you seen Gaius and Quintus?'

'They walked past a while ago. Do you think they're in danger?' Kendra asked.

'Gaius is because Quintus is Zeryn,' Max replied.

'Quintus? He's such an innocent, bullied young man,' Kendra said.

'Another Zeryn act,' Simo snapped. 'I swear he'll not hurt another family ever again.'

'How can you be so certain that Quintus is Zeryn?' Kendra asked.

'Because we found Quintus's body in the basement of Tamphilus's domus,' Cal said.

'Can we save the discussion until later? Which way did Quintus and Gaius go?' Simo demanded.

'Manius, I'm going with my friends to catch that Zeryn I mentioned,' Kendra shouted across the stall.

Manius looked at Kendra and then at Fabia. He frowned before saying, 'Okay, Kendra, but be careful.'

Kendra set off, followed by Max and the others. They headed through a labyrinth of alleyways leading off from the Forum, passing the enticing air of fresh bread and roasting meats from nearby taverns and thermopolia.

'I know where you're headed. Livia and I used to go to a marcellum this way, which sold Caesar's favourite cooked and raw meat,' Max said, taking the lead from Kendra.

They passed a group of scholars in a lively debate about the political future of Rome, and Max smiled as one said, 'We should make Caesar the leader of Rome, a dictator perpetuo.'

After an eternity of twists and turns, they entered a plaza full of fresh and cooked meat stalls.

The place buzzed with activity, a vibrant and chaotic hub of Roman life that engulfed them in a whirlwind of sights and sounds.

Amidst the crowd, people jostled and shoved, each vying for their place in the busy marketplace. Traders shouted their wares in booming voices, while customers haggled fiercely, their exchanges punctuated by colourful insults and heated gestures. Animals added to the clamour, their bleats and cries blending with the cacophony of human activity.

In the midst of this chaos, the task of finding Quintus and Gaius became increasingly daunting. The distractions of the lively plaza threatened to divert or confuse their attention at every turn as the bustle and heat hindered their search further.

'This is hopeless,' Cal moaned.

'We need to spread out,' Simo suggested.

'I agree,' Max replied, scanning the crowd. 'Luc go round the left side of the square, and Cal head to the right. Simo, you go to the right of the centre through the crowd, I'll go left of the centre, and Kendra head straight through the middle. Be ready to use your immobilisers.'

The group split, and Max started to fight through the crowd. His eyes darted across the mass of people, searching for Gaius or Quintus.

'Gaius!' Max shouted, his voice struggling above the deafening noise and bustle of the market and the stifling air.

He pushed onward, dodging carts laden with fresh produce and stalls surrounded by shoppers. Beads of sweat trickled down his body due to the sweltering heat of midday Rome and the press of bodies in the busy plaza.

'Come on, where are you?' Max thought to himself.

'I'm going to find you, and then I'm going to avenge what you did to my family,' Simo snarled, scanning the bustling shoppers.

There was a scream to Cal's left. He gripped his immobiliser and ran towards it. As he drew near, he relaxed his grip, seeing that the noise was merely a shopper startled by an excited chicken.

Fewer shoppers were on the market's edge, giving Luc a better vantage to scan the hot and flustered shoppers. After what seemed an age, Luc noticed Max and headed towards him. 'M-M-Max, have you seen Q-Q-Quintus or Gaius?'

'Luc, is that you? I'm still struggling as I see Livia, but hear you,' Gaius replied. 'I'm Gaius.'

'G-G-Gaius? S-S-Sorry, I thought you w-w-were Max,' Luc replied.

'That's alright. Why are you here? I thought you, Max and the others were hiding in Tamphilus's domus,' Gaius replied. 'Quintus said you were staying there for a few days.'

'It was a t-t-trap, Q-Q-Quintus is—'

'Quintus is standing right behind you with an immobiliser pressed against your back, Lucraxin,' Quintus replied.

'Zeryn, we know it's you,' Luc replied.

'How strange, it seems you forgot to stutter, my friend,' Zeryn sneered.

'I'm n-n-no f-friend of yours, Zeryn. My s-s-stutter g-goes under s-s-s-stress,' Luc said.

'I thought stutters worsen under stress,' Zeryn challenged.

'That's the m-m-most c-common way. But s-s-some like m-me improve if s-stressed,' Luc said.

'Is that right?' How about this for stress? Tell me where Max, Simo and the others are and lead me away from them, or else I immobilise and kill you right here,' Zeryn snarled, pressing the immobiliser more firmly into Luc without pressing the button and holding his other hand in front of Luc, revealing a dagger.

'N-N-Never, you can k-k-kill me if you w-want, b-b-but they will g-get you,' Luc replied.

Zeryn sighed. 'So be it.' With a quick jab of the dagger, he stabbed Gaius in his left side. The wound wasn't fatal, but it was enough to draw blood, and Zeryn felt it made his point clear enough.

Luc watched Gaius clasp his side as a trickle of blood seeped between his fingers. 'Okay, I'll do it, b-b-but leave Gaius and his f-f-family out of it.'

'I'm sorry, but you seem to think you're in charge. I'm the Deputy Supreme Leader, and once I've transmuted through Caesar, I'll become the Regent Supreme of this desolate planet,' Zeryn sneered.

'The DSL title m-m-means nothing here. B-B-Besides Timezel r-revoked your title,' Luc replied.

'Timezel? That washed-up nobody has no authority here,' Zeryn replied. 'Now, which way avoids Max and his cronies?'

'They're heading towards the Porta Carmentalis,' Luc sighed.

'So, we need to head back around the Capitolinus towards the Forum,' Zeryn replied.

'Yes,' Luc said.

Zeryn paused and watched Luc intently. 'You didn't stutter.'

'What?' Luc replied.

'When you talked about the Porta Carmentalis, you didn't stutter,' Zeryn said, frowning. He held his dagger close to Gaius, who was still trying to stop the bleeding.

'I d-d-did,' Luc replied.

'No, you didn't, and as you admitted, your stutter goes under stress. You're trying to lure me into a trap,' Zeryn snarled.

'I'll make you pay for that. Now head towards the Porta Carmentalis.'

'Okay, b-b-but l-leave Gaius here,' Luc begged.

'I'll be okay, Luc,' Gaius said.

'I give the orders, now move,' Zeryn snapped, shoving Luc forward and grabbing Gaius.

Luc turned and saw Zeryn holding the dagger against Gaius's side.

'You've made it clear you don't care about yourself, but you do care about these pathetic Romans,' Zeryn smiled.

'Oi, who are you calling pathetic?' a man said.

Zeryn ignored the man and went to walk away, but the man grabbed his arm. 'I said, who are you calling pathetic?'

Zeryn turned swiftly, plunged the dagger into the man's chest, pulled it back out, and wiped it on the man's tunic as he crumpled to the ground.

'Now get moving, Lucraxin,' Zeryn ordered as they rushed away from the screams rising from people crowded around the dying man.

Max heard the screaming and rushed towards it. He reached the crowd, gathered around the dying man and started pushing through.

'What happened?' Max asked.

'A boy stabbed him and then ran off with two friends,' a woman in the crowd said.

'No, there were only two, not three,' a man replied. 'But one of them was bleeding, like he'd been stabbed too.'

'I saw four boys,' another man argued.

'Actually, one was a girl,' another person said.

'Which way did they go?' Max asked.

'That way, towards the Forum,' the first woman replied.

'No, they headed towards the Porta Carmentalis,' another woman insisted.

An argument broke out between several people about how many were involved, in which direction they ran, and how many were male or female.

Simo arrived, quickly followed by Kendra and Cal.

'What's happened?' Simo asked.

'I think Zeryn knows we're onto him,' Max replied. 'He's got at least one hostage who's bleeding, possibly Gaius, and he might have Luc too.'

'We need to find him,' Simo said. 'Do they know which way he went?'

'Half think he went towards the Porta Carmentalis,' Max replied.

'What about the others?' Kendra asked.

'He ran off towards the Forum with his friends,' a man who had been listening to them said.

'Kendra, you and Cal head to the Forum and Simo and I will go towards the Porta Carmentalis,' Max said.

'I swear by the end of this day, Zeryn will die, or I will die trying,' Simo said.

Max looked at Simo and said, 'Only one person dies today, and that's Zeryn.'

Max ran in the direction of Porta Carmentalis, followed by Simo.

Ahead of them, Zeryn snarled at Luc, 'If I see any sign of Max, Simo or any of your enforcers, Gaius dies, followed by you.'

29
REBORN

'W-W-What are you g-going to do?' Luc asked.

'Do you think this is some old-fashioned Zephyrion play, where the bad guy tells you the plot?' Zeryn sneered. 'Just hurry up to the Porta Carmentalis.'

'It's just ahead of us,' Luc replied anxiously.

'When we get there, go through the gate,' Zeryn ordered. 'Then go a little to the left.'

'B-B-But if you get through the P-Porta and beyond the walls of R-R-Rome to escape, you'll never be able to transmute inside Caesar,' Luc said.

'I'm not escaping, and I will be Caesar,' Zeryn snarled.

'B-B-But if you're not escaping, then the only thing beyond the gate is the Ludus, the g-g-gladiator training camp,' Luc replied.

'Stop talking and hurry up, or Gaius gets another little jab in his side.' Zeryn snapped.

'Please, Quintus, I've not wronged you or Zeryn,' Gaius pleaded as the slow but steady blood loss made him feel weak.

'Shut up, Gaius,' Zeryn snapped. 'Nobody cares about you.'

'You're wrong, Zeryn,' Max shouted.

Zeryn turned and saw Max rapidly approaching, closely followed by Simo. 'Stay back, both of you.'

'Zeryn, you've got no authority here,' Max replied.

'Maybe not, but this dagger does,' Zeryn sneered, holding it to Gaius's throat. 'Lucraxin, get in front of me, facing your pathetic friends.'

Luc stepped forward, glancing to his left at Zeryn.

'Don't even think about it, raxin. Make any attempt to attack me, and Gaius dies.'

'Please, Luc. I'm scared,' Gaius begged, welling up with tears.

'I won't let him hurt you, Gaius,' Max said.

As Luc moved into position, Zeryn stepped behind him. 'Noble words, Maxohal, but totally worthless, of course. Oh, look, more of your feeble gang have joined you.'

Max glanced to his left and saw Kendra and Cal running towards them.

'Sorry, we started running to the Forum, but everyone kept saying they hadn't seen them, so we came back,' Cal said, gasping.

'Luc, are you and Gaius okay?' Kendra asked.

'I'm okay, b-b-but Zeryn has stabbed G-G-Gaius, and he's b-bleeding,' Luc replied.

'You're far from okay, raxin,' Zeryn replied, holding up the immobiliser. 'Now, Max and Simo, make sure you and your friends do exactly what I say, or they both die.'

Kendra gasped and said, 'Max, that's the—'

'Yes, that's one of the immobilisers Manius made for me,' Max replied. 'Zeryn must have stolen it when I was transmuting.'

'I took it well before then, and it's a good job I did, as I could barely get near you when you were transmuting because of that meddling Marcia,' Zeryn snarled.

'Don't you dare insult my Mater,' Gaius said feebly.

'It seems like your transmutation in this feeble Roman has emboldened him,' Zeryn replied, slowly walking backwards towards the Porta Carmentalis. 'Lucraxin, stay close. You and Gaius will ensure the others do as they're told.'

Max pulled Simo, Kendra and Cal into a huddle and whispered to them while keeping an eye on Zeryn. As they turned back, they started to spread out.

'No, you don't. Get back together, or more people will die,' Zeryn snarled.

'You killed my family, but that's still not enough death for you,' Simo snapped back.

'They were my family too, nephew,' Zeryn replied.

'You're not family. You're a twisted, sick and ruthless killer,' Simo spat back.

'And you killed my partner and probably my brother,' Max said.

'Are they the only ones I get credit for?' Zeryn smiled at Max.

Max frowned. 'What do you mean?'

'Oh, you never joined the dots with your parents then?' Zeryn smirked.

'What?' Max exclaimed.

'The death of your parents. You didn't think it strange that they died in a crash while investigating vote rigging?' Zeryn challenged.

'I've always queried their deaths, but everyone told me I was crazy. They said it was an accident,' Max replied.

'Oops. It was an accident of my making,' Zeryn replied, smiling. 'I couldn't have them proving the son of the new Supreme Leader tried to fix the vote, even if it wasn't about making my father Supreme Leader, but actually about putting me into power. It was so easy to upload the computer virus into their flight system.'

Max lunged forward. 'You sick, twisted narcissist.'

'Careful, Maxohal. You might make me nervous, and if I start shaking, I might accidentally plunge this dagger into young Gaius's throat,' Zeryn replied.

'You're never going to escape, Zeryn,' Simo snarled.

Zeryn paused and tilted his head as if confused. 'Why does everyone think I'm trying to escape?'

'Because if you stay here, we'll kill you,' Max replied.

'That'll be hard to do when I'm going to be the only one of us still alive,' Zeryn replied.

'How are you going to defeat all of us?' Cal challenged.

'Simohal, pull out your immobiliser,' Zeryn ordered.

'I don't take orders from you,' Simo replied.

'Okay,' Zeryn said before stepping forward and jabbing his dagger into Luc's left arm.

Luc screamed and clutched his bleeding arm in agony. A couple of passersby glanced towards Luc but decided this wasn't their argument and carried on towards the gate.

'The next time, I may go for something worse than his arm, but don't worry, I'll immobilise him, or should I say her first,' Zeryn replied. 'Now let's try it again. Simo, please pull out your immobiliser.'

Simo glanced at Max, who nodded, so he begrudgingly pulled out his immobiliser.

'That's better. Now immobilise those two,' Zeryn replied, nodding towards Kendra and Cal.

'No,' Cal and Kendra protested in unison.

'I'm not doing that. They could be killed while they're immobilised,' Simo protested.

'Oh yes, I hadn't thought of that,' Zeryn replied.

Simo sighed in relief at the reprieve.

'No, actually, I had thought of that. Just do it before my patience runs out,' Zeryn ordered.

'But,' Simo started to say but was cut short by Zeryn stabbing Luc in the other arm.

As Luc screamed, Cal pleaded, 'Please, there must be another way.'

'You don't have to do this,' Kendra argued. 'You could leave and go anywhere on this planet.'

'Why would I go anywhere else? If I stay here, I can transmute inside Caesar and rule the planet instead. I hear they're going to make him dictator perpetuo. So, he'd be the ruler for life, and I'd ensure it passed down his family,' Zeryn laughed. 'Which, of course, means down to me as I transmute through his family.'

'Making you Regent Supreme in all but name,' Max said.

'I can introduce the title later, once I've taken control,' Zeryn smiled. 'Now, nephew, please do as I asked and immobilise those two.'

'No,' Simo snapped.

'No? What would dear Shazon say about her darling son being so disobedient,' Zeryn sneered.

Simo lunged at Zeryn at the mention of his mother. 'Don't you dare mention my mother.'

Zeryn sidestepped Simo's lunge with ease, but Simo grabbed Gaius's arm and dragged him free of Zeryn's grasp. As Simo and Gaius tumbled onto the floor, Zeryn grabbed Luc. Simo quickly recovered and tried to grab Zeryn's leg, but Zeryn moved quickly, stamping on Simo's hand.

Luc struggled, trying to break free, but Zeryn wrapped his arm around his throat, with his immobiliser tight against the side of Luc's neck.

Zeryn stepped back and felt the wall behind him. He started to edge along it towards the gate, dragging Luc with him. 'That wasn't a clever move, nephew.'

'You killing my mother wasn't the smart move, Zeryn,' Simo growled, standing up and helping Gaius to stand.

'How can such a feeble Shadower have the same heritage as me and the great Zyrenev?' Zeryn sneered.

'You killed my grandfather. You have no right to say his name,' Simo replied.

Zeryn sneered and mocked Simo's voice, 'Don't mention my mother's name, don't say my grandfather's name.'

'Don't rise to it, Simo,' Kendra insisted. 'He's only doing it to get a reaction because he knows he'll lose.'

'Wow, she's a smart one. I bet she could have made it to the top with that degree of insight,' Zeryn replied sarcastically. 'Of course, I mean to the top of a Zingle burger serving counter!'

Max watched the events unfold before him and slowly moved away towards the gate while Zeryn and Simo argued. He signalled Cal and Kendra to stay where they were before disappearing around the corner of the wall.

Luc slowly pulled out her immobiliser from the pouch hanging from her waist, but Zeryn noticed.

'What is it with you enforcers?' Zeryn demanded, knocking the immobiliser from Luc's hand and slicing off the belt holding the pouch. 'You're all so predictable.'

Simo helped Gaius stumble to Kendra. 'Go and find a medicus before Gaius bleeds to death. Then take him home.'

'Yes, Simo,' Kendra replied.

'Where is she going with Gaius?' Zeryn demanded. 'I never gave permission for them to go.'

'You don't get it, Zeryn. You have no power or authority here,' Simo said.

'Simohal, you're the one who doesn't understand,' Zeryn sneered. 'I don't need a title to have authority or power. This dagger gives me all the power I need.'

'If that dagger is all the power you need, let Luc go and fight me fairly like a man,' Cal bristled.

'Like a man? You used to be one of Dronin's henchmen. You know nothing about fighting fairly,' Zeryn sneered, edging along the wall until he felt the corner of it with his heel.

'Max, there you are. Have you seen Cal and the others? We haven't seen them since we started the final stage of transmuting,' Paulie said, accompanied by Keri. 'We even went to the gladiator training camp when we couldn't find you in Rome. There's a man there looking for you too.'

Max put a finger to his lips to indicate they should be quiet.

'What's going on,' Keri whispered.

'I need you to create a distraction. Zeryn is Quintus, and he's holding Luc hostage,' Max replied. 'Simo and Cal are keeping him busy against the wall, but as soon as he comes round this corner heading through the gate, I need to get to him quickly.'

'You'd know all about Dronin. He was on your payroll,' Simo growled.

Max turned and saw Simo, and then he noticed Zeryn's foot tapping the corner of the wall as it opened into the gateway. 'Now,' he hissed.

'But, what—' Paulie started to say as Keri dragged her into the open.

'Cal, there you are. I've been looking for you,' Keri said at the top of her voice before running towards him.

Paulie glanced at Luc and then Simo, noting where Zeryn was. 'Simo, Luc, it's big hug time.'

Paulie held out her left arm to embrace Simo, grabbed Luc's arm, and tried to pull him away from Zeryn's grasp, but Zeryn's grip was firm.

Zeryn was startled by this sudden interruption, but his mind was clear on what to do. 'If you want him or her, then have them, but be quick.'

Zeryn drove the dagger into Luc and then jabbed his immobiliser into her neck. As Luc started to collapse, Zeryn thrust Luc forward and darted around the corner of the wall, expecting to make a clean escape from Rome.

'Hello, Zeryn,' Max said, coldly staring at him.

'You need to save your friend Luc, Maxohal. I'm afraid my dagger slipped,' Zeryn smirked.

'I'm sure Luc will live to fight another day, even if she has to build a new shell,' Max replied emotionless.

'Ah, about that. You see, I happened to find your immobiliser, and during the little skirmish, I may have jabbed her with it. If you hurry, I'm sure you can save her, though,' Zeryn said.

'Luc may die, but then we all die eventually,' Max stated, never breaking his cold, empty stare from Zeryn. 'Lin died, Zym has probably died, my parents died, even your father and sister died. Not forgetting your friend Nico, the enforcers with me tracking Dronin and many more.'

'Okay, so many have died, and so many more will, but you can save Luc if you hurry,' Zeryn replied nervously.

'Luc is being looked after, but nobody is going to look after you, Zeryn,' Simo snarled.

Zeryn turned, pressing his back against the archway wall forming the Porta Carmentalis. 'Simo, my dear nephew.'

'I've told you already; you are not related to me or my family,' Simo replied.

Zeryn looked at the bristling, burning hatred of Simo and then back to Max's cold, icy stare.

'Simo, Max, we have a new planet here where, with our knowledge and skills, we can make incredible things happen,' Zeryn pleaded.

'Why would we want to do anything with you?' Simo snapped.

'Because this planet is so backward, we can advance them so quickly they'll worship us,' Zeryn replied confidently.

'This planet needs to be left alone,' Max replied. 'We helped destroy our world; we don't need to accelerate the Roman technology, so they do it to their planet.'

'Oh, Max. Lin always used to say you were a pessimist,' Zeryn smiled.

Max stared at Zeryn blankly and said, 'Don't mention my partner's name. You killed her, and that's why I will kill you.'

'I never killed her,' Zeryn protested. 'How could I know the rings detonator would be left behind when the Exodus machine sent me here.'

'Because you knew the Exodus machine can only send energy,' Max replied. 'I guess you shot Zym by accident, too?'

'Oh no, Zym deserved to die. He and your parents stopped me from making Zephyrion a better place,' Zeryn smirked.

Max knew Zeryn was trying to provoke a reaction, so he stared at him emotionlessly, gripping his immobiliser tightly.

Simo noticed Zeryn was focused on Max and lunged towards him, intending to grab Zeryn's dagger. However, Zeryn saw Simo move and flicked his wrist, arcing the dagger across Simo's chest, leaving a deep, curving cut that started bleeding as Simo fell to the floor.

A soldier manning the Porta Carmentalis shook his head as if disoriented and then noticed the commotion from three young men fighting. He went to investigate. 'What's going on here?'

'It's fine, Sir. We are just having a friendly disagreement,' Zeryn replied.

'It doesn't look that friendly, given the blood coming from that cut across his chest,' the soldier said, nodding in Simo's direction. He reached over, grabbed the dagger from Zeryn's hand and threw it on the floor. 'That's better, now you're both unarmed.'

There was a scream just before the gate, and Simo stepped back to see past the edge of the wall. Keri and Paulie were holding the limp body of Luc with Cal looking on. 'It's Luc, I think she's dead.'

'Go and check,' Max said. 'Zeryn isn't going anywhere while I'm here.'

The soldier turned to Simo and said, 'Go ahead. I'm sure Keri, Paulie, and Cal would appreciate you checking on them. They can also help with that cut. We wouldn't want another person bleeding to death on the streets of Rome today.'

'Okay, but if Zeryn tries to escape, shout,' Simo replied.

'I will,' Max said reassuringly.

Zeryn looked at the soldier and Max, noting they were watching Simo, and he lunged toward Max. They both fell to the floor, rolling around together. As they stopped, Zeryn jabbed his immobiliser against Max's neck and hit the button. He looked for his dagger on the floor just beyond arm's reach. He climbed off Max, grabbed the dagger and turned back towards Max.

'Luc, give me your sword,' Max shouted.

The soldier threw his sword to Max, who caught it. Max held the sword firmly and slowly stood up.

'But I immobilised you,' Zeryn protested.

Max smiled. 'Oh dear, you must have picked up my demonstrator model.'

Zeryn threw the immobiliser on the floor and noted Max had also lost his. He glanced around and spotted it on the floor, near the wall.

'Give up now, Zeryn, and I'll make it quick,' Max growled.

'Why don't you give up, Max, and I'll make it slightly less painful,' Zeryn replied, slowly circling Max as he moved towards the wall.

'Max, he's going for your immobiliser,' Luc shouted.

'Throw me yours, Luc,' Max replied.

'I don't have one. Zeryn knocked it out of my hand when I was in my Livia shell,' Luc said, moving towards Zeryn.

'Stay back, raxin. I've killed you once today, but next time, I'll do it properly,' Zeryn sneered, waving his dagger.

Max swung his sword towards Zeryn, but Zeryn easily parried it with his dagger. 'Is that the best you've got?'

Max saw Luc bending to pick up the immobiliser, but Zeryn saw it too and plunged his dagger into Luc's shoulder. Luc fell to the floor in agony, still grasping the immobiliser.

'Luc, throw me the immobiliser,' Max screamed, swinging his sword at Zeryn.

Zeryn ducked under the sword and lunged towards Max just as Luc threw the immobiliser.

Max dodged to avoid Zeryn, but despite sticking out his hand, the immobiliser flew past him and hit a passing citizen as Max crashed to the floor.

'Oi, who threw this,' the man said, bending down and picking up the immobiliser.

'Sorry, Sir. My friend Luc threw it to me, but I'm a terrible catch,' Zeryn replied, standing up and walking towards the man and hiding the knife behind his back.

'Max,' Luc shouted, clutching his shoulder.

Max scrambled to his feet. 'Please, Sir. Don't give the immobiliser to Zeryn. He's already killed our friends and family.'

'Don't listen to them, Sir. There's two of them, and they jumped me,' Zeryn whimpered like a weak, feeble victim.

The man looked at the device and then at Luc lying on the floor, clasping his shoulder, which Max was checking. 'It looks like you fought back well.'

'It was a lucky strike, Sir,' Zeryn replied dolefully.

'I thought you said Luc was your friend?' the man challenged.

'He was, but, uh, that other guy turned him against me,' Zeryn flustered.

'What is this thing?' the man asked, turning it over. He pushed the button down and noted the two pins sticking out. 'This could hurt someone. You young'uns seem to keep finding new ways to make weapons.'

'Sir, give it to me,' Zeryn demanded, holding out his hand.

Max walked towards Zeryn and the man. 'Please, Sir. If you don't know who to give it to, then keep it or throw it away, but don't give it to Zeryn.'

Zeryn drew the knife from behind his back with his other hand still outstretched. 'I really must insist you hand it over, Sir.'

The man looked at the immobiliser and then at Zeryn's dagger. 'What's your name, boy?' he asked, looking at Max.

'Max, Sir.'

'Well, I'm sorry, Maxo, but it looks like I have no choice but to give it to Zeryn,' the man said, pushing the button down on the immobiliser and plunging it into Zeryn's hand.

Zeryn realised what was happening in that split second and swung the dagger towards the man. Max reacted even faster and plunged his sword into Zeryn with all his strength, causing them both to fall to the ground. Zeryn's eyes widened before he slumped unconscious. A few seconds later, there was a flash of light, and Zeryn was dead.

Max rolled off Zeryn's body and stood up.

'What's happened?' Simo asked as he and Cal rushed into the gate area.

'Yeah, we saw the flash,' Cal said.

Luc shouted to some colleagues, 'Hey Simonus, we've got a dead thief over here. Get some lictors to clear it away.'

'Okay, Sextus,' a soldier replied.

30
NEW BEGINNINGS

'Zeryn tried to kill me, but Luc and Zym saved my life,' Max said.

Cal sighed, 'Sorry, Max, but Luc is dead.'

Max looked at the soldier and then back to Cal and Simo and smiled, 'Luc's Livia shell is dead, but here is...'

'Sextus at your service, guys,' Luc replied. 'But how did you know, Max?'

'Simple. You referred to Cal, Paulie, and Keri by name. How would a gate soldier know the names of strangers?' Max replied.

'Hang on, you said Zym as well,' Simo frowned.

Zym coughed.

'Sorry, Sir, can we help you?' Cal asked.

'Well, if you happen to know anywhere round here that serves a decent Brackles, it would be a good start,' Zym replied.

'How the hell are you here, Zym?' Max asked.

'It's nice to see you too, little brother,' Zym laughed as he hugged Max. 'We've got plenty of time to discuss that. Let's check on the others first.'

'Talking of the others, Luc was immobilised as he was dying,' Simo challenged. 'so how did he end up in Sextus?'

'Don't our immobilisers work properly?' Cal asked.

Max bent down, picked up the immobiliser by the wall, and threw it to Simo. 'Use it on Luc or Cal.'

Simo caught the immobiliser and turned it over, noting the subtle differences in its design from the one Max had handed out from the batch Manius had made. 'It looks almost identical to the others.'

'Use it on one of them,' Max insisted.

Simo frowned at the thought of immobilising his friends.

'Oh, for the love of gods,' Max sighed. 'Try to immobilise me with it then.'

Simo hesitated but then leaned forward and jabbed Max in the neck, pressing the button to immobilise him.

'Oww, that hurts,' Max said.

'Aside from the two small puncture wounds in your neck, you seem fine,' Luc said.

'I am. I've suspected Quintus for some time. So, I asked Kendra to make a special immobiliser, which I knew wouldn't work,' Max replied. 'All I had to do was make sure when Zeryn came looking for my immobiliser, he found this one.'

'But we saw him immobilise Luc and kill him,' Simo challenged.

'You saw Zeryn jab Luc with a device that couldn't immobilise him!' Max replied.

'Which meant when my Livia shell died, I could find a new host, which is why I'm in Sextus,' Luc said.

'Good grief. You were a right smartarse on Zephyrion. It seems coming to this place has moved you to a whole new level,' Zym laughed.

'How long have you been here?' Simo asked Zym.

'I've been on this planet for around two months, but I've only been in Rome a few days. Cicero had been in Sicily which is where I landed in him. He later headed back to Rome, stopping in Naples, when we heard about the long-sleep disease striking someone down in Pompeii and a lot more people in Rome. I had a feeling it was you lot transmuting,' Zym replied.

'The person in Pompeii was Juli,' Max said.

As they were talking, a group of Romans arrived and started to clear up the remains of Zeryn.

'Who are these people?' Cal asked.

'They're lictors. They work for magistrates, and part of their duties include clearing away dead thieves and other individuals' bodies from public spaces,' Luc explained.

'I don't know whether to be impressed or scared that a dead person is just cleared up like a piece of litter,' Simo said.

'I can't think of a more fitting end for that piece of rubbish, Zeryn,' Zym replied.

'Let's leave them to it and check on the others,' Max said.

They returned to Paulie and Keri, who were still hugging Luc's deceased shell.

'That's so touching to see, but it's only a shell you're crying over. I'm still here,' Luc said. 'Or would you b-b-believe it m-m-more if I said I'm s-s-still here.'

Paulie looked at Sextus and then back to Keri. 'Is it?'

'I think so,' Keri replied.

'Give me a hug. I am Luc,' Luc replied.

'Luc,' Paulie said, grabbing and hugging him.

'Hello, I am here, you know,' Zym said.

Keri looked at the man in front of her. He must be at least fifty and clearly from a wealthy position, given his portly figure. 'I'm sorry, do we know you?'

'It depends if anyone round here can do me a triple Zingle burger with spicy sides?' Zym replied.

'Zym?' Keri frowned.

'Well, I'm currently the guest of Marcus Tullius Cicero, but yes, it's me,' Zym replied.

As Cal and Keri joined the hug of Luc and Zym, Simo turned to Max. 'I'm so pleased Luc and Zym survived, but I feel so empty.'

'In what way?' Max asked.

'I thought seeing Zeryn dead would bring me closure,' Simo replied.

'Revenge never brings closure,' Max replied. 'Because no matter what happens, nothing will ever bring back any of our loved ones.'

'But I just thought knowing he can never hurt again would be enough,' Simo sighed.

'It'll never be enough. If we're still here in a thousand or even two thousand years, we'll still have moments where the thought of Shazon, Lin, or Kazi will still burn brightly,' Max replied.

'Do you think we'll still be here then?' Simo asked.

'I don't have a clue. We know Zeryn brought a lot of his Deceptor friends with him. Maybe they'll kill us, or maybe not. Perhaps we'll both have partners and children,' Max laughed.

'Can you imagine me partnered with two or three children?' Simo laughed.

'I think you'd have children anyone would be proud to know,' Max replied.

'As long as they're happy and healthy, anything else would be a bonus,' Simo smiled. 'You might have several children too, Max.'

'I don't think so. I feel like every time I have someone I love, they get ripped away,' Max replied.

'But you can't spend your life alone,' Simo challenged.

'I won't be on my own,' Max sighed. 'I have all of you, plus Zym, Gaius, Livia and the other Roman hosts. Having good friends, no matter how many or how few, and being with them is the important thing.'

'Hey, what's going on with you two looking so serious,' Paulie asked as the group hug ended.

'We're just thinking about the future,' Simo replied.

'Blimey, if the future makes you look that miserable, we're all doomed,' Luc laughed. 'Besides, now that Zeryn is dead, we can start working out how to get home.'

'We need to speak to Juli to see if that's possible,' Max replied.

'Paulie and I received a message from her this morning,' Keri said. 'She's transmuted and said she should be in Rome by tomorrow.'

'It'll be good to see her again,' Keri said.

'See him, you mean,' Cal corrected.

'Oh yes, I'd forgotten Juli was in Cornelius,' Keri laughed. 'It'll be nice to see him again.'

'Talking of seeing people, I wonder how Gaius is?' Paulie said.

'Who's Gaius?' Zym asked.

'He was my host. He's a servant in the domus of Caesar. Let's go and check, and I can introduce you to him,' Max suggested.

'Caesar? As in Julius Caesar?' Zym asked.

'Yes, have you heard of him?' Max asked.

'Let's just say your host's Dominus and my host have a challenging relationship,' Zym laughed. 'You check on your old host, and I'll catch up with you later. No, sorry, tomorrow. Cicero tells me we have a busy evening.'

'Okay, Zym,' Max smiled broadly. 'I still can't believe I've got you back. We're meeting by the old derelict buildings near the market in the morning.'

'Yes, I know where you mean. I'll see you there in the morning,' Zym replied.

'Come on then, let's go and see Gaius.' Max said.

'We can, but you can't,' Simo said.

'Why not? I didn't hurt him,' Max replied in confusion.

'It's nothing to do with that. I'm pretty sure Marcia might be shocked seeing two versions of Gaius,' Simo laughed.

'I've got an idea,' Paulie replied. 'Let's all meet near the Temple of Saturn in an hour. Simo, Cal and Luc try to get some foreign-looking clothing. Keri come with me and Max.'

Max, Keri and Paulie headed towards the Temple of Saturn an hour later.

'I look ridiculous,' Max protested, trying to brush down the thick, long, curly wig and pulling it back in place for what seemed like the hundredth time.

'I think Atia's hairdresser has done a wonderful job considering she only had an hour,' Paulie replied.

'I think long hair suits you,' Keri replied, stifling a laugh.

'See, even Keri can't control her laughter,' Max complained.

'Hello, Paulie and Keri. Who's your new female friend?' Simo chuckled.

'Don't you start,' Max muttered.

'It'll be fine once we've dressed you,' Paulie said reassuringly. 'What clothes did you find?'

'I got him this pileum cap,' Luc said, handing over the red, brimless, felt, conical cap.

'Perfect, that'll help Max keep his hair on,' Paulie laughed, putting over Max's wig and pulling it down tightly.

'Okay, don't make it too tight,' Max grumbled.

'Come on, Max, keep your hair on,' Cal laughed.

'I think that phrase could catch on,' Simo chuckled.

'You'll catch something in a minute,' Max moaned.

'Did you get any clothes?' Paulie asked.

'Just this Gallic cloak,' Simo said, passing across the dark green hooded cloak.

Paulie wrapped the cloak around Max, tied the belt at the front, and pulled the hood up. She stood back and admired her handiwork. 'Even Gaius's mother wouldn't recognise you,' she said.

Keri stepped forward. 'Just one little tweak,' she said, pulling some of the wig's hair over his face. 'Perfect.'

'I can only just see,' Max protested.

'Which also means it's harder for others to see you,' Keri replied.

'Can we go and see Gaius now?' Max asked.

Simo stifled a laugh and started to say, 'I don't see why not, erm...'

'Now what?' Max asked frustratingly.

'We can use our host's names, but what do we call you?' Simo said.

'Why don't we just use his name?' Cal asked.

'Yeah, just call me Gaius,' Max said.

'We've just got you a disguise, but you're going to use Gaius's name?' Paulie sighed.

'I don't mean your host's name. I mean, use Max,' Cal explained.

'Use me for what?' Max asked, confused.

Cal rolled his eyes. 'I mean, you use your real name. We call you Max.'

'Well, why didn't you say so?' Max asked. 'But is my name very Roman? I've not heard anyone called Maxohal.'

'No, but Maximus is,' Cal replied. 'It means greatest or largest.'

'The thought of Max being the greatest will have Zym roaring with laughter,' Simo chuckled.

The mention of his brother's name made Max smile. 'Come on, let's go and check on Gaius, and don't you dare tell Zym.'

Kendra welcomed them when they arrived at Caesar's domus.

'How's Gaius?' Simo asked.

'He'll live. The medicus put a poultice of fungi and other substances on his wound, and he's recovering well,' Kendra replied.

'Can we come in?' Simo asked.

'Sorry, yes, of course. Caesar insisted he be put in the same guest bedroom some of you were in when transmuting,' Kendra replied.

As they filed past, Kendra grabbed Paulie to one side and whispered, 'Why is that soldier here?'

Paulie replied, 'That's Luc. Zeryn killed his Livia shell, but because Max got you to make that false immobiliser, Luc escaped into Sextus.'

'Did Zeryn escape?' Kendra asked.

'No. Max killed him,' Paulie replied.

Kendra looked at everyone heading towards the guest bedroom. 'Talking of Max, where is he?'

'He's at the back with the green cloak and red hat,' Paulie said.

'I thought he was a vagabundus that you'd all taken pity on,' Kendra laughed.

'I heard that,' Max said, turning. 'I'm no vagabond.'

'With that much hair, you wouldn't have to worry about getting cold if you lived on the streets,' Kendra chuckled.

'It's what's living in this wig that scares me,' Max replied, scratching his head.

'Oh, there's more of you,' Marcia said, coming out of the bedroom as Paulie headed towards her across the atrium, followed by Max and Kendra. 'I'm not sure about this without my Dominus's approval. I must find him.'

'And what, by the gods, do you seek my approval for,' Caesar roared, entering the atrium.

'Caesar, Sir. These people turned up to check on Gaius,' Marcia said apologetically. 'They just came in, Sir. I couldn't stop them.'

'Calm down, Marcia. I heard there was an altercation at the Porta Carmentalis involving some boys. When I saw Decimus, Atia, and Fabia with a soldier, one of Gaius's friends and a couple of others coming this way, I thought I should follow,' Caesar replied.

Upon hearing the great Caesar's voice, Sextus hurried into the atrium. 'Salve, Caesar.'

'Salue, soldier. What is your name, and what is happening here?' Caesar asked.

'I'm Sextus, Caesar. Gaius was attacked by another boy called Quintus.'

'Quintus? Wasn't he that boy we hired when the deep sleep struck Gaius, Livia and the others?' Caesar asked Marcia.

'Yes, Dominus,' Marcia replied. 'I never trusted that boy. His eyes were too close together.'

'Where is Quintus now?' Caesar queried.

'I'm afraid he was killed attacking another boy,' Sextus replied.

'Is that boy alright?' Caesar asked.

'Oh, he's here, Dominus. I heard them talking about it to Gaius when they came in. I didn't hear everything as I came out to find you,' Marcia rambled. 'I think they said his name is Max or Zeryn.'

'Marcia, just relax and fetch some bandages for this soldier's shoulder before he spills any more blood on the floor,' Caesar replied. 'Sextus, bring this boy to me.'

'Yes, Imperator,' Sextus replied.

Sextus quickly ran into the bedroom. 'Max, Caesar wants to see you.'

'Me? Why?' Max asked.

'Marcia heard the others mentioning you and Quintus fighting and that Quintus was killed, so Caesar wants to meet you,' Luc replied.

'But what if he recognises me?' Max asked.

'I don't even recognise you,' Gaius laughed.

'Come on, we can't keep Caesar waiting,' Luc replied.

'So, this is the brave lad who stood up to an attack by Quintus,' Caesar said. 'What's your name, boy?'

Max looked at Caesar and scratched his head again, wishing he could get rid of the wig. 'I'm Maximus, Sir. My friends call me Max.'

'Good to meet you, Max,' Caesar replied, studying this scruffy, long-haired boy before him, scratching like crazy. 'Are you hungry?'

'Erm, I guess so, Sir,' Max replied, trying to avoid directly looking at Caesar.

Caesar noted that Max was averting his gaze and said, 'Do I know you, Max?'

'No, Sir. I don't think so,' Max replied, scratching his head.

'Look at me, Max,' Caesar ordered.

Max gulped, slowly lifted his head, and looked at Caesar.

'I do know you,' Caesar said.

Max started to panic. The heat of the cloak, the pileum cap and the wig combined with whatever was infesting the wig and making his head itch like the fires of hell. Sweat started trickling down his face as he said, 'No, Sir. I'm sure we've never met.'

'Yes, I do. You've been begging by the Temple of Janus,' Caesar replied. 'Do you know who Janus is?'

'No, Sir,' Max said.

'Janus is the god of transition, endings and new beginnings,' Caesar said.

'Oh, he sounds like a god of hope, Sir,' Max replied, wishing Caesar would let him go and scratching his head simultaneously.

'Indeed so, Max. Well, I'm going to give you a new beginning,' Caesar said. 'Sextus, when you return to your castrum, take Max with you and enrol him in your unit.'

'Yes, Caesar,' Luc replied.

'Max, the army will give you structure, discipline, and opportunities for advancement. Your time on the streets is over,' Caesar said.

'Thank you, Caesar, Sir,' Max replied, scratching his head.

'Sextus, thank you for taking care of Gaius. I am grateful, and I know Marcia is,' Caesar said.

'Yes, thank you so much, Sextus,' Marcia said gratefully, rushing back with a bowl of water and cloth bandages. 'Please let me tend the wound on your shoulder.'

'Marcia, please ensure that our guests are fed, and make sure you dress that wound in Sextus's shoulder well. Now, please excuse me. I must attend the Senate. I bid you farewell,' Caesar said.

'Thank you, Caesar, Sir,' Max answered.

As Caesar headed across the atrium, he stopped and turned. 'Maximus!'

'Yes, Caesar?' Max queried.

'Lose that horrendous wig. Nobody cares if you're bald in the army.'

'Yes, Sir,' Max replied.

Max and Sextus returned to the guest bedroom as Marcia hurried away to prepare some food and to get an outer bandage for Sextus, while summoning Livia to help.

'What happened?' Gaius asked.

'I'm joining the army,' Max laughed.

The following day, Juli sat on a boulder, waiting in the derelict building where their time in Rome seemed to start.

'Juli, it's great to see you,' Max said, running over and hugging him.

'How did you know it was me and not Cornelius?' Juli asked.

'Because I'd recognise Lin's sister anywhere,' Max replied.

'What's happened to your hair?' Juli asked.

'I'm in the army now. They said I needed to have it short, but thanks to an infected wig, I decided it was best to shave it off,' Max laughed.

'Need to keep him in order,' Luc added, entering the building.

Juli looked at the soldier and frowned.

'It's Luc,' Max explained.

'What happened to Livia?' Juli asked.

Luc and Max explained everything that had happened while Juli was in Pompeii, with the story being embellished as Keri, Paulie, Kendra, and the others arrived.

'Well, Jeric may be out there somewhere, but the target was Zeryn, and he's gone, so what next?' Juli asked.

'Jeric's not the same danger to this planet as Zeryn was,' Cal said. 'Why don't we look for him while we build an Exodus machine, and when it's built, go home?'

'Brilliant idea,' Juli replied. 'But...'

'Why is there always a but to everything in life,' Simo sighed.

'I'm a technician and junior engineer, so I know the principles of how to build it, but we need a scientist like Gran to calculate the way it needs to work and a senior engineer like Fion to calibrate it to work properly,' Juli explained.

'Max is an engineer,' Simo said.

'I was an engineer. I can't do this,' Max protested.

'Max is the best engineer I've ever known,' Zym said, walking into the room.

'Do we know you?' Juli challenged.

'Most people in Rome know me as Marcus Tullius Cicero, but you can call me Zym.'

'Zym!' Juli ran and wrapped his arms around Zym tightly. 'I never thought I'd see you again.'

'I must admit I never envisaged an encounter like this either,' Zym laughed.

'Max, you have to be our engineer if we are ever to go home,' Paulie said.

'We knew this could be a one-way trip,' Luc said.

'I know it was a risk, and losing Gran and Fion makes it even worse, but surely we have to try?' Cal challenged.

'We can try, but we have a significant problem,' Juli replied.

'There's that but again,' Simo said.

'What's the problem?' Kendra asked.

'Even if we found the materials to make an Exodus machine work, the technology here could never machine the lenses and equipment to fine enough tolerances to make it safe,' Juli replied.

'I can see another problem,' Keri laughed. 'Does anyone have an electricity cable that'll reach Zephyrion?'

'That is a bit of a problem,' Juli replied.

'What do we do then?' Cal asked.

'We've got no choice. We stay on this planet and live our lives until the technology is available,' Max replied.

'It looks like I'm staying with Fabia and Manius then,' Kendra said.

'Atia said she likes having me, Keri and Cal living with them,' Paulie replied. 'I assume you'll stay with Cicero until you transmute, Zym.'

'Absolutely. He's got some fascinating ideas about life,' Zym replied.

'What about you, Simo?' Max asked.

'I guess I'll have to move away. Decimus has been kind, but he's made it clear I can't stay with him,' Simo sighed.

'Come and live with me,' Juli suggested.

'Live with you where?' Simo asked.

'Cornelius has asked me to live with him, and I know he likes you, too. We could have a lot of fun in Pompeii,' Juli replied. 'You'll need a name, though. I'm going to be Julius.'

'Sounds good to me. Sextus shouted a name earlier I think I'll use,' Simo said.

'I did?' Luc queried.

'Yeah, that soldier you called over to about clearing away Zeryn. Simonus wasn't it?' Simo said.

'Oh, yeah,' Luc laughed.

'Then say hello to Simonus Marcius. What about you, Luc? I assume you're in the army, at least while you're transmuting again,' Simo replied.

'Yep, I've gone from enforcer to Roman soldier, and Rome's latest recruit joins me,' Luc laughed, pointing to Max.

'So, you weren't joking? You're in the army?' Juli laughed.

Max smiled, 'Yep. Maxohal is history. Let me introduce Maximus Janus, a new Max with a new beginning.'

ALSO BY D.P. BOWKETT

MAX JANUS - THE BOBBY YEARS

A Modern-Day Young Adult Science Fiction Fantasy

Max And The Hidden Visitor

About the Author

D.P. Bowkett qualified as an accountant in 1997, auditing a diverse range of businesses and preparing the accounts and tax returns for people as varied as builders to military leaders and the landed gentry. A career in the automotive industry and financial services saw him become a Group Chief Financial Officer for a multi-billion-dollar multinational business before starting his own management consultancy business. He now advises companies across Europe in growth and expansion, managing risk and working on due diligence for investments, acquisitions and divestment.

His love of writing stemmed from creating articles for numerous websites and producing regular reports for clients who use them for marketing and business intelligence.

This love of writing and reading science fiction culminated in his latest project, documenting the life of an alien, Max Janus, who came to Earth over two thousand years ago.

Outside his professional endeavours, Dean cherishes moments with his family, which includes five grandchildren.